W9-CBX-128

DECEPTION

DECEPTION

A Harry Tate Thriller

Adrian Magson

This first world edition published 2012
in Great Britain and in the USA by
SEVERN HOUSE PUBLISHERS LTD of
9–15 High Street, Sutton, Surrey, England, SM1 1DF.
Trade paperback edition first published
in Great Britain and the USA 2012 by
SEVERN HOUSE PUBLISHERS LTD.

British Library Cataloguing in Publication Data

Magson, Adrian.
  Deception. – (A Harry Tate thriller)
  1. Tate, Harry (Fictitious character) – Fiction.
  2. Intelligence officers – Fiction. 3. Great Britain. MI6 –
  Fiction. 4. Great Britain. Army. Royal Logistic Corps –
  Fiction. 5. Military deserters – Fiction. 6. Suspense
  fiction.
  I. Title II. Series
  823.9'2-dc22

ISBN-13: 978-0-7278-8130-4 (cased)
ISBN-13: 978-1-84751-409-7 (trade paper)

All Severn House titles are printed on acid-free paper.

Severn House Publishers support The Forest Stewardship Council [FSC],
the leading international forest certification organisation. All our titles that
are printed on Greenpeace-approved FSC-certified paper carry the FSC logo.

Typeset by Palimpsest Book Production Ltd.,
Falkirk, Stirlingshire, Scotland.
Printed and bound in Great Britain by
MPG Books Ltd., Bodmin, Cornwall.

For Ann, who, in the heat of battle, has to put up with the thousand-yard stares and the questions not always receiving immediate answers. I'm right here.

ACKNOWLEDGEMENTS

With thanks as always to the wonderful Kate Lyall Grant, James, Michelle, Edwin and the whole team at Severn House, for turning my words into a complete book; to my agent, David Headley, for his help, energy and enthusiasm; to M, K, and W, who prefer to remain anonymous, and the team at Brackley Fire Station, for their kind advice.

ONE

'*Three minutes to landing.*' The pilot's Texan accent
sounded terse through the comms unit. '*Three minutes.*'
'*Roger that. Three,*' echoed the crewman on the port
side M60 door gun. He lifted his chin at former MI5 officer
Harry Tate, who nodded to show he'd got the message. The
crewman on the opposite gun flicked a hand in acknowledgement, busy scanning the gathering gloom below as the MH-60L
Black Hawk, a sinister, sand-blasted war machine stripped of
markings, clattered across the vast, darkening sprawl of Baghdad
city.

Harry peered through the open doorway to where the snake's-
head outline of an Apache AH64 attack helicopter was running
parallel some 300 yards away and slightly to the rear. Another
AH64 held the same position on their starboard side. None of
the aircraft showed running lights.

It had been the same since he'd come aboard; no smiles, no
welcome. If they had any curiosity about what Harry was doing
here, or the man with him who was now handcuffed to his seat,
they kept it in check. Just a few terse words of safety from the
crew chief, and an agreement about what they were to do when
they reached their destination. There was more chatter, this time
between their pilot, Postal One, and the escorts – referred to
as Shotgun One and Two – confirming direction and coordinates,
the talk stripped to its essentials, almost unintelligible to an
outsider.

Subhi Rafa'i, the reluctant cargo, showed no interest. The
former Iraqi cleric was dressed in plain tan pants and a white
shirt beneath a flak jacket. He looked listless and withdrawn,
staring at the rooftops flashing by below and occasionally shaking
his head. If ever a man looked like one going to meet his doom,
Rafa'i was it.

Forty minutes earlier, two military policemen had hustled
him out of a covered truck parked in the corner of a secure

section of the US operations base – where they had been driven immediately on leaving the main airport – and straight up into the belly of the Black Hawk. Rafa'i had been in the open for no more than twelve seconds, watched by several armed guards.

It had been the longest twelve seconds of Harry's life.

'He'd better be worth it,' US Army Colonel Seymour White, the Assistant Operations Officer, had muttered. He watched the transfer, the skin around his eyes pale with tension. 'These guys got better things to be doing than playing cab driver.' He didn't add 'for British spooks and their rag-head prisoners', but the meaning was there.

Harry ignored it. The colonel was flexing some psychological muscle, showing that he didn't have to like what he was being asked to risk men and equipment for, but he had his orders and would do whatever was required. In this case it was the unusual job of delivering an insurgent back to his people.

The two crewmen reached down and grabbed Rafa'i and hauled him aboard with little ceremony. They were in their late thirties, lean and tanned, forearms covered in exotic tattoos. Although dressed in combat fatigues, Kevlar helmets and flak jackets, and wearing side arms, little about them echoed regular US forces. They wore no badges or insignia, had shown no reaction to Colonel White's arrival, given none of the normal snappy US military response to an officer being within shouting range. It was as if White didn't exist.

'Who are they?' Harry queried. He wasn't expecting an answer, but Colonel White surprised him.

'PMCs,' the American replied. 'Private military contractors. We use them when we can't spare our own crews or . . .' He left the sentence hanging and tilted his head slightly.

'You don't want to?'

'You said it, not me.' White shifted his weight and tugged at his waistband, eyes flicking around the base perimeter. 'We use whoever we can get. And these boys are good and willing.' He glanced at Harry. 'And they're expensive, so don't go getting them busted.'

'I'll try not.'

White nodded. 'This is the best time to fly. They'll take you in low once you're near the coordinates, then go down fast. You'd better hold on to your lunch.'

'I understand.'

'Hope so. You'll off-load your cargo and get straight back out of there. No chit-chat, no fond goodbyes and try not to start a firefight. Just in case of trouble, they're sending over two Apache six-fours to run interference; they'll join you as soon as you leave here. Do exactly what the crew tell you and you'll be back in time for dinner.' He nodded once and walked away, stiff-backed; the mention of dinner clearly not an invitation.

Now they were approaching the Al-Jamia district west of Baghdad, where Rafa'i had once had his heavily fortified base and centre of operations. Until he had blown it up, anyway. Part of a failed plot to gather support against the Western Coalition Forces, he had sacrificed a number of his closest followers in a bid to disappear, believed killed by the Coalition. Tonight he was being returned home to face those he had left behind. Nobody expected the outcome to be a good one.

But it solved a tricky problem the UK government had faced only a few days ago: what should they do with a former cleric-turned-insurgent who had tried to gather sufficient financial and terrorist support to throw out every westerner still in Iraq? Having him die on UK soil was unthinkable – although that had been the plan if a group of shadowy Coalition businessmen and others had had their way. Equally, imprisonment in a UK jail on terrorist charges would have turned any establishment holding him into a tinderbox. The solution was brutally simple: send him back home.

Harry felt the seat shift beneath him as the Black Hawk changed direction. The gunners focussed their attention on the ground. The escorting Apaches kept station with them and the houses below suddenly sprang into view as the nose dipped. They were coming in fast. Colonel White hadn't been joking.

TWO

'*Ready for landing.*' The pilot again, his voice strangely calm. '*Postal One going straight in. Shotguns One and Two, hold course and check for unfriendlies. Over.*'

The escorts responded, and Harry saw the port side craft pull away. He didn't envy them their task. They would be using night vision equipment to scout a confusing jumble of narrow streets, back alleys, open lots and rooftops, checking for any threat to the Black Hawk's safety and hoping to spot it before it happened. Only the most foolhardy of insurgents would stand out in the open to fire on them, but there were plenty of those. Most preferred the illusory safety of houses and walls, where the night vision 'eyes' couldn't always reach. Any incoming fire from ground level would be on them before they saw it.

The helicopter dropped again, the engine note changing and the vibration increasing. The noise echoed back from the surrounding structures and the top of a tree flashed by at floor level, straggly and bare. Harry saw the flare of a paraffin lamp on a rooftop, the flames glinting off an array of aerials, wires and satellite dishes, and highlighting the upturned faces of a family gathered around it.

'*Postal One, we have three SUVs near the designated landing area. Three SUVs, over.*'

'*Shotgun One, Roger that. Estimate eight, repeat eight people. No weapons in sight. No weapons.*'

'*Let's get down and do it.*' The pilot dropped them with stomach-churning speed and dust billowed around the open doors as the helicopter settled, sending up a whirlwind of scrap paper and other debris. The two crewmen were at their guns, flicking off the safeties and settling their feet, the senior man waving to Harry to get ready to disembark. They both looked on edge, their movements rehearsed and economical, but tight, and Harry could feel the tension between them.

He released his seat buckle and took out the keys to the

handcuffs, then unplugged the helmet comms lead and swung across to Rafa'i's seat. The former cleric smelled of sweat and fear, and one of his legs was shaking uncontrollably, but he looked Harry in the eye and said nothing while the cuffs were being unlocked.

A loud whistle. The starboard crewman was pointing towards the opposite door, where his colleague had picked up an M4 assault rifle, ready to lead the way out. He slapped his hand against his side to indicate that Harry should draw the M9 pistol he'd been given before take-off.

Harry eased the gun from the grip of the holster clip, then pushed it back. The last time he'd drawn a gun was still raw, in a place about as far removed from this scenario as it was possible to get: St James's Park, central London. He could still smell the discharge, still hear the gunshots, still feel the recoil through his wrist.

Still see the body falling.

He cursed silently and urged Rafa'i out of his seat and across to the door, which was facing the open square where they had landed. The quicker the welcoming committee saw Rafa'i, he'd been advised, the better. If all they saw were two armed men piling out of the helicopter, things could get complicated.

He took a deep breath as the smell of dust, hot metal and engine oil swirled around him. He kept one hand on Rafa'i's arm just above the elbow and followed him through the door, dropping to the ground right behind him and going into a crouch while the crewman with the assault rifle took up a position ready to watch Harry's back. The noise was deafening, battering the air around them, sand particles stinging every square inch of exposed skin and defying concentration.

Across the square and just visible in the gloom, a number of men watched their arrival, loosely scattered around three four-by-four vehicles. In the background, keeping watch, the two Apaches were constantly shifting position just above the rooftops.

The crewman waved Harry forward, sliding sideways to give himself a safe field of fire. Harry pushed Rafa'i and followed closely behind, drawing the M9 and holding it down by his leg. None of these men would expect them to come unarmed, but waving weaponry in the air like some of the cowboys of the PMC community was asking for trouble.

The men watched him come. The agreement had been to take Rafa'i to the centre of the designated landing site, then leave. That suited Harry just fine, but he'd have felt a lot better if he could have seen how many more were lurking in the shadows. It suddenly struck him how incredibly insane this was.

Then one man detached himself from the group and walked forward. He was unarmed, heavily built and dressed in a white shirt and pants. He immediately became the focal point for a beam of high-intensity light from the helicopter. At a shout from Harry, he very cautiously lifted his shirt to reveal a bare torso. Harry gave the OK and urged Rafa'i on. When they were down to a dozen paces apart, the light beam was switched off and Harry stopped walking. He backed away, ordering Rafa'i to continue alone.

Seconds later Harry was back in the Black Hawk and the crewman was giving the OK to lift off.

The pilot was as calm as ever. '*Postal One, we're out of here. Thank you, Shotguns One and Two. Delivery completed.*'

Rik Ferris was waiting when they got back to the base, left arm in a tan-coloured sling. He had a US army baseball cap jammed on his head and looked pale and restless.

'You took your time. I thought you were just going to fly over and throw him out?'

'We were,' said Harry. 'But we decided it would be polite to land first.' He eyed the sling, which had been plain white when they'd arrived here. 'That looks fresh.' The sling and bandage covered a bullet wound sustained in St James's Park a few days before, courtesy of a rogue female Special Forces bodyguard. Rik still hadn't brought it up in conversation, but Harry knew he would when he was ready.

Getting shot wasn't something you forgot for long.

Rik grinned. 'Yeah, that's the only good bit about coming here. A US army medic noticed the sling and insisted on taking a look. When she saw it was a bullet wound, she was well impressed. Her name's Tammy and she lives in Florida.'

'Lucky you. You've only got a few thousand competitors, then.'

'Very funny. How did it go?'

'Fine. We had an easy ride.' Thank God, he thought. He could still see the faces of the two crewmen and their businesslike, wire-tight movements. They'd been out here too long, he guessed; living on the edge and expecting every trip to be their last. It had a way of eating away at you. No wonder Colonel White was concerned for them; although it was probably more to do with logistics and paperwork if he had to replace them than concern for paid mercenaries. But it was none of his business.

'And Rafa'i?'

'Forget him.' Harry walked into the operations building. He unloaded the pistol and watched the man behind the desk check the breech, then signed the log. 'Did you get anything on the car registration?' He'd asked Rik to run a photo past what Rik called 'the community' – his contacts in computer geekdom – to see if anyone recognized the buildings or the part of the car registration plate that was showing.

'Nothing yet. I wanted to chase it up while I was waiting, but the security guys wouldn't let me use my laptop.' He nudged the shoulder bag lying at his feet. 'Said it was a security risk.'

'Don't worry about it. I need something to eat.' What he needed more was to lie down somewhere for a week. He was still feeling the bruises from the contact in London, when he'd been shoulder charged by a man intent on killing him.

'Mr Tate, sir?' A man wearing the insignia of a Specialist handed Harry an envelope. 'I was instructed to give you this, sir, compliments of Colonel White. There's a driver waiting to take you to the airport when you've eaten, and your flight leaves at oh-six-hundred, sir. Have a safe one.' He flipped a half salute and walked away.

Harry ripped open the envelope. It contained a sheet of paper with a brief message: *The Italian off Wigmore. 10.30 Friday. RB.*

Richard Ballatyne. It took him a moment to think about what day it was. Wednesday. He needed some sleep.

Rik said, 'There's a great cafeteria across the way. They serve steaks the size of a mattress.'

'Good. After that we head home.'

'What's on the agenda?'

'If Ballatyne keeps his word, we're going hunting.'

THREE

Richard Ballatyne was sitting in the same Italian restaurant off Wigmore Street, in London's West End, where Harry had first met him. It had been less than ten days ago, but seemed longer. Much had happened since then, and a rapid series of events piled one on another skewed one's perspective on time. The MI6 officer looked tired, as if the past few days had drained him of energy, his dark hair limp and the eyes behind the glasses blank and hollow.

A hard-case in a suit was sitting to one side of the room, hands out of sight beneath the table and an untouched glass of water in front of him. Other than a brief nod of professional acknowledgement, he paid no further attention to Harry, but concentrated on the street outside.

'Coffee?' Ballatyne nodded at a side table set up with cups, saucers and an ancient aluminium percolator. 'Georgio's own coffee maker. Probably the best brew in London.'

Georgio was the restaurant owner and, Harry suspected, a local asset for MI6. He poured himself a cup and tasted it. Not bad. He sat down. 'You didn't ask me here for the coffee.'

'No, I didn't. How's Ferris?'

'Recovering. He shouldn't have come to Baghdad, though.'

'I know. But it couldn't be helped. It was for his own good – yours, too. If he'd stayed here, he'd have got himself a front page press release. We didn't want that.' He paused. 'That was a good job you did in Baghdad. Rafa'i's friends—'

'Spare me the details,' Harry cut him off. He didn't want to know. It was over. Done. He didn't feel particularly good about dumping the man back among his former friends and supporters, but he could live with it. Rafa'i and whatever may have become of him was no longer his concern. 'What's the public story with the shootings in St James's?' Three killers – two men in military uniform and a young woman, all sent to kill Rafa'i – shot dead in front of a sizeable crowd of witnesses, was bound to have caused a fuss. Harry hadn't even looked at the newspapers, less concerned by public opinion than Rik Ferris's gunshot wound and the need to keep a low profile.

Ballatyne looked unconcerned. 'It's off the front pages, although a few shaky scenes came up on YouTube before we could stop them. Fortunately, the shooting was all over before anyone could zero in on the gory details. Best we can hope for, I suppose. There've been questions in the House . . . tourists terrified, appalling lack of security in the nation's capital, gunmen on the loose just yards from Westminster, that kind of thing. And lots of foreign press coverage, which isn't so good. Still, give it a few more days and they'll have something else to occupy them. There have been arrests, too, and resignations here and in the US and Europe.'

'Archer's employers?' The plotters behind the attempt to snuff Rafa'i. Oil interests, mostly, with grey-faced politicians and others hovering in the shadows. They'd be lucky to get all of them, he thought. Some of the financiers and corporate movers and shakers had better security cut-outs to protect themselves from unwanted investigation than most spies.

'Yes.' Ballatyne shifted his cup and saucer and placed a photo on the table. It was the one he'd shown Harry immediately after the shooting in St James's Park. It showed the man Harry knew as Henry Paulton, Operations Director of MI5; the man who had posted Harry to Georgia following a disastrous drug bust and nearly succeeded in having him eliminated by a government 'wet' operator known as the Hit. Paulton was pictured about to get into a car in an unnamed street. Harry had been counting on analysing the photo to begin the hunt for his former boss.

'The situation's changed,' Ballatyne said, before Harry could pick up the photo. 'Paulton's moved on.'

Harry was disappointed but not surprised. He'd been hoping Ballatyne was better than this, though.

'Handy.'

Ballatyne blinked at the cynical tone 'No, I'm serious. I meant what I said: you take Rafa'i to Baghdad and I'd tell where the photo was taken. It was Brussels, in case you're still interested. Just off Avenue Louise. He's not there now, though.'

'But you know where he is.' It was a statement.

'Not exactly. He was seen two days ago by an embassy security staffer, leaving Frankfurt airport. Unfortunately, he lost him in the crowd. He could be anywhere by now.'

Harry watched the MI6 man's face, trying to determine what was true and what was misdirection. There was something there, under the skin. A glint in his eyes which showed that this wasn't all he had to say.

'But you have an idea?'

'Yes. A slim one, but it sounds plausible.' He cleared his throat and took another sip of coffee. 'As you probably know, the British army has anything up to two thousand personnel listed as absent without leave at any one time. Most of those are short-term, through illness, family problems, drink, drugs, fights, arrests and so forth. And trauma. A few are long-term, meaning they don't intend reporting back. Most are from infantry regiments with a few scattered among other units. It's a problem, but manageable. However, there's a core group who have gone absent and can't be found. They're spread as far as Australia, Canada, South Africa, Thailand . . . and lots of other places where we can't get at them. Within that core group are a few personnel of particular concern.' He flicked at a sugar grain on the tablecloth and gave a wintry smile. 'They're listed as SDPs, or Strategic Displaced Personnel, would you believe?'

'Meaning what?' Harry couldn't quite see where this was going, but it had to involve him somehow; whatever Ballatyne was leading up to, he wasn't going to leave here without exerting some kind of official pressure to do a job of work. 'Does this involve Paulton or not?'

'Yes.' No room for doubt.

'How? He's not on this list, is he?'

'Hardly. But we believe he's got something to do with it.'

'In what way?'

'Of the maybe two dozen names on the SDP list, there's a handful who are too important to let go.'

Harry felt his spirits sink. 'You want me chasing down a bunch of squaddies? I don't think so.' He made to stand, but Ballatyne put out a hand to stop him.

'Wait. That's not what I'm leading up to. Well, not entirely.'

He waited for Harry to relax before continuing. 'The people I'm talking about are not your average squaddies, too pissed to find their way back to their units. All of them have tactical, planning or technical information in their heads; information that if let out, would be a disaster for our operational and strategic capability.'

'Let out?'

'Sold.'

Harry breathed out. He began to see where this was going.

'In the business world,' Ballatyne continued smoothly, 'people like this would be head-hunted from one corporate body to another, valued and appraised for their technical skills, education and potential. Most would have been fast-tracked from university on career-management paths. Well, these specialists are no different . . . only, the interested bodies involved are not our friends.'

Nice, thought Harry. Russia. Iran. North Korea. China. And a few smaller countries who'd love to get their hands on our latest weapons technology. Throw in al-Qaeda for the fun of it and the nightmare was real.

'And you think Paulton's involved in horse-trading military specialists?'

'He's got the background. And he's got a living to make. He wasn't like Bellingham and a few others we could name, born with the benefits of a silver spoon; he was a normal wage slave like the rest of us.'

'He's nothing like the rest of us.' Harry's words come out as sharp as tin tacks, his hackles rising. Paulton, along with Bellingham, his MI6 opposite number, had conspired to have Harry, Rik Ferris and several other security and intelligence services staff terminated. That put him well outside the pale of normal.

'Forgive me. Clumsy comparison.' Ballatyne looked genuinely sorry. 'But I think you know what I mean. There's a lot of money swilling about out there looking for the right information. Paulton's got contacts built over a lifetime in the business, he has a first class brain and knows his way around every kind of negotiating situation. He dealt with the IRA for years, he's mixed it with numerous other terror groups and their front men, and he's very good at keeping people onside. He's also an expert at disappearing. As you'd expect, he has numerous passports in a variety of names.' He held up a hand and began to count off his fingers. 'Some MI5 personnel knew him as Henry. Others knew him as George. To his neighbours in the block of flats where he lived, he was George Henry, civil servant. Other names we've discovered are Patrick Towen, George Bartholomew and Paul McHenry. There's a John Arthur Millar and a Colin Bracewell out there, too, although documents in both those names have turned up recently, so he's probably ditched them by now. He seems to have made an art out of playing identity games with everyone he ever came in contact with, just for the hell of it.'

'And nobody picked this up?'

Ballatyne shrugged. 'Apparently not. Shows how good he was. His life was carefully compartmentalized, so one group never met the others. Classic undercover technique. Only he took it several stages further.' He smiled coldly. 'If it happened and two separates did meet, he probably had a good explanation for it. Having two names is not uncommon. I'm still known by my family as Paul – my middle name. Apparently I never liked Richard as a kid. Once I started work, though, Richard was on my records, so Richard I became. In a perfect world, a psych evaluation should have seen Paulton's budding paranoia, but he appears to have avoided close examination for years.'

Harry felt himself being hemmed in, dragged slowly against his will into a separate kind of chase, one not of his choosing. Hunting down Paulton was all he'd been thinking about for months. But he'd been planning on doing it on his own terms. Having got this close to a possible location, he was now recognizing a carrot being dangled before him; a carrot intended to get him to do a job of work in exchange for knowledge about Paulton's whereabouts.

He tried one last method of stepping sideways. 'You've got people who can do this. You don't need me.'

'Sure we have. But this is delicate. And we'll pay you for your time, sub-contract rates. Ferris, too, if you need him.' Ballatyne sighed. 'Look, the MOD has a squad of recovery officers chasing down overdue squaddies and persuading them to come in. But they have limited skills and authority. Redcaps are good, too, there's no denying, but they go best where they're pointed.'

'So?'

'I want you to do the pointing. You're good at finding people – you've already proved that. We want you to follow the trails. Find the SDPs and you'll find Paulton.'

'And when I find them – and him?' He'd been down this route before.

'Sit on him and call it in. You'll have twenty-four-hour back-up.' Ballatyne fixed him with a cool stare. 'Just so there's no mistake, we really would like him back to answer for what he did.' He reached into an inside pocket and placed a five-by-three photo and a folded slip of paper on the table. 'This is the first name we want brought in – and the nearest. He disappeared while in transit overseas three months ago, was spotted in Sydney, then again in Thailand. He just surfaced out of the blue in London. He was either daft or desperate enough to use his credit card in Stockwell and got lit up. Where he's been since Thailand, we have no idea. He might be waiting for a contact . . . or is on the point of running. We'd like to get him before he does.'

Harry glanced at the photo. It was a head and shoulders shot of a lean man in his thirties, smiling into the camera. He looked relaxed and tanned. He scanned the brief details. *Cpl Neville John Pike, age 36. 251 Signals Squadron. Specialties include ECM (electronic countermeasures) and IT systems design. Service in Iraq, Somalia and Afghanistan. Unmarried, no family.* It was followed by Pike's eight-digit service number and an address in Clapham, south-west London.

'Is this all?'

'How much do you need? There'll be full backgrounds on the others, mainly because they're out in who the hell knows where. But this one's probably the simplest.' He flicked a hand at the suit, who stood up and carried a black nylon bag across the room and placed it by Harry's side. 'Taser and cuffs,' Ballatyne explained. 'Just in case. We don't need any more shooting for a while. I'm sure you'll be able to use them if you have to.'

'I'll do my best,' said Harry. He'd done a two-hour course once, part of a new equipment training module. It hadn't been a great success. He'd forgotten to switch the Taser on and got stamped on by an instructor posing as a rioter. 'This is all a bit personal for someone on your level, isn't it?'

'Level?' Ballatyne blinked.

'Well, you're, what – Ops Director at least? Handing over bits of paper and bags of equipment is below your pay grade, I'd have thought.'

'I suppose so. But I owed you the first couple of meetings at least. Later on you'll be dealing with a man named Cullum. He's currently putting together the file for you, along with personal data and background on the absentees. He'll provide you with whatever other information you need. I'll need a secure code for the data – something you've never used before.'

Harry thought about it and gave him the six-digit number from the back of his watch. Ballatyne wrote it down. 'What's that – your mangled birth date?'

'No. The model number of my iPad.' It wasn't, but he didn't think Ballatyne would check. He picked up the slip of paper. 'What makes this so important to Six? You don't normally go chasing deserters.'

'You're right. It shouldn't be our problem, but things have changed in the last few years. People like Pike are highly trained and educated; they carry enormous detail in their heads about new developments in equipment and tactics, systems and strategies. And Two-Five-One Signals Squadron takes the best. Even their average member these days is a mine of saleable information to the right people. What we'd like to do is find out who's doing the buying.'

'That doesn't explain why Six and not Five.'

'It's the way it is.' Ballatyne tapped the table before standing up. His minder moved to the door and checked the street. 'Two military cops are keeping watch on the house where Pike's gone to ground. They'll assist you in collecting Pike, and take him to Colchester. Before they do, however, we'd like you to question him and find out where he's been for the last three months. It's a little outside the standard procedure, but if you can get anything out of him it might help. Good luck.' With a brief nod he walked out on the heels of his minder, leaving Harry alone with the black bag.

FOUR

The house where Corporal Neville Pike had gone to ground was a tired-looking Victorian pile near Clapham Common, south London. Yet to be swept up by developers and gentrified, it seemed to be resisting change, unlike many of its neighbours which were proudly displaying radical facelifts and makeovers. Pike was in number 11 on the third floor, according to Ballatyne's watchers, where he'd been holed up for three days living off pizza deliveries from a shop on the corner.

Harry buzzed the array of buttons until someone let him in, then climbed the stairs and knocked on the door. No answer. The floorboards squeaked as his balance shifted, but there was no answering shift from inside. He knocked again, waited, then slid a card underneath the door and walked back downstairs, trying not to breath in the sour atmosphere of damp walls, ancient carpets and stale cigarette smoke. He was deliberately making enough noise for Pike to hear him, and the card said he'd be waiting outside and why. He was hoping the soldier was going to come down without any drama.

If he didn't, he and the MPs – military police – would have to go in and get him.

Fifteen minutes passed, during which a cat wandered across the unkempt rear garden, jumped over a rusting metal wheelbarrow and disappeared through a ground floor window propped open with a saucepan. Traffic noises sounded out in the street, kids laughing, the distant rattle of road mending machinery. A woman's head popped up from behind a fence two gardens down and stared hard at him before disappearing again. Life was going on as normal.

Then Pike appeared.

He had a holdall in one hand and was wearing a denim jacket and jeans, with a baseball cap mashed down over his eyes. He was tall and lean, sporting the remains of a tan from his last tour in Helmand, or maybe his stay in Thailand. But underneath it he looked soft and pasty, and wobbly on his feet. Too long spent indoors behind curtains, waiting for the sound of footsteps. Instead of looking for Harry's offer of a chat, though, he came out of the back door and down the garden path as if the place was on fire.

Harry let him come. He guessed he was heading for a green left-hand drive BMW 5 Series in the service alley at the rear. Four years old, good condition and a bit flash, the left-hander had been a sure giveaway, a cheap pick from the vast backstreet car market of south London.

Something silver glinted in Pike's free hand.

When Harry stepped out from behind the garden wall, Pike looked shocked and skidded to a halt. Up close, his eyes held an unreal light which might have been from too little sleep, too much alcohol or too many pills. Drugs were the most likely, drugs to keep him awake, alert and ready to go, as available among active service units as they were on the streets. But there was something else in there, too: the look of a man who had travelled beyond reason and couldn't stop.

He gave a small, high-pitched moan, more child than man, and dropped the holdall. It landed with a soft thump. Spare clothes, whatever he could carry that wouldn't slow him down. Going AWOL means travelling light.

'Don't,' Pike muttered, and motioned for Harry to get out of his way.

He had a compelling argument; he was holding an SA80 British army bayonet in his hand, blade up, the light glinting off the clean metal. The edge looked razor-keen, which went a long way to explaining what Pike had been doing to pass the time in his bolthole. There was no point wondering if he knew how to use the weapon.

He would know.

Harry waited for him to make a move. There were two options for dealing with Pike: one was under Harry's jacket on his right hip. He could simply pull out the 9mm Steyr semi-automatic and shoot him – especially now he'd seen the bayonet. Under the rules of engagement, such as they were, armed defence was permitted. But he didn't want to do that.

He waited instead while the seconds ticked by.

Pike launched himself on six.

The second option was less fatal, but risky if it didn't work. Since he really didn't want to shoot a man for being desperate and traumatized, he took out the Taser and pulled the trigger.

He had forgotten to issue the required warning, but that was just a technicality.

The twin probes hit Pike in the chest, the charge of electricity to his nervous system taking his legs out from under him and dropping him like a sack of cement. He lay trembling on the path, one foot kicking uncontrollably, the bayonet clutched in frozen fingers.

'He'd have filleted you with that.'

The voice belonged to a big Londoner named Wallace. He was one of two Royal Military Police sergeants on standby in case Pike got lucky, and responsible for taking him in when Harry gave the nod. Wallace had been playing backstop in the lane by the BMW. He looked disappointed that the fun was over before he could join in. His partner, Collins, whom Harry had automatically thought of as Gromit, was covering the front door in case Pike tried to go that way.

After he'd disengaged the Taser probes, Wallace bent and prised the bayonet from Pike's grip. He flipped it twice, tested the blade and hissed sharply. 'I could shave with this.' He gave Harry a sideways look. 'Why didn't you shoot him?'

His tone meant, you've probably shot people before, so why not now?

'I didn't want to start the day on a bad note.' Harry bent and checked Pike for vital signs. It wouldn't look good if he died on them. When he was sure the man was breathing steadily and showing signs of rallying, he gave Wallace the OK to take him to the nearest A&E for a check-up.

'That'll be King's College,' the MP replied. 'Are you sure you want to bother? He looks OK to me. We've been told to get him to Colchester.'

'I know. I want to take a look inside first. Wait for me at the hospital.' He packed up the Taser and walked through to the front of the house where Gromit was lounging against a lamppost looking bored. He nodded moodily when he saw

Harry and went round to join his colleague. Harry walked back up the stairs and found the door to Pike's room open. The interior was surprisingly neat, with the bed made, blankets folded and everything in military order. Some habits died hard. A coffee table held a tidy pile of magazines and newspapers, and the only attempt at disorder was the sink drainer, which held three flattened pizza boxes and two empty soda bottles. An overhead cupboard held crockery, glasses and an unopened bottle of wine.

He took a look round, but it was clear that Pike had been on his way out and wasn't coming back. If there had been anything of value, he wouldn't have left the door open.

As Harry reached his car, his phone rang. It was Ballatyne.

'Any joy?'

'We've got him. The MPs are taking him to King's College, Denmark Hill, for a check-up, then on to the Military Detention Centre, Colchester.'

'What's to check? Did one of the redcaps help him down the stairs?' Ballatyne's tone was as dry as dust.

'I had to use the Taser.'

'You really don't mess, do you? OK, be at Langham Place Starbucks tomorrow at ten. Gordon Cullum will be there with the rest of the information.' The phone went dead.

FIVE

The young doctor who checked out Corporal Pike treated Harry and Sergeant Wallace to the kind of look he probably reserved for axe-murderers and Saturday night deviants. He ran an expert eye over the patient, with pointed attention to where the Taser darts had entered his skin, then nodded. 'He's OK. He looks undernourished, but if he's been hiding from you lot, I'm not surprised. Where are you taking him?'

'Off your hands,' said Harry. 'Can we use a side room for a few minutes?'

The doctor pointed along the corridor. 'First on the left. Don't take too long – we might need it for real-life problems.' He hurried away without a backward glance, white coat-tails flying, while Wallace helped Pike to his feet and walked him along the corridor.

'Mind telling us where you were going, Corporal?' Harry asked, emptying out Pike's bag once they were in the room. Pike sprawled on the examination table, eyes on the opposite wall. As Harry suspected, the bag contained a change of underwear and socks, two T-shirts, a pair of trainers and a slim washbag. Nothing in the side pockets and nothing under the baseboard.

'You've no right going through that,' Pike muttered without looking at him. 'It's private.'

'You're right,' said Harry quietly. 'And a private is what you're going to be as soon as they bust you for going AWOL, theft of military equipment and assault with a deadly weapon. Where were you going?'

'I don't have to answer that.'

'No, you don't. But it'll help if you do. You have a wallet?'

Pike reached round and took out a thin leather wallet, handed it over. It contained a Visa credit card, driving licence, a family group photo and a mix of sterling and euro banknotes to the tune of £300. On the back of the photo was a telephone number.

'If I rang this, who would answer?'

'Nobody. It's discontinued.'

Harry handed his mobile and the photo to Sergeant Wallace, who dialled the number. After a short wait he looked up and shook his head. 'Unobtainable.' He returned the phone and photo.

'We know you've been overseas for a while, Neville. Can I call you Neville?'

Pike shrugged. 'Break your neck.'

'You were in Sydney, then Thailand, we know that. Where else?'

'Helmand. That do you? Now fuck off and leave me in peace.' He lay back and stared at the ceiling.

Harry drew up a chair and sat alongside him. Wallace stood the other side, tall and imposing. The silence lengthened, broken only by the pink of the heating system and the squeak of shoes on tiles along the corridor outside. Pike ignored both men, but a strong pulse was beating in his throat.

'Were you approached by anyone while you were away?'

No reaction. Harry wondered about Pike's background. The slip of paper hadn't said, but it was obvious the NCO was no idiot. At a guess he'd been to university or technical college, maybe even through industry, before joining the army. His voice and speech were middle class, even if his language wasn't.

'How did you support yourself for the last three months? Did you have help?'

Still nothing.

'Man like you, you'd be a valuable commodity to some people . . . all the knowledge you've got in your head. We know there's a market out there, and buyers. If you spoke to anyone, you really don't want us finding out later on. It would help your case if you said so now. Who approached you?'

'Nobody approached me, so leave me alone.' Pike spoke through clenched teeth. He was clearly hiding something. Whatever it was, he wasn't going to talk about it here.

Harry took out a card and slid it into Pike's hand. It carried his name and a telephone number. 'Please yourself. My name's Harry. If you change your mind and want to talk, get them to give me a call.'

Harry walked outside and took a short cut through the hospital car park towards the road where he'd left his car, his thoughts on what Pike could have been doing in Clapham. The man had been virtually home and dry, if what Ballatyne had said was true. All he had to do was horse-trade some information in return for a new identity and a new life, away from whatever had driven him to go AWOL in the first place. So, with no family ties and no baggage, why had he come back?

Then a thought struck him. Baggage. Pike's room had been clean. After five days cooped up in a single room, wouldn't there have been some rubbish?

He stepped back as a grey estate car drifted down the street and swung into the visitors' car park right in front of him. The two men inside gave him a steady look as they passed. They wore the air of two individuals going about their duty, rather than visiting the sick, and Harry pegged them as police.

He watched them go, then dialled Ballatyne's number.

'Are you having me shadowed?'

'Not me. I don't have the personnel. Why?'

'No reason. Must be getting paranoid.' He rang off feeling mildly embarrassed. This job was already starting to get to him.

The street in Clapham where Pike had been staying was quiet, with only an occasional vehicle and a scattering of pedestrians. Harry found a space and climbed out of the car. As he approached the house, he passed a woman putting out a pile of bound news-papers on the front step. It was the same woman he'd seen looking over the fence at the rear while waiting for Pike to emerge. She looked the confrontational kind, and he wasn't disappointed.

'I saw you earlier,' she said, brushing back a stray lock of hair. 'You were out back with that chap. You know we've got Neighbourhood Watch in the street?' She blinked furiously and he wondered at the fragile state of mind which allowed her to face a total stranger like this.

'Glad to hear it,' he said pleasantly. 'Do you have a bin collec-tion, too?'

'Of course, we do,' she muttered. 'Cheeky bugger. You think we're a third world country or something?'

Mad, he thought. Beyond seeing danger. 'When do they come? The bin men?'

'Tomorrow.' She moved back to her front door. 'It's papers today. School collection. I should call the police!'

He thanked her and smiled, which finally seemed to unnerve her, and she disappeared inside, slamming the door.

He walked up the steps to Pike's house and pressed the cleanest button.

'Yeah?' A male smoker's voice, dry as sandpaper.

'Tenant come to see the empty flat on three. The agent's parking his car.'

A buzzer sounded and Harry pushed the door, thankful for people who probably didn't even know there was a Neighbourhood Watch. He climbed the stairs and stopped outside No. 11. It was still open.

He stepped inside and saw that the scavengers had beaten him to it. The coffee table had gone, the magazines and newspapers tossed on the floor, and the blankets had been turned inside out. He opened the overhead cupboard. No bottle of wine.

He checked the window, which overlooked a corner of the
rear garden. It explained why Pike had been surprised to see him.
What it didn't explain was why he'd come out armed and ready
for a fight.

The place was clean, he already knew that, but he had another
look, anyway. Then he closed the door and went back downstairs.
Turned right at the bottom and walked down a short passageway
to a rear door, and out to the service alley. Two bins were out
ready for collection. They contained standard household rubbish:
bottles, pre-packed food bags, supermarket packaging and other
discards. Nothing indicating a bachelor lifestyle in hiding.
Alongside them were two plastic bags, one secured with a wire
tie. He opened the first one, which contained vegetable peelings,
a hair conditioner bottle, coffee grounds and a craft magazine.
Quilting and sewing. Definitely not Pike's rubbish, then, unless
he had a secret hobby. And he was no cook; he'd preferred his
food ready made and full of fat.

The second bag held a scrunched kitchen roll, an old T-shirt
with a torn sleeve, an empty milk carton and two crushed beer
cans . . . and three flattened pizza cartons.

And down at the bottom, a torn ticket stub from Eurostar,
Brussels to London.

He thought about letting Ballatyne put his people on to it, but
that would take too long. He rang Rik Ferris and read out the
ticket number. 'Find out who it was issued to and where from,
can you?'

'Thank God for that,' breathed Rik. 'I'm going stir crazy, my
shoulder's itching and my mum's driving me nuts with all the
phone calls. I was just about to go out and stab some car tyres.'

SIX

'You want a tab?' Sergeant Wallace held out a cigarette
packet to Corporal Pike, who was huddled in the rear
seat of their unmarked Vauxhall Vectra, staring out of the
window. They were on the A12 heading north-east and had just

got police clearance to filter through a two-lane accident. The delay meant other traffic was getting through in bursts, and they were surrounded by open road.

'I don't smoke.' It was the first thing Pike had said since leaving the hospital, in spite of Wallace and his colleague's attempts to start up a conversation. Neither of them enjoyed taking in men who'd gone AWOL; their stories were usually far from straightforward, and certainly too complex for snap judgements, even by hardened military policemen. But they tried to keep things civil.

'You saw the Green Slime off,' said Collins, using the derogatory term for members of the Intelligence Corps. 'Tate, I mean. Put a right dent in his day.' He grinned in the rear-view mirror, received a look of contempt in return. He shrugged. 'Please yourself.'

'What makes you think he's Intelligence?' said Wallace, snapping his lighter and drawing in a lungful of smoke.

Collins looked surprised. 'What makes you think he's not?'

'You didn't see him use the Taser.' Wallace spoke quietly, although there was little chance their prisoner couldn't hear what he was saying. 'Faced with a bayonet sharp enough to cut my old lady's rock cake, he left it to the last second, then bam. If he was really I-Corps he would've got sliced and diced. Or panicked and shot the poor bastard.' He shook his head. 'Don't know what he is, but it's not army intelligence.'

Collins sniffed and checked his rear-view mirror as they passed a junction. Pike was lolling against the side window, eyes closed. The road behind was clear. Then a silver-grey Mercedes estate joined the carriageway and slid up fast on the outside lane. Two up, he noted automatically. Business types, probably, lucky gits. Nice car with lots of muscle. Better than this heap of overdriven crap they were forced to use.

The Mercedes drew level with them and slowed.

Collins glanced across, expecting to see the car cruise by, but the bonnet was now close alongside, keeping pace. He felt a jolt of alarm when the rear nearside passenger window slid down and he saw a face appear. 'Hey, what the fuck's this idiot playing at?'

'Who?' Wallace was fiddling with the radio. He looked round, squinting through the smoke from his cigarette.

The first bang was shocking in its intensity, and Collins felt the back of his head showered with glass fragments. He ducked instinctively and felt the car wobble as his grip faltered. Wallace shouted something, but the words were lost in the sudden roar of road noise coming through the shattered rear door window and the increase in engine noise as Collins automatically hit the accelerator.

Then Collins saw the blood. It was sprayed across the mirror, on the roof and even across the side of Wallace's face. And something warm was trickling down the back of his neck. *We've been hit!* He whipped his head round to check the back.

'Pike! You OK?'

But Pike was slumped back, the side of his face gone and his one good eye staring up at the roof.

Another two bangs very close. A car horn blared loudly and Collins realized it was him; he'd hit the button with a reflex action. Then the Mercedes surged away, leaving them behind, and Collins was fighting to hold on to the steering wheel as the shredded offside tyres began a terrifying *whump-whump-whump*, bits of rubber flew past the side windows and the air was filled with the screech of tortured wheel rims on tarmac.

Seconds later, before Collins could slow down, the steering wheel was ripped from his grasp and the car began a lazy, unstoppable spin and roll, and everything blurred into in a sickening whirlwind of broken glass, gravel, ripped metal and the sickly smell of blood and spilled diesel.

'Felicity calls you my International Man of Mystery.' Jean Fleming helped Harry take off his jacket and hung it up. A tall and willowy redhead who ran an upmarket flower business just down the road from her Fulham flat, she accepted Harry's unexplained absences with equanimity and never asked about where he had been. As the widow of an army officer killed in Iraq, she knew that questions rarely brought a true answer and never true peace of mind. She possessed an irreverent sense of humour and a throaty laugh which made Harry's toes curl. Felicity was her business partner, a committed Sloane Ranger who knew everybody who was anybody and was vital to the business.

'Well, I am,' Harry agreed, 'and Felicity's a romantic.' He

accepted the large glass of red wine Jean handed him, and the kiss that followed. Since his divorce, Jean was the nearest he'd come to a long-term relationship, although neither of them had made any moves towards taking it to another level. Jean teasingly introduced him as her occasional date or OD, which suited them both.

She sat on a leather-covered footstool in front of him and chinked glasses. Her eyes were light brown, the gaze disconcertingly direct. 'You look tired. What've you been up to, Charlie Brown?'

He knew she didn't want the fine print; she knew better than that. But she'd heard about the shooting in St James's Park and Rik's wounding, and had put two and two together. 'Rik and I had to take someone overseas. It was a long flight and I'm glad to be back.'

'Long? Iraq long or Afghanistan long?' She knew Harry's previous area of operations, if not the precise details, and she knew he was still connected with the intelligence community, albeit by a long cord. She was also perceptive, armed with a former military wife's expertise at telling the difference between job tiredness and the slow wind-down from operational stress.

'Iraq. Baghdad.' Ballatyne would have had kittens hearing him admitting this to anyone, but he didn't care. He smiled and took a sip of his wine, feeling himself relax. 'Is this a Merlot? It's very smooth and . . . let me see – fruity with a touch of blackberries.'

'You are so full of bullshit, Harry Tate,' Jean said with a laugh, and leaned forward for another kiss, bringing a faint smell of lemons. 'It's a Shiraz and you know as much about wine as you do about flower arranging, so don't change the subject. I just like to know you're OK, that's all. How's Rik?'

'Trying to avoid his mother's phone calls and getting stroppy, which is a good sign.' He sniffed the air. 'Is that something cooking?' It reminded him that he hadn't sat down to eat properly for a couple of days. The ration pack he'd been handed on the flight back from Baghdad had been uninspiring, and had found a good home in the stomach of the private contractor in the next seat.

Jean lifted an eyebrow. 'You mean you want to *eat*?'

Harry gave an elaborate shrug and fought hard to keep a straight face, burying his nose in his glass. 'Well . . . eventually. Why, what are you suggesting?'

She stood up and took his glass off him. 'Follow me, International Man of Mystery, and if you're a very good boy, I'll show you.'

SEVEN

The Langham Place Starbucks had a line of office workers waiting to collect their morning fix of caffeine from the end of the counter, and a middle-aged man in a rumpled pinstripe suit. He was sitting and flicking impatiently through a travel brochure with the dislocated nervous look of a patient about to see his dentist. He looked up as Harry stepped through the door and gestured for him to come over.

'Tate? Good of you to make it. Gordon Cullum.' He gestured to the chair and put the brochure to one side, then sat back without offering to shake hands, eyes flicking over Harry, assessing. The table was in a corner, away from its nearest neighbour, and Harry guessed Cullum had used this place before.

'Who sent you?' he asked.

'You know who.' Cullum gave a hint of a sneer, keen to demonstrate that as far as he was concerned, playing security games wasn't necessary. 'Ballatyne.'

'Where is he?'

'Not mine to ask and they don't tell. He's Six.'

Which meant Cullum was not. Five, probably.

'You have some information for me,' Harry said, keeping it simple. He'd never met Cullum, didn't know his history. For all he knew, he and Paulton might have been secret bridge buddies, in which case this was a waste of time.

'Yes.' Cullum delved in a pocket and produced a data stick on a key ring. He placed it on the table but kept it close by. 'How was Baghdad?'

'Hot. Unfriendly. Same as always. What's on the stick?'

Cullum sniffed. 'Never been, myself. Belfast was more my time. So you got him there, then – Rafa'i? Back with his own kind.'

The man's only trying to be friendly, Harry told himself, although he questioned the man's lack of tact – in here, especially, less than a sticky bun's throw from the BBC and its wasp's nest of journalists. He decided to humour him. 'The last I saw, he was back home and walking.' He nodded at the data stick. 'Is that what I think it is?'

Cullum ignored the question. 'That was good work, especially after what you went through with Paulton.' It sounded genuine but his eyes gave him away. The praise was hollow; he didn't care one way or another. This was just a job to be ticked off, one among many in a busy day. He finally tapped the stick. 'In here is the information Ballatyne asked for. It's all in the file: names, units, dates, backgrounds. It will ask you for an unlock code. That's whatever you agreed with Ballatyne.'

'Does it include Paulton?'

'What about him?'

'I need whatever you've got; family, friends, contacts, where he went to school.'

'Why would you need that?'

'Because it's how I find people.'

Cullum chewed it over then nodded, playing the generous benefactor. 'It's all there. Heavily edited, of course, but there's plenty to be getting on with.' He slid the stick across to Harry. 'I can imagine what you'll do when you find him.'

'Really. And what's that?'

'Well, some would like him to fall under a bus, but that's not my decision. There's a note for interested parties should you need it, and a form to sign. You can print it off.'

'A form?' Harry wondered if he was about to be offered his old job back. That would be a shocker. He wasn't sure he could take that.

'We're assigning you a nominal position of WO-Two.' Cullum smiled thinly, and took a card out of his pocket. It showed Harry's MI5 file photo. 'I know you were a captain in a previous life and it's a bit of a step down, but an officer would be all wrong for what you'll be doing. It's a cover in case a situation arises.'

'Situation?'

'You know what I mean.' He folded his chubby hands on the table, the lecture over and enjoying the brief power it gave him.

Harry pocketed the data stick and card and stood up. 'Forget it.'

'What?'

'I won't be signing anything, now or later.'

Cullum scrambled to his feet. He was shorter than he'd looked. 'There isn't room for compromise, Tate,' he muttered. 'This isn't some kind of lone warrior mission, you know. We need that form signed.'

Harry's phone rang. He checked the screen. Ballatyne.

'Harry.' The MI6 man's voice was flat. 'We've got a problem. Are you alone?'

'I'm with Cullum. We've just finished,' he added heavily. Cullum looked annoyed. He must have guessed it was Ballatyne. He turned and walked out without a word, scooping up the travel brochure as he went.

'Good. Lose him and get down to Victoria Embankment Gardens. Urgent.'

'He's gone. What's up?'

'Pike and his escorts never made it to Colchester.'

EIGHT

Harry took the underground to Embankment, changing trains twice on the way as a precaution. If Pike had been killed or taken, someone must have been watching him. It followed that Harry might now be on someone's watch list. He emerged into bright sunshine. Behind and to his left across the river was the London Eye, revolving slowly under a blue-grey sky. In front of him was a paved pedestrian area leading up towards Charing Cross station. Victoria Embankment Gardens opened to his right, with the usual cluster of office workers on a smoke break, managing to look somehow miserable in their enjoyment.

He checked the immediate area but saw no sign of Ballatyne, so he turned right and walked into the gardens. Bordered on one side by tall buildings and on the other by the river and the rush of traffic along the Victoria Embankment, the gardens presented an oasis of sorts, overlooked by a number of large trees with lush foliage. The area was roughly triangular in shape, narrowing at one end, with wooden benches dotted at regular intervals around the central lawn, facing outwards. It was a good place for a meeting, Harry noted; busy enough for a person to merge with the office workers and tourists, central enough for anyone to be there with good reason, and with space for a discreet conversation without being overheard. He'd used places like it over the years, although not always so pleasant.

Ballatyne was sitting on one of the benches down the river side of the triangle, next to a young woman in a blouson jacket and jeans. He was nursing a disposable mug and reading a newspaper. His minder was standing a few yards away, chewing on an apple. The minder spotted Harry and gave a brief nod, then walked over and threw his apple into a waste bin. It seemed to be the signal for the young woman to get up and walk away, leaving the seat next to Ballatyne vacant.

Harry walked along the path and sat down.

'Smooth,' he said. 'Do you all practise that on the terrace at Vauxhall Cross?'

'Well, we have to spend the allocation on something,' said Ballatyne, not bothering to check that anyone was near. The background noise of a train passing over Hungerford Bridge and the roar of traffic along the Embankment would ensure privacy. 'Pike and his escorts were in an RTA on the A12 north of Brentwood. Pike and Wallace are dead and Collins is in intensive care, condition critical.'

Harry felt his gut drop at the news. 'What happened?'

'It was a hit. Witnesses said another car – a Mercedes estate – came off the intersection with the M25 and drew alongside. There were some bangs and Pike's car swerved and flipped. The witness said they were travelling fast. The Merc was gone by the time anyone could take the number. Did you get anything from him?'

'No. He wouldn't talk. But I know he came into the country

on Eurostar via Brussels. Someone else must have known it, too.'
He ran back over the past eighteen hours. Pike's trail must have
been picked up and followed at some stage. He thought back to
the two men he'd seen in the car at the hospital. That had been
a grey estate, too, but he couldn't recall the make. The men had
stood out only because of their look. It didn't mean they were
responsible for killing Pike, but it was a possibility. He told
Ballatyne about them. No, he hadn't noticed the registration.

Ballatyne nodded. 'I'll get the Plods to see if the local cameras
picked them up. What time was this?'

Harry told him. 'I'll follow the Eurostar lead, backtrack his
journey in. If he came in from Thailand, he could have flown in
to Amsterdam, then by train on through Brussels to London.' He
had a sudden thought. 'That photo of Paulton in Brussels; how
recent was it?'

Ballatyne gave a ghost of a smile. 'I can see your thinking.
But whatever Pike was doing in Brussels, it wasn't meeting
Paulton. That photo was four months old, before Pike went on
the trot. We do have a lead, though. A flag just came up on Pike's
Visa card. He used it twice to draw cash from a machine near
The Hague. Approximately four hundred pounds in two lots.'

Harry thought about the money in Pike's wallet. That would
be about right, given ticket money to London and some kind of
deposit on his room rental in Clapham. Yet laying such an obvious
trail was inconsistent with a man deciding to bunk off to foreign
parts and pick up a new life in exchange for selling sensitive
military information.

'He wasn't running anywhere,' he said finally, as the realization hit him. 'He was coming home.' He thought about the bayonet
and its keen edge, and the expression in Pike's eyes when he
saw Harry standing in his way. It had been a reactive process:
Harry was there to stop him, ergo he was the enemy and to be
taken out. 'Pike was damaged goods. He needed psychiatric help,
not a return to combat.'

'I wouldn't argue with that.'

The young woman in the blouson returned and sat on a section
of low wall a few yards away, while the minder in the suit
wandered off to watch the traffic on the Embankment. The young
woman turned and lifted a mobile phone to squint at the screen.

'Tell her to knock it off,' said Harry mildly. 'You've got my picture on file.'

Ballatyne looked irritated and glared at the young woman until she got the message and moved away. 'Sorry,' he said. 'That wasn't part of their orders. Bloody mobile phones, given them all *carte blanche* to record everything they see.' He sighed. 'Many more downloads of worthless crap and the system will crash altogether.' He leaned over and dumped his cup into a waste bin alongside the bench. 'There's a rum thing about Pike, though, Harry: he can't have been all that damaged. We came across an offshore bank account in his brother's name. Popped up out of nowhere. Four days ago he received a deposit of fifty grand from sources unknown via an account in Grand Cayman.' He squinted at the sky. 'The Pikes of this world don't get money from offshore centres – certainly not that much – not unless it smells of drugs or terrorism. Or espionage.'

'I didn't know he had a brother.' There had been no mention of close family in the notes. Pike was alone in the world, a free agent.

'He doesn't. He did once, but little Davy fell out of a tree when he was five. Died of a brain haemorrhage.'

Harry let it go. It sounded as if Ballatyne had Pike's past activities all sewn up and the evidence to prove it. There was nothing more he could do except find out where the man had been. 'Do you have the location of the cash machine Pike used in The Hague?'

'I thought you might ask that.' He took a brown A5 envelope from his pocket and passed it across. 'It's in there. A place with an unpronounceable name on the coast.' It seemed a curiously furtive action and Harry wondered how often Ballatyne got out of his office.

'We're trying to track the route of the Mercedes that totalled Pike and the others, but I'm not holding out much hope. Some of the cameras have been turned off to save money. It's probably been torched in a field somewhere by now.' He paused, then said, 'There's another runner out there who's causing a bit of a fuss at the moment. No need to concern you overly, but like Pike, she has potential value to the right people.'

Harry opened the envelope and slid out a sheet of paper and

a five-by-seven photo of a young woman with black hair and a confident, steady gaze. She had even, white teeth and the kind of smooth, latte-coloured skin most women would kill for. There was Asian blood in there, Harry thought. Her mouth looked as though it might be about to break into a smile, and he wondered what had made such a high-flyer break for the hills.

'Vanessa Tan,' Ballatyne intoned quietly. 'Age thirty, daughter of a Hong Kong Chinese father and English mother. Currently a lieutenant with the Royal Logistics Corps. Did impressively well at Cambridge, came away with two Firsts and decided on an army career. Came out top of her intake, shook off the competition and got herself seconded as a junior aide-de-camp to Deputy Commander, International Security Assistance Force, Afghanistan. She speaks Pashto and Dari, which puts her in the upper point-five per cent of serving personnel in the region.'

'Really?' Harry grunted. 'It's a miracle she didn't get assigned to a depot on Salisbury Plain counting bootlaces. When did she run?'

'Two weeks ago. She failed to report for her flight back to Afghanistan after leave. That's all we know. She's reputed to have what some call an eidetic memory. It means she has the ability to recall hundreds, maybe thousands, of images, pictures, graphics, you name it, as well as sounds and objects. She's a walking bloody digital recording unit, in other words.'

'Ouch.' Harry could only imagine what that meant in planning meetings; dozens of maps, schematics, video presentations and data, let alone the reams of stuff an ADC would be handling on a daily basis. And all there to be absorbed and retained, a veritable human databank. 'Conversation, too?'

Ballatyne shrugged. 'We don't know for sure, but colleagues claimed instances when she had recalled pretty much word-for-word discussions which took place days before. That aside, she's got a head full of battle plans and logistical information, as well as an unspecified amount of detail about forthcoming operations and key personnel in southern Afghanistan. Detail which can't be changed or erased.'

'And you want her back.'

'I don't. The army does. No arguments.'

Like Pike, then. Tan was someone who couldn't be allowed

to simply go adrift. She was cursed with knowing too much for her own good. He felt an instinct to avoid this one, without knowing why. Perhaps because it was a woman. 'Haven't you got a female recovery officer to handle this?'

'If I had and she was experienced enough, she'd be on it already.' Ballatyne flicked a glance at the next bench where two girls in shorts and boots were dumping heavy backpacks on the ground. One of them looked across and gave a vague smile. 'Tan puts Pike right in the shade,' Ballatyne added, 'value-wise.'

Harry slid the photo and sheet of paper back in the envelope and put it away inside his jacket. 'Why did she run?'

'Does it matter? She's got a head full of top-secret information which we don't want anyone else to have.'

'Somebody must have an idea what spooked her. It might help me find her.' Somebody always knew, in his experience; friend, colleague, unit chaplain or family member. Look deep enough and there was always a hint. People on the edge dropped clues, gave off vibes, voiced concerns or worries, responded negatively to something they would customarily have treated as common-place. Whatever had tipped Tan over the edge was unlikely to have been front-line battle trauma, however. As an aide to the regional deputy commander, she'd have been remote from any front-line action. Serving in Kabul didn't automatically preclude stress or danger, but it wouldn't have been the kind picked up from ducking bullets or going face first into a darkened alley, not knowing if the bump in the ground you were stepping on was goat shit or an IED – an improvised explosive device – about to erupt beneath your boots.

'If there is someone she took into her confidence, we haven't found them yet. She seems to have kept pretty much to herself, although that's no surprise; as ADC to the Deputy Commander ISAF, she'd have been kept on the run more than most.'

Harry looked at him. The 'yet' implied they were still looking, which meant he wasn't the only one on this. An indication, perhaps, of Tan's perceived value. Yet Ballatyne seemed remark-ably calm about her, as if she were just another member of the forces adrift out in the open.

Ballatyne seemed to read his mind. 'She's only unusual in that she's a woman. The others are just as critical, if not more so;

they have detailed equipment information which the brass don't want let out. We need to find all of them, find out who they've been talking to and re-introduce them to the concept of duty.' He waved a hand. 'You know the stuff.'

Harry wasn't sure he believed that, especially with someone like Tan. Anyone with her service background who cut and bolted would never be allowed near the brass again. She'd be watched, followed, monitored round the clock, even kept under lock and key if necessary while her knowledge degraded. Any concept of 'duty' had been rendered invalid the moment she'd jumped the fence.

Ballatyne, though, was on a roll. 'There's a far bigger problem than her simply deserting.'

'Go on.'

'We suspect she might have been targeted by the Protectory.'

NINE

'That's campfire stuff.' Harry had heard the stories, like everyone else. The Protectory was the subject of military water-cooler gossip, up there with UFOs, Area 51 and Elvis sharing a condo in Florida with Michael Jackson. Rumoured to be a group of disaffected ex-soldiers, deserters or discharged, they had allegedly formed a loosely knit band of sympathizers after the first Gulf War to help others of their kind. Shadowy and elusive, their numbers and identities unknown, they were mostly dismissed as the creation of cranks and too much barrack-room chatter. Harry was surprised Ballatyne was giving the matter much credence. Unless he knew a lot more than gossip allowed.

Ballatyne didn't even blink. 'I wish it were. But if she's with any kind of group, I'd rather she was cut adrift before she does any damage.'

'So you believe the rumours?

'Doesn't matter what I believe. Others believe it, that's my problem.' He shifted in his seat. 'About eight years ago a Major Colin Nicholls in the Intelligence Corps went AWOL after being

wounded in a firefight in northern Iraq. He was working undercover ahead of conventional forces, and it was his third time
down – an unlucky bugger to share a bunker with, if you ask
me. He was sent back to the UK and treated; given the usual
review and post-op psychobabble, but it didn't stick; he bugged
out before the shrinks could lock him on a programme.'

'They missed the signs.'

'Maybe. Don't forget he was Intelligence; hiding stuff is in their
nature. Before Iraq he'd been playing secret squirrel in Northern
Ireland, snooping on the Real IRA. Anyway, after his third strike
in Iraq he dropped out of sight and nobody's seen him since; no
contact with family or friends, no footprint from bank accounts or
plastic. It was like he'd dropped off the edge.'

'As you said, it's what they do.'

'I suppose. Anyway, about twelve months ago a former
colleague thought he spotted Nicholls in a restaurant in Sydney,
talking to two men. The colleague took a photo on his mobile
and sent it in. It's not a confirmed sighting because the man
turned away, but the other two were identified as long-term
deserters. Their names had cropped up before in connection with
others who'd done a bunk and gone underground. We think they
were with Nicholls for a reason.'

'The Protectory?'

'Correct. The word is old – it means protecting waifs and
strays. Someone's twisted idea of a joke, if you ask me, consid-
ering some of the people they'll be helping.' He smiled without
humour. 'Still, it would fit the kind of man Nicholls was said to
be: idealistic, apparently; good family; highly intelligent but
emotionally a little naïve.'

'There's no guarantee the Protectory will have helped Tan.'

'I wouldn't want to find out the hard way by having her
knowledge sold on the open market, would you?'

'She might have slid off the radar all by herself and gone to
ground.'

'Don't bet on that, either.' Ballatyne leaned closer as a pair
of suited office workers crept by, eyeing the bench covetously
as if looks alone would render it vacant. 'If the Protectory is
operating the way we think they are, it's likely they need a regular
flow of operating capital for expenses, accommodation, bribes

and travel. It's a costly business slipping people off the radar. One way of doing it would be by selling the information deserters have. And some of them are very bright bunnies indeed. Bloody scary, the details some of them carry in their heads.'

'Going AWOL doesn't automatically make a traitor. Someone like Tan might refuse to play along with them.'

'It's not just about Tan.' Ballatyne's eyes were cold. 'We can't count on the Protectory passing up on anyone with her specialized knowledge. They go on fishing expeditions for the people they want and they play hard.'

'Go on.'

'We have reason to believe that while he was sunning himself in Thailand, Pike was contacted by a man named Thomas Deakin. He's a former captain in the Scots Guards who went over the fence six years ago. Since then, he's rumoured to have tried forming his own group, called Highway Eighty, which as you probably know is the main route out of Baghdad.' The flinty smile came again. 'The man clearly has a sense of irony. Anyway, we hear they've now merged with the Protectory, although they would appear on the surface to be like chalk and cheese.'

'How so?'

'In another life Deakin would be a mercenary. It's not fighting that frightens him; it's the lack of freedom to do his own thing. My guess is the Protectory is a useful stepping stone. Nicholls and his crew are probably a bit too soft for the likes of Deakin, too touchy-feely . . . not aggressively commercial enough. In the end, though, they're the same animal, sharing similar traits; they help other deserters, check them out, give them money, sanctuary, documents and point them towards a new life.'

'A benevolent society.'

'Originally, maybe. But Deakin's turned them into a regular business; they concentrate on targeting new deserters within days of them leaving, and finding those with saleable talents. They drain them of any specialized knowledge, then sell it to the highest bidder. It's an attractive deal for someone on the run: just tell us all you know and we'll give you money, a new ID, freedom . . . and no more fighting.'

'What about the ones with no saleable talents?'

'That's where the touchy-feely face comes in. Your average

squaddie gets some cash and a promise, and is told to get lost. Helps perpetuate the myth. But there've been rumours that they don't react well to any specialist talent turning them down once they've got them in their sights. Two Armoured Regiment bods who'd bunked off after testing a new battle tank were approached but said no. They ended up dead in a drive-by shooting in Melbourne. These people are in it for the money and they don't play nice.'

Harry studied Ballatyne's face. He was too experienced to be giving anything away, but the way he was talking gave a hint of something which made the hairs stir on the back of Harry's neck.

'You've got an insider,' he said softly. Ballatyne had just revealed a little too much detail for this to be idle speculation. 'Someone in the Protectory.'

'Nothing like that.' Ballatyne's response was bland. 'We've been getting a few hints, that's all. Stronger than gossip; enough to know that it's not, as you put it, campfire stuff.'

'And where does Paulton fit in?'

'He and Deakin know each other from way back. Deakin was also spotted hanging around at Frankfurt.' He produced another photograph from his pocket and held it out for Harry to take. It was the same shot he'd shown him on the day of the shooting in St James's Park: Paulton crossing a pavement in an anonymous street, about to get in a car.

'I've seen this already. So?'

'I know you have.' Ballatyne gave a knowing smile. 'I also know you've got your little mate Ferris analysing the details to see if he can come up with a location.'

Harry didn't rise to the bait. Maybe Ballatyne didn't get the opportunity to show off much, surrounded as he probably was by Sixers who thought themselves smarter, sharper and more ambitious. 'And?'

'Forget it – you're wasting your time. It was taken in Brussels.' Ballatyne's finger was tapping on a man standing back from Paulton. He looked to be in his forties, dressed in a pale suit and looking relaxed and fit. 'This is Deakin. Remember the face.'

Harry stared at the two men in the photo, trying to remain calm at the knowledge that Ballatyne had been playing him with

this photo, drawing him in. It was part of the game; he should
have known.

'Paulton's with the Protectory?' It was a hell of a jump from
waging war on spies, terrorists and anyone threatening the country's security, to actually helping its enemies gain vital military
information. Had he really gone that far overboard? Or had that
always been his plan, working towards this goal? The possibilities were unsettling. No wonder someone on Ballatyne's level
had been put on the case.

'Almost certainly. But Deakin's the one to watch. Nicholls has
moved into the background. It's possible he doesn't like what's
happened and has cut himself off. He's an idealist. But Deakin's
an attack dog. He rarely goes anywhere without a couple of
Bosnian wingmen with him, guarding his back. They do the
heavy lifting.'

'Thanks for the warning.' Sensing there was nothing more to
come, Harry stood up to leave, then turned back. In the background, Ballatyne's minders stirred. 'There's one thing.'

'I know,' Ballatyne said. 'Gordon Cullum. He rang me. You
upset him.' He didn't seem too put out by the revelation.

'Is he for real?'

'Real enough. He was in Five for years, worked undercover
in Ulster back in the early days. He's now a sort of floating
liaison between the MOD and the Intelligence community, used
whenever there's an overlap of responsibilities, like now. He's
due for retirement soon, but he's solid enough. It's only a signature, you know, on the form. Bureaucrats need signatures like
bees need pollen; it's how they survive.'

'It won't happen. Last time I signed on the dotted line for
Five, they tried to kill me, remember?'

'Fair point. I can see that would be a problem.' Ballatyne
seemed to be enjoying himself. 'OK, forget the bloody signature.
I'll sign it for you.'

'Fine.'

'So what's the real problem?'

'Cullum. He feels . . . odd. Could he have known Paulton?'

There was a brief silence while Ballatyne chewed that over.
Eventually he said, 'You asked before why Six is on this rather
than Five. The answer is Paulton. Thames House was seen as

too close to be objective, even after what he did. They could well screw it up by going after him mob-handed, just to put the books straight. That was enough to give us primacy even though this is not our normal area of operations.' He gave a quizzical look. 'You sure you're not letting Paulton become an obsession, Harry?'

'Probably. I get that way with people who try to have me terminated.'

'I'll bear that in mind.' He chewed his lip and added, 'We've got professionals you can talk to about that, you know. Just a thought. And remember one thing: we rarely get the resolution we crave.'

'Thanks. Have you finished?'

Ballatyne tilted his head. 'Sorry . . . getting philosophical in my old age. Back to Cullum. You're wondering if he'll get in the way?'

'I wouldn't want to rely on him in a snow storm.'

'In that case, you won't have to. I'll handle the control end of things myself.'

Harry was relieved. It confirmed what he'd been thinking. Cullum was just filling in and not to be relied on long term. He hadn't been looking for a holding hand, but someone who wasn't full of old baggage was far preferable as a contact, especially if all hell broke loose and he needed a quick response. Nothing in Cullum's attitude had given him that reassurance.

'One thing more.' Ballatyne wasn't looking at him now, but staring out over the river towards the London Eye. 'Your mate Ferris.'

'What about him?'

'All the information you need is on that data stick. Any more, you ask me and, within reason, I'll make sure you get it. I know Wonder Boy's reputation for letting his electronic fingers do the walking; it's what got him into the last spot of bother. But you'd better make sure he knows that snooping on the peccadilloes of our illustrious members of parliament will be like nothing if he even considers intruding on my bailiwick. Got me?'

'I'll tell him.'

Ballatyne turned and looked at him, the light flashing off his glasses and lending his eyes an oddly sinister tone. 'I'm deadly serious, Harry. If he goes ferreting about anywhere he shouldn't, if I pick up a hint that he's been hacking into SIS files, truly nasty things will happen.'

With that, he stood up and walked away, trailing his security team behind him.

TEN

'Sounds like someone didn't want Pike talking,' said Rik. 'It was quick work, though, nailing him like that.'

'Too quick,' Harry agreed. Pike was no anti-surveillance expert; he was a squaddie and would have left a trail a mile wide. Even so, getting someone on to him so quickly would have taken resources and expertise.

They were sitting over takeaway coffees in Rik's flat near Paddington. Harry had brought him up to speed on events so far, and was going over what had happened to Pike, and what it implied.

'It would have taken some organizing,' Harry surmised, 'and the timing had to be spot on. Hitting someone on the move takes practice . . . or experience. And out in the open, it takes nerve.'

'You saying it was a professional hit?'

'Had to be. One to drive, another to shoot. It shows the Protectory has got the reach and the talent. But Pike wasn't the first. Ballatyne says at least two others are known to have walked away and died.' He sipped his coffee and wondered if they had seen him at Pike's bolthole. He didn't think so, but he decided to keep his eyes open from now on. 'Makes you wonder what Pike could have known that made taking the risk to kill him worthwhile.'

'The names and faces of the people who approached him, presumably.'

Harry couldn't argue with that. It was the single biggest danger for anyone in the intelligence gathering business, on whichever side of the fence they stood: the moment they came out of the shadows of their cover and stood face to face with their target. If they had overplayed their hand and their contact was actually playing them in turn, they were exposed. He took the data stick from his pocket and slid it across the table. 'This has all the info Ballatyne can give me on the deserters they think are at risk of being poached . . . if they haven't been already. And there are sections from Paulton's personnel file. Can you run the details and see if you can pick up a trace?'

Rik dragged a laptop across the table with his good arm and plugged in the stick. When a pop-up box asked for a secure code, Harry read out the number from his watch. The file opened to reveal six screen icons, with a name against each one.

Sgt Barrow G.
SSgt McCreath G
Cpl Pike N.
SSgt Pollock M.
Lt TAN V.
Paulton H. G.

'I'll check them out,' said Rik. 'You want me to print the summaries?'

'Yes. I'll need to read up on them.'

Two minutes later, he was absorbing the basic details of each of the missing personnel and paring them down to even barer essentials.

Sergeant Graham Barrow of the Intelligence Corps was thirty-five years old, divorced and in debt. He was listed as a specialist in counterintelligence and electronic warfare, industry and army trained in electronic countermeasures and penetration systems. He'd spent time in GCHQ in Cheltenham, working with their experts on building protective security and the use and counter-use of satellite technology, and had extensive knowledge of the security measures surrounding some of the country's most sensitive installations, including nuclear sites and strategic arms depots. His FTR – Failed to Report – notification was dated two months ago.

Staff Sergeant Gerry McCreath, 38, widowed with no family, was from 251 Signals Squadron like Pike, but attached to 16 Air Assault Brigade. Extensively trained in operational networks, he had been testing a new and critically important forward battlefield communications system when he had been wounded by an IED and returned to the UK for treatment and recuperation. Two weeks into his stay, he had walked out of Selly Oak Hospital and disappeared. His FTR was dated six months ago.

Staff Sergeant Martin Pollock, 39, of the Royal Armoured Corps. Divorced, no children. After working in every branch of the corps, from battle tanks to reconnaissance units, and with extensive service in Iraq and Afghanistan, he had transferred to the Joint Chemical, Biological and Nuclear Regiment, where he had been undergoing specialist instruction. The summary did not specify what that instruction was, but the name was enough to make Harry's blood run cold. Like most orthodox military men, he disliked the very idea of chemical or biological weapons. Pollock's FTR was dated two months ago while training in Germany.

Lieutenant Vanessa Tan, 30, single, no family. Of all the missing personnel, she probably had the widest exposure to strategic information, including current battlefield plans and thinking. If she had the eidetic memory Ballatyne claimed, then anything that had passed before her eyes, whether plans, proposals, strategy or Force distribution, was firmly lodged in her head. Add to that the untold hours of conversations she would have been privy to in her work as ADC to the Deputy Commander ISAF, and the flow of paperwork it would have produced, taking in UN, American and Joint Task Force personnel, from General David Petraeus on down, and it was a hell of a lot of exposure. But nothing technological. Did that make her any less saleable? He didn't know.

He flicked through the notes and saw that the absentees' homes were being monitored along with known family members, a reminder of how much the MOD and government valued their retrieval. A margin note stressed the difficulty involved due to the spread of the families, with a question mark regarding extra funds to be made available to cover the inevitable shortfall if the hunt continued for too long. Phone and email logs were being trawled for clues, and mobiles were being tracked for possible signals. These were proving difficult to follow due to the variety of networks involved in the UK and overseas.

Harry wondered aloud how long any of them had got.

'How do you mean?'

'If what Ballatyne says is true, Deakin and his crew don't beat about the bush. If they think someone knows too much about them, but isn't keen on joining, they take them out. If these four have been approached already and haven't jumped on board, they'll be living on borrowed time.'

'How real do you reckon Paulton's involvement is? Doesn't sound very likely to me; getting his hands dirty with deserters, trauma victims and misfits.'

Harry didn't have an answer to that one. He'd been thinking about Paulton more or less constantly. He'd have been happier being able to give Rik some specific clues to follow, rather than the supposition he was working on. He'd shown him all the names the MI5 man had used, but was almost certain they would lead nowhere. Paulton was too canny; he'd work on the old adage of never revisiting old territory. That included using old aliases and code names. The risk of bumping into figures from his past was too real. And wherever Paulton was right now, he wouldn't be living in a straw hut with a donkey for transport, the ageing white man standing out like a tart at a tea party. He'd feel trapped and ultimately vulnerable, something a man with his background of intrigue and double dealing would find intolerable. Wherever he was, it would have to be close to good lines of communication, multiple routes in and out and surrounded by a community where he could blend in and become part of the backdrop. The invisible man.

Rik was reading his mind. 'Spain would be good. All those creaky old expats to hide among. Modern, sophisticated, good transport, fleshpots. Everything.'

Harry shook his head. 'It's a retirement community; probably crawling with ex-cops, former spooks and civil servants, all bored out of their skulls and looking for excitement. Paulton may have been secretive and with a mania for different names, but he wasn't faceless. Someone would recognize him sooner or later. They'd want to grill him, chill him or turn him in for the reward.'

'Good point, Holmes.' Rik glanced at the screen and did a double take. 'Well, that's another one accounted for. Staff Sergeant Pollock's turned up alive and well.'

Harry looked. It was an email from Ballatyne. Pollock had

walked into a police station in Ripon, Yorkshire, accompanied by his former wife, and handed himself in. He'd been hiding near Bournemouth for the past seven weeks after skipping from Germany and had run out of money. And he was homesick.

It proved one thing: the Protectory didn't get to everyone. Or maybe they were being extra choosy about the talent they went after. He noticed one common factor: all the people listed were single, widowed or divorced. Pollock, although divorced, was the only one with a significant other who still seemed to care about him.

He went back to the records. Home addresses and telephone numbers were listed and were being monitored around the clock. Harry assumed that meant in person by the Royal Military Police and electronically by GCHQ. There was always a chance they might call without thinking, but he wasn't about to hold his breath. Interestingly, there was a note that Sgt Barrow's was the only mobile still active, although no fix had been made on it so far.

He thought about it for a few seconds, trying to decide who to focus on first. If Rik came up with anything, that was a bonus. In the meantime, he hated inaction and needed to get on with something concrete. He decided to get on Lt Tan's case. Whatever Ballatyne thought about the other men and their equipment and technical knowledge, the Protectory might well have other views. Signals, Intelligence Corps and other personnel were relatively plentiful, and they would be counting on more coming along sooner or later. But someone from a central command position was a rarity, and that alone would command a good price to the right taker. If he could get a line on Tan's movements, then the Protectory – and Paulton – wouldn't be far away.

It was a few minutes before he noticed that Rik was unusually quiet, and scratching absent-mindedly at his shoulder beneath the bandage. He had said little on the long return journey from Iraq, and Harry wondered when he would reach the tipping point; when it would become too urgent for him to hold in any longer what was surely bothering him. Shooting someone for the first time was bad enough, no doubt about it. Not that the second time was any better. And Rik had done it just a few days ago. Worse, he thought he'd killed a woman.

'Would you have shot him if things had gone bad?'

Harry guessed Rik was referring to Rafa'i. There had never been anything explicit said about dealing with the former cleric once they arrived at the delivery point in west Baghdad; and he had taken it as read that being seen to shoot the Iraqi, no matter that his own people probably wanted him dead before long, would be the worst possible action to take. It had been a simple drop-and-leave mission, and what Rafa'i's former friends wanted to do with him once they'd heard of his deception and betrayal was up to them. But Harry wasn't naïve; if it had all kicked off the moment they touched down and they'd found themselves under fire from supporters still loyal to Rafa'i, he knew he would have been expected to ensure that there was no comeback.

'We'll never know. Probably.'

'So it does get easier.'

Harry kept his head down, eyes on the papers. It was a question with no easy answer and one he didn't think he could tackle right now. But he knew this was the tipping point he'd been waiting for.

'You didn't kill her.'

A short silence. 'What?' Rik's voice was hoarse. It wasn't the answer he'd been expecting. On the surface, he appeared ready for anything, but Harry knew it wasn't that simple. He was human. 'You don't know that.'

'Your shot didn't kill her. It went high and to your left. Hit her in the right shoulder.' Rik had been sitting on the ground, hands already shaking with the adrenalin rush of being in a firefight and the trauma of a gunshot wound from Joanne Archer's pistol. He'd been calm enough, aiming, then shouting a warning, but it would have been amazing if he'd been able to pull off an accurate kill under those conditions. It had been Harry who'd fired the fatal shots.

'But I saw her. She fell.'

Harry nodded and looked at him, saw his confusion . . . and the beginnings of what might have been relief. 'Ballistics confirmed it,' he continued, keeping it casual. 'I can show you a copy if you like.'

'Why didn't you say?'

Harry shrugged. 'There was no point. You wouldn't have

believed me anyway. That kind of thing, after what you'd been through . . . you have to be ready to hear it.' He grinned deliberately. 'Don't worry, when your shoulder's better I'll take you down the range and teach you how to shoot properly.'

'Is that all you've got to say?'

'What else do you want me to tell you?' Harry reached for the summaries again, then stopped and turned back to face Rik. 'Actually, there is one other thing: no, it doesn't get any easier.'

Rik didn't respond, so Harry picked out a summary at random; it was Sgt Barrow. That would do. There was an active mobile number, so he picked up the phone and dialled. It rang out six times before going to a standard robot voicemail. He decided to leave a message. It seemed too simple, somehow, but he wondered if anyone else had thought of it. 'Graham, my name's Harry Tate,' he said carefully. 'I want to help you. I work in conjunction with the MOD, but I imagine you're not sure who to trust right now, so I won't waste time trying to sell you a deal. Call me and we'll talk. This isn't as bad as you think.' He added Rik's landline number, with the overseas dialling prefix for the UK, then cut the connection. If Barrow was out there and listening, and became desperate enough, he might call back.

Rik was looking at him. 'What am I – a call centre?'

'No, you're walking wounded. If he rings back and I'm not here, I'll need you to talk to him and find out where he is. Then let me know.' He paused, remembering Ballatyne's cold-as-permafrost warning for Rik to keep his nose clean. If he was going to get Rik to help, he needed his understanding of the background to the job, and that included the dangers involved. 'If we get into this, there's no straying into official files. Ballatyne knows your history and he'll be watching.'

Rik had held up a hand. 'No problem, boss,' he promised with a sly grin. 'I'll be as good as gold.'

'You'd better. Otherwise I'll save Ballatyne the trouble and shoot you myself.'

ELEVEN

Anglesey was shrouded by a squally curtain of drizzle as Harry drove along the coast road and turned into a small lane leading to the bungalow where Vanessa Tan's parents had lived for many years. It was set on a slope, an extended building in mature grounds overlooking the Menai Strait. At any other time he would have enjoyed the scenery and tranquillity away from the city, but right now he had other things on his mind.

After drawing a blank with Barrow's mobile, he had decided to take a closer look at Tan's background. It had meant a long drive, but the solitude had allowed him to trawl for ideas and let his brain focus on the best ways of getting to Tan and the other personnel, and, through them, the Protectory. Along the way, he had stopped at irregular intervals, doubling back for short distances to check he wasn't being tailed. It was basic stuff, and time-consuming, but necessary to ensure he stayed clean.

He parked on the side of the lane just across from the Tan bungalow and studied the building. Set some eighty yards from its nearest neighbour, it looked closed off, remote from the world, with the empty look of something long abandoned. The rain was doing nothing to dispel the air of stolid gloom, aided by the unkempt lawn, weed-filled flowerbeds and paint peeling from the wooden window frames. A glut of moss and leaves had filled the guttering and rainwater was trickling on to the ground from numerous points where the blockage was most acute. He left the car and walked up the open paved drive to the front door. It was fitted with a heavy brass knocker in the shape of a fish. He lifted it and let it drop with a hollow *boom*.

No reaction. He waited, then knocked again. The fish was tarnished, unused, and the letterbox had been sealed shut. No sounds from inside, no sense of movement. He took out his mobile and rang the landline. No good trying Tan's mobile number, it was showing unobtainable. He could hear the phone ringing inside. It had that empty quality.

'Can I help you?'

The voice came from the lane behind him. He turned and saw a tall, trim woman in her fifties standing at the end of the driveway. She was wearing a green waterproof and walking boots, and had a lock of wet hair plastered down one cheek, courtesy of the rain. Harry walked back down the drive and smiled to put her at her ease.

'I'm looking for Vanessa Tan,' he said. 'I thought she might be in.'

'Vanessa?' The woman lifted one eyebrow. 'Goodness, she hasn't been around for years. May I ask who you are?'

Harry took out his wallet and showed her his card with the official portcullis logo in one corner. It was a useful leftover from his MI5 days, although it didn't say anything about the Security Services in writing.

'Oh. Government.' The woman looked impressed. 'Sorry – only we have to be so careful these days, don't we?' She tucked the stray hair back behind her ear. 'Excuse the state of me – I like walking in the rain. I find it therapeutic. I'm Margaret Crane; the next house up. I'm afraid I can't help you, Mr Tate. Vanessa left home to go to uni some years back, and that's the last we saw of her. Maureen, her mother – she died just over a year ago now – always told us Vanessa was doing well, but she never came home to visit, as far as I know.' She glanced up at the sad-looking bungalow. 'Such a shame, leaving the place empty like this. I think Maureen must have hoped Vanessa would come back one day, and she'd have this waiting for her. It needs someone living in it, though, rather than simply being patched up. But that's young people for you, isn't it? A different sense of respon-sibility, I suppose.'

Harry saw what she was referring to: a wooden panel had been fitted over one of the smaller windows. It had the appearance of what his father had once called a long-term temporary fix, some-thing that would do until a better alternative came along. 'So who does the patching up?'

'A management chap comes round every now and then, but he never says anything. Checks it's sound, I imagine, does what-ever needs doing, then goes away.' She gestured vaguely in the direction of the coast road. 'There's quite a few like this, though;

empty year-round, never a sight or sound of who owns them, makes you wonder why they bought them in the first place. And they say there's a housing shortage.' She shook her head at the absurdity of it.

'Do you know which company?'

She nodded. 'They're local. Menai Management. In the centre of Caernarfon.'

'Thank you. I don't suppose you know if Vanessa has any friends in the area?'

'I doubt it. She was such a quiet girl growing up – and her mother always kept her nose to the grindstone. Wanted her to go to university and get a good job. She was too hard on her, in my opinion, always pushing her to excel, poor kid – as if she might make up for being a bit plain by having a string of letters after her name. Her father wanted it, too, don't get me wrong, but he died when she was in her teens.' She looked sad. 'I'm not surprised she never came back, not once she got away. All that pressure – it was bound to tell in the end. Still, if hard work was the way to succeed, Maureen made sure that was how Vanessa would do it.' She waved a vague hand towards the bungalow. 'Makes you wonder why she keeps this place on, though, doesn't it? If she's never coming back.'

In exchange for her number, Harry left his card with Mrs Crane with a request that she call if she thought of anything useful, and returned to the car. Mrs Crane stood and watched him leave. Maybe, he thought, strange men calling on houses in the area constituted real excitement up here.

He got the number of Menai Management and got through to the office manager, Ian Griffiths, who said, 'Sorry, Mr Tate. Can't help you. There's a standing order for the management fee, paid up to date. Instructions are to continue until notified otherwise. We don't have authority to sell, if that's what you're after. I can't give any further information, though, not over the phone and without proper authority—'

Harry cut the connection and drove into Caernarfon. The man was only doing his job, but he could do without the confidentiality runaround. He found the offices of Menai Management next to a chemist and stepped inside. The staff consisted of a pasty-faced man in his early thirties with a premature comb-over. He was sprawled behind a PC looking bored, and glanced up as Harry entered. He tapped a key, shutting down the screen.

'Can I help?'

Harry flashed his MI5 card and said, 'MOD police, Mr Griffiths. I'm trying to trace Miss Vanessa Tan.'

Griffiths jumped up.' Oh, you're the bloke who rang earlier. Police, you say? What's happened to her, then? Nothing serious, I hope.'

'That's what we'd like to find out.' Harry gave him a level look. 'Are you going to help me or do I need a warrant?' He looked at the PC humming on the desk and tapped the monitor reflectively. 'Are all your records computerized?'

'Of course. Why?'

'We'd have to impound that, for a start.'

Griffiths looked stunned. 'What? But there's nothing on there. I mean . . . work stuff and a few games, stuff like that. Nothing that would interest the police, though.' He put a protective hand on the monitor. 'Um . . . what exactly do you need?'

'A contact number or an address. Either would do. I presume you have one?'

'Of course, yes. Standard practice. I'll just call it up.' The manager's throat sounded dry, as if he was having trouble gauging how much damage could be done by having his computer taken away. He slid behind the desk and tapped at the keys, then frowned. 'That's odd.' He tapped again but the frown stayed. He looked up at Harry in a mild state of panic. 'I don't understand it; there's nothing on here. No address, telephone – nothing. But we *always* have contact details . . .' He stared at the screen as if willing it to give up its secrets. 'Just the house itself.'

'How long is it since you last looked at the file?' Harry was sceptical about the man's air of surprise. Whatever had happened, whether by accident or design, he was willing to bet that a long-term arrangement with automatic payments made through a bank would soon become part of the wallpaper, rarely checked or updated because anything more would be too costly. Until something went wrong.

'I don't know.' Griffiths looked embarrassed. 'A while, I admit.'

'You did some patching work on a window recently. Is that part of the agreement?'

'Yes. I mean, it doesn't include anything major or structural – we'd have to get permission to do that. But we had instruction to look after the basic skin, if you like, make sure the property's secure, no burst pipes and so forth. I saw the cracked window on my last visit about three weeks ago – a blackbird had hit it – so I placed a panel of three-ply over it until I get the owner's agreement to replace the glass.' He pulled a wry face. 'I suppose I can whistle goodbye to that, if she's gone missing.'

He had a thought. It was a long shot, but Griffiths was about the same age as Vanessa Tan, and the catchment area for schools here would probably have covered a fairly wide patch. He took out the photo and said, 'Is this the owner? You might have known her.' He was to be disappointed.

'No idea. I never met her.' Griffiths looked at the photo and made a soft whistling noise. 'I wish I had, though. Would've made life a lot more interesting.'

Harry thanked him for his help. The fact that they'd never met cut down the need to ask any further questions. He returned to the car. On the way, he rang Rik and asked him to access the phone records for the Tan number. Then he set off back to London. There was nothing to be gained by staying around here. It was a blind, going nowhere.

Thirty minutes later, Rik sent a text.

Subscriber Ms V Tan, address as given. Bills paid by DD – Barclays. Call record shows no outgoing, no voicemail.

Harry switched off the phone. At least the drive back gave him plenty of time to think. Mainly about what had happened to Vanessa Tan, hard-working, nose-to-the-grindstone student with ambitious parents. Had the enforced studies coupled with military service been a push too much, or had something more sinister happened to make her disappear?

He took out the photo and glanced at it as he drove. Something was tugging at the corner of his mind. Something Mrs Crane had said . . . and Griffiths, too. But whatever it was wouldn't come. Instinct told him it was significant, but knowing that didn't help.

TWELVE

In a small bar in Wandsbek, a district of north-east Hamburg, three men sat around a table in a back function room. One of them was talking quietly on a mobile. The other two waited patiently. The room lights were on and the broad Friedrich-Ebert-Damm outside hummed with the rush of traffic. Four glasses and a chilled carafe of Mosel stood on a tray in the centre, but none of the men had yet taken a drink.

'It's done.' The man on the phone switched it off and dropped it into his breast pocket. Then he reached for the carafe and poured three measures of wine. Thomas Deakin was slim, fair-haired and tanned, with quick eyes and a way of checking his surroundings on a constant rotation. It was unsettling to anyone meeting him for the first time, but a habit those around him had come to accept. He had the antennae of a guard dog and his instincts had served him well since going AWOL – a useful function for a man permanently guarding his back. He hadn't stepped foot inside the UK since walking away from his unit in the Scots Guards while in transit through Germany, and was constantly on the move from one country to another, regularly changing identities to stay ahead of anyone hunting him. Infrequent meetings in anonymous bars like this, with routes in and out guaranteed and locations never used more than once, were what had kept him out of trouble for so long.

'Which one?' The man to his left was in his early forties, whipcord thin, balding and ascetic-looking. Former Master Sergeant Greg Turpowicz, a Texan, had taken his own leave of the US 101st Airborne Division and joined Deakin after surviving too many close shaves in a job he had long ceased to care about.

'Pike. The Signals wonk. They iced him on the way to Colchester. That's the British Military Detention Centre,' he added, for the American's benefit.

'What a waste.' The third man was Colin Nicholls, once a

major in the Intelligence Corps. 'I was counting on getting Pike
on board. What went wrong?' His tone was soft but accusatory.
He'd made it clear already that he considered Deakin's general
approach to deserters far too aggressive, and likely to frighten
off those who really needed help.

'He got cold feet, that's what went wrong.' Deakin's lip curled
in derision. 'Maybe they're all like that in Signals and the Green
Slime: no guts when it comes to carrying through a decision.'

Nicholls ignored the nickname; he was long accustomed to it
in a job where name calling was as much for self-protection as
it was for denigrating other branches of the military. But the
implied insult rankled and he took in a deep breath, eyes growing
dark with dislike.

'Hey, guys, cool it.' Turpowicz tapped the table and looked
from one to the other as an almost electric charge sizzled in the
air between them. 'Shit happens, right? We win some, we lose
some. There'll be others.'

Nicholls eventually nodded and relaxed. Deakin shrugged.
He'd rarely shown any great liking for the former major, and
they regularly disagreed on the tactics the group should use to
earn funds. But he knew not to push him too far. Nicholls was
older, but he'd worked undercover for months on end in Iraq and
other dangerous locations, and a man didn't do that without
having powerful inner resources and a determination to survive.

The three men sipped their wine while the atmosphere returned
to normal. Then Deakin said by way of explanation, 'Pike turning
us down I could put up with; but not after we'd transferred the
money. That was taking the piss.'

'We'll get it back,' Turpowicz said quietly. A former bank
worker before enlisting in the US military, he handled the financial
transactions on behalf of the Protectory and regularly fed a stream
of funds through offshore financial centres around the world. It
meant the Protectory could have access to money in numerous
countries at short notice, for paying helpers, informants and
contacts, as well as supplying cash to help the deserters they
targeted. 'I put a reversal code on all the transfers, operable up
to seven days after confirmation. One push of a button and the
transfer comes right back, minus an abort fee.' He smiled at his
own ingenuity.

'So push it, then,' Deakin muttered sourly. 'Without the info to sell, we're behind target.'

'Will do. What about new leads?' He was referring to their insider in the Ministry of Defence in London, a nameless voice who was their information feed to personnel on the 'Failed to Report' list. With the names came all the relevant information about regiments, background, rank and home addresses, allowing the Protectory to get a trace on the missing personnel before they went cold. The fact that only one in twenty FTRs were of a grade worth following up to the fullest extent did nothing to deter their efforts with the remainder. Any serving member of the military had something they could trade, given the right pressure, even if only about senior officers and force strength. The Protectory's trade was in information, and there were many eager buyers out there.

'I'm on it. Our man's having to be extra careful going through the records in case he leaves an electronic footprint. For now, though, we've got a few to work on.'

'How did they do it?' Nicholls queried. He plainly hadn't finished with the matter of Pike's death.

'Why?' Deakin countered. 'Will it help, you knowing that?'

'He'll find out eventually,' said Turpowicz, 'when it hits the news channels. And I'd be kind of interested, too.'

Deakin relented with ill-concealed reluctance. The Signals NCO would have stood no chance against Zubac and Ganic, the two Bosnian enforcers he'd sent to England to deal with him. They had learned their craft over years of turbulent fighting in their homeland and in a dozen different places since. Once locked on to a target, they were lethally committed and had no 'off' switch other than Deakin's word. 'They tailed him and took the car out on the A12 east of London. They got Pike with a head shot; one of the MPs died, the other's not going anywhere. Clean job.' He related the details with a clinical lack of emotion.

'And Barrow?'

'I'm waiting to hear about that. Ganic and Zubac flew to Berlin immediately after the hit on Pike and caught up with him heading for the Polish border.'

'Are they going to bring him in?' Nicholls asked.

Deakin stared at him without expression. 'What do you think?'

'There's gonna be questions about Pike, though. Right?'

Turpowicz looked between the two Englishmen. The UK was their territory, but his question was clearly valid; had it been in the US, there would be a major investigation by both military and federal authorities. Nobody took out two military cops and their prisoner on a public highway without causing a firestorm. Surely the UK was no different.

'Let them ask. Who cares? Our men are clear and gone. Point is, it works in our favour.' Deakin spoke calmly, unaffected by what he had ordered done. 'It sends a message to anyone else who thinks they can stiff us. The word is: don't. And that includes our clients.' He smiled and finished his wine, leaving the other two men with no doubts that he was extreme enough to go after anyone who tried to cross him, whatever their nationality or location.

The phone in Deakin's pocket buzzed, and the sound of voices drifted through from the front section of the bar. Turpowicz and Nicholls stiffened instantly, but Deakin held out a hand to stop them getting alarmed.

'It's OK,' he said. 'This is someone I want you to meet. He's going to take our organization to the next level.' He spoke into the phone. 'Send him in, please.'

'You didn't think to warn us first?' Nicholls looked angry. 'What the hell are you playing at, Deakin? We're all equal in this. We should each have a say about who we meet and when.'

Turpowicz nodded in agreement, his eyes bleak. He stayed calm, but said, 'Not cool, man. You should've run it by us first.'

Deakin was unfazed by their reactions. He laid a hand on his chest. 'Sorry, guys. It was a last minute thing and I didn't have time. He was in the area, that's all. I promise, this will be to our advantage.'

Nicholls leaned forward. 'How do we know we can trust this man? Are you going to vouch for him?'

Deakin gave a flinty smile. 'Of course, Colin. Why? Do you doubt me?' He looked at them in turn as if daring them to object. 'No? Good. We know where we stand then.'

Amid the stiff silence that followed, there was a knock at the door and a man entered. He was in his fifties, conservatively dressed in a suit and tie, with a light coat slung over one arm. He could have been a simple businessman, his nationality northern

European but not clearly defined by his clothes. He looked thin, as if he had recently lost weight, but fit and tanned, with neat, grey hair. He smiled at the three men with what looked like genuine pleasure.

'Good evening, gentlemen,' he said, his accent middle-class and English. If he sensed any hostility in the atmosphere, he ignored it. 'Am I interrupting?' He chuckled as he took a chair indicated by Deakin, who poured the fourth glass of wine. He took an appreciative sniff, raised the glass in salute and said, 'My name's Paulton, by the way. But please call me George.'

THIRTEEN

One kilometre north-east of Schwedt, a small industrial town on the German side of the border with Poland, a small white pickup truck churned along a narrow, isolated track riddled with muddy puddles and wallows. Darkness was coming in fast and the driver's face was beaded with perspiration as he fought to control the steering wheel. He was praying that he didn't get a puncture. Running on sidelights only, which were barely enough to show the banks on either side or the potholes in the surface, he was constantly having to wrench the vehicle back on course as he felt the bumper brushing against the tangle of overgrown grass and bushes bordering the track.

'Come on, come *on* . . .!' he swore softly, as the truck failed to respond to his foot pounding on the accelerator. The worn-out engine was pinking in protest at the half tank of cheap petrol he'd been sold with the vehicle, a last-ditch attempt to stay clear of bus or train routes, and the noisy heater clamped under the dashboard sounded laboured and tinny. With the approaching night came a curtain of rain sweeping across the countryside towards him, and he was shivering with a mixture of cold and despair that not even the ancient camouflage jacket he'd bought in a market two days ago could stave off.

He checked the wing mirror, but the bouncing vehicle made seeing anything behind him impossible. He thought he'd caught a glimmer of lights back there earlier, but had seen nothing since. Maybe he'd lost the pursuers he knew were on his tail. Or maybe he'd been imagining it, a result of exhaustion. He flicked on the yellow interior light and risked a quick glance at the folded map pinned to the dashboard. Schwedt was behind him, and if he could believe the single dotted line showing just west of the town, the track he was on led towards the Polish border and the river Oder. He was counting on finding a way of crossing the water when he got closer, and avoiding the road where there would certainly be border controls. The pickup was barely roadworthy and would not stand close scrutiny if a bored official decided to give him the once-over.

He checked the mirror again and pulled to a halt alongside a clump of pine trees silhouetted against the sky. He climbed out and watched the track behind him for a moment, straining to hear the sound of a vehicle engine. But there was nothing. Satisfied that he wasn't being observed, he then went round to the rear of the vehicle. Two sharp kicks and the tail and brake lights were smashed. If anyone was following him, they'd have nothing to fasten on. If, on the other hand, he ran into a border patrol or the police, he was already in deep enough trouble and broken lights would be the least of his problems.

He unzipped his pants and relieved himself against a rear tyre, eyes on the track behind him. It would be just his luck, he thought wryly, to be caught taking a piss. A couple of guys in his unit in Helmand had done the same, to their cost; one got taken out by a sniper, the other had stepped on an IED hidden behind the bush he was watering. Bastard insurgents.

When he was finished, he zipped up and walked away from the pickup, scanning the darkened fields and woodland for signs of life. Other than the up-glow of lights from Schwedt, and the furtive scurry of a fox or rabbit in the undergrowth, he was certain there was nobody about. He sniffed the air, catching a trace of pine sap and a waft of brackish water from the river. Then, as he stepped round to climb back behind the wheel, he saw a movement out of the corner of his eye. He stopped dead, overcome by a wash of despair.

A man was standing by the front wing, the thin glow of the sidelights reflecting off the gun in his hand.

FOURTEEN

'You should have taken the deal, Sergeant Barrow.' The newcomer spoke softly, his accent east European with a faint American inflection. He was from Bosnia, and Graham Barrow had met him before, in the company of the man named Deakin. His stomach went cold. This one's name was Zubac and he was a killer. And wherever Zubac went, so did his mate, Ganic. Two halves of the same tool. 'All you had to do was agree to trade what you knew,' Zubac continued. 'Now you have . . . no value.'

'Wait.' Barrow held up a hand. He was breathing fast, eyes sliding sideways as he estimated his chances of making it to the side of the track and the surrounding darkness. Once out there, maybe he'd have a chance. But he knew it was slim. He'd been a long time out of action, stuck behind a desk in GCHQ Cheltenham before his last posting to Sangin, Afghanistan. Quite apart from not being physically capable of taking on monsters like these men, he wasn't combat fit. He glanced around, trying to see into the darkness. Where the hell was Ganic? 'I got confused, OK? I thought Deakin was going to screw me and I couldn't risk going back. Tell him . . . tell him I'll do it.'

Zubac said nothing, merely stared at Barrow. He was of medium height and muscular, his dark hair peppered with grey, and looked exactly like what he was: an ex-soldier. Ganic was taller, with a shaved head, but they could have been brothers.

Barrow opened his mouth to say something else when suddenly a large shape flew soundlessly out of the trees right over their heads, flashing white in the glow of the truck's lights. There was no sound, and both Barrow and Zubac ducked instinctively before realizing it was a night predator, a snowy owl, the *qweck-qweck* alarm call echoing through the trees.

Barrow reacted first, throwing himself off the track and running straight into the night in sheer desperation. He had only the vaguest impression of the layout of the trees, and aimed for where he thought there was a gap in the straggly trunks. He stumbled as he hit a hollow, his teeth snapping together with the shock as his foot finally hit solid ground. Then he recovered and continued in a mad dash, his breathing loud in the night and his chest heaving with the effort. He swore repeatedly without realizing, a litany of self-blame, regret and anger, but powered on by fear. He slammed through a growth of what he guessed was blackthorn, felt the skin of his cheeks and forehead laid open and a sudden coldness where the cuts were deepest. Behind him came a shout, and he knew Ganic had joined the chase. Two against one. Two killers against a tech. No contest.

He sobbed and turned instinctively towards the border, splashing through a muddy wallow. Coldness enveloped his lower legs, the wet cloth of his pants clinging to his skin, slowing him down. One of his shoes was coming loose, grating against his heel. He tried to remember what was in his camo jacket: passport, phone and some cash. Not much to shout about after what he'd been through. What a stupid waste. He was sure he'd heard the phone ringing earlier, but he'd ignored it, too busy concentrating on getting away to take calls from mates trying to convince him to turn himself in, or worse, the bastard Deakin trying to pinpoint his location. He wished he'd answered it now; maybe it was the cavalry, ready to jump in and save his skin.

Some bloody hope. He slowed just enough to rip off the jacket and, balling it up, threw it away from him and hoped his pursuers would miss it. Maybe someone would fasten on it later . . . afterwards.

He coughed as the pain of running caught up with him and his lungs fought to compensate for too long without exercise. He zigzagged in a vain attempt to throw the men off his trail and immediately felt his legs weakening. No good; it was too much effort and he was running out of gas. He heard a shout off to his right and instinctively veered left away from it.

Christ, this was a shit way to go, wasn't it? Better to have stayed in Sangin . . .

Then he was running through lighter vegetation and his speed picked up. He felt a bust of exultation as he pictured the two

Bosnians left way behind. Perhaps they were no better at running through this shitty terrain than he was!

He swerved once more as he saw the distant glow of lights on his left. Christ, *left*? What was that? There was nothing on his left, only . . .

Schwedt.

He'd run in a circle.

Barrow retched and slowed, then stopped, and sank to one knee, his legs finally giving up on him, the muscles shaking with cramp. He felt beaten. In front of him, not thirty yards away, the truck lights came on. The motor was still chugging, the heater clinking like a line of tin cans on a wedding car.

And there was the tall shape of Ganic, standing by the front wing and grinning. Barrow heard a scrape behind him and knew without looking that Zubac was here, too, hardly breathing for all the running.

He felt tears of frustration and rage pulsing down his cheek. They'd herded him like a bloody sheep, forcing him to go round and come right back to where he'd started. Was this what happened to all deserters, to all those who couldn't take any more and chose to cut and run? An ignominious end in a shitty back-water? Or did some of them actually make it and survive?

Fuck it. With the last of his resolve, he took a deep breath and charged right at Ganic, screaming with anger, wanting to pulverize that grinning face to a pulp.

He almost made it, too, catching the Bosnian by surprise. Ganic lost the grin, his mouth rounded with shock. Then Barrow saw a flare of light from the gun in the man's hand and felt a hammer blow in his chest, and then darkness enveloped him.

Zubac walked forward and knelt by the body, checking for life signs. Nothing. Without waiting for Ganic's help, he grasped the dead man's arms and, huffing with the effort, dragged the body through the wet mud and grass until he was in a thin strand of pine trees. Even though he was sure the body wouldn't be seen from the track, he felt around in the dark and scraped soil, grass and pine needles over it and brushed his hands together before returning to the truck. Then he stood for a moment, trying to recall whether Barrow had been wearing a coat. Well, if he had, he wasn't now. Too bad. Time to get out of here, before someone came.

Ganic clambered behind the wheel, and when Zubac gave him the nod, drove off the track and slammed his foot down hard, propelling the nose of the vehicle into a tall thicket of hawthorn, nettles and wild grass. There was a dull crunch as one of the front wings collided with another heap of rusting metal which had once been a car and was now becoming part of the vegetation. The engine stalled and died. All around were the twisted and rusting hulks of other rubbish which had been thrown here over the years; an old refrigerator, tangled bicycles, ancient garden and farm machinery – even the rotting remains of an old World War Two Jeep.

Ganic considered torching the vehicle; he liked a good fire. But he dismissed the idea. Too much trouble, and it would attract attention. He walked back along the track until he reached a small BMW parked off to one side. Zubac followed, puffing on a cigarette. He climbed in and Ganic drove them back towards Schwedt, then branched off before reaching the first signs of habitation and headed for the Berlin–Stettin Autobahn.

Behind them, the rain swept in hard, covering the landscape and dripping through the trees, gradually washing the thin layer of grass and pine needles from the body.

FIFTEEN

Deakin's phone buzzed. He excused himself and checked the screen. A text message had come in. When he put the phone down he looked troubled. 'That was our man in London. The MOD sent an investigator to ask questions about Lieutenant Tan.' He looked at Paulton and explained, 'Our latest target is an aide to the Deputy Commander ISAF. She went walkabout after leaving Kabul. We don't know what she's got in her head, but the MOD's blowing up a shit storm about her. This investigator is a new development. They must really want her back.'

'I'm not surprised,' Paulton murmured. 'It's bad news for the MOD, losing an officer in her position. Highly embarrassing for the British military establishment, too. The Americans in particular won't be too impressed.'

'It could be good for us, though.' Deakin twirled his glass on the table. 'If they've put someone on her trail, it means they have no idea where she is. That gives us time to find her first. This could be a big one, gentlemen; someone in her position probably has more current strategic information at her fingertips about the campaign in Afghanistan and the command staff involved than any of the others put together. If we get her onside and ready to trade, I believe we can name our own price.'

'Except that we don't know where she is either,' Nicholls pointed out.

Deakin sat back. 'True. But if she's plugged into the network the way the others are, she might get in touch.' The information grapevine which guided many absconding soldiers into reaching out to the Protectory for help was amazingly efficient, yet did not betray any details of the men who ran it – Deakin and his colleagues worked very hard at keeping it that way. It had proved effective so far, with Pike and Barrow being two recent examples of where doors had to be slammed shut to prevent a leakage of information by runners who changed their minds.

'As long as she plays ball,' said Nicholls.

Nobody disagreed with that. The one weak point in the way the Protectory operated was that not all their 'projects' were guaranteed to trade information for the promise of a new life and new identity. Serving personnel decided to jump the fence for all sorts of reasons, including fear, sickness, religious principles, right through to a change in philosophical outlook. Not all of them felt so disenchanted with their lot that they could easily break the oath of loyalty they had taken and sell country, regiment and – most importantly – former comrades for the chance of a new life.

'She sounds a real prize.' Paulton was holding his wine glass to his nose, breathing in the aroma and staring at Deakin with a measured gaze over the rim. It gave him an almost professorial air of superiority.

'Hang on a sec. Aren't we getting ahead of ourselves?'

Turpowicz gave Paulton a sideways look, then glanced at Deakin. 'Exactly how much does he know about this?' His tone suggested that if it were true, Deakin had gone too far in revealing details of their targeted deserters to an outsider.

'Everything.' Deakin paused for a moment to let that sink in. 'George already knows what we do. I briefed him on our current projects because he has a line on some new contacts in the market place; contacts who will guarantee us a better price for what we sell. He knows the current thinking in the British and American security establishments, which is vital to us if we are to continue in safety, and I felt he had a right to our confidence in return for his help.'

'In that case,' Nicholls said coolly, 'it's rather too late in the day to argue about it, isn't it? But what makes George here so all-knowing? Does he come with special credentials?' He stared hard at Paulton as if challenging him to say otherwise.

'I do, actually,' said Paulton calmly. 'I spent many years working for the British government . . . in the Security Services, should you be interested.' He smiled at the look of shock on the faces of Turpowicz and Nicholls. 'Sadly, we had a little disagreement and I was forced to leave. I now find myself at a loose end and, knowing Thomas here, I decided to get in touch and offer my services.' He fixed a steady gaze on Nicholls. 'Is that satisfactory or would you like to check my shirt size?'

'We'll have to see, won't we?' Nicholls looked calm enough, and nodded for Deakin to continue. Before he could speak, however, Paulton chipped in, leaning forward to add emphasis and authority to his words.

'I realize you have reservations about me, gentlemen – which I understand, believe me. I would, too, in your place. But let me say this: Tom's absolutely right about the opportunity here. From what you've told me, an extremely bright young woman joins the British army and moves into a position of vital importance, working alongside the Deputy Commander ISAF in Kabul. She will have seen documents, data, plans and people from David Petraeus on down. There are very few at her level who would have had this kind of access. Very few.' He looked around but nobody interrupted him. It was a clear sign that his position was already established, even after such a brief time. 'And now

this bright young woman with a superior brain has gone walkabout . . . and the British MOD has put an investigator on her
trail. Believe me, gentlemen, they don't do that lightly. It must
mean they think she's worth it for whatever information she
has in her head.' He paused again, demonstrating his skill at
holding an audience. 'It won't be just the British concerned
about that, either. Your former bosses, Mr Turpowicz, must be
equally keen to see her returned to the fold of the godly before
she can unload what she knows about Petraeus and his home
team.'

'Maybe.' Turpowicz was unconvinced. 'Get to the point.'

'My point is simple. If we find Lieutenant Tan . . . locating a
suitable buyer for what she knows will be a matter of course. In
fact, I may already have one in mind.'

SIXTEEN

On his way back to London, Harry rang Ballatyne to
arrange a meeting. There were things he needed doing
which he hadn't got the clout for, but which Ballatyne
had. The MI6 man agreed to a rendezvous at the Italian restaurant
off Wigmore Street later that evening.

Next he rang Rik Ferris, who already had news about the
Eurostar ticket.

'It was bought through a ticket office in Scheveningen, near
The Hague, in the name of Fraser,' said Rik. 'I checked his
background; it was Pike's mother's maiden name.' He gave Harry
the address of the ticket office. 'Still no other hits on his or any
of the other names, and Tan's so common it's like wading through
seaweed.' He yawned. 'Can I come out to play? I'm getting
bunker fever here.'

'Sorry,' Harry told him. 'I might need your back-up later,
though.' It was a small lie; he couldn't see any scenario arising
where he would need that kind of help, and Rik was in no shape
to go around being physical. But he didn't want to depress him
further.

This time when he arrived at the restaurant, there was no coffee on offer and the suited hard-case stayed with the car.

'Sorry about the rush,' Ballatyne explained. 'I can't spare much time – we've got some rockets going up. Nothing to do with our business, though. What've you got?'

'I've drawn a blank so far on Lieutenant Tan. No family, no background to speak of and nothing yet to show even a sign of where she might be.'

Ballatyne looked unconcerned. 'So she's gone to ground. I'm sure she'll surface sooner or later. I think you should forget about her for the time being. Weapons technology and systems are the hot topics right now; personnel with that kind of saleable knowledge are the ones being sought.'

Harry was surprised. It was such a change of emphasis that he got the uneasy feeling Ballatyne was stonewalling him. Or maybe he had developed a new set of priorities.

'You mean who's got the biggest gun?'

'Exactly. Boys' toys, Harry. Boys' toys.' He looked pleased at the analogy.

'I still think Tan's worth looking at, that's all. You can be sure the Protectory will, too.'

'What are you looking for, specifically?'

'I haven't got the punch to gain access to Cambridge University graduate files or unlock the MOD's records. You do. Did something happen while she was at university which could have had a delayed reaction – made her vulnerable? Did she meet someone after joining up who could have influenced her in some way? Anything like that could be a lead to help track her down. There's certainly nothing else out there.'

Ballatyne looked unconvinced, but appeared to relent. 'Very well. I'll see what I can find.' Then he changed the subject. 'On my way here, I got word from the security boys at London City airport. Two supposed German males boarded the scheduled Lufthansa flight to Frankfurt at seven fifteen, the same evening Pike and Wallace were killed. The timing fits; it wouldn't have taken them long to get from the A12 to the airport. They could have lost the Merc anywhere along the way; left the keys in the ignition on a side street in east London and the local bangers would have done the rest. It's probably gathering a thin layer of desert sand on a dock in Dubai even as we speak.'

'Sounds like it was planned,' Harry agreed, 'if it was the same two men. Do we have pictures?'

'Not good ones – and nothing from the hospital cameras. They were offline. Highways Agency computer problems made their pictures grainy. Both men were heavily built, one medium height with dark hair, the other tall, but bald, possibly shaven.'

'What made them stand out, then?'

'One of the girls on the desk is German. She said their German wasn't that good and believed they were either Czech or Bosnian. She thought it odd enough to mention it to her supervisor who called it in.' He shrugged. 'We got lucky: the supervisor used to be in Immigration and thought it worth passing on.' He checked his watch. 'Got to go. What are you doing next?'

Harry explained about his intention of following Pike's trail back to Holland. 'Wherever Pike started his return journey, he must have had a meeting prior to that, presumably to sell what he knew, which generated the payment through Grand Cayman. Getting a line on where he came from right before he used the cash machine in The Hague will help me backtrack him from there.'

'We know he was in Thailand,' Ballatyne pointed out. 'Long way to go.'

'It's also too big and crowded. You could hide an entire regiment out there and nobody would know.'

'Fair comment. But why travel anywhere? We've got people who can do the research online and on the ground. Ferris could do it, given the right equipment. How is our wounded soldier, by the way?'

'He's fine. He'll be all right when he's rested up and got something to concentrate on.' He paused, then said, 'I want to rattle a few cages over there, to see what I turn up. If I cross the Protectory's trail along the way, they might get to hear about it. That won't happen working online.'

Ballatyne pursed his lips. 'It's a risky strategy, rattling cages. You never know who or what you might wake up.'

'I know. But I'm short of ideas at the moment.'

'Fair enough.' Ballatyne nodded. 'Just watch your back.'

He walked out, leaving Harry to shut the door.

SEVENTEEN

A sickly dawn was lifting over the horizon as former railroad worker Wilhelm Dieter plodded slowly away from Schwedt, following his ritual daily walk, a determined but joyless defence against advancing old age. He absorbed little of the surrounding scenery to interest him; he'd been seeing it for too many years to count and doubted it would bring anything new to arouse his curiosity or brighten his day. It was why he alternated between this route and another going north, hopeful that maybe the change would keep his mind engaged along with his body, and throw up something distracting to look at once in a while, even if only some wildlife.

As he neared the strand of pine trees running along the border like a prickly rash, he noticed a group of carrion crows in the upper branches. Nothing unusual in crows, he reflected, the bloody things were everywhere. But clumped together like that? They looked like a bunch of priests on a day out, dark and faintly shabby, united in their bickering.

Tyre tracks in the mud – and recent, too. He'd have noticed them if they'd been here on his last walk two days ago. Nothing much came down here these days other than the occasional border patrol, although they were rare, too. There wasn't the same need now, for patrols. Not since the Wall had come down.

He stopped and gave vent to a hacking cough, the result of too many cheap cigarettes, a lousy diet and damp living conditions, and tugged irritably at the woollen cap with the ear-flaps flying loose about his head. He shivered and thrust his hands deep into the pockets of his trench coat, feeling the cold easterly wind coming across the trees and surrounding grassland. Christ, if only we could have a bit more sunshine, he thought. It would liven up this bloody back-of-nowhere place for a start.

He continued walking and skirted a puddle, his ears prickling with tension. He stopped and studied the ground. Footprints everywhere, and more than one set, by the look of it. The tyre tracks ran on through the mud, leading towards the bend and the thicket where a few irresponsible louts from the town were forever dumping the rubbish they couldn't be bothered to dispose of properly.

He decided to take a look. There was nowhere down here for a vehicle to go, not unless it was military or police. The track ended in a heavy gate, although if one were determined, it might be possible to blast through. But why bother? It only led to Poland for God's sake; same scenery, different language.

He followed the track, his curiosity aroused. If there was anything salvageable, he could maybe get some cash for it in town. Anyway, what else did he have to occupy himself? Then he noticed a shallow furrow leading off to one side of the track, as if something heavy had been dragged through the grass towards the trees where the crows were gathered. A sack of something, perhaps? Probably somebody's worthless shit, but worth a look at least . . .

As he stepped off the track he noticed a coat spread over a tangle of blackthorn, the khaki colour darkened almost black in places by moisture. An old jacket, he decided, military surplus by the looks of it and widely available in places if you knew where to look. But why was it here? He felt the beginnings of a worm of excitement beating in his chest, and stepped forward to retrieve it.

Two hours later, less than two kilometres away, a former government office worker named Sylvia Heidl sat in a bare flat on the second floor of an ugly concrete block looking out over a featureless landscape. She was staring at a shiny black object on her kitchen table. It had a small green power light in one end which was flashing intermittently like a deficient ceiling bulb. It was a sign of energy and life, seemingly mocking the fact that her own vital signs were fast diminishing.

Outside, thin rain pattered against the windows, cold and relentless. In the quiet of the room, her breathing was quick, bird-like. It matched the throbbing of a pulse at her temple, visible under the translucent skin marked by the blemishes of old age. But old age wasn't the problem. She looked down at her hands. They were like a collection of bony sticks; sticks which had lost their strength over the past few months and weeks along with the rest of her body, the disease which had overtaken her turning her into an old woman in no time at all.

A sound outside brought her head up, fear clutching at her breast. Then she relaxed, recognizing old Bendl's asthmatic coughing. He shuffled down the foul-smelling stairs in the darkness each morning, on his way to the refinery where he worked as a clerk. Like the few who had jobs here, he started early and finished late, eager to work punishing hours for next to nothing, since earning nothing was simply to fade and die.

As the footsteps receded, she wondered what Ulf would say. Her brother was a doctor, although not the kind who could help her. An army medic for many years, he knew a lot about battle wounds but precious little about cancerous growths caused by the toxic air which attacked you as you breathed. But with his part-time job at the hospital, he knew people he could ask . . . people with access to drugs which helped manage the pain she was suffering with increasing regularity.

She reached over and picked up the mobile phone, and brushed off a thin smear of mud, where old Wilhelm had handled it.

'See if Ulf can sell these in town,' he'd suggested tentatively, pushing the mobile and the slim red book into her hands. He had come straight round after his walk and woken her up, pounding on the door as if his life depended on it. 'He might even be able to return them to the owner . . . for a reward. We can share in whatever he gets.' He'd gone on to explain where he'd found the jacket and, in the pocket, the mobile phone and the British passport. 'I would do it myself, but I don't know who to speak to. I don't get into town much these days.'

What he meant, Sylvia thought cynically, was that Ulf had been in the East German army and Sylvia had been in the . . . the job she'd been in. To Wilhelm, that meant they had contacts . . . people who knew things. He was one of very few people who knew about Sylvia's past, although he cared nothing about it. History is history, he often said pragmatically, best forgotten.

She took the passport from the pocket of her apron, listening for the sound of footsteps on the landing. Such caution was second nature to her; the grate of steps in the night, the rustle of thick serge cloth, the rumble of heavy boots and the clink of weapons moments before the door burst open and the future ceased to be. It had been a way of life for everyone here once. Now all she had left was the bite of ingrained paranoia.

The book was slim, dark-red, the colour of dried blood. The pages were rich and stiff, the paper of good quality. In the back was a photograph of a man with short hair and broad cheekbones. He wasn't smiling, so she couldn't tell what he would be like. A smile told you so much about a person. A doctor, she thought wistfully? A handsome man, anyway. Probably rich.

These things must be worth something, she hoped fervently. Down by the station, in the seedy backstreet cafés where she never went, there were people who would pay for such things; foreigners, mostly, from all quarters of the world. One had to be careful to get the money before handing over the goods, so it was no good her trying it. She'd be no match for a man in that situation. She would have to speak to Ulf.

EIGHTEEN

The KLM flight from London City dropped Harry into Rotterdam airport under a leaden grey sky. He was thankful that none of the other passengers – mostly businessmen, bleary-eyed after early starts – had attempted any conversation. It had allowed him to close his eyes for a short while and catch up on some sleep, a trick he had worked hard on perfecting over the years. He made his way through the terminal and enquired at the information desk about travelling to Scheveningen. The woman rolled her eyes and wagged a finger, saying quietly, 'Sir, you must not take a car to this place. It is impossible to park and very expensive. Taxis are cheaper and quicker.' She handed him a basic map of The Hague and its surrounding districts, and directed him towards the taxi rank.

Scheveningen was a neat, modern and busy resort, and virtually a suburb of The Hague. It boasted sweeping sands, an impressive pier and an abundance of smart hotels and restaurants for the clean-living burghers of Den Haag, or the conference delegates too intent on business to have any interest in the various fleshpots of Rotterdam. In the background were a number of modern high-rise buildings which seemed to blend in perfectly with the holiday setting.

Harry asked the cab driver to drop him off and walked along the front, getting a feel for the place. He shivered slightly at a stiff breeze sweeping along the promenade, stinging his face with a light touch of fine sand. He was trying to see the place from Pike's point of view, and what might have attracted him here. Was it purely for a meeting with the Protectory, to barter over what he could bring them and how much he was worth? Or had he come here in the final stages of deciding to return home?

He walked past the magnificent structure of the Kurhaus Hotel which, according to a brochure the cab driver had thrust at him, had been central in location and social standing to the resort since 1885. It boasted a fine restaurant and facilities, including a famous concert hall – the Kurzaal – and for that reason Harry decided Pike wouldn't have gone anywhere near it. A deserter on the run would find such places too open, too threatening. He'd also spotted at least two cameras along the front, and Pike would have avoided them, too.

He turned inland and found his way into a collection of back streets. Elegant and orderly, but much less open, this was more likely a setting for a fugitive wishing to stay out of the limelight. Casual clothing was the norm and Pike would have blended in well here, just another man prowling the streets with time to kill.

He checked the address of the ATM machine Pike had used, and found it in a branch of ING Bank. It was just along the street from a ticket agency offering holidays to the Maldives and cruises down the Nile. The same agency where Pike had bought his Eurostar ticket.

He did a slow tour of the neighbourhood, ostensibly window-shopping while noting the various bars and cafés, a sex shop and a nightclub. The rest were small shops and businesses, and neat, red-brick houses topped by bright-red roof tiles. The sex shop aside, the area could not have been more anonymous, more normal. It was almost small-town compared to the vibrant modernity of the beach front area, and offered no clue as to what Pike could have been doing here other than blending in. Keeping his head down. Yet he'd used the machine twice. It suggested he'd stayed somewhere nearby. Anyone keeping a low profile wouldn't risk walking far in broad daylight to use an ATM or to buy a train ticket – there was too much danger involved. Duck out, do what was necessary, duck back in, all with the minimum of exposure, would be the norm. The excursions to a bar-café were different; that would have been at night when it was easier to stay in the shadows.

Harry wondered at what point Pike had made up his mind about going home, in spite of having allegedly taken the Protectory's money, if that was where it had come from. Even those intending to sell secrets they had promised to keep might suffer the equivalent to a seven-day cooling-off period, a crisis of conscience highlighted rather than salved by an influx of illicit cash.

He entered the tour agency and showed the man behind the desk the photo of Pike. 'I'm looking for my brother-in-law,' he explained. 'He stayed in the area and bought a Eurostar ticket to London, but never arrived home. His name's Fraser.' He had written the ticket stub number on the back of the photo.

The manager hesitated for a moment, then shrugged as if answering questions from relatives whose brothers-in-law had not arrived home was not an uncommon occurrence. He entered the number in his computer, waited for a second, then said, 'Mr Fraser gave his address as the Monro Hostel. It is very popular with people on a budget. Go down Keizerstraat for two hundred metres, then take a left. It is not far.'

'He paid cash?'

'Yes.'

Harry thanked him for his help and followed the directions to the Monro Hostel, a red-brick building set back from the street with a large awning over the front. He went inside and stepped over a pile of backpacks to the small desk, and rang the bell. A large woman with bright-red hair came out through a beaded curtain and nodded. '*Goedemorgen.*'

Harry explained about his wayward brother-in-law, and how his sister was worried about her husband. The woman listened without comment, then checked a register.

'*Nee,*' she said eventually. '*Mijnheer* Fraser was here two days, but no more.' She pointed back towards Keizerstraat. 'Try the Continentale Café. I see him there two times, at night, with friends. I hope he is OK, your brother.' Then she turned and disappeared through the curtain.

With friends. That could mean anything or nothing. Drinking buddies for the evening . . . or something more focussed and deliberate.

The Continentale was sleek, modern and furnished with polished wooden bench seats and tables, and a scattering of ethnic cushions under subdued lighting. A small dais at the end was overlooked by a row of coloured spotlights and held two large amplifiers and a microphone. The barman was a spit for a young Bruce Springsteen, right down to the blue jeans and waistcoat, and nodded as Harry approached the bar. There were no other customers, in spite of it being close to lunchtime, and he guessed the place probably came alive at night.

He ordered a coffee and slid Pike's photo across the bar. 'Have you seen this man recently? His name's Fraser.' He didn't bother with the brother-in-law; any pro barmen would automatically clam up when faced with a story like that.

The man put down the glass he was polishing and studied the picture, his expression blank. 'Sorry, pal.' His accent was pure American, the voice a growl nurtured on late nights and too many cigarettes. 'Don't remember him.' He dropped the photo and turned to pour a cup of coffee from a percolator on the back counter. He placed the cup in front of Harry and added cream and sugar alongside. 'Come night-time, this place rocks, y'know? People come and go all the time. Just faces, most of 'em. It's like Grand Central. What's he done?'

Harry wasn't in the habit of making snap judgements. He usually had to know people a while before judging their character . . . unless they were brandishing a weapon or wearing a body belt of explosives strapped to their chests, then he felt able to make all the judgements in the world. But this man was different. Whether it was his tone, body language or accent, or the knowledge that Pike had been here more than once with 'friends', he knew without a shadow of doubt that the barman was what he'd been looking for. He was crossing the trail of the Protectory.

It felt like stepping over a snake.

'You never saw him.'

'Not what I said. I said I don't remember seeing him. Different thing altogether.' He gave a tough-guy smile, as if pleased with his response, and picked up the glass and resumed his polishing.

'You're right,' said Harry. 'It is different.' He sipped the coffee. It was stewed and bitter on the palate. He decided to push harder. 'Why, if you don't remember him, have you just polished that glass three times since I came in?'

The barman stared at him and flushed. He'll remember this, thought Harry, watching the anger rise in the man's face. He'll remember and pass the word.

'I think you'd better leave.' The barman put down the glass again and lifted his chest. 'Right now. The coffee's on the house.'

The barman waited for five minutes after the Englishman had gone. Then he went over to a payphone at the rear of the premises. He dialled a number from memory, and when it was answered, identified himself.

'Wait there,' said a woman's voice on the other end. 'Keep the line free. He'll call back.'

He placed an 'Out of Order' sign on the phone and went back to the bar, where he continued polishing glasses. When the phone rang, he picked it up.

'What have you got?' The voice was male, the accent British.

'It's Daniels. I just had a guy in here asking questions.'

'About what?'

'You know. The guy on the run . . . Fraser. This fella showed me a photo. It was definitely him.'

'What was his name? What did he look like?'

'He didn't say his name. I didn't ask. Just a guy, y'know? British, forty-something, good build, not a business type, though. Smelled like a cop. Hard-nosed.' He had his own reasons for avoiding cops; especially those from countries with extradition treaties. He recalled the way the man had looked at him, and how he'd felt a sudden chill in his stomach. Drunks sometimes had the same look. But they were rarely dangerous. Drunks he could deal with. But this one had been stone cold sober. He considered the answer he'd given the visitor, and decided on a small lie. 'I told him I'd never seen the guy before.'

There was a short silence, then, 'That was a mistake. Not remembering is a better answer.'

NINETEEN

In Schwedt, Sylvia Heidl struggled into a thin overcoat and ·headscarf, picked up a shopping bag, then cast around for a moment before gathering together a pair of worn shoes and an old towel. She placed the phone and passport in the bag, and covered them with the towel. After checking the bag to make sure nothing could be seen, she slipped on her shoes and left the flat.

The air on the landing was cold and damp. She took a deep breath, feeling the customary stab of pain in her chest. It hurt more today than it had in a while, and she wondered if Ulf had managed to get her any more painkillers. She wasn't sure she could take another day without them.

As she emerged from the prefab concrete block, one of the few cheap workers' buildings that hadn't been flattened in the wake of reunification and development, the smell from the refinery and factories engulfed her like a cloak. They had said you would get used to it, but she never had. She followed the path into town. A steady stream of heavy trucks caked in mud thundered along the narrow road, their slipstream tugging at her coat and whipping a spray of damp grit across her face.

She passed only two other women on the way. Both ignored her. The streets in the centre were quiet, with a scattering of cars and one or two pickup trucks. If there was any new wealth from the reunification, it had not yet penetrated this far in any major way, seemingly bypassing the town like the trucks.

She entered a doorway along a narrow street and climbed a steep flight of uneven stairs, her breath rasping in her throat. As she reached the landing a door opened and her brother Ulf peered out. He beckoned her in and closed the door.

'Do you have them?' she asked, slumping into a chair. She was struggling for breath, her face a pallid grey and her eyes narrowed to pinpoints.

He nodded and took a twist of paper from his pocket. 'Only when you have to,' he reminded her. 'When the pain is too much.' He said it each time he gave her the painkillers, but the intervals between her asking for more were getting shorter all the time. Very soon the tablets would fail to make any difference at all.

She took the paper with trembling hands and undid the twist. A tiny tablet slid into her palm, and with a brief nod she put it between her lips and swallowed, her fleshless throat working to push the painkiller down. She smiled. It was too soon for the tablet to have worked, but the act of swallowing seemed somehow to work its magic on her. She carefully re-twisted the paper and placed it in her coat pocket.

'Let me look at you,' he said softly, touching her face with a gentle hand. She pushed his hand away with a gentle shushing sound. The clinic had already explained that her exposure years ago to a range of deadly toxins had eaten away at her internal organs and left precious little to save. All Ulf could do was try to make life as bearable as possible.

He poured some of the good coffee he got from a porter at the hospital, and watched as Sylvia breathed in the heavy aroma. She didn't come here often, although he'd tried repeatedly to get her to share the flat with him, to reduce the burden of a lonely life without her husband. But she always refused stubbornly.

'No news of Claus?' He had never cared for her husband, contemptuous of his work for the *Stasi* – the *Staatssicherheitsdienst* – East German Security; the same organization which had employed her too, until the Wall came down. But he always asked. Claus had been away ever since, God alone knew where. Running from his enemies, most likely. Or dead.

Sylvia put her mug down and reached inside her bag. Placed the black mobile phone and blood-red passport in front of him. 'Can you sell these?' she asked him.

Ulf stared at them in astonishment. He poked the phone with a stubby finger and saw a winking green light. Some of the better-placed army officers carried them down at the hospital in Freienfelde. Kids, too – even the ones with no money. *Handys*, they called them.

'Where the hell did you get these?' He didn't possess one himself, but understood the basic functions. This one, with a picture screen and lots of little images, looked as if it could track a rocket all the way to the moon.

'Old Wilhelm found them down by the border. He wants you to sell them and share the money. He's afraid to try in case he gets ripped off.'

'Have you shown them to anyone else?'

She shook her head. 'I was too scared.'

'God, the old fool must be getting senile!' he muttered. 'It's a good job you didn't use it. They can track these things from space. Thirty thousand metres up and a satellite tells them just where you're calling from. "Yes, Commander, we have an old lady in Schwedt, a nowhere spot on the bloody map, and she's using a stolen phone to call her friends around the world."' He sighed guiltily. He was exaggerating. Anyway, who would she have called? He flicked open the passport, his tone softer. 'Sorry. I'm worried about you, that's all. These things, they're like gold dust in the right places. But if you got caught with it . . .'

He picked up the phone again and tapped some keys. A list of numbers scrolled up the small screen, showing which ones had been dialled last. Three were to the same number, and began with an overseas code, 00 44. He seemed to recall the number 44 was for the United Kingdom. No doubt he would soon find out if he dialled it. But was it safe?

Then he recalled that these things had a message facility, like ordinary landline phones. He played with the keys until he found the voicemail. It held one message. If the date setting was correct, it had been left nearly two days ago. 'Listen,' he said earnestly, placing a reassuring hand on Sylvia's. 'We'd get virtually nothing from those thieves at the station. They'd rip us off – or worse. But maybe the owner would pay something to get them back – especially the passport.' He tapped the phone. 'This might help me find them.'

'How will you know you have the owner?'

That was something he didn't want to think about. 'I won't,' he admitted. If the wrong people heard about this, he could end up as a guest of the police – or worse, in a muddy ditch courtesy of the local *Mafiya* . . . and with no money to help Sylvia. He was already having problems getting the painkillers; the man who supplied him was becoming more greedy and threatening as he sensed Ulf's desperation. In fact Ulf was sure the man had heard of Sylvia's past and would one day use that knowledge to demand more money.

He re-read the passport. It was of little help to him; the section at the back under the heading 'Emergencies' had been scratched through, maybe as a precaution, although he thought doing that was probably illegal. Maybe a wife, brother or sister no longer available to help, taken by death or divorce.

He played the voicemail message, listening intently. *'Graham, my name's Harry Tate. I want to help you. I work in conjunction with the* MOD, *but I imagine you're not sure who to trust right now, so I won't waste time trying to sell you a deal. Call me and we'll talk. This isn't as bad as you think.'*

Ulf listened to the voice message several more times with a growing sense of excitement, trying to gauge what kind of man was speaking. If he understood the words correctly, the owner of this phone was in some kind of trouble, and this caller, this Englishman, Harry Tate, was offering to help him. But what was this 'MOD' he mentioned? He played it again. And again.

Eventually he switched off the phone to conserve the battery. Clearly the man Tate did not know this Graham Barrow. Yet he was offering to help him. Why? And the talk about trust; it sounded like a man offering reassurance of some kind. There followed a number, which Ulf had already written down, in case the battery died. Luckily, the caller had spoken slowly, carefully.

He began to compose in his head what he was going to say. His English was rusty, learned at university a long time ago while studying for his medical degree. But that had been no grounding for conducting a negotiation over a lost *Handy* and a passport.

TWENTY

Harry was eating a late lunch at Rotterdam airport when Rik called.

'We got an answer from Barrow's mobile. I was out but the caller left a message.'

'Hold on,' said Harry. A nearby group of elderly men in colourful tracksuits were making too much noise to hear properly. 'I need to get somewhere quiet.' He stood up and walked around the terminal until he found an alcove used for storing luggage trolleys. There was no background noise other than the faint sound of the tannoy. 'OK. Can you play it?'

'Sure thing.'

He waited while Rik held his mobile close to the answering machine. A voice crackled with surprising clarity, the tone at first halting, then gaining in confidence. *'Hello. Please believe me . . . we have not caused anyone any harm. This Handy was found and we wish to return it for a fee . . . a reward for service. Also we have a passport . . . the name is Graham Barrow . . .'* The voice struggled with the first name *'. . . from England. Please, this is not a trick. We wish only to send back what is not ours to keep. Please call . . . but quickly as I think the battery is weak. Thank you.'* There were a few moments of forced breathing, some dull clunks, then the call ended.

Harry found he'd been holding his breath. He asked Rik to play the message again. It sounded genuine enough, but there was no way of knowing. Someone after a reward, as he had claimed? Or some elaborate ploy?

He told Rik to count to ten, then play the message again, giving him time to set up the recorder on his own mobile. Once that was done, he played the message over and over, pausing for coffee and prowling the terminal lounge, trying to read in the deep, slow voice a sign as to the identity of the caller. Educated, obviously. Articulate, too, although English wasn't his first language. Maybe not used much. Middle-aged by the tone and depth, even courteous in his request. And then the word *Handy*: it was what they called mobiles in Germany.

He dialled the number.

It was answered on the tenth ring, as he was about to give up.

'*Ja*?' A man's voice, flat and hesitant. In the background Harry heard someone whispering urgently. A woman's voice, cut off by the man saying something sharp.

Harry introduced himself. 'You were kind enough to call about this phone, the *Handy*,' he said carefully, avoiding any sign of accusation. 'And the passport. Are you willing to trade?'

'Trade?' the man sounded wary.

'Sell. Are you willing to sell them to me?'

A whispered conversation and the man came back. '*Ja* . . . Yes . . . We wish to return both items. Your name is Harry?'

'Yes. Harry Tate. What about the man who owns these things? Is he hurt? Have you seen him?'

'*Nein* . . . no. We have not seen the man in the *Pass* – the passport. Only this and the telephone.'

Harry decided to cut to the chase before the man lost his nerve or the phone died on him. 'Where can we meet?' he asked. 'Can you give me your name?'

There was a silence, and for a second or two Harry thought he had gone. Then the man said, 'Schwedt. You must come to Schwedt. You will bring money?' His voice faded on the last question, suddenly unsure . . . or embarrassed.

'Where is Schwedt?'

'Near the Oderbruch,' the man said. 'Fifty kilometres north-east of Berlin, by the border with Poland. You must come to Tegel, I think, then by car to here.'

Berlin. Barrow hadn't gone far, then.

'Mr Harry . . . are you there?'

'Yes, I'm still here. How will I know you? Where will we meet?'

A second or two of silence, then the man said briefly, 'You come to the church in Oderstrasse. Then ring this number and I will find you.'

The phone went off.

Harry returned to the main concourse and bought a ticket for Berlin on an early Air Portugal flight the following morning. It meant an overnight stay, but at least he could get his head down in a hotel, ready for whatever lay ahead. Next he went to the bureau de change and bought a thousand US dollars. With no idea what the mystery man in Germany might be asking for the return of phone and passport, it was better to be on the safe side.

He called Rik and told him of his plans, then Ballatyne. The MI6 man was concerned.

'You might have dug a stick in the wasps' nest, Harry.'

'That was the intention. I'll never get anywhere following vague trails. I need them to come to me.'

'If Paulton is involved with the Protectory and this is a trap, he might bolt the moment he hears your name.'

'That's the risk I have to take. I'll call as soon as I hear anything.'

In the flat in Schwedt, Ulf Hefflin sat back with a sigh. His chest was hurting with the strain of making the call, but he felt good. He glanced at his sister. She seemed to have gone into a trance, eyes fixed on some distant horizon, and he wondered how many of the blue tablets she had taken. Too many for her own good, probably. On the other hand, he wasn't the one fighting the pain.

'He will come,' he said softly, and went to make more coffee. He would have liked something stronger, but once he started down that road, it would be hard to stop. The stress of getting Sylvia's tablets was burden enough; now he had to meet this Englishman and go through the humiliation of asking for money for the phone and the passport. 'Harry Tate will come.'

Back at the Continentale Café, the barman, Daniels, was staring at the screen of the security monitor in the back office which showed a still picture from the CCTV camera over the front entrance. It was the British guy, frozen as he stepped through the door. It was a good shot, and should be easy to get a make on him for someone with the right contacts.

And the man he'd been talking to earlier, the one he knew as Deakin; he would have the contacts.

He took a copy of the frozen frame and added a brief identifier: *'The Brit who came in asking questions. D.'* Then he sent it off to a Google Mail address where Deakin could pick it up.

TWENTY-ONE

S taff Sergeant Gerry McCreath stood by the door of his bedroom and listened for sounds of movement. The hotel he was being kept in was large, square and anonymous, fancy enough to be expensive, yet still a soulless block of glass and steel, a couple of miles from Brussels city centre. He hadn't slept more than a couple of hours straight in the past three days, but that wasn't down to the bedding or the decor. First had been the unfamiliar, of not being constantly under orders. Even in Selly Oak Hospital, his timetable had been fixed from morning until night. Second came the pricking of conscience after agreeing to do what he'd never thought himself capable of. Now it was fear, plain and simple.

Oddly enough, fear was something he could deal with. Christ, he'd known enough of it recently.

He scooted across to the bedside cabinet and gathered his few belongings together. Cash, watch, wallet, a cheap paperback he couldn't get into. He tossed the book aside and dropped the rest into his pockets, resolve suddenly spurring him on. Then he picked up his overnight bag and paused to take stock. He was dressed in a jacket, white shirt and dark slacks, which the men who'd brought him here had made him wear. It fitted the ambiance better, one of them had joked. A man named Deakin, ex-British army. He seemed to think it was amusing, a serving soldier agreeing to trade the information in his head in exchange for cash and a new identity. Like it was some kind of game.

He was breathing fast – too fast. He had to keep control. Ever since his wounds had been patched up, he'd been getting anxiety attacks. The slightest thing could set them off, from a door slamming, to the sound of someone shouting . . . The medics said it was normal and they'd subside in time. But if anything they seemed to be getting worse. And now this situation wasn't exactly helping. He forced himself to calm down, focussing on the wall and trying to find a picture of somewhere serene. Sometimes it worked, sometimes it didn't. Right now it had to.

Since deciding to seek the Protectory's help, he'd been doubtful about what he was getting into. Going on the run had been done on a whim, high on prescription drugs and the after-effects of his injuries, when he was desperate to be away from the stuff he'd been doing with 16 Air Assault Brigade. It wasn't going to work out over there, he told himself. The lads would be at it for years, slowly losing numbers. Eventually the politicians would have to admit defeat, or have Afghanistan as a permanent killing ground, a gross war of attrition. How could you fight an enemy you couldn't even see most of the time? Where they hid among civilians and came at you out of nowhere, and the next time you stepped down from a Chinook in a swirling dust cloud you could be right on top of an IED—

He breathed deeply until the thoughts receded. Too late for all that. *Focus*. He'd made the jump and now he had to face the consequences. Whether he did the trade the Protectory wanted him to, emptying his head of everything he knew or . . . he did what his brain was telling him to do right *now*, before anyone came back, he was out on a limb and would have to make the best of it. Trouble was, he now knew, after what he'd just heard, changing his mind might be the last thing he ever did.

So much for the support the head man of the Protectory – Deakin? – had promised. Help us, he'd said, and we'll help you. If you don't want to, no fault, no worries. We'll give you a ticket out and new papers, even a couple of names and addresses where you'll find work and a chance to disappear into the undergrowth. He was certainly persuasive, that Deakin, no messing. Made it all sound so simple. Only it wasn't. Not now. Now it was shit serious and . . . Christ, what would his mum have said . . .?

He gripped his bag tight, his breathing coming under control, every muscle and nerve telling him he should be on the move. He had to make a decision. *Now*. Stay here and sell out . . . or go back and face whatever shit they wanted to throw at him. There were no half measures. Only, if he was going back, he'd have to move quick, while the two Bosnian minders were out of the way. They'd disappeared suddenly, but promised to be back. It must have been them who did for Neville Pike. They had that look about them. The call to his mate earlier, who'd put him in touch with Deakin in the first place, had been a shocker. News from England, he'd said, then told him about a hit on a car carrying two redcaps and a third man named Pike.

Is that what they did to people who changed their mind?

He'd tried to ignore it, thinking there had to be more to it. Maybe Pike had blown it and threatened to dob them in. Then another thought came creeping, one that stopped him getting to sleep at the thought of the Bosnians. Was it only the doubtful who got slotted? Or was it everyone's fate?

He eased the door open and peered through the crack. Saw a long corridor with a light-tan carpet lit by yellow overhead lights. Follow the yellow brick road to . . . what? He took a deep breath. He could make it down there, no problem, like a greyhound on whisper mode. If anyone else showed up, either Deakin or his Yank mate, he'd run right through them. He already had his exit route scoped: down the back stairs and out through a side door near the kitchens. In a place like this, the fire escape door was probably rigged to show up on a security screen if it was opened. He couldn't risk that. But he'd seen the staff sneaking out for smokes through another door, and figured that would be his best way. He'd noticed how taxis were always coming and going here, too, all through the night, so there would be no problem flagging one down and flashing some notes. Quick trip to the station and he'd be heading for the coast.

And England. London. Home.

He stepped out and started running.

TWENTY-TWO

The terminal at Berlin's Tegel airport was a frantic mass of meeters and greeters. Harry fought his way through the crowd and found a car-hire desk where he signed for an anonymous VW Golf. The clerk behind the desk handed him his collection slip and directed him to a kiosk where he could find detailed road maps. He picked up his overnight bag and thanked her, and walked away.

The man immediately behind Harry stepped forward to take his place, then appeared to remember something and changed his mind. Throwing a glance at Harry's back, he hurried out to the front of the terminal.

When Harry left the airport, following the map towards the east of the city and the E74 Ring and the E28 leading north-east towards Stettin, Poland, he was being followed.

The city had changed beyond all recognition since he'd last been here, a result of reunification and EU funding, and he was forced to concentrate on the traffic around him to avoid being spun off in the wrong direction. It was this concentration which made him realize that he'd picked up a tail.

A dark-blue VW Passat had nosed out from the airport behind him, and was sticking rigidly behind him a hundred yards back. It wasn't significant given the volume of traffic, and he wouldn't have thought anything of it, except that two manoeuvres later, when he'd deliberately turned off the Ring and regained it, the Passat was still there. The driver was male, but holding too far back for Harry to get a clear sight of his face.

When the car was still behind him twenty minutes later, but showing no signs of doing anything other than following, Harry decided this was the first indication that his plan to get the Protectory interested was working. But he needed help. He rang Rik.

'How's the arm?'

'Itching like a bugger. Why?' Rik sounded bored and irritable.

'Saddle up, Tonto. I've got a tail and I need to find out who he is without letting him know that I know.'

'Thank God!' Rik muttered fervently. 'Where to?'

Harry gave him directions to Schwedt and read out the Passat's registration number. 'Get the details on that and grab the first flight available,' he suggested. 'Be ready for an overnight stay.' He had no qualms about billing Ballatyne for the double expense; there were times when operating two-handed was the only option. And having this man on his back was the nearest yet to a definite show of interest from the Protectory. 'You might do well to hire an automatic, with your arm.'

'What are you, my mother?' Rik muttered. 'I'll be fine, don't worry. I'll put the word on the car out with the community; they'll soon get me a name.' His fellow-hackers and IT geeks loved nothing more than nosing around in official files where they had no business, each venture a new challenge to be overcome. He paused. 'Ballatyne's people could get this, too, you know.'

'Yes, they could. But he'd have to go through official channels, and it would take too long. And I'm not sure how leak-proof those channels are. Hire something inoffensive and try to be inconspicuous.' Rik usually drove a vivid blue Audi TT, and his spiky hair and choice of garish T-shirts were hardly unmemorable.

'Hey – I can blend,' he protested. 'I mostly choose not to.'

Harry thought that was rich, remembering how Rik had been canned from MI5 for nosing into restricted records and leaving a footprint, but he let it go. 'Take my advice and blend. These people don't mess. Remember what happened to Pike.'

'Gotcha, boss. That all?'

'Yes. Ring me when you get close.'

He disconnected and checked the map. Schwedt wasn't far. Another forty minutes and he'd be there. He put his foot down and watched as the Passat gradually matched his pace. He slotted himself between two large trucks and the Passat began to overtake, then dropped back. Not a professional, he decided, or a cop. Just a man doing a job of work. But who for?

TWENTY-THREE

'Who the hell is this bloke?' Deakin was on his laptop studying the photo-snatch sent by Daniels in Scheveningen. It was clear enough to use, and he'd earlier forwarded copies to watchers at the airports of Amsterdam, Rotterdam and, to be safe, Berlin. These were all cities where he had contacts he could use at short notice. Most were gofers, available for simple tasks requiring no elaborate skills other than mobility and freedom of movement in exchange for a small fee. They usually had contacts with the local police, town halls and other agencies. A few were capable of more serious work if it was needed, or knew others they could call on. They cost more but it was a price Deakin was prepared to pay for his prolonged security.

Right now, he was waiting to see if anyone would spot the face.

He and Turpowicz were staying in the Goldenstedt Hotel in Delmenhorst, a southern suburb of Bremen. At two storeys and forty rooms, it was big enough to be anonymous, and close enough to the city's commercial zones for two foreign visitors to pass unnoticed. He and Turpowicz had made the move from Hamburg as a natural precaution, and would be moving on the following day. Staying ahead of trouble was something that had kept them all free for a long time now, and would do for the foreseeable future.

He traced a map laid out on the table alongside the laptop, trying to second-guess the man's movements. If the mystery investigator Daniels had warned them about chose to head south towards Antwerp or Brussels, both routes back to the UK, then the trail would go cold. But there was always the Eurostar terminal in London. Someone might pick him up there.

Greg Turpowicz looked over his shoulder at the screen. 'Certainly looks like a cop to me,' he muttered. 'Most likely military. Can your MPs operate anywhere they choose?'

Deakin shrugged. 'You know what it's like: since Nine-Eleven everything's changed. It used to be they had jurisdiction only around British bases. Anywhere else, they'd have to get the local police involved. But now . . . now I wouldn't bet against anything.' He bent and peered closely at the man on the screen. He was stocky and solid, an ordinary dresser by the look of it, not flashy; one who would blend in anywhere. A hunter. He switched off the screen. 'I don't really care who or what he is. He's chasing a dead man. What I do care about is where he goes next.' He checked his watch. They had a meeting coming up on the other side of Bremen. And this was of major importance for the group's financial future. More importantly, if it went according to his plans, it would establish his position as undisputed leader of the Protectory.

*   *   *

Harry Tate entered the town of Schwedt on the main road and let it take him towards the border crossing, which his map showed him was through the centre. He was working on the basis of German logic placing Oderstrasse in the direction of its nearest stretch of well-known water, and wasn't disappointed. Two minutes later, he saw a sign for a church to his left. He checked his mirror. No sign of the Passat, but that had been the case for the last fifteen minutes. Maybe he'd got a puncture.

He turned left and saw the church rising above the surrounding houses. He parked against the church wall and turned off the engine. *'Ring this number and I will find you'*, the man had told him, before hanging up. That could mean he either lived in the centre of town and spent all his time watching for new arrivals, or he was someone of substance who had others to do his watching for him.

Harry got out and locked the doors, sniffing at the smell of petrochemicals in the air. From a panel on the map, he'd learned that Schwedt had been largely modernized since reunification, and although it had lost some of its population in recent years, it had not entirely ceased being an industrial centre for the region.

Across the road was a small expanse of green. Two elderly women were chatting, while a couple of small children played with a ball. On a bench nearby, an elderly man in working clothes was smoking a pipe over a newspaper. It was peaceful here, and off the main road, secluded.

He decided to take a scouting tour first. It took him all of forty minutes to make a rough tour of the centre and get his bearings. Just before arriving back at the church, he dialled the number of Barrow's mobile.

'*Ja?*' It was the same voice.

'It's Tate. I'll be at the church in two minutes.' He switched off and continued walking. When he arrived at the car, an elderly woman was standing alongside it, as if keeping guard. She had grey hair and was poorly dressed in a thin coat and worn, faded shoes, although she carried herself with a certain dignity. Her eyes were ringed with dark shadows, and Harry thought she looked sick.

'*Herr* Tate?' The old woman's lower lip was trembling slightly, and she looked frightened. Harry wondered what she had to be concerned about.

'That's right,' he replied. But before he could say anything else, the old woman turned and walked away at a surprising clip, leaving him to follow. He had no choice but to hustle after her.

The woman led him down a narrow walkway between houses and gardens, and stopped near a large block of flats. The building was old, unlike its neighbours, and made of concrete; a throw-back, it seemed, to another era, and called a *Plattenbau*, Harry remembered. Originally for workers, most had been torn down or renovated.

The old woman beckoned him inside. A flight of bare concrete steps led upwards, and she wheezed ahead of him, then motioned him along a landing and opened a door. She ushered him inside and pointed to a clean, sparsely furnished room with a table and three hard-backed chairs. The flat smelled musty, and the light was poor, blocked by heavy net curtains. He sat down on one of the chairs.

'You must wait,' the old woman told him in heavily accented English. 'He comes soon.'

'What's his name?' Harry asked, but she shook her head and walked through into a small kitchen area, where she put a saucepan of water on to an ancient stove. Then she produced a small tin of coffee from a cupboard and with almost genteel care, set down a clean mug before him. Her eyes gave nothing away, although he could have sworn the trembling in the old woman's frame might have been generated by some kind of expectation or excitement, rather than the frailty of old age.

While the water was boiling, he tried in his limited German to get some response from her, conjuring up phrases from his time in Berlin.

'When's he coming . . . *Wann kommt er?*'

But she refused to play, staring instead at the saucepan as if too nervous to meet his eyes. When the water was boiled, she made the coffee, then placed sugar alongside his mug. There was no milk. After stirring the saucepan, she poured the black mix into the mug, sniffing in evident pleasure as she did so.

'*Danke.*' He stood up and walked to the window, mug in hand.

The coffee was very strong, good, pure Colombian. If he was at all suspicious, he would have begun to think this was all turning into a wild goose chase. But since when did con artists drag someone across Europe, then leave the mark alone with a little old lady to ply him with expensive coffee?

The view of the houses opposite showed cracked walls and peeling window frames. There were no vehicles in the street, merely a bicycle propped against a house further down. Just above the houses rose the church spire, where his car was parked. By leaning close to the glass he could see the length of the street, and, beyond it, the roofs of the town centre.

As he watched, a car drove by. It was a dark-blue Passat with a white mark on the front wing.

Harry felt the hairs move on the back of his neck. 'I have to go out,' he said, putting down the mug.

The old lady looked alarmed, and he raised both palms to reassure her. He struggled for the words, hoping they were right. *'Ich bin gleich wieder da . . .'*

She seemed to understand, but there was no way of knowing. He left the flat and ran down the stairs, startling a child sitting on a front step. By the time he reached the end of the street, there was no sign of the Passat. He walked back to the church, staying close to buildings, and stopped at the corner. He could see the area in front of the building, and his car. Nearby was a beer delivery truck with the driver hauling himself into the cab.

No sign of the Passat.

Harry wondered if his nerves were getting the better of him. Yet he was certain he'd recognized the car just a few minutes ago. As he turned to leave, the beer truck started up and pulled out on to the street. Behind it was the dark-blue Passat. It was empty.

Harry froze and waited. He wondered if he was being watched right now from another vantage point, and resisted the temptation to turn and scan the surrounding buildings. Moments later a large man in jeans and a leather jacket emerged from a narrow side street and walked over to the Passat. He stood for a moment, staring at Harry's VW, all the while talking on a mobile phone.

TWENTY-FOUR

When he returned to the flat, Harry found a bear of a man sitting at the table drinking coffee. Although several years younger than the woman, he looked drawn, as if he had not slept in a long time. But he stood up readily enough and offered his hand.

'Ulf Hefflin,' he said, and looked awkward, as though he wasn't sure what to say next. He shrugged and murmured to the old woman, who poured more coffee for Harry before slipping into her coat and leaving.

Hefflin studied Harry from beneath heavy eyebrows. The look was steady, and gave Harry the impression of a sharp mind, in spite of the tired exterior.

'Did you bring money?'

Harry nodded, relieved that the man was getting to the point. The coffee was strong enough to float a brick and he was already beginning to feel the effects of the caffeine pounding through his system.

Hefflin stood and took a small cardboard box from the top of a cupboard near the kitchen sink. He took out a burgundy-coloured passport and placed it on the table with what seemed almost reverence, then took a mobile from his pocket and placed it alongside.

Harry picked up the passport and turned to the back. Barrow's photo stared up at him.

'Where did you get them?' he asked quietly.

Hefflin motioned him to sit down. 'Please . . . I will tell you what I know.' He crossed his hands on the table in front of him and looked squarely at Harry. 'Sylvia, my sister,' he said, nodding towards the door, 'has cancer. She needs drugs. Drugs we do not have here. I can get them . . . but not easily.'

'I'm sorry to hear that. Is that why you want money?'

'Harry – I may call you Harry?'

'Of course.'

'Thank you. I am Ulf. You have heard of the *Staatssicherheitsdienst*, Harry?'

'The *Stasi*? Yes.'

'They employed many people. Young, old . . . ordinary people, some of them. Their job was to watch others. Spies for the state, spying on foreigners, on travellers, dissidents, artists . . . but mostly each other.' He tapped the table nervously. His fingers were strong but clean and smooth, Harry noticed. Not a labourer's hands.

'Sylvia and Claus – her husband – both worked for the *Stasi*,' Ulf continued. 'Until the change, of course.'

Harry nodded. 'They were disbanded. I know.'

'Disbanded, yes. But life for them is not easy. Many became known after the Wall came down. They suffered – some disappeared. Sure, they did wrong . . . they spied on their friends, even their own families. But it was the way of life here. You worked for the state . . . and sometimes you found you were working for the *Stasi*, also.'

'What has this to do with this passport?'

'Sylvia worked in a weapons factory. Research and development. The safety systems were non-existent. They were exposed to chemicals.' He sighed deeply and stared through Harry, remembering.

'What about you?' Harry asked.

'Me?' Ulf grunted. 'I was a doctor in the army. Sometimes with the East German army, sometimes with the Russians . . . we went where we were told.' He studied Harry's face. 'You were military, too, I think?'

Harry nodded. 'Yes.' Ulf being a doctor explained his command of English and the smooth skin of his hands. 'How much do you want for these?' he asked, indicating the passport and mobile.

'Five hundred dollars.' The answer was calm, unemotional, with just a hint of a reservation in the tone, as if it might be asking too much . . . or too little.

Harry counted out the money and pushed it across the table. Added another two hundred. Ulf let it lie, as if good manners wouldn't allow him to touch it.

'It is for Sylvia,' he explained. 'You understand?'

Harry nodded. 'Of course.' He gathered up the passport and

phone, adding, 'For the extra money, I need to know exactly where they were found. Can you take me?'

Ulf looked puzzled and wary. 'Of course. But why do you want to go there?'

'Because things like these don't just appear as if by magic. Someone left them, lost them or threw them away. I'd like to find out which it was.'

On the other side of the street, in the shadow of a doorway, the driver of the Passat watched as Harry Tate and another man came out of the block of flats and walked back towards where Tate had parked his Golf. The watcher hurried back to his car. He was already dialling the number of the man who had hired him.

Ulf refused to say more as Harry drove, other than giving directions. Towards the river, he said. Towards the border. Other than that, he slumped in his seat, rubbing his hands on his knees and staring out at the passing countryside, his expression troubled.

A few minutes later, they left the streets behind them and entered a narrow track leading into open countryside. The land was lower here, and Harry caught a glimpse of water in the distance. The surface was deeply rutted and puddled by recent rain, and the vegetation on either side brushed against the wings of the Golf with a soft hissing sound. When they came in sight of some trees, Ulf signalled for Harry to stop.

'People do not come down here now,' Ulf said quietly. 'Only the young who do not care for history. For others there are too many bad memories still. Just beyond the trees is the border and the river Oder. It is not encouraged to approach. But there is one man named Wilhelm who walks here often. He found a coat containing the phone and the passport. Someone had thrown it away.' He looked at Harry. 'We should not be here, Harry. For Wilhelm, who found the coat, it is OK . . . because everyone knows he is a little mad.'

Harry got out of the car and stood for a moment, scanning the surrounding countryside. It was pleasant enough, although a little bleak compared with the other side of Schwedt, but that may have been due to the circumstances. He tried to imagine what would have brought Barrow and his passport and phone down here, and where he'd been going.

There was only one way to find out.

He walked along the track away from the car. It was overgrown and showed signs of little use, and any tyre tracks further back were no longer evident. Behind him, he heard Ulf open and close the car door.

'Where did he find the jacket?'

Ulf explained, pointing towards some bushes near a strand of pine trees. A clutch of crows in the upper branches watched as Harry approached, then took off with a clatter of wings and coarse cries of alarm.

Harry checked the bush, but saw nothing to indicate why the jacket had been left here. He shivered. It wasn't cold, but the atmosphere here, close to the pine trees, was suddenly gloomy, as if a dark cloud had drifted across the sky above them.

Or maybe it was the crows, and what might have happened here.

He turned as Ulf joined him, and walked towards the trees. Trees and crows, he thought, remembering a small village in south-western Kosovo. That had been a pleasant place, once. A place for picnics and children playing, a secluded spot in the evenings for lovers to walk and find each other. But horror had come calling early one morning as dawn was breaking, and everyone in the village had disappeared. Several days later, in a copse of pine trees just outside the village, someone from a neighbouring hamlet scouting for pine cones had reported a gathering of crows. An investigation by UN personnel had found the trees were now concealing a mass grave.

Harry found the body moments later. The grass leading up to it had been disturbed, the flattened path pointing like an arrow. The first thing he saw was the blaze of pale flesh and the darkened crust of dried blood where the birds had been feasting on the soft tissue of the face and chest. There had been no real attempt to bury the man or conceal what had been done here.

'Ulf,' he called, and pointed to the flattened area leading up to the body. The doctor joined him, treading carefully, and muttered an oath.

'This is the man?'

Harry nodded. 'It's him.'

TWENTY-FIVE

Thirty minutes later, the scene was the focus of attention of a cluster of local police vehicles and an ambulance, all bustling for space on the narrow track. While waiting for them to arrive, Harry had taken a look around the immediate area and found the pickup truck with a map on the dashboard. The paper was too fresh to have been here long, and he knew it must have belonged to Graham Barrow. Other than that, the pickup was clean.

At first Ulf had argued about the wisdom of calling the police. But Harry had prevailed, explaining that Barrow may have been a deserter, but he'd been a soldier first. It would be the only way he would ever return home.

It would also bring to the attention of anyone watching that the body had been discovered. As a precaution, he had called Ballatyne and explained what he'd found.

Ballatyne seemed unperturbed at Harry's decision to involve the police. 'Probably the best outcome. Keeps it officially believable. What cover story are you using?'

'I'll use the WO-Two cover, chasing down a missing squaddie.'

'OK. I'll get on to the MOD and our embassy in Berlin and prep them. Tell the cops you're operating out of London. It'll save any of our bases being dragged into it.'

The senior uniformed officer nodded at Ulf and the two men had a brief exchange. Then Ulf turned to Harry. 'I know this man. I have worked with him. He is from the local state police. He has asked me to look at the body before they move it.'

'Good idea.' Harry looked at the policeman. 'Thank you.'

A few minutes later, Ulf stood up from the body and said, 'He was shot once. It came near the heart. No other wounds that I can see. Only the . . . the birds.'

Before he could say more, another vehicle arrived. Two men climbed out and approached the trees. Their arrival seemed to have an effect on the other officers present, and Harry heard Ulf take in a sharp breath.

'*Bundespolizei*,' he murmured. 'Federal investigators. They have responsibility for the borders and will take over from the local police. They will not approve of us being here.'

The first man, short and balding, stepped forward and spoke to the senior uniform, leaving his younger colleague, who had a ginger tinge to his hair, studying the body.

'You are?' the short man said, turning to Harry. His English was unhesitating and fluid.

Harry considered his response, but there was only one way to play it.

'My name's Tate,' he said, and handed over his passport. The policeman flicked through it and passed it to his colleague.

'For your information, my name is Drachmann and my colleague is Müller. Why is an Englishman here –' he gestured around him at the trees and bushes, and then at the body – 'in such a quiet place?' His eyes flickered coolly across to include Hefflin in his words. 'Perhaps you do not know, but this is a restricted area, Mr Tate. Do you not have restricted areas in England?'

'I'm sorry,' Harry said carefully. 'That was my fault. I put pressure on Mr Hefflin, here.' He indicated Ulf, who looked relieved but still worried.

'Pressure?'

'Yes.' He produced the Warrant Officer card and passed it over. 'I came looking for a member of our military who has gone missing. Mr Hefflin was handed his passport and a mobile phone, and called my number. I came to see if the soldier was in the region.' It was as near to the truth as he wanted to get, and he hoped Ballatyne had the clout with the British Embassy in Berlin to back it up when the official questions progressed further along the diplomatic and police lines.

'And why would this . . . man be here?'

Harry shrugged. 'We can only make a guess at that. He left his unit and disappeared, that's all we know.'

'A deserter?' Drachmann looked faintly disapproving.

'Technically, yes. But there may have been extenuating circumstances. He has been under severe stress recently.'

'Afghanistan?'

'Yes. We wanted to find him before he did anything drastic. My job is to persuade men like this to return to their units.'

The policeman nodded and pursed his lips. 'It is understandable. He is important, this man?'

Harry hesitated. Drachmann was quick on the uptake. 'He has – had – specialized knowledge, yes. We wouldn't want it to fall into the wrong hands.'

'Of course. I understand.' Drachmann nodded slowly. 'But I have two questions: how did you know he was here? And how did Herr Hefflin know to contact you?'

Harry took a deep breath. This could be tricky and he hoped Hefflin was quick on the ball. 'I was in London. I was keen for Barrow to get in touch with me, so I left a voicemail message with my number. When Mr Hefflin called me to say he'd found the passport and phone, it seemed reasonable to come and look around. I thought Barrow might have been in a car accident. I asked where the items had been found, and when Mr Hefflin told me, I persuaded him to bring me down here. Any blame for him being here is mine.'

The policeman lifted his eyebrows, but did not seem overly impressed. 'You did not think to work through the proper channels? We have a common interest here.'

Harry smiled briefly. 'I was impatient. I thought if I could find Sergeant Barrow and persuade him to go back, it would involve the minimum of fuss . . . for him as well as us. I'm sorry if I've gone about this the wrong way, but I'm sure you understand.'

To his surprise the man nodded and handed back his passport. 'And is this definitely Barrow? You can formally identify him?'

'Yes. It's Graham Barrow.' Harry handed him Barrow's passport.

'We will need to keep this, Mr Tate. And you will have to make a statement at the station in Schwedt. Perhaps you would be good enough to go there. One of my men will accompany you.' He stared at Ulf. '*Herr* Hefflin also.' He motioned to the waiting ambulance men to take the body away. 'I will have the area sealed while we carry out more intensive investigations, although I do not think there will be much to tell us who killed this man.' He didn't look happy at the thought, and Harry got the impression that if things got sticky, he was going to have to rely on Ballatyne to call in some favours, status non-attributable or otherwise. Being stuck in the German justice system wasn't going to help him find Paulton or Vanessa Tan.

TWENTY-SIX

F ar away from Schwedt, in Bremen's discreet Bürgerpark, a short drive from the city centre, Deakin was pacing the elegant columned foyer of the Park Hotel, his face taut with anger. He had just taken a call from the man following the mystery investigator. 'I don't bloody believe this,' he hissed. 'Petersen picked up our man coming through Tegel and tracked him to some place called Schwedt, on the Polish border. First thing he does on arrival is talk to a local guy, and less than an hour later they find Barrow's body and call in the Federal cops.' He snapped the phone shut with venom. 'Christ, of all the places . . . how in God's holy name did he find it so quickly? They might as well have fitted Barrow with a bloody tracking device!'

Greg Turpowicz was unmoved by Deakin's mood. He thought the Brit was getting way too stressed for his own good. It was something that had been showing more and more just recently. Instead he gazed thoughtfully at the magnificent domed ceiling above them and said softly, 'I know Schwedt; it's in the middle of nowhere. Petrochemicals and paper, mostly. Jesus, if that's where Beavis and Butt-head did their jig with Barrow, and this guy found it already, they didn't exactly break their necks trying to hide the evidence, did they?'

'They do a job we don't want to,' said Deakin defensively. It had been his decision to take on the two Bosnians and he disliked any criticism of their methods. 'They're not sophisticated but they're good at what they do.'

Turpowicz shook his head, recognizing the futility of arguing, and walked over to a coffee table in one corner of the foyer, where they had been sitting waiting for their meeting. He turned the open laptop to face him, calling up the photo from the Continentale in Scheveningen, and stared at the picture as if trying to read beneath the face. 'This guy's smart; he moves quick and he asks all the right questions.' He looked at Deakin. 'Why do I find the hairs lifting on the back of my neck, Deak? Who the fuck is he and what are we going to do about him?'

Deakin shook his head. 'I don't know yet. Let me think about it.' He sat down and took out his phone, and dialled a number. He checked in case anyone was close, but the hotel was quiet and nobody was paying any attention save for a slim Chinese man in a neat suit, standing by the reception desk. They had marked him down as a security man the moment they arrived. 'Petersen? Are you still in that place . . . what's it – Schwedt? Right. Stay put. I don't care how you do it, but I want the name of the man you've been tailing. Drop some money on the local cops if you have to.' He switched off the phone and looked at Turpowicz. 'Good enough for you? We'll find him and deal with him.' His face was bleak.

Turpowicz grunted and checked his watch. 'Where's Paulton got to? I thought he was supposed to be in on this with us, putting up some front.' It was a reminder that they had agreed on a united display to show the Protectory's substance, something the Chinese were in favour of when negotiating.

Deakin waved a hand. 'He's busy on something else; sent a text to say go ahead without him. Anyway, once the monkey we're seeing hears what we have for him, I don't think he'll care about how many we are. He'll just want results.'

'If you say so. Better not let him hear you call him a monkey, though. They can be a bit touchy about body image.'

But Deakin was ignoring him, his mind already on something else. Seconds later he was on his phone again, talking to Nicholls. 'Did you get the photo I sent you?'

'Yes. Is there a problem?' Nicholls sounded cool.

'There could be.' He brought Nicholls up to date on the discovery of Barrow's body. 'Whoever this bozo is, he's getting too close.'

'I agree. But what do we do about it? Or are you planning on setting your tame bouncers on him?' Nicholls had no more love

for the Bosnians, Zubac and Ganic, than Turpowicz, an opinion
he had never bothered to conceal.

'Forget them. You need to contact our man in the MOD. Send
him the photo and see if the face comes up on the official files.
If he's an investigator, he'll be on record somewhere.'

'All right. But it's risky. He might get jumpy if he thinks we're
after one of their own.'

'Tough shit.' Deakin's tone turned savage. 'He gets enough
easy money out of us for supplying names and numbers; now
let him earn it. I want to know who this tricky bastard is!' He
shut off the phone again just as a uniformed under-manager came
gliding across the floor and gave a hint of a bow. In the background, the Chinese security man stood waiting, hands crossed
in front of him.

'Gentlemen? Mr Wien Lu Chi will see you now. Follow me?'

Deakin nodded and picked up the laptop. As he turned to
follow the under-manager, Turpowicz grabbed his arm, and said
softly, 'You didn't really answer me, Deak. You said you'd deal
with this investigator. What does that mean exactly?'

Deakin brushed off the American's hand. 'Simple. He's a
threat. I'm going to stop him. Permanently.'

TWENTY-SEVEN

'You are free to leave, Mr Tate . . . *Herr* Hefflin.' Drachmann
handed both men their documents. He didn't look pleased.
They had been in the local station for over three hours,
providing detailed statements along with answering a list of
supplementary questions. It had all been very low-key, but there
had been no mistaking the intensity behind the queries. 'If it
were my choice,' he continued bluntly, 'I would have you stay
in Schwedt until we had completed our investigation. But I have
my instructions from the *Bundesministerium* – the Ministry of
the Interior.'

'Thank you. What now?'

'As long as there are no problems, the body will be released

in a few days, after our Senior State Medical Examiner has satisfied himself. After that you may make arrangements for it to be
returned to England.' He stared at Harry for a long moment,
giving the impression that he wanted to ask a lot more questions,
but could not. 'Our forensics personnel say that in their opinion
the lack of gunshot burns indicate it cannot be a death by suicide.
Somebody unconnected with the shooting may have found the
body and removed the gun – perhaps to sell. We will never know.
It would be useful to know who might have wished harm to
Sergeant Barrow, a complete stranger in this area.' He lifted his
eyebrows and waited.

Harry shrugged easily. The tactic was one he recognized, meant
to draw him into saying more than he might want to. 'I wish I
could help,' he said eventually. Ballatyne must have intervened
at a high level to facilitate their release. If so, it would explain
Drachmann's general air of reluctance to let the matter drop. 'I'm
as puzzled as you are. I can only think they might have been
criminals acting on chance.'

'Criminals.' Drachmann considered the word as if it were new
to him. 'Ah. You mean the *Mafiya*?'

'Of course.'

'A possibility. They are everywhere.' He didn't look as if he
believed it, but he nodded and walked away.

They were heading towards the hotel where Harry had booked
a room in expectation of an overnight stay, when his phone rang.
It was Rik.

'Daddy, I'm home!' he sang cheerfully.

'Where are you?'

'I'm about ten minutes out. Where shall we meet?'

Harry gave him the name and location of the hotel. He hadn't
seen the Passat for a while but he could almost feel its presence
out there. The man wouldn't have followed him all the way here
from Tegel just to lose interest and leave. 'Come up to the room
whenever you can. I'll see if I pick up the tail on the way there.'

He drove Ulf to his flat and said goodbye. They would be
unlikely to meet again, and for Ulf's sake he wanted to put some
distance between them. His story about finding Barrow's phone
and passport would only stand up for as long as it remained

convincing and uncomplicated. If Harry stayed with Ulf too long, Drachmann might start to wonder why and dig a little deeper.

He arrived at his hotel, a functional, two-storey block near the outskirts of town, and saw Rik in the car park behind the wheel of an anonymous Nissan. He was taking his low profile instructions seriously. There was no sign of the Passat.

Five minutes later, there was a knock at the door of his room. He checked the spyhole. It was Rik. He was dressed in jeans and a casual jacket, and wearing glasses. His normally spiky hair was only just this side of tidy.

'Your man's outside,' Rik told him. He slumped on the nearest bed. He looked drained and was nursing his shoulder. 'He pulled in on your tail but stayed out on the road.'

'Well done. Who is he?'

'The car's registered to a Carl Petersen. He's listed as a security specialist, but for that read private eye. Ex-German military, sometime heavy for a small gang in Berlin, he does low-level divorce and commercial stuff.'

'That fits.' The man's surveillance skills were hardly top drawer. He was a watcher, hired to follow and report. He brought Rik up to date on finding Barrow's body. 'My guess is this Petersen will have called it in already. What we don't know is how much he knows or who he's speaking to. If he's any good, he'll be looking for someone to contact in the local police department – possibly posing as a journalist. The *Bundespolizei* will be keeping it close to their chests, so it might take him a while. But he'll get there eventually.'

'Isn't that what you want him to do?'

'Yes, but I want to be the one he sees, not you.'

'No problem. I'll get out there and watch him.' Rik saw the mini-bar. 'Any chance of a Coke? I'm parched.'

'Help yourself. I don't know what Petersen's main purpose is, or what he's doing other than watching me. What's with the specs?' When he'd first met him, Rik was wearing oval spectacles which seemed a must for the geeky look. But over time he'd dropped them without explanation. Now they were back.

'It's part of my disguise. You said inconspicuous . . . and as my mum always says, men don't look at people who wear glasses.'

'I think your mother was referring to girls.' Harry watched as he groped about inside the fridge, inspecting the bars of chocolate and small bags of peanuts and crisps. He was worried about the effects of the journey on Rik's wound, but decided against saying anything. 'Don't let me keep you.'

'Right, I'm going.' Rik grabbed two cans of Coke and some chocolate, then left, promising to stay in touch. Harry decided to get his head down and recharge his batteries. Food could wait.

He was woken an hour later by a knock at the door. Rik was back.

'Petersen's been down at the police station,' he reported, walking over to the mini-bar and helping himself to another Coke. 'He was inside ten minutes max. He came out and was texting someone. He looked pretty pleased with himself, like someone who'd just got a pay day. I think you're now more than just on the radar: you've been lit up like a Christmas tree.'

Harry nodded. Now the Protectory – if that was who Petersen was working for – knew his name. What they didn't know was that his WO-2 status was a cover. He hoped it stayed that way for a while longer. For now, it would put the pressure on them to decide what to do about him. And pressure led to mistakes.

'Is he still around?'

'No. He headed for the Autobahn. Looks like he got called off.'

Harry nodded and got his things together. 'In that case, they don't intend any further action. Time to head home.'

TWENTY-EIGHT

In the Park Hotel in Bremen, Deakin and Turpowicz were ushered into a luxurious suite on the second floor. It was exquisitely furnished, with moulded ceilings and gold brocade at the windows, large armchairs and sofas, and a tented canopy over the king-size bed. It had the air of a sheikh's tent and declared unashamedly that this was the temporary lodging of a very wealthy and influential man. The security guard who had followed them up from the foyer stayed long enough to check both men with a security wand, then withdrew without a word.

'You don't trust us?' said Deakin. He looked slightly ruffled at the electronic body search.

'I don't trust anyone, Mr Deakin,' Wien Lu Chi replied softly. 'It is how I have survived so long in my business.' He was portly and sleek, with black hair and a purple port-wine stain on one cheek, and immaculately dressed in a dark grey suit and silk tie. A pair of black English brogues sat by the desk where he had been working on a laptop. He gestured at the shoes with an apologetic smile. 'Please excuse me – I prefer to relax whenever I can. Feel free to do likewise.'

'We're good, thanks,' said Deakin, and put down his laptop bag. Turpowicz, on the other hand, nodded with a touch of graciousness and kicked off his shoes, squishing his toes into the thick pile carpet.

'So what is your business, Mr Chi?' Deakin asked.

If Wien Lu Chi was offended by the careless misuse of his name, he gave no sign. He gestured instead for the two men to sit. 'I am a facilitator, Mr Deakin – what you might call a middleman. You have a product to sell, I have clients who wish to buy but also to remain at arm's length. I bring the two entities together in an amicable fashion, and we do business. It is a system as old as time.'

'May we ask,' said Turpowicz, 'how you heard of us?'

'I have many contacts in all walks of life, Mr Turpowicz. It is my job to know who is trading in what, and where certain products can be found.' He eyed Turpowicz with a degree more warmth than he had Deakin. 'I have been hearing of your organization for some time now. You are a unique undertaking.' He paused for a moment, searching for the right words. 'Not precisely replicated elsewhere, but your business model is understood by my clients. Thus, it seems we may have interests in common. Would you like a drink? I always have a whisky at this time. It helps my digestion. Mr Turpowicz, a bourbon for you, I think?' Without waiting for a reply, he leaned over and picked up the telephone and ordered drinks from room service, then sat back and chatted politely about the weather.

The drinks arrived very quickly, an indication that they had been pre-ordered. Wien Lu Chi picked up his glass and took a sip with evident pleasure. Turpowicz exchanged a look with Deakin and did the same. The preliminaries were being observed.

After a few moments, their host put down his glass. 'Gentlemen, I think we all know why we are here. I had my . . . associates call you because I have need of certain information which I believe you have access to.' He was referring to a phone call Deakin had received two weeks ago after making tentative forays through a middleman in Hong Kong. It had been their first open venture towards that area of the world, instigated by Deakin and a move against which Colin Nicholls had been forcefully vocal. It clearly had one market in mind: the People's Republic of China. It had come as a surprise to them all when a response had followed so quickly; among many things, the Chinese were noted for taking the long view, especially over any action involving deals with foreigners. Deakin had immediately agreed to a meeting to discuss details, and lay out what the Protectory could do for them.

Neither Deakin nor Turpowicz was in any doubt that one of Wien Lu Chi's main functions was to act as an agent for the Ministry of State Security (MSS or *Guoanbu*), responsible for the dual role of intelligence gathering and internal security. With a standing army of over two million soldiers and vast military spending, and a growing strike capability extending far beyond its borders, China was considered by some to have no need of foreign secrets; but that was far from the truth. Part of the MSS remit was the acquisition of technology from whatever source they could find, whether friendly or not, and via personal contacts, middlemen or, as was increasingly the case, through electronic hacking.

'You name it,' said Deakin warily, 'and we'll try to meet your requirements.'

'Really?' Wien Lu Chi looked sceptical. 'That is a very broad claim, Mr Deakin. My clients have very . . . specialized interests.' He folded his hands together. 'Since you clearly believe in getting to the point, perhaps you would give me an idea of what you can currently supply from your . . . portfolio?' His face creased and he giggled gently. 'I love the English language; you have a way of dressing up a meaning so delicately.'

Deakin looked at Turpowicz in puzzlement, then said, 'Very well. As I explained to your contact in Hong Kong, we currently have access to specialists in the latest generation of battlefield communications, network structures and high-level firewall systems. You need details of counterintelligence strategies and penetration systems, we can provide those. Current battlefield armaments, light and heavy, are continually changing but we keep abreast of those and future plans. One of our latest contacts has been working on electronic warfare and electronic countermeasures – ECMs. Another brings the latest data on British and NATO armoured capabilities for battle tanks and reconnaissance units, and another has been extensively trained in the area of biological and chemical warfare delivery and detection.' He stopped and waited, and silence dropped on the room like a blanket.

Wien Lu Chi said nothing for a moment, eyes blank. Then he stirred and picked up his whisky glass, emptying it in one gulp.

'Let me ask you a question, Mr Deakin,' he said softly. 'Much of what you talk about is already "out there", as Mr Turpowicz's countrymen might say. My clients are constantly watching developments in these matters, as I'm sure you are aware. That being so, why would I come on a shopping trip for weapons technology which is already a generation behind some of the best available elsewhere? IT countermeasures, too, are something my clients are developing all the time, with applications for battlefields and . . . other areas. In short, they already have access to many of these things.'

Deakin looked momentarily nonplussed, but recovered quickly. 'I was laying out our stall, Mr Chi, that was all. You tell me what you need and we'll see how we can accommodate you.'

Wien Lu Chi smiled briefly and put down his glass. He straightened his already immaculate tie and stood up. 'Admirably blunt and to the point, Mr Deakin. I like that. In which case, let me reciprocate. It has come to my attention that one of the "specialists" currently available – and one which you have not mentioned – is someone with information of a far more . . . shall we say, non-combatant nature.'

'I don't follow.' Deakin was surprised. He had come here

expecting a shopping list of hardware data, but he'd been side-stepped. 'What non-combatant nature?'

Wien Lu Chi glanced at Turpowicz, who seemed much less puzzled. 'I think your colleague understands,' he said. 'But to save us all time, I will be more direct. I am talking about a young woman who has recently gone absent without leave – another delightful dressing up of words – from a position of considerable . . . shall we say, delicacy . . . in the high command structure in Kabul?' He looked from one to the other as their faces slowly showed their understanding. To help them, he added, 'A Miss Tan, gentlemen? An aide to the British Deputy Commander ISAF?' He walked over to the door and knocked twice, and the security guard appeared. He was carrying a small aluminium briefcase. 'Bring *her* specialized knowledge to me, gentlemen, and I think we will do business.' He gave a signal for the guard to hand the briefcase to Deakin. 'As a sign of good faith, we are making a down-payment of fifty thousand dollars, non-refundable. For the correct quality of this particular item, delivered in prime condition, I am authorized by my clients to go up to one million dollars.'

Deakin stood up, his face flushed, and took the briefcase. Behind him, Turpowicz slipped his shoes back on. 'I think we can accommodate you,' Deakin said calmly. 'Just give us a week or so to come up with—'

But Wien Lu Chi held up a hand to stop him. 'No. For a down-payment such as this, Mr Deakin, it is my clients who make the conditions. And this one is non-negotiable. You have five days. Five days from today and you must have the item in question ready to ship.'

'But that's very short notice.' Deakin looked stunned, but was reining himself in. 'Why only five days?'

Wien Lu Chi remained unperturbed. 'Beyond that time, her value reduces day by day as her superiors amend or block any useful information she may have taken with her.' He gave a humourless smile. 'It is like a supermarket, no? She has a sell-by date, beyond which, she is –' he flicked a careless hand – 'dispos-able. You understand?'

'We get it,' said Turpowicz. 'But what happens to Miss Tan afterwards?'

Wien Lu Chi looked faintly puzzled. 'Come now, Mr Turpowicz;

surely you realize that this is what the one million dollars is for: you do not need to know, and should not ask.' He stood up and clapped his hands. 'Thank you for coming, gentlemen. My colleague will show you out.'

Less than three minutes later they were outside the hotel. Turpowicz turned to Deakin and muttered, 'Christ, Deak, what did you just sign us up to? You promised Charlie Chan back there that we'd bring him Tan within five days? We don't even know where she is!'

Deakin looked unconcerned as he walked back to their car. 'Then we'd better find her, hadn't we? You heard him: they're interested and they'll pay big bucks. That's good enough for me. This would be the biggest sale we'll ever make.'

'That's if we get her to the church on time. But how? She's out there in the frigging wind! So far there's been no sign of her, none of the usual flags going up when someone cuts and runs. All your guy in London can give us is her service details and some useless crap about home, but there's no substance.' He shook his head and got in the passenger seat. 'If we don't deliver on time, that guy back there will cut our balls off. Nobody gives away a case full of money that easily, especially the Chinese.'

Deakin shrugged and switched on his mobile, checking for messages. There were two texts. The first was news from Ganic, and made him curse aloud. They had lost another one. While the Bosnians were busy dealing with Barrow, another target had had a change of heart. He'd slipped away from the hotel outside Brussels where they had installed him and was heading for the UK. They had missed him by minutes but had picked up his trail and were asking for instructions.

'What's up?' said Turpowicz.

Deakin ignored him, and was already composing a reply. There was no point in trying to persuade the target to come back; it was too late for that. But he'd met Deakin and could identify Turpowicz and the Bosnians. To prevent him talking, there could only be one outcome. He sent a terse text back to Zubac. *Cancel the contract*. The Bosnians would know what to do. He finally looked at Turpowicz. 'Another one down.

McCreath's done a runner from the hotel. They think he's heading for London.'

'I thought we'd him won over to the idea.'

'Me, too. He must have had a change of heart.' He gave an almost buoyant smile. 'Never mind, there's plenty more where he came from. Get hold of Nicholls and Paulton and get them to focus harder on Tan's trail. She could make up for all of the losses so far. Someone must have an idea of where she is.'

The American took out his phone ready to make the call, then said, 'What about the guy who found Barrow? If he's so hot he might lead us right to her.'

Deakin nodded. 'Maybe he will. I don't care what we have to do, but this one's not getting away from us, you hear?' Deakin checked the second text message and grinned. 'Well, speak of the devil. Our man's name is Tate . . . and he's a bloody warrant officer in the British army. How about that?' He switched off the phone and dropped it in his pocket, then turned the ignition, suddenly energized by the news. 'You were right, Turp; all we have to do is find Tate and see where he goes next. And when he leads us to Tan, we'll have her *and* we can get him out of our hair. Permanently.'

TWENTY-NINE

It was seven the following morning when Harry's bedside phone rang. He rolled over and took the call, wincing at stiff muscles after the journey back from Germany. It was Ballatyne and he sounded hyped.

'Some news,' the MI6 man said. 'We might have a serious lead on Deakin and his crew. Staff Sergeant Gerry McCreath just walked into a south London police station and asked for protection. He says his life is in danger.'

'I think I know the feeling.'

'He had a meeting with Deakin and an American in Belgium. They pitched him a deal to provide a ton of information on the latest trial versions of NATO operational networks and communications in return for cash – a lot of it. He agreed in principle, and was told to stay low and given an open-ended account at a hotel outside the city. They said they'd call him with details of the next stage and make a first payment. Can you believe it? "Agreed in principle". These people amaze me. They think selling secrets is like signing up to a bloody mortgage.'

'What made him run?'

'He heard about Pike. Seems they trained together, although he hadn't seen him for a while. McCreath had been away from his home base playing Action Man stuff with the Air Assault Brigade. He got wounded and decided he'd had enough of being chucked out of helicopters and being shot at, so he went on the run to sort himself out. He got a lead from a mate about the Protectory, and next thing he knows is, he's been approached by Deakin and offered a way out.'

'Deakin wouldn't have told him about Pike, though.'

'No. He says he heard about it from the same friend. He started to get worried that he might end up in a ditch somewhere, so he ducked out and headed back to England by train and boat.'

'Why south London?'

'He used to live in the Brixton area. Probably figured he could go to ground and get lost.'

It was no surprise to Harry. Most runners headed for the familiar by instinct, looking for comfort in any place where they felt safe. They usually didn't realize that it was the worst thing they could have done until a knock sounded on the door.

'He claims he saw a face in the crowd on the way over,' Ballatyne continued. 'A man named Zubac – a Bosnian. He travels with a man called Ganic. McCreath says they're enforcers for the Protectory, ex-militia or military, he reckons, and highly nasty. Sounds as if they're the men who killed Pike and Barrow. If they're that close behind McCreath, they've only got one thing in mind. I've cleared your entry down at Brixton. The sooner we question him the better.'

Harry swung out of bed. 'I'm on my way.'

THIRTY

Milan Zubac was studying a small electronic box on his lap, eyes on a set of coloured lights numbered Level 1 to 5. He was slowly turning a dial on its side. When the level 5 light glowed red he nodded to his friend and former Bosnian army colleague, Zlatco Ganic, who was behind the wheel of their car, an anonymous Vauxhall Corsa.

'He is here. Time to go.'

Ganic took a last drag of a Marlboro and flicked it out of the window, where it bounced in a shower of sparks before dropping through a drain cover. From where they were sitting, they could see the rear gates of a large building, and through the bars, the colourful flash of police vehicles. It was barely nine in the morning and everything seemed quiet apart from an irregular flow of police cars entering or leaving the compound behind the gates. But they had no illusions; this was a busy station and things would change dramatically the moment they got inside. Once they began, there was no going back.

Ganic gave a wry smile and uncoiled his heavy, six-foot frame ready to get out of the car. 'This time,' he said with exaggerated courtesy, 'I think you should go first, my friend. It is only fair.'

Zubac shrugged and reached for a heavy rucksack between his feet. 'OK by me,' he said. 'You can play the tail of the dog if you like.' He opened the bag and took out two 9mm Ruger SR9 handguns and half a dozen black cylindrical objects each with two pull rings and a safety lever. American-made M84 stun grenades or 'flash-bangs', they held a mix of magnesium and ammonium, and were designed to distract and disorientate anyone in an enclosed space. He passed Ganic one Ruger with a seventeen-shot magazine and a spare, along with three stun grenades, then slung the bag with the remaining handgun and grenades over his shoulder. If they had to use all seventeen shots plus spares, then they were in trouble. But he didn't plan on that happening. You won in these situations by always going prepared.

They climbed out and checked the street in both directions. Police activity this close to the station was likely to be heavy, and although the car was done with and they wouldn't be coming back to it, there was no future in being stopped by a policeman or traffic warden for parking in a restricted area before they even began the next stage of their plan. When Zubac was satisfied, he nodded to Ganic and the two men walked along the street and turned in at the barred gates.

Zubac, whose accent was less noticeable then Ganic's, pressed the call button on the intercom.

'Yes?' The voice was tinny, with a faint wheezy quality. Too old to be a cop, Zubac noted. Probably a retired officer reduced to playing security guard.

He read the prepared sentence. 'Hi. Wilkins and Collier from the MOD, to assist with the interview of Staff Sergeant McCreath.' Short and sharp, was the advice he'd received from Deakin; sound businesslike and don't take any shit. They get people coming and going all the time. You're just following orders like everyone else.

The priority was to get through the gates. Once inside, the rest would be easy.

'Hold your ID up to the screen, please.' The man sounded bored, going through the motions.

Zubac did so. This was the weak point. If the guard saw or heard something he didn't like, they weren't going any further.

'OK. Come across the yard to the red door and wait.'

The gates swung open with a whine of an electrical motor. Both men stepped through, walking past a line of empty police vans, patrol cars and a couple of transits with swing-down mesh riot screens. No people, though; the yard was deserted.

Zubac slid his hand inside the rucksack, fanning himself with the fake ID with his other hand to distract attention. He glanced at Ganic and said, 'Remember, we need directions. After that, anything goes.'

Ganic nodded and stuffed small rubber cones into each ear. Whatever else happened, the next few minutes were going to be very noisy. Zubac would put his in place once they got past the security guard. After that it wouldn't matter because they would have no need to talk or to listen.

THIRTY-ONE

S taff Sergeant Gerry McCreath was looking every one of his thirty-eight years, with a yellowish tinge to his skin and dark hollows beneath each eye. His white shirt and dark slacks were creased, evidence of a long journey without being able to change, and he looked strung out, eyes searching for a way out like a rat in a box. He'd take some stopping, thought Harry, if he decided to get up and go. Operating with 16 Air Assault Brigade in the hills of Afghanistan had toughened up the Signals NCO in a way that playing with communications equipment never would have.

Harry sat down opposite him and dropped a packet of cigarettes on the table. A pair of large constables were stationed by the door, and one of them, with ginger hair and pale skin, shifted his feet.

'Can't do that in here, sir.'

Harry looked at him. 'Don't worry, officer, I think he's got more pressing problems than breaking the smoking ban.' He took out a cheap Bic lighter and slid it across the surface. 'You want to smoke, go ahead.'

McCreath shook his head. 'I'm trying to give up. Who are you?'

'You can call me Harry. I want to help you get out of here in one piece.' He sat back. 'I hear you've got Ganic and Zubac on your tail.'

'You know them?'

'I've seen their handiwork.'

McCreath grunted and looked around the room. 'Then you know this place won't stop them. Nor will the two plods on the door.'

'You think they'll come inside? Why would they risk it?'

'Because they're mental, that's why. I've seen their type before – even served with one or two like them. They get off on proving how tough they are, thinking they can go through anything or anyone. If Deakin sets them on a target, that's all they need.'

'And you think he's set them on you?' He sounded deliberately sceptical; he wanted McCreath to become unsettled, even angry. It would lead to the truth that much quicker.

McCreath blinked. 'Of course. I bugged out, didn't I? Left his cosy hotel and fancy meals and legged it back here. It was saying I didn't want to play his game or take his money. He wouldn't like that. If they can't get me in here, they'll wait for me to go out . . . just like they did Pike.'

Harry ignored that for the moment; he wanted to get McCreath talking about the Protectory. 'Tell me about Deakin; how you met him.'

'Will it help my court martial?'

'I can't guarantee that, but your cooperation will certainly be taken into account. Did he order Neville Pike killed?'

'He's the only one who could have. I'm not sure he's all there, to be honest; there's something behind his eyes, know what I mean? I saw the same thing in some of the prisoners taken in Afghanistan, even in some of the subcontractors out there. Like they're living on a hair-trigger, waiting to blow. But he's different when he's talking; then he's all good ideas and friendly, just like you want to hear when you're on the run. Then, when I heard about Pike, I just . . . I decided it wasn't for me.' He shifted in his seat as if embarrassed to admit it. A faint burst of shouting sounded somewhere in the building, muffled and distant. A door slammed followed by another, and the overhead lights flickered.

Harry glanced at the constables, but they hadn't reacted. In a busy station like this, shouting was the norm, doors slamming a sound everyone learned to live with day and night.

'How did you get in touch with him in the first place?'

'I didn't.' McCreath's breathing rate had increased and his fingers were tapping out a rapid staccato rhythm on the table surface. His nails, Harry noted, were bitten down to the quick. 'I was bunking with an ex-army mate in Antwerp after leaving Selly Oak.'

'That's where you had treatment?'

'Yes. The place got on my wick . . . people coming and going like it was a bloody theme park . . . charity visitors treating us like a bunch of mental cases, doing their good fucking works . . . It finally got to me when one woman spoke louder to me because I'd been wounded – can you believe that? She thought because someone mentioned trauma I was a bleeding cabbage case. Then there were the therapists and psych people, all telling us how we'd soon recover and how we had to stay positive, how it'd be all right in the end and look at how some amputees were even trekking to the North frigging Pole and climbing mountains on their false fucking legs!'

As McCreath started breathing faster, gradually becoming more and more worked up, one of the constables shifted his feet and prepared to step forward. But Harry held up a hand. He had to see where this would lead. McCreath was venting his frustration. If they shut him down now, he might never tell them what they needed to know.

McCreath gradually regained control. He took a deep breath, placing his hands flat on the table and shaking his head. Then he continued in a calmer voice. 'I'd had enough so I got up and walked out. When I got to Antwerp, my mate said he knew someone who could help me; someone he said was part of a group who helped out guys like me. I thought he was taking the piss. Next thing I know, this guy Deakin's at the door, saying he was from the Protectory, like it should mean something. I mean, it sounded like some sort of loony religious order to me. I nearly told him to piss off, thinking what could a bunch of bible bashers do to help me?' His head came up as a dull concussion sounded. 'What was that?' This time the two guards looked at each other.

Harry said to them, 'Can you call the desk from here?'

The ginger-haired constable shook his head. 'From out in the corridor if we have to. Why?'

Harry stood up and signalled McCreath to get to his feet. 'I think we've got company. That was a stun grenade. The station's under attack.'

'What?' The second officer laughed. 'Don't be bloody stupid. This is Brixton nick—'

'He's right.' It was the ginger guard. 'I've heard them before . . . used them, too. Recognize the sound.'

Suddenly McCreath was coming round the table and nodding animatedly, his face draining of colour. 'He's right. It's Zubac and Ganic. They've come for me. They'll kill anyone who gets in their way.'

'Where does this corridor lead?' Harry asked, pointing away from the noise.

'To some stairs, a storage room and more cells. But we can't leave here.'

'You want to stay, be my guest.' Harry walked over and kicked the door. It shook in the frame. Solid but not solid enough to withstand grenades or bullets. 'They'll come through that like cheese and they won't be using stun grenades. We need to get out of here. Now.'

'There are the cells,' said the second guard. 'The doors are reinforced with rolled steel. We'd be safe in there.'

But his colleague shook his head. 'No way. They'd blast right through them, too. Anyway, we'd be trapped.'

The second guard opened the door and peered out. Two bangs sounded, muffled but closer, followed by another concussion, this one causing a small vibration through the walls. 'There's people running,' he reported. 'I can see them through the security door at the end.' He looked pale but calm. 'Follow me, yeah?'

Harry grabbed McCreath by the arm and hustled him out, and pushed him along the corridor in the wake of the two guards. More bangs and some screaming this time. As they reached a junction in the corridor and the constables disappeared, he felt a ripple effect in the air followed by a blast of sound, and a sliver of wood flew past him and bounced along the floor.

THIRTY-TWO

'*R*oom *B16!*' the gate security guard had screamed, his shoulder shattered by a round from Ganic's Ruger. '*Down the stairs and along the corridor . . . to the right . . . with a man named Tate.*'

Ganic pulled the safety ring on one of the M84 stun grenades and paused, glancing at Zubac. The time delay fuse on the device was a maximum of two seconds once the safety lever was released.

Enough time to step back and avoid the worst of the blast, but too short for any hero to scoop up the grenade and throw it back. He nodded at the nearest camera, then mouthed the words, 'What about the cameras?' Then he flicked the safety ring away and hurled the M84 round the corner of the corridor, ducking back before it could explode.

'Forget them.' Zubac mouthed back with a grin, checking his weapon. 'So we get famous . . . our faces on television. You don't like that?'

If Ganic understood the words, his reply was drowned out as the grenade's blast filled the corridor, the sound wave snapping around the walls and intensified by the confined space. The vivid flash of light lit the air, adding to the confusion, then it was gone. The sound of tinkling glass in the background was almost musical but it was doubtful that any of the policemen or support staff in the corridor was able to appreciate it.

Zubac stepped wide round the corner, his weapon held two-handed, knees slightly bent. Two officers were on their knees, hugging their ears in agony and confusion. Further along, a short, plump woman in a white shirt and dark skirt was sitting inelegantly against one wall, mouth open in shock, eyes closed tight.

One of the officers looked up and saw Zubac. His eyes fastened in disbelief on the Ruger. Coughing, he reached instinctively for his waist. Zubac shot him in the throat.

The officer fell back, a telescopic baton rolling away from his hand.

Zubac shook his head at the man's idiotic courage, and the two attackers advanced along the corridor, Ganic clubbing the second officer as he passed, ignoring the woman and hurling another M84 as two shapes appeared out of a door at the end. He and Zubac stepped inside an open doorway until the blast came. It breached a soft door, hurling fragments of glass and pieces of softwood through the air. They stepped out and moved on.

An alarm began wailing followed by a volley of shouting as the Bosnians' progress was tracked along the lower floor. Footsteps pounded on the floor above, filling the stairwell until a commanding voice ordered them back.

Ganic saw movement up ahead. He fired twice to keep any

heads down, then turned to his friend as Zubac slapped him on the shoulder and made a pistol sign with his fist and forefinger. The meaning was clear.

So far they had dealt with unarmed opposition only. But the ones with guns would soon be here, which meant they hadn't got long to find their target.

Ganic puffed out his lips and loaded a fresh clip of ammunition. His meaning was clear: even if they came with their weapons, they would die.

THIRTY-THREE

'Keep going!' Harry shouted, and pushed McCreath towards the turn in the corridor. Somehow the Bosnians had found out where the prisoner was being held and had worked their way down into a secure part of the station. How they'd done it was appalling, but it didn't matter right now; they were far too close. He pushed on, feeling an itch of vulnerability in the middle of his back, and wished he was armed. No bloody good being carded, he told himself, if he wasn't actually carrying a gun. Should have learned by now that being in London didn't guarantee safety. Not that he would have been allowed to bring a weapon down here, anyway, authorized or not.

A shot echoed down the corridor and ricocheted after them, buzzing past Harry's head and gouging a long, ugly chunk out of the plaster on one side. Ahead of him the two constables had reached a door with wire-reinforced glass, holding it open for Harry and McCreath. In the background, footsteps pounded after them. The pursuers were moving with frightening speed, bulldozing their way through the station and disposing of any resistance with terrifying ease, working on the knowledge that they had no friends here, only enemies.

They weren't going to make it. Then he and McCreath were through and into another corridor, and the door was being slammed behind them.

'Keep going!' ginger hair shouted. 'I'll lock this.'

Harry turned. 'No, don't! The door won't stop it—!' But he was too late. A shot echoed beyond the door, and a large hole appeared in the fabric, just below the glass. Slivers of wood and flecks of paint flew in all directions and the constable was lifted off his feet and hurled to one side, a spray of blood flicking across the wall behind him.

'Go!' Harry shouted at McCreath. 'Keep going!' He grabbed the other constable who was staring at his colleague with an expression of dumb disbelief and pulled him away. 'You can't help him – go!'

They ran, passing several closed doors with no lights showing and no sign of anyone inside, and arrived at a flight of stairs going up. An open door revealed a storage cupboard. Harry glanced inside. No good as a hiding place; it was crammed with fire extinguishers, mostly battered and with a large handwritten sticker warning that they were not to be used.

'They're due to go back,' the constable explained, his voice neutral, breathless. He was on automatic pilot, Harry recognized, retreating in on himself and looking for the familiar and everyday. A safe place to go.

'Where do the stairs lead?'

'What?' He blinked.

'*The stairs.*' Harry slapped his arm, shaking him out of his daze.

'To the delivery bay and back yard.' The constable shook his head, his expression clearing. 'Wait . . . it's open out there . . . There's nowhere to run.'

'Gates?'

'Locked and controlled from inside the building. There's a motion detector for going out, but it'd take too long.'

They heard shouting coming closer. A series of bangs; but not explosions. Doors being kicked open and rooms being checked. It would slow the attackers down but not for long.

'Better than staying here,' Harry muttered, and on impulse, grabbed one of the fire extinguishers. He followed the other two men up the stairs, thigh muscles burning with the effort and the adrenalin rush. Their footsteps were loud in the open space, echoing back down and telling their pursuers precisely where they were—

How did they know? In all this building, how could they tell exactly where McCreath was?

They arrived at the top and the constable gestured to a fire door with a security bar. 'This is it. It locks automatically behind us. We'd have to use the entry-phone system to have the guard open up the staff entrance.' He stared at the extinguisher. 'What are you doing with that?'

'Delaying tactic. Open the door. And you,' he looked at McCreath, 'stay close and don't try running.'

But McCreath was one step ahead of him. He said, 'Tie the handles together, otherwise it'll never stay on long enough.' He shrugged. 'Used to let them off at school when I was a kid.'

'Here.' The constable ripped off his tie and handed it to McCreath, then turned and slammed the security bar down and pushed open the door. Harry pulled the safety pin on the extinguisher and placed the canister close to the top step, with the nozzle hanging over the stairs. McCreath waited for him to squeeze the levers together, then wrapped the tie around them and knotted it firmly. The contents began to gush out, filling the air in the stairwell with a choking spray of white powder that hung like a mist, completely shielding them from the men below.

Then they were sprinting across the open yard to the door where the gunmen had made their entry. It was a close call; as they ducked inside, bullets tore into the door-jamb, ripping off great slivers of wood. Harry turned and saw a CCTV monitor showing two men running diagonally across the open space, one of them pausing to slap a hand against a motion-detector panel to open the automatic gates. Seconds later, they were out into the street and gone.

THIRTY-FOUR

'How did they get weapons? It's not as if they could pick them up at the nearest branch of bloody Tesco!' Ballatyne was raging at the ease with which the attackers had entered the country, equipped themselves and stormed the secure structure of a police station, taking it apart as if it were no more than a training exercise.

Harry said nothing; Ballatyne knew as well as he did that determined men with connections had access to weapons and the people to supply them. They wouldn't have risked bringing guns and stun grenades in on the boat, but with a source in London or the south-east, one phone call was all it would have taken to have someone waiting to meet them with a full kit as soon as they landed.

Ballatyne turned as a sergeant walked towards them down the corridor. His shirt was bloody and he looked grey with shock. In the background, armed officers from the firearms support unit were controlling the entrances and turning away members of the public and press, while paramedics hurried about their business and senior officers stood around looking grave. None of these, Harry noted, came anywhere near Ballatyne, but they were clearly aware of his presence and constantly throwing nervous looks his way. Ballatyne's minder stood waiting, not bothering to hide the sidearm he was wearing and somehow aloof from all the activity. 'What's the damage?' Ballatyne asked.

The sergeant stopped. 'Two of my men dead, five wounded, one PCSO critical. It's a bloody nightmare.' He shook his head. 'I'm ex-army and I've never seen anything like it. It was text-book stuff: in, assault, pull back and out again, all inside four minutes. They must have been ex-military . . . Special Forces or commandos. We didn't get so much as a bloody touch.'

The timing had seemed a lot longer to Harry, but he knew the man was right. 'How's the guard on the rear door?' When he, McCreath and the other constable had run out of the fire door and approached the rear entrance, they'd found the door open and the security guard on the floor in a pool of blood.

'He'll live. He was lucky, though.' His face twisted in disbelief. 'He says two men on foot came to the back gate and showed what looked like an MOD badge on the security camera. They said they were here to assist with the interview of Staff Sergeant McCreath. There was no reason to question it, so he let them in to check further. As soon as they got inside, they kicked off. The guard took a bullet in the shoulder before opening the inner doors.'

'Can't he tell a foreign accent when he hears one?' Ballatyne grated.

The sergeant gazed back at him, undaunted by Ballatyne's position or the credentials he'd shown on arrival. 'You spooks bother to spend a little time around here and you'll hear every accent under the sun – and I'm not talking about outsiders. We get all sorts; foreign cops on liaison, police delegations from wherever, security representatives from every country you can name.' He sighed and added quietly, 'What we don't get is a pair of fucking headcases treating the place like a kill zone. Now, if you'll excuse me, I've got people who need my help.' He turned and marched away without waiting for a reply.

Ballatyne let him go, his anger subsiding, and looked at Harry with a wry expression. 'Me and my big mouth. He's right, of course. What's your take on all this?' He had come south of the river in response to the full city-wide alert to a station under attack, knowing that it could only be for one reason: to silence McCreath.

'Very simple. He met with Deakin, but backed out before going through with it, so Deakin and his buddies sent the Bosnians after him to teach him a lesson. It's what they do.'

Ballatyne nodded. 'And I bet the guns have already been dumped – or passed on.'

'What I'd like to know,' said Harry, 'is how they located McCreath so quickly inside the building. They knew exactly where to go.'

'I'm hoping we'll have the answer to that shortly.' As Ballatyne spoke, a thin, grey-haired man in plain clothes arrived and nodded to him.

'This is a bad business,' said the newcomer.

Ballatyne made introductions. 'Chris Paynter, Harry Tate. Chris works with SO15, advising on surveillance techniques. I asked him to pop down and tell us what he thinks.'

Harry shook the newcomer's hand. He'd worked with SO15, the Met Police surveillance unit, many times, and could guess why this man was here. For all his raging at people, Ballatyne had been cool-headed enough to call for expert help when he needed it.

'I've had a look at the camera footage,' said Paynter. 'Those cowboys weren't too fussed about being seen, were they? Come see.' He beckoned and walked away towards the rear of the building, and into a small room with blinds at the windows and a number of video monitors. A support officer in a white shirt was standing at a printer, tapping instructions on to a keypad. He pointed at a monitor showing a still shot of an internal corridor.

Paynter ran his fingers across the monitor's keyboard, and the picture changed to show a section of corridor with a flare of daylight at one end. A man in a white shirt was lying on the floor, legs jerking in obvious distress. He had a dark patch on one shoulder. Another man with close-cut hair was bending over him, and holding a semi-automatic pistol pressed into the wounded man's chin.

'The security guard working the rear gate,' Paynter explained. 'He's just been shot by one of the attackers. We can't get a sound feed, but my guess is the attacker's asking where the prisoner is being held.'

The gunman stood up and pointed his weapon down at the guard's head. But before he could open fire, another man appeared and tapped him on the shoulder. This man was shorter and stockier, Harry noted, with dark hair. The gunman lowered his weapon, then stepped over the guard and walked away along the corridor with his colleague, passing beneath the camera.

Neither of them looked up, and Harry wondered if they were unaware of being filmed or simply didn't care. He stared hard at each of them, impressing their images on his memory. Both men looked hard and fit, heavy across the shoulders, and moved easily, with the purposeful manner of trained soldiers.

'They've done this before,' he said softly.

'Watch this.' Paynter tapped another key and this time the scene jumped to show a junction of two corridors. The two attackers were approaching the camera, walking quickly past a series of doors on each side, seemingly undeterred by any possible resistance. They paused at the junction and the taller of the two pulled an object from his pocket and peered round the corner, where three figures were clustered around a doorway, looking each way. 'M84 stun grenade,' Paynter commented softly. Without hesitating, the taller attacker pulled the pin and tossed the grenade around the corner, where it rolled and bounced towards the three police officers. The attacker stepped back and waited. The picture dissolved momentarily as a bright flare of light illuminated the corridor where the officers were standing. When the image cleared, it showed two men on their knees, holding their heads, and a woman officer slumped against one wall. As the shorter attacker stepped into view, one of the officers, recovering faster than his colleagues, looked up and reached out for the equipment belt at his waist.

'God, you fool,' whispered Ballatyne, just as the gunman braced himself and shot the officer, who was flung over backwards by the force of the bullet.

The shooter stepped forward, shaking his head, while his companion paused only to lash out at the other officer with his pistol, knocking him unconscious. He then hurled another grenade along the corridor before stepping smartly with his colleague inside an open doorway to wait for the blast.

'This is unreal,' said Ballatyne. 'Didn't they see the cameras?'

'Far from it.' Paynter tapped the keys again, and the scene showed the two men passing beneath another camera. This time the shorter of the two looked up and grinned, then winked before calmly shooting out the lens. 'They knew they were being filmed all right. They just didn't care.'

Ballatyne walked over to the door and back, puffing his cheeks in frustration. 'I know why, too: because they'll be gone and out of the country before we can get a lead on them. Can we have prints of these two?'

Paynter nodded. 'Already done.' He turned to the support officer, who handed him a stack of still photos. 'These are already going out to all units and ports.'

'Too bloody late!' Ballatyne muttered with unaccustomed venom. 'Harry?'

'Like McCreath said, it's Ganic and Zubac,' he replied. 'He reckoned they'd come for him. He wasn't wrong.'

THIRTY-FIVE

'Right. Next question: how did they find him?' Ballatyne was suddenly calm again, working logically through the situation and assessing what had happened . . . and how. Paynter was already ahead of him. 'Is the prisoner still here?'

'McCreath? Yes, downstairs. Why?'

'If they located him inside a building like this, they either had someone on the inside or he's carrying a tracking device.'

'He claims he chose the place on impulse,' said Ballatyne. 'They wouldn't have had time to set up an insider.'

'Then it's a device. I already checked his personal effects in the property box, and they're clean. We'll have to do a body search.'

'Bloody Nora,' Ballatyne murmured. 'You can wear the rubber gloves, then. Come on.' He signalled to the support officer to lead them downstairs to where McCreath was being held. In spite of his close shave with death, the staff sergeant looked remarkably calm, as if the sudden burst of action had regenerated him and settled his nerves.

Paynter asked him to stand up, then examined his clothing, checking the collar and cuffs of his shirt and moving down to his shoes, which he'd been allowed to keep but without the laces.

'If he's carrying any kind of tracker,' Paynter explained as he worked, 'it will be located in the shoes, the belt or the thicker parts of his clothing. There's no belt, which is the easiest place to put it, so that narrows it down. Can you remove your shoes and trousers, please?'

McCreath did so. Paynter checked the shoes first, placing them to one side. Then he studied the trousers, working through the front, pockets and waistline. When he reached the turn-ups, he grunted and took out a slim knife. Slitting open the turn-up on the right leg, he removed a lightweight brown resin biscuit, no bigger than a mobile phone SIM card.

'Neat,' he commented. 'GSM tracker. Not one of ours, but

nice.' He held it up for the others to see, turning it over to reveal a small silver disc embedded in one side. 'Battery. Probably lasts a hundred hours, with a range of fifty metres or so.' He handed it to Ballatyne. 'If they knew which building he was in, all they'd have to do was get close to an outside wall with the monitor and wait for a signal. Once inside, though, they'd still need directions to find out which floor he was on.' He took a small device from his pocket. It had an array of buttons and a tiny aerial. He switched it on and one of the lights lit up.

'If it's so simple,' Ballatyne growled, 'why didn't you use your little toy in the first place?'

Paynter gave him a patient look and said, 'I like to keep my hand in. Like reading a map book instead of a satnav, technology doesn't always provide the answers.'

'Smart arse.' Ballatyne looked at McCreath, who was pulling his trousers back on. 'Did you know about this?'

McCreath gave him a look of contempt. 'What, you think I'm suicidal? I wanted to get away from the bastards, not have them jumping all over me. They must have got at my clothes and planted that thing when I was asleep in the hotel.'

Harry caught Ballatyne's eye. 'We need to find out more. Do you have time?'

'Why not?' He nodded to Paynter, who waved a hand and left, while Harry signalled for McCreath to take a seat and pulled up a chair opposite.

'Tell me who you met, give me descriptions, names – even nicknames – and anything else you can think of.'

McCreath nodded. 'I'll try, but there's not much to tell. Tom Deakin was first. He must be mid-forties, hard-looking, not easy to talk to. But he's the boss; seems to make all the decisions. I found him pushy, to be honest. Impatient and edgy, as if he was living on his nerves.'

'Who else?'

'A Yank. I didn't get his name, although I heard Deakin call him "Turp". Forty-ish, skinny but looks as hard as nails. Calm, though, unlike Deakin. Ex-US airborne.'

'He told you that?'

'No. He's got a One-oh-One Airborne tat on his wrist; an eagle's head and banner. I saw it once when he scratched his arm. I've seen them before. From the way he talked, I got the impression he's the admin guy.'

Harry made a note. 'How's that?'

'He talked about the money . . . how they'd get it to me, the transfer through bank accounts offshore, how I'd need to choose passwords and where I'd want the deposits made. I mean, I handle my own financial stuff, like insurance and bank accounts, but he was using a whole different language, like an expert. He was "Turp" and Deakin was "Deak". They seemed pretty tight.'

'Anyone else?'

'Apart from the nut-jobs who stormed this place, you mean? I met them at the hotel Deakin kept me in near Brussels – a four-star block near the ring road. They never said much, and they weren't there all the time. They'd turn up without warning, then disappear again. But it was like they were letting me know they were watching me all the same. They said there was another guy around when they weren't going to be there, but I never saw him.'

'Names?'

'Ganic and Zubac. Don't know their first names – we never got that friendly. They're Bosnians . . . ex-military or militia, I'm not sure. Zubac's the boss; he's the smaller one, but not by much. Ganic is scary and doesn't care who knows it. There's not a lot goes on behind the face, if you know what I mean. I've seen guys like him before: dead on the inside. Wouldn't surprise me if they've buried a few where they come from.'

Harry didn't bother asking him where the hotel was; he was sure Ballatyne already had that covered. Besides, he was sure that the Protectory would have had it cleaned, checked and sanitized of anything incriminating.

'There was another name I picked up,' McCreath continued. 'Someone called Nicholls. Deakin didn't seem to have much time for him, but he was obviously part of the group. He never came to Brussels, though, as far as I know.'

Funny how Brussels kept cropping up, thought Harry: first with Pike, then Paulton and Deakin, now McCreath and the Bosnian storm-troopers.

He made McCreath go through the descriptions again, getting him to paint a picture and give him every bit of detail he could recall. It was standard debriefing procedure tailored to drain the mind of every scrap, even to the point of recalling material that would serve no specific purpose, in the hopes that it would drag out something he could use.

But Deakin and his crew had been very clever.

'Tell us about the Protectory,' said Ballatyne. 'Names and numbers.'

'They never told me much – and nothing about themselves,' McCreath replied. 'I got the impression that there are three main guys running it, but Deakin hinted at others he could call on if needed. He laid it on that the Protectory was there to help people like me who'd been asked to do too much for Queen and country.' He grunted. 'He made it sound like a charitable organization for damaged squaddies. I fell for it, I admit. Christ, it was a no-brainer; I was in a mess, no life to speak of, no way back and they were offering me a way out. It was a bloody sight better than what I'd been living with for the past four years, so I said yes.'

'And what exactly were they offering?' Ballatyne asked.

'A new identity, ready cash and help with relocation. There were places I couldn't go, Deakin said, because I'd be vulnerable. But that left plenty of places I could disappear to, no bother.'

'Like where?'

'Low cost countries like Thailand, Cambodia, a couple of places in Latin America, even Australia and Canada. He said a fair number of Americans have ended up there.'

'What did they want in return?'

This time McCreath hesitated, and Harry guessed it was probably out of shame at having considered trading information for a better life. 'They wanted anything new, especially on comms systems, networks, satellites and ECMs – electronic countermeasures. They were particularly interested in the new battlefield communications system I'd been working on when I got wounded.' He scowled. 'They seemed to know quite a lot about it already, though. I think they'd already done some work on it.'

Pike, thought Harry. They'd have got something from him before he turned and ran. With another 251 Signals Squadron expert on their hands, Pike wouldn't have been worth trying to hold on to, not once he'd made his intentions clear.

'Did they ever mention any other British army personnel they were after?'

'Not to me. The focus was all on me.'

'Anyone named Tan?'

'Tan? No. They didn't mention and I didn't ask. They didn't seem the kind of people to mess with; I got that message pretty quick.'

'So what made you back out?'

McCreath sighed. 'They were asking too much. No way did I want to go back to Afghanistan, but that didn't mean I was prepared to sell the kind of information I had to the highest bidder.' He frowned and twisted his hands together. 'I know it's easy to say it now, but I realized it was my mates I'd be selling down the river . . . exposing them to God knows what, now or in the future. It wasn't like I'd planned on becoming a traitor, you know? I just wanted . . . out. Anyway, I wasn't supposed to call anybody from the hotel, but I needed to talk to someone. So I bribed a cleaner to let me use her mobile and rang the mate I'd been staying with before Deakin turned up. He told me about Pike; said he'd heard on the grapevine that Pike had arrived back in London, ready to call it a day, but he'd been taken out.' McCreath looked down at the table. 'I knew it had to be Zubac and Ganic. They'd been away for a couple of days by then. I was a bit slow on the uptake, but I figured if I stalled or tried telling them I wasn't going to sell, I'd be next.' He gave Harry an empty look. 'So I bugged out and headed back here.'

'To do what?' said Ballatyne.

'I don't know. Hand myself in, I suppose. I wasn't exactly thinking clearly, but I knew if I stayed where I was, I'd most likely end up dead.'

Harry let the silence lengthen, then said, 'You were lucky.'

'I know. I should say thanks, but I suppose it would be pointless, wouldn't it?' He looked miserable and suddenly couldn't meet Harry's eye.

'No, I mean you were lucky before today. You heard names, saw two of the Protectory and the two Bosnians face to face. That was a lot of exposure for someone who was going to be allowed to disappear into the sunset with a new ID and a load of cash.' He stood up. He needed to keep moving. 'Fact is, from that moment on, you could identify all of them and that made you a liability. Whatever else we know about the Protectory, one thing's clear: they've survived for a long time now. They only let out the kind of personal information you got for one reason.'

McCreath swallowed as the full realization of his position began to sink in. 'Go on.'

'Because once they'd drained you of the information they wanted, you weren't going to be allowed to live long enough to pass anything on.' He walked to the door. 'There was nothing in this for you and never has been. Just like Neville Pike and at least three others we know of. No future, no money, no new ID. You were expendable.'

THIRTY-SIX

While Harry and Ballatyne were talking to McCreath amid the wreckage from the attack on the police station, Zubac and Ganic were closing in on the M25 motorway, the east–west link south of London, their sights set on taking a ferry to France. Their exit from the attack site had been a close-run thing; as they left through the rear gate, they had run into an armed response vehicle responding to an all-units call. But they had been undeterred; a few rounds of fire from the Rugers had disabled the police vehicle and they had managed to walk away amid the confusion and screams from pedestrians ducking for cover.

Two hundred yards further on, they had made a pre-arranged hand-off of the rucksack containing the weapons to an elderly Jamaican at a grab-and-go craft stall. It disappeared under the table and in return they got a holdall and keys to an anonymous grey Renault waiting in a pub car park off Coldharbour Lane. From there it had been a simple route through the back streets to take them south and out of immediate trouble before a cordon could be set up.

Zubac was feeling humiliated by the results of their attack. They had not failed to carry out an assignment like this in a long time – especially on a lightly armed facility where resistance should have been minimal. With superior firepower and the element of shock backed up by the M84s, it should have been a cake-walk. They should have been able to clear a route to McCreath and eliminate him with the minimum of fuss and walk away before anyone could stop them. Instead, they had been drawn like amateurs on a chase of their quarry through the corridors of the police station, only to run into a choking cloud of potassium bicarbonate in a stairwell. Zubac suppressed the desire to rub his eyes and scrabbled around in the footwell where he found a plastic bag containing a bottle of water, a change of clothing, packs of sandwiches and a packet of antiseptic wet-wipes.

He ripped out a handful of wet-wipes and handed them to Ganic, who was driving. His friend was red around the eyes from the effects of the potassium, but had avoided the worst of the powder. Zubac had been leading the way and had started up the stairs just as the first wave had come down, cloaking him in its embrace before he could back off. He poured water into his cupped hand and splashed it over his face, swearing fluently at the man who had done this to them.

'*We had guns and stun grenades!*' he howled angrily, splashing more water. 'How could this happen? They had silly little sticks, that's all!'

Ganic shrugged and lit a cigarette one-handed, and Zubac swore at him in frustration. His knew his friend of old; Ganic wasn't so concerned with failure. For him, the occasional setback was an operational hazard. It happened when you were least expecting it and was something you lived with, even Zubac had to admit that. Not that Deakin would see it that way.

He drank some water and tried not to think about the head of the Protectory. The former Scots Guardsman didn't even come close to scaring him, but he was undoubtedly living on a hair-trigger and liable to go off at any moment. And unpredictable men like him were always a worry. Fortunately, Turpowicz was calmer, a restraining influence on his colleague; but he, too, was a former soldier and would do whatever Deakin told him. God knows what they would say about this setback, though.

Once they had cleaned their hands and faces as thoroughly as they could, they stopped long enough to remove their jackets, shirts and trousers, which they emptied and bundled into a plastic charity shop collection bag and dropped out of the window. Give it an hour or so and the contents would be recycled on the street or sitting in a shop somewhere, waiting for a grateful customer. The holdall they'd received from the Jamaican contained replacement clothing, cheap, commonplace and untraceable.

'You going to call him?' said Ganic. He was steering one-handed, twirling a triangular metal ring on his finger and flicking it with his thumb with an irritating pinging sound.

'Is that what I think it is?' Zubac gave him a sour look. Tough as he was, his friend was disturbingly childish in the things that amused him. Here he was playing with a pull ring from one of the M84s.

'Sure.' Ganic grinned and studied the ring. 'This is neat. I think I'll have it silvered and put it through my *kurac*. The girls, they go for that weird shit. What do you think?'

'I think you're the weird one.' Zubac took out a disposable mobile phone with a pre-programmed number. He wasn't looking forward to this, but was feeling sour enough to not give a damn.

He pressed the speed-dial key.

Deakin listened in open disbelief to the call, then cut the connection without comment. He looked at Turpowicz and shook his head. They had moved to a hotel on the outskirts of Nürnberg awaiting the outcome of the Brixton assault, and a meeting with Paulton to discuss future plans. Zubac had just called with the bad news.

'Problems?' Turpowicz tried not to look unsurprised. Lately he'd come to expect almost anything of the men he referred to as Beavis and Butt-head, given their unsubtle methodology of eliminating the people Deakin sent them after. Following the attack on Pike in broad daylight, and the careless manner in which they had left Barrow's body to be found, he'd had his doubts about the wisdom of making a suicidal assault on a police precinct, even with the traditionally unarmed British policemen they'd be up against. But Deakin hadn't listened, intent only on teaching McCreath a lesson and sending a warning to anyone else who changed their mind about cooperating with the Protectory.

'Bastards!' Deakin looked ready to spit. 'They missed McCreath! God Almighty, how hard can it be to walk over a bunch of noddies? All they had to do was get inside and finish him off.' He paced up and down, then jumped as his mobile rang again. He listened for a second, then said, 'Yeah, come on up.' He disconnected and said, 'Paulton's here.'

'Are we going to tell him about Tate?'

Deakin shrugged. 'Why bother? What difference does it make?'

'You said Paulton knows his way around. He might give us a line on getting this guy stopped. We could do without this right now – especially as we still haven't located Tan. Every time he interferes, he's eating away at our deadline.'

'You worry too much.'

'Yeah, well, worrying has kept me out of trouble so far. But this is moving on to a whole new level.'

'What are you talking about?' Deakin scowled.

'This.' Turpowicz waved a vague hand in the air. 'Pike, Barrow, those guys in Australia, now going after McCreath in a police precinct building. We've changed the rules of engagement, Deak – don't you see? We've come out and given the establishment the finger, saying "take this, suckers, we do what the hell we like!"' His face twisted. 'They'll only stand so much of that shit before they come after us with all guns blazing.'

Deakin squared up to him. 'What's the matter, Turp? Not losing your nerve, are you?'

'No, I'm just saying we should back off a little. We're—'

He was interrupted by a knock at the door. It was Paulton.

'Hello, boys,' he said smoothly. 'Am I interrupting something? Much louder and the whole hotel will know our business.' He dropped his coat on a chair and headed for the mini-bar. 'Come on, what's the problem? Mr Wien Lu Chi putting the pressure on, is he?' He opened a miniature of whisky and poured it into a glass. 'I told you getting into bed with the Chinese was a risky business. They don't play like the rest of us, believe me.'

'It's not him,' Deakin growled. 'I sent Zubac and Ganic after McCreath. They missed him.'

'Never mind. It wasn't necessary, anyway. What happened?'

Deakin told him in a few brief sentences, ending with a description of Harry Tate.

Paulton paused mid-sip. 'Did you say Tate?'

'Yeah,' said Turpowicz. 'He's a warrant officer with the army. One of the recovery officers they send after deserters.'

'I know what recovery officers do.' Paulton stared reflectively into his glass. 'How long?'

'Huh?'

'How long has this Tate been in the picture?'

'He first turned up in The Hague,' said Deakin, 'chasing Pike's trail. Then he found Barrow not long after the Bosnians had dealt with him. The man's like a bloody sniffer dog.'

'I thought you said Pike was dead.'

'He is. They were checking his back trail. Don't worry, it's a dead end. Like Barrow.'

'That's two of two,' said Paulton enigmatically.

'What does that mean?'

'The odds. Two of two is what an old boss of mine called lousy odds – unless they were on your side. Two good contacts meant we were in business. Two bad ones and we were in trouble. This feels like trouble.'

'And what exactly was your business?' asked Turpowicz. 'You never really said.'

Paulton smiled. 'No, I didn't, did I? Let's say I was in a similar line of work to this man, Tate.'

'A man hunter? Spy catcher?' Turpowicz was quick off the mark. 'Don't tell me . . . MI5? Special Branch?'

'Something like that. Do you know what Tate looks like?'

'Sure.' Turpowicz turned to the laptop and switched it on. The machine booted up and he found the shot of Harry Tate. Paulton bent and studied it carefully, then walked over to the window and peered out while the other two men waited. He seemed to have gone very still, as if frozen in mid-thought, but neither of the other two seemed to notice.

'So how do we stop him?' said Deakin. 'Can he be called off?'

Paulton shook his head. 'Not by me, he can't. I don't have the reach. People like Tate are independent. They follow their own lines of enquiry. Stopping them is not that simple.'

There was a lengthy silence. Turpowicz was the first to speak. He said with a nervous laugh, 'Hell, you sound almost like you know the guy.'

'Me?' Paulton turned and shook his head, glancing briefly at the laptop screen, then checked his watch. 'Shall we have lunch? I'm famished.'

THIRTY-SEVEN

As Paulton followed the other two men downstairs, he was reflecting on how quickly and dramatically the past could come back and haunt you. Even with a quick glance at the laptop, he'd had no trouble recognizing his former MI5 subordinate, Harry Tate. The realization made satisfying his appetite the last thing on his mind, but he wasn't about to let these men know the size of the problem they were facing. Not that Tate was unstoppable – no man was. Paulton had once described him as solid and resolute, outwardly a plodder, the kind of man who crept up on the fence; the kind you never saw coming until it was too late. It had been meant as a criticism, a dismissal of a man he had seriously underestimated. How ironically prophetic that had turned out to be. His gut tightened unpleasantly at the memory, and what it had led to. He'd made a mistake with Tate. It had brought serious consequences, especially for Paulton's fellow conspirator and opposite number in MI6, Sir Anthony Bellingham. He had suffered a particularly nasty fate on London's Embankment, a spit away from the SIS headquarters, courtesy of one of his own disgraced officers, Clare Jardine.

Paulton was damned if he would make that mistake again.

He caught up with Deakin and Turpowicz just as they reached the restaurant, and drew them out of earshot of the maître d'.

'Those men you use – the Bosnians?'

'What about them?' Deakin looked defensive, expecting more criticism.

'Tell them not to leave the country.'

'Why not?'

'Because we need them to cover your tracks. This man Tate isn't going to stop.'

'What are you saying?'

'Take my word for it – we must take him out of the picture.'

'That's what I was going to do,' Deakin looked pointedly at Turpowicz, 'but others disagreed.'

'It's too risky, that's why,' the American insisted. 'Go after Tate and it'll bring down the big battalions on our heads. There'll be nowhere to hide.' He stared hard at Paulton. 'Or is there something you're not telling us?'

'No.' Paulton kept calm, his face blank. 'But I know the type of man Tate is and I know how this will end if we don't stop him now.' He knew he was too experienced to betray any misgivings he might have; he had, over the years, kept greater secrets from better and far keener intellects than these. But he was realistic enough to know that if he didn't handle this very carefully, it could all go very badly indeed. The fact that he knew Harry Tate was going to come out; these things always did. And being the men they were, even with his long-time acquaintance of Deakin, if they suspected there were personal reasons for a man hunter to be on his trail, they'd dump him in a heartbeat. He'd be too much of a liability to keep around for their continued survival, as small and self-contained as the organization was. He had joined them, promising to bring specialized contacts and resources, because he had seen an unrivalled opportunity to profit by the kind of assets they had passing through their fingers. It was something he did not want to lose. He was looking forward to many years of productive life yet, and for that he would need a regular supply of operating capital and the means to keep himself out of trouble.

'We're all ears, George,' Deakin prompted him impatiently. 'How do we get to Tate and how do we stop him for good?'

Paulton gave a knowing smile. 'We distract him. Everyone's got a weak point, and Tate's no different. We hit him where it will hurt and draw him out. Then we take him out of the picture. And I think I know just the way to do it.'

THIRTY-EIGHT

'I wish I'd been there.' Rik Ferris looked disgruntled at having missed out on some fun. Harry had called at his flat to bring him up to date on events and to see how he was progressing with his trawl for information on Vanessa Tan.

'Good job you weren't,' said Harry. 'You'd have slowed us down.' He smiled to show he was joking and took a pair of pistols out of a leather briefcase he'd brought with him. They were German H&K VP70 semi-automatics.

Rik's eyes widened in surprise. 'Jesus – what's this?'

'The difference between life and death.' Harry handed him a magazine. 'Nine millimetre, eighteen-round mags, courtesy of a now defunct south London gang. If Zubac and Ganic come after us, we're going to need them.'

'How did you get hold of them?' Rik picked up one of the guns and checked the mechanism. Both weapons had the patina of past use, but were clean and ready to go.

'Ballatyne pulled some strings. They're not logged to anyone, but if we have to lose them, make sure they stay lost.'

'You think they'll come, even after what they did in Brixton?'

Harry nodded. 'Especially after what they did in Brixton. They don't take failure very well, nor does Deakin. With McCreath banged up and out of reach, they'll be concentrating even more on going after a prime target like Tan . . . that's if they haven't already found her. But to do that, they'll want me out of the way.'

Rik looked at him. 'How do you know that?'

'Because it's what I would do.'

Rik put the gun down on the table with the magazine aligned alongside it. 'Apart from watching our backs, where do we go from here?'

'We keep looking for Tan. She's the key to this. If we find her, we'll eventually find Deakin and the others.'

'And Paulton.'

'And Paulton.' It always came back to Paulton. Maybe his

former boss had become an obsession, just as Ballatyne had suggested. But trying to ignore his part in the picture wasn't going to help; he was a constant, hovering in the background like a ghost, an itch Harry couldn't scratch. He rubbed his face and forced himself to rationalize. After the events of the morning and the dramatic flight through the police station, he was feeling numbed, as if he'd come down off a chemical high. The truth was, though, he'd been concentrating so much on the other runners, he'd given little more thought to finding Tan. And she was worrying him. For a high-profile young female army officer, Tan had disappeared completely. Too completely. With no back-story he could use to figure out where she might have gone, and no family history or recent employment details other than the sparse MOD material, it was like staring into a dense fog.

'I haven't found anything yet,' Rik admitted, as if reading his mind. 'I even checked all the social network sites like YouTube, Twitter, Facebook and others, but there's been nothing. I've got a couple of friends working on the name, too – and one is using the photo to link in to FR systems at airports. It's slow going, though.'

Harry nodded. It was a long shot. Facial recognition systems were still not readily available in all international airports, and the chances of Vanessa Tan doing them a favour by appearing on one at the right moment were slim. But it was another avenue to explore. He sat down and stared at the ceiling, trying to work through the problem. There was something right there, back at the beginning, which was bugging him. 'Why would someone on the run,' he said aloud, 'set up a system for managing a property left to deteriorate, and pay phone rental on a machine which is never used? What would be the point? It doesn't make sense.'

'Keeping a bolthole, just in case?' said Rik.

And what about the bank details? There had to be a link somewhere, Harry reasoned. 'Anyone arranging regular payments through a bank has to leave some kind of trail. Christ, they certainly know how to chase me quickly enough when something goes wrong.'

Rik shook his head. 'I checked and double-checked. Nothing doing. Somehow the system got wiped, but left instructions and funds enough to keep paying.' He glanced at Harry and added,

'Of course, there's always the possibility that it was done deliberately. But why would they?'

There was only one reason Harry could think of. It was a major one and went right to the heart of international espionage practice: that of penetrating a foreign bureaucracy or military infrastructure and working on the inside. It would mean the current Vanessa Tan was a sleeper, a spy gathering information, data and the confidence of some of the most important military officers in the world. Yet, if that had been her sole role, whoever was running her could not have guaranteed the Cambridge graduate ever making it into the army, let alone gaining access to any of the information they wanted. Getting run over by a Cambridge bus would have been just as high on the cards.

Unless she had been just one of a handful of sleepers, her controllers playing the odds that at least one of them would succeed and find their way inside. If so, it spoke of people playing very long odds indeed. And that narrowed down the field considerably. Harry put that thought to one side. There was nothing he could do about it right now. Instead he had to concentrate on finding Tan. If she was a sleeper, the switch must have been made after leaving Cambridge and applying for the army. If so, that cut down the timeframe. But it still didn't tell him who was running her.

And why would she drop out at such a crucial moment and position in her career? Had someone blown her cover? If so, Ballatyne would have been the first to know. Unless she'd simply lost her nerve and taken flight. She was thirty years old, still young, and the intense pressure of working in that kind of environment, storing away information while staying below the radar of constant security reviews, would have been enormous.

That raised another question: how did the people running her get the information out of her head? They couldn't exactly download it like a stored computer file. Unless she took huge risks and put everything down in writing and passed it on by secure electronic means. He mentioned it to Rik, who looked doubtful.

'It's possible, but risky. Transmissions of any data going out from anywhere in Afghanistan would stand a high chance of being picked up, and an encrypted satellite phone would only be any good as long as nobody found it. Would she be allowed to carry one in her position?'

Harry had to agree. But if she didn't pass the information online, it had to be by personal contact. That was also highly risky, but providing she was careful, she could have done it by booking into a hotel somewhere and having pre-arranged meetings with her controller in the next room.

He decided to call Ballatyne. The MI6 man came on within seconds.

'Were there ever any doubts about Lieutenant Tan in the weeks leading up to her disappearance?' Harry asked him.

Ballatyne hesitated, then said, 'Not as far as I know.' He sounded puzzled. 'Why do you ask?'

'Her disappearance doesn't fit. The whole set-up is odd.'

'Odd?'

'There's no trace of her before or after she signed up. That's not normal. Everyone leaves something, no matter how small.'

'Are you suggesting she's a sleeper?' Ballatyne had caught on fast.

'It's possible. But if she is, why leave such a prime position if she didn't have to? It's a waste of an asset.'

There was another pause before Ballatyne said, 'All I can say is, she had a spotless record, with exemplary conduct. But then,' he continued, 'if she was a sleeper, her controllers would have made sure of her legend, wouldn't they?'

The legend – the cover story for operatives working undercover. It had to be good enough to stand up to rigorous examination, with enough strands of truth to sound convincing, yet not so many that a reasonable check would reveal unexplained holes. If Tan was a spy, her legend must have been exceptional, given the position she had achieved. Either she was genuinely clean and original or she was the cleverest insert anyone had ever put in place.

'Whether original or a plant,' Ballatyne pointed out, 'we still have a problem: a person of importance has gone missing. What we don't know is how much she has taken with her or how much she may have already passed on.'

He was right. If a foreign power had managed to strike gold by placing an asset in Tan's position, they wouldn't sit back for long without taking delivery of every nugget they could get their hands on. And neither would the Protectory.

'There's another point bugging me.'

'Only one?'

'How does the Protectory get a line on the deserters, and how do they identify who's a talent and who isn't?'

'That's been worrying us, too. So far I don't like the answers we're getting. I'll keep you informed. Anything else?'

'Yes. The American McCreath referred to as "Turp". I'm guessing he's a deserter like Deakin. There can't be too many One-oh-One Airborne men out there on the run. Do you know who we can ask?'

'You need to speak to the Army Deserter Information Point at Fort Knox. A Major Kenwin Dundas. He's been cleared to help you.' He gave Harry the relevant telephone and fax numbers to call. Harry was impressed. It showed Ballatyne had been listening carefully to McCreath and had already prepared the way for him to make contact.

'There's just one thing,' Ballatyne continued. 'If Tan is a sleeper, I think we can be fairly sure it isn't the *Guoanbu* running her.'

'How do you know that?'

'We've had an interesting circular bulletin from German Counterintelligence. A "person of interest" named Wien Lu Chi has been staying at a luxury hotel in Bremen for a few days. The reason he was noticed was that a member of the German parliament was staying there with a young woman who is not his wife, and they were keeping a close watch to keep the press away. Wien Lu Chi happened to pop up on the radar. He's a known middleman for the Chinese and a few select Middle Eastern clients, usually dealing in arms and weapons technology. Nobody knows why he was in the country, but it's a safe bet he was up to no good. If the Chinese are running Tan, they wouldn't need him to be involved – they'd deal direct.'

'I take it there's been no sighting of her in the area?'

'No. They've interviewed the staff and bugged his room, but nothing has shown up yet.' He paused, and Harry picked up on it.

'There's a but in there.'

'There is. Wien Lu Chi received two visitors in the hotel before the Germans could get a bug in place. One American, one British. They left no names but the watchers got a look at the hotel's

CCTV system.' Ballatyne's voice contained a smile. 'One of the men was Thomas Deakin.'

THIRTY-NINE

I t was nearly eight in the evening before Harry was able to pin down Major Dundas at Fort Knox. When he finally came on, the officer sounded efficient and brisk, yet there was an undertone of reserve, as though he was not altogether pleased at having to assist a British subject about an American deserter. Harry put it down to pride and launched into his request.

'Sorry to bother you with this, Major,' he said smoothly, after an exchange of names and positions, 'but we have reason to believe that one of yours is helping channel British deserters to new identities and lives in exchange for information.'

'What kind of information?'

'The sensitive kind: technology, security, intelligence, armaments . . . anything they can sell.'

'They?'

'A group called the Protectory.' Harry gave him a summary of what they knew without adding any names. 'They approach deserters from strategic regiments or specialist units and offer a deal: a new life in exchange for whatever information they will trade.'

'Sounds quite a scheme, Mr Tate. And where do they sell this "strategic" information?'

'To the highest bidder. I'm sure I don't need to tell you who they are.' Harry wondered if he was getting through to this man. Dundas sounded less than enthused. His next words confirmed why.

'I guess you don't at that. Thing is, these are British military personnel, right?'

'That's right, but—'

'Selling British military data?' The level of interest had dropped instantly and the implied focus for Dundas was clear: a British problem remained just that. British, not American.

'We don't know that for sure,' said Harry, who understood his reasoning, 'or how long it may last. One of their targets said he was introduced to an American working with the group. He was wearing a One-oh-One Airborne tattoo, eagle's head and banner, and was referred to as "Turp". We suspect this man is high up in the pecking order.'

'Well, sir,' Dundas replied eventually, 'I can tell you now, there are more men out there wearing the flying eagle tattoos than ever served in airborne. Same with Vietnam vets who wear the right tags and tell all the right stories. Some of them never even enlisted, but they like to claim some kind of credit on the backs of the men who did. What makes you think this Turp character is for real, anyway?' His voice had drifted off now from professionally interested to openly sceptical.

'It takes a soldier to recognize another one, Major. The target thought he was real enough.'

'That doesn't mean he'll target American personnel.' The response was automatic, and Harry wondered what it said about Major Dundas's open-mindedness to the men and women he was responsible for processing – or his perspective on America's military partners.

'If he does, they'll have a field day. You want to bet against them coming across another Bradley Manning?'

The line clicked and buzzed as Dundas digested the implications of that. It was a brutal argument to use, but the revelations that a member of the US army had systematically released classified information which eventually found its way on to the Internet had been a hard pill for the military establishment to swallow, and the reverberations were likely to go on for years. Even someone like Dundas must know that it could happen again.

Before the major could put him off, Harry continued, 'All I'm asking, Major, is if you would be good enough to get one of your staff to see if the name Turp comes up in your records. Then we can close off that avenue of investigation. It sounds like an abbreviation of a real name to me, wouldn't you think?'

There was a lengthy pause. Harry was counting on Dundas, sceptical or not, finding it hard to refuse such a simple request.

'I guess that's true, Mr Tate. Let me put you on to our Lieutenant Garcia and she'll run a quick check. I sure hope you find what you're looking for. You have a nice day, now.' There was a click and Dundas was gone as suddenly as he had come on. His voice was replaced by a young woman's, asking how she could help.

'Lieutenant, my name's Harry Tate, attached to the Recovery Office in the Ministry of Defence, London. I think we work in the same line of business.'

'Sounds like we do, Mr Tate. What's the problem?' Garcia sounded businesslike, but her tone was a good deal warmer than that of her boss.

Harry gave her the details. While he was talking, he heard a burst of conversation in the background at the end of the line, then the sound of a door closing. A man's voice said something close by and there was an intake of breath as if Garcia were mouthing something in reply. Another rumble of background conversation was followed by a door closing, this time with a firm snap. Garcia said, 'Uh . . . thank you, Mr Tate. I'll have to get back to you on that.'

'Is there a problem?' Harry's antennae were twitching. Something told him that Garcia had just received a visitor, most probably her boss, Major Dundas. She sounded distracted. What the hell was going on?

'Uh, no . . . not really. I've been advised that our system's down for a routine maintenance check, so I'm not able to access those files right now. We should be up and running again later . . . say in an hour?'

Harry gave her his email and phone number, then thanked her and rang off, puzzled by what had sounded like a blatant delaying tactic. If what he'd heard about the amount of money being thrown into the Department of Defense for IT systems was true, they should have an answer very quickly. But instinct told him that wasn't going to happen.

An hour and a half later, Lieutenant Garcia still hadn't called back. Harry gave it another twenty minutes, then called Fort Knox and asked to be put through to the lieutenant's extension.

'I'm sorry, sir,' said the receptionist after a few moments. 'I'm afraid Lieutenant Garcia's in conference.'

'Can you interrupt it? It's very urgent.'

'I'm afraid not, sir. There's a strict protocol on this session: no calls allowed.'

'I see. The system's still down, then?'

'Sir?' The receptionist sounded puzzled. 'There's no problem with the system. I've been on it all day and it's fine.'

Harry thanked her politely and cut the call.

Someone wasn't telling the truth.

FORTY

A few miles away, Ganic and Zubac had pulled off the M25 motorway at the first available exit and were heading north at a fast clip. A phone call from Deakin had given them fresh orders, and they were to report to an address in east London.

'C'emal?' Zubac was on the phone, arranging a meeting in a part of the city called Hackney. Neither man had been there before, but they had been assured of a safe reception.

'Yes, brother. It is good to hear from you again.' Their contact's voice was softly familiar, the same voice which had arranged the guns and stun grenades for the attack on Brixton police station. 'While you are on vacation in the city,' he continued quickly before Zubac could say anything else, 'you should call and see your uncle Bakir.' He gave no address, but Zubac knew it meant they should go to a store in Dalston Lane. 'Come and visit. We will eat and help you shake the dust from your journey. Eight o'clock. Drive carefully.'

The call was ended. Zubac put the phone away and gave his friend directions.

It was dark by the time they reached Hackney and parked in a side street just off Dalston Lane. They were a few blocks away from the address they had been given, but the car would be safe enough here. Just in case, they used wet-wipes to go over everything they had touched and made sure they left nothing of themselves behind.

They walked the rest of the way, noting familiar smells and sounds, of music and conversation, eyeing the eateries with interest but resisting the temptation to go inside. Being seen in the open around here would be a mistake; if the police had released photographs of them attacking the station, it would not take long for someone to see them and call it in.

Eventually, they found a store trading in all manner of goods from groceries to clothing and kitchenware. The lights were still on although no customers were in evidence. Zubac tried the handle. The door was locked. He tapped on the glass. Seconds later, they were admitted and ushered to the rear of the store, where the air was heavy with the smell of fruit and spices, and the mustier aroma of soft goods and clothing. Three men were standing by the counter at the back, watching the two new arrivals. The man who had let them in remained by the door, watching the street.

Two of the men were in their twenties and dressed in jeans, trainers and jackets, the uniform and appearance of a million others. The third was a large individual with a shaved head, a heavy stomach and beard, and piercing eyes. His hands were resting on the counter.

'I am C'emal Soran,' he said, and swept a hand towards the others in introduction. 'Antun, Davud.' He did not introduce the man by the door, but it was clearly one of his sons, since he possessed the same build and posture.

Zubac and Ganic nodded and shook hands all round with steady formality, then Soran led them through a door at the back, to a storeroom with a central table and four chairs. The air here was heavy and gritty on the tongue, the floor scattered with a variety of packing materials. The table held a large platter of food, bread and fruit, and alongside stood glasses of juice and bottles of water.

'Sit, my brothers, sit,' said Soran and waited for the visitors to take their places, then offered them food and drink. 'I apologize for the surroundings, but we have a growing mail-order business and not enough room.' The two younger men sat but did not eat or drink.

'So,' Soran said eventually, when Zubac and Ganic were refreshed. 'How can I help you?'

'Did the rucksack come back to you?' asked Zubac, pushing his glass away. 'There should have been two handguns, some ammunition and three grenades.' He smiled to soften any implied suggestion that he did not trust the Jamaican who had handled the weapons after the attack. 'Our thanks for everything – and the car.'

'It was nothing.' Soran waved a vague hand. 'And yes, we have everything back.' He gave a humourless smile to show that he understood the reason behind the question. 'We have a good relationship with the Jamaicans. They help us, we help them. Because nobody expects it, it works to our mutual satisfaction. You have need of these things again?'

Zubac nodded. 'The guns, yes. But first we need these two.' He lifted his chin to indicate the two younger men, who had so far remained silent, summoned by Soran to listen and be ready to follow instructions.

'That is why they are here, brother.'

Ganic leaned forward. 'Are they any good, though? They look very young to me, just out of school.' He seemed less comfortable with the ritual Zubac had insisted they should observe, and more intent on getting down to business. He stared hard at the two young men, who blinked nervously before looking to Soran for guidance.

'They are sons of my cousin,' the older man rumbled, and looked calmly at Ganic as if daring him to question it further. The message was clear: these two are blood relations and therefore vouched for. 'They have lived here two years and know the city well. They have also been trained in another place. They have many skills.'

Zubac nudged Ganic's knee under the table, and the taller man shrugged and sat back with a muttered, 'Very well.'

'What do you want them for?' asked Soran, eyes switching back to Zubac.

'Surveillance work,' Zubac replied. 'That is all. Watch and report on a target . . . on who comes, who goes, what she does. We will pay well for their time.'

'She? You want them to watch a woman?' Such an idea, Soran's question implied, was both beneath them and could lead to trouble, in spite of the money offered. A man could only get so close to a woman for so long before someone noticed – usually the woman herself, if she had her wits about her.

'Yes. Why? Is that a problem?' Zubac spoke firmly but without heat. He knew that Soran was probably looking for any reason he could find to raise the fee. Having a difficult, even well-known target would make any surveillance all the more complex to carry out.

'You tell me.'

There was silence, lengthening as wary looks were exchanged between Soran and his two men. Then Zubac added carefully, 'She is nobody of importance, I give you my word. Simply a connection in a chain.' He rolled a finger through the air as if winding in a length of string. 'Watch her and we find the person we want.' He smiled and lifted his chin. 'Is that acceptable?'

Soran nodded. He wasn't about to turn away valuable business. The young men, Antun and Davud, said nothing, their opinions not required. 'You have a name and address for this woman?'

Zubac took a folded sheet of paper from his pocket and slid it across the table. Soran picked it up and opened it. The paper had a small photo clipped to one corner. He read the details written down, his lips moving slowly, then slapped the piece of paper and photo down in front of the man named Davud.

'It is agreed.' He smiled as if he had signed an international treaty, and poured more juice. This time he included his cousin's sons, who raised their glasses and drank in turn. 'They will go immediately and watch and report on this woman of no importance,' he said, eyes glinting with dry humour. 'In the meantime, you can sleep if you wish. I have made arrangements.' He jerked his head at the two young men and they got up and left the store without a word. Then he looked again at the paper and said, 'This woman named –' he tilted his head to one side, curling his tongue with difficulty around the words – 'Jean Fleming, a seller of flowers.'

FORTY-ONE

Six thirty next morning, and Harry found sleep elusive. It was too early to call Fort Knox, so he ran through Paulton's details on the data stick. He came up for air at one point

and phoned Rik to see how he was progressing with his search
for Vanessa Tan.

'Nothing yet,' said Rik. 'But it doesn't mean there isn't something out there.' There was the sound of key taps in the background, then, 'Point is, we're not the only ones looking.'

Harry gripped the phone. 'Explain.'

'I put a couple of mates on to it . . . told them it was a simple
trace for an insurance job. More hands make light work, that sort
of thing.'

'And?'

'They both came back with the same message. They'd bumped
into other searches for the same name. Queries left on forums,
the name Tan fed into search engines to see what came up –
pretty much what I've been doing. There was even a back-door
search made through an airline database, but it bombed out when
the searcher tripped an alarm.'

The Protectory.

This had turned into a race. 'What's your best guess?'

'If we haven't found anything so far, it means she went off
the grid as soon as she ran. In fact . . .' He paused. More taps
on the keyboard.

'What?' Harry fought to remain patient. Rik often mused aloud
as he typed, as if using his fingers to drive his thought processes.
In Harry's experience, it was best to let him mumble away, but
this was getting urgent.

'To have disappeared so completely, she'd have needed to stop
leaving a trail way before that. But there's nothing.'

'How do you mean, nothing?'

'You sure you want to hear this?'

'Can you hear my hand coming down the line?'

'It's like she never existed.'

Harry was stumped. Not even the dead vanish so completely
that they don't leave some trace behind. Unless . . .

'Could someone have erased her back-trail, or whatever you
call it?'

'History. I don't know. I've heard whispers about a programme
that can do it, developed by webmasters working for the National
Security Agency. They'd certainly have the budget and the means
to carry it out, but it would be a hell of a task. If it's true, though,

it would be like a giant search engine which simply gobbles up any mention of the target name and wipes it off the records. There one second, gone the next. The main problem is, if they weren't very careful, it would wipe out all other Tans, too. But I know that hasn't happened.'

'How?'

'Easy. I fed the name into Google. If I told you how many hits it got, your head would explode. The main question is, even if they've managed to wipe out her individual history, why go to those extremes for one junior officer? What are they trying to hide?'

Another answer Harry didn't have. But they couldn't give up now, especially with the Protectory out there, too. 'Keep looking.'

'Sure. How deep do you want me to go?' The question was casual, but the tone of voice wasn't. Rik was getting impatient, both with not being able to turn up something useful and being cooped up nursing his shoulder. As Harry knew well, when that happened, he was in danger of letting his fingers do the walking into areas best left alone – the very thing that had got him assigned out of MI5 in the first place.

'You know the answer to that,' he said neutrally. Rik possessed skills that could save a lot of time and legwork. Preventing him using those skills for what could be a global search seemed a chronic waste of talent. But if he took care, what could be the harm? 'Can you use a . . . what is it called – a proxy?'

The smile was evident in Rik's voice. 'Oh, dude,' he drawled, 'you're so beyond ancient it's like . . . prehistory. Fortunately, I know what you mean. I'll get back to you.'

Harry switched off the phone and went back to studying the file on Paulton. It amounted to precious little, and nothing to get his teeth into. The official records had been pared down to the bare minimum, large chunks of text having no doubt been black-lined at source to conceal sensitive information. What was left contained no personal clues to the man behind the name – or names, in Paulton's case – giving only a skeleton of facts from a life spent on the move, serving in various locations including Northern Ireland, the US, Afghanistan and Colombia – the last two on attachment with the Drug Enforcement Administration, waging war on the Cartels and other traffickers – and with many

gaps in the narrative which Harry translated as working undercover, and therefore classified for all eternity. It seemed ironic
to him that a man like Paulton, who had been running an illegal
operation that broke all the rules of the Security Service, should
now be protected by the official protocol he had so clearly
despised.

But railing against it would do no good; he had to work with
what he had. And that, he was forced to conclude after reading
and re-reading the files, was next to nothing. Paulton had turned
out to have been a master of security, even among his peers. A
list of fellow MI5 officers was attached, all of whom had been
interviewed. Their names were blanked out, but their comments
confirmed what Harry already knew: that George Henry Paulton
had lived and worked among them, yet had remained an unknown
quantity, even within an organization that prided itself on its
sense of family, of shared ideals and goals. Paulton had been
the odd fish, with no leads, no handy family connections to be
pressured, no habits which might betray him and reveal his
location, no long-term friends. He had been a true everyman,
colourless, self-effacing, leaving no trace and nothing in his
wake.

Harry stared at the wall with a mild sense of frustration. There
was only one thing for it: if he couldn't get to Tan and ultimately
to Paulton, he would have to wait for Paulton to come to him.

Seconds later, his phone rang.

'Harry?' It was Jean.

Her voice brought an instant feeling of disquiet. 'Hi, you.
What is it?'

'Umm . . . I don't want to ask silly questions,' she said carefully, 'but . . . are you having me followed?'

FORTY-TWO

Harry felt his gut go cold. Vetting of families and friends
when working for the security and intelligence services
was an occupational hazard you lived with. Having

strangers delving into every aspect of your life and background wasn't pleasant, but it was part of the job and something you learned to live with. But why would Five or Six choose to take an interest in Jean now, of all times?

'Why do you ask?'

'I couldn't sleep last night, and got up for a drink. When I glanced out of the window I saw two men sitting in a van just along the street. They were still there this morning, although they'd changed position slightly.'

'They're probably watching someone else.' Even as he said it, instinct told him it wasn't likely. London was a huge city, and no doubt there were plenty of individuals currently under a twenty-four-hour watch by the authorities and private security companies all over the metropolitan area. Yet why should Jean be one of them? And any official surveillance would be a lot more discreet.

It could only mean one thing: the Protectory.

'It feels a lot more personal to me,' said Jean. 'After Michael was killed and journalists hung around hoping for a story, I got into the habit of checking the street. I still do it.'

'What do they look like?' He had to remain calm, to avoid feeding any sense of concern through to Jean. She had been through the mill after her husband, Michael, had died in Iraq, with a small media buzz surrounding her for what seemed like weeks. This would certainly have reminded her of those times.

'Young, mid-twenties. Short haircuts but not military. Mediterranean types, wearing blouson jackets and jeans. They're sitting in a red VW van – I'm not sure of the model. Are they from Thames House?' Jean knew enough about Harry's work to venture a reasonable guess at where any security related interest might originate.

'I'll get it checked.' He knew it would be waste of time, even though the descriptions didn't match Zubac or Ganic. These two were too young. He guessed the two Bosnians were keeping a low profile at the moment after the attack on the police station. But how difficult would it be to get two men – probably fellow countrymen – to do some basic legwork for them? They wouldn't need specific skills apart from patience, the ability to keep their eyes open and a healthy fear of failing.

Unless they had been given specific orders to do something else.

'Can you stay where you are for a while?' He hoped he sounded casual. 'I'll come round.'

'OK. I'll ring Felicity and tell her I'll be in later. Is this dangerous?' She came across as amazingly calm, and Harry wished he was with her right now.

'I doubt it. They're probably looking for someone else.'

He rang off and went to a locked drawer inside a cupboard, and took out the VP70 semi-automatic and inserted the magazine. Then he rang Rik.

'You need some fresh air,' he said. 'And I need your help. Bring the Heckler. I'll pick you up.'

Rik knew by his tone not to question it. 'I'm ready.'

As Harry drove fast towards Rik's flat in Paddington, he realized that he had got precisely what he'd wanted: the undiluted attention of the Protectory. Except that instead of watching him, they had latched on to Jean. The one weak link in his background. And there was only one person he could think of who could have told them about that.

Paulton.

FORTY-THREE

The door of Jean's flat swung open with a faint puff of sound on the carpet.

Harry breathed in the familiar smells of her perfume and felt his stomach turn to ice.

This door shouldn't be open.

He'd come in through the back entrance to the block, avoiding the street where the two watchers were sitting in a red VW Kombi. Rik had stayed in a side street nearby, keeping an eye on them while Harry came in to check on Jean.

He stepped across the threshold, nerves humming with anticipation. If anyone was waiting for him, they would not be able to conceal their presence completely. A scrape of fabric, an unguarded intake of breath, something would always give them away.

There was nothing.

He moved along the hallway. No furniture out of place, no signs of a struggle, no debris . . . or worse.

He checked each room, leading with the gun. Each space was empty save for a lingering trace of Jean's presence, tantalizing and almost painful. Where the hell had she got to?

He made his way back to the front door of the flat, beginning to feel a desperate sense of panic. Surely they couldn't have—?

'Harry?' Rik's voice was a soft murmur coming from the mobile in Harry's top pocket. He tapped the mobile twice in response. *Go ahead.*

'The two guys are still in the VW van. You OK?'

Harry breathed out and lowered the gun. 'She's not here,' he said. 'Her door was open. Can you see inside the van?'

'Shit. Give me two . . . I'll do a walk by.'

He heard the sound of breathing and the rub of cloth as Rik moved out into the main street, then an increase in traffic noise. Ten seconds, twenty seconds; he was beginning to get impatient and on the point of going down when Rik spoke.

'Two young guys trying to look hard. They look half asleep to me. Definitely a surveillance job. Can't see inside the back, though. What do you want me to do?'

'Stay on them. I'll join you.'

Harry pocketed the gun and walked back downstairs, gut churning with fear at what might have happened to Jean. Had the watchers called in help and had her lifted? Had she panicked and fled? No and no. If they had taken her, they wouldn't need to hang around. And Jean didn't do panic. She must still be around here somewhere. So, there must be another explanation. She had to have slipped out for some reason.

That still left the watchers to deal with.

Harry left the block of flats by the rear entrance and made his way round to the street where the two men were stationed. Instead of heading straight towards them, he took a narrow street at right angles to the one where they were parked, passing Rik on the way. Rik was wearing his sling and clutching a clipboard, playing street canvasser and stopping the occasional pedestrian, able to act out in full view of the watchers while keeping an eye on them.

Harry reached an intersection and turned left then left again, eventually completing the circumference of the block until he came back to the main street. On the way, he picked up a black garbage bag bulging with old telephone directories, a throw-out from a renovation job in a nearby house.

Nobody expects a tail to carry a garbage bag.

He was now in front of the Kombi, which was parked thirty yards away. A crushed Coke can lay in the gutter by the driver's door. The two men inside watched him appear, then saw the rubbish bag in his hand and lost interest.

Sloppy tradecraft, thought Harry. They had parked facing against the traffic, which was a big no-no and made them stand out. It meant they weren't professionals, but that was a good thing. Professionals would already have detected something not quite kosher about him and would be driving away fast. Or shooting.

Rik had broken off talking to a young woman further along the street and was walking towards him, the clipboard in evidence and his other hand parked inside his sling. He was limping noticeably, too.

Harry smiled in spite of the circumstances. It was a neat touch, if a bit dramatic. Who would expect any kind of threat from a man with a gimpy leg *and* his arm in a sling?

He approached the Kombi, timing his pace to coincide with Rik's arrival at the rear of the van. Five paces short of the vehicle, he moved to the kerb and dropped the garbage bag alongside a bin, shaking his head in a disgruntled resident look, then moved off to continue on by. As he did so, he checked the pavement both ways. No pedestrians close by, nobody watching. No collateral risk if anything should kick off. Otherwise, a few passing cars, a FedEx delivery truck just pulling in along the street, but most of the drivers too intent on their progress to take any notice.

As he drew level with the Kombi's front wing, Harry turned and stepped in fast against the driver's door, preventing it from opening. In the same instant, Rik moved out into the street and walked up to the passenger door, tapping on the window.

The men inside scrambled to sit up, the passenger upsetting a plastic bottle of mocha milk drink over his lap with a shout of protest while the driver turned to stare at Harry with a look of alarm. He began to reach for the ignition.

Then he saw the gun in Harry's hand, resting against the glass. Harry made a circular motion with his hand, and the driver hesitated, then lowered the window. A loud tap from Rik and the passenger saw the gun's twin not two inches from his shoulder, hidden inside Rik's sling. He also lowered his window, but with reluctance.

Both men were in their twenties, dressed casually in jeans and jackets, and would have passed unnoticed in the street. Neither had shaved for a couple of days, and had short, scrubby hair. The driver was suffering an outbreak of acne. The passenger stared across at Harry, deliberately ignoring the gun right next to him. Harry identified him as the leader of the two, all attitude and bravado.

'Police,' he said, and reached in and removed the keys from the ignition. He nodded at Rik to check the back. Rik disappeared for a moment, and there was the sound of a door opening, then closing. He reappeared at the passenger window and shook his head. No sign of Jean.

'Can I see your driver's licence?'

The driver looked surprised and shook his head. 'We are waiting for job,' he said, his accent thick. 'Sorry, officer. We are painters. What is this? Are we doing wrong?' His look of wide-eyed innocence would have been convincing had the passenger not fisted him in the leg with a muttered warning.

Harry didn't understand what he'd said, but murmured, 'Ah, Bosnians, I see. Now we're getting somewhere.' He decided to rattle them, to keep them off-balance. 'Did Zubac and Ganic send you? Get you to keep an eye on a flat across the street?'

The driver's mouth dropped open in recognition, but the passenger said something else and he snapped it shut again.

Rik said, 'You've got a lot to say for yourself, sunshine.' He pushed his gun forward until the barrel was resting against the passenger's shoulder, which got his full attention. At such close range, there would be no dodging a bullet. 'What are you doing here?'

'Painters,' the passenger answered dully. 'Like he said. You not police, so what you want?' He stared at Harry with knowing contempt, but there was no hiding the doubt in his eyes. British police he understood; they had rules and regulations in situations such as this. But anyone else carrying guns in London was an unknown quantity, and therefore to be treated with caution.

Harry pushed the tip of his gun barrel up against the driver's nose, forcing his head back so that his companion could see what would happen if he pulled the trigger. He didn't care right now whether anyone saw them, he was growing angrier at the threat to Jean. 'Wallets. Now!' It was sharp and brutal, and the driver grunted with pain, his eyes streaming, but it achieved the desired effect. Both men handed over their wallets, which were of cheap leather and slim.

There wasn't much to help. The driver's name was Antun Goranuvic and his colleague was Davud. Brothers or cousins. There was no way of telling if they were their genuine names, and Harry doubted it mattered anyway. The wallets held a few notes in sterling and euros, some credit cards and one or two photos, but nothing to say who they worked for or where they came from.

He looked at Rik and nodded at his gun. 'How many shells have you got in that since the last job?'

Rik didn't miss a beat. He gave a lazy smile and said, 'Enough. Why?'

'Shoot them both. Now.' Harry turned and walked away.

FORTY-FOUR

'**W**ait!' He had taken just three steps before the driver, who he figured was the weaker of the two, decoded the instruction and his nerve broke.

Harry turned back and stood by the window. Now it was the passenger who looked the most worried. His attitude was gone and his knuckles were clenched tight on his knees, the cloth wet with the spilled drink.

'We have not seen her,' he muttered. 'The lady. I show you.' He reached up and gingerly took a slip of paper from behind the sun-visor. It held Jean's name and address written in ink and a photo clipped to one corner.

'Who gave you this?'

There was a momentary hesitation before the driver said, 'What you say before . . . Zubac and Ganic. They came to us and said we should do this.' He wasn't looking at Harry, instead staring rigidly to his front as if holding on to the last bit of courage he could muster and not doing too well.

'And what were you to do, exactly?'

'Watch and report. That is all.'

'Report where?'

But the man shook his head. 'You will not shoot us. But the one who hires us . . . for this he will kill us both.' Harry saw his lip beginning to tremble and a sheen of sweat lining his forehead. He exchanged a look with Rik, who raised his eyebrows. Whoever had hired these two had got them terrified. He wondered how. They should be able to cobble together some kind of story about being caught napping, surely. It happened to everyone—

Then his instincts kicked in. He'd missed an obvious trick. Why were these two sitting out here in a red van? Red vans weren't exactly uncommon, but nobody mounted a surveillance so openly . . . unless they were meant to be seen. And these two being so petrified could only mean one thing: *they knew they also were being watched.* He leaned against the van and glanced surreptitiously along the street, following the driver's line of sight. The only way these two would have been so easily scared was if they knew the watchers were close by. The street was getting busier, with several cars moving in each direction, gradually building towards peak traffic. Other vehicles were lining the kerb, including the FedEx truck a hundred yards away. The driver was sorting packages at the side door, then carrying them to a nearby shop.

There was too much going on; it was impossible to tell where the watcher might be.

'Wait here.' Harry stepped back from the van and rang Ballatyne. 'I need a favour.' He told the MI6 man where he was and why, and gave him the number of the van and the names of the two men. 'Whoever employs these two has them scared. They won't talk to me and I think someone else is in the area keeping an eye on them.'

'Is Jean all right?' He heard Ballatyne snap his fingers at someone in the background, already issuing instructions to get some men on the move.

'I don't know yet—' He broke off, glancing automatically towards the block of flats. Jean was standing by the side of the building, out of sight of the street. She waved and gave a signal that she was OK, and Harry heaved a sigh of relief. He said, 'Forget that . . . I see her. She's fine.'

'Glad to hear it. There's an undercover unit not far from you. They'll pick them up and tail them. Leave it with us from here on.'

Harry thanked him and tossed the driver his keys through the window. It was time for some play-acting to fool the watchers. 'One thing you should know,' he said coldly. 'If I see you again, I'll kill you.' He jerked his thumb in dismissal.

'That went well,' said Rik, as the Kombi disappeared along the street. He looked at Harry. 'I don't know what that order to shoot did to those two, but it frightened the crap out of me.' He frowned. 'What's going on?'

'My guess is,' said Harry, 'they were meant to be seen and someone else wasn't. They were decoys. Follow me and don't look round.'

They crossed the street to the cover of the block of flats, and Harry folded Jean in his arms. 'You all right?'

'Yes.' Her voice sounded firm, but he could feel a faint tremor running through her. 'Well, I am now.'

'Where were you?' he asked, biting down on an instinctive desire to reproach her. 'Your door was open.'

She pulled back from him. 'I did what your colleague said.'

'Colleague?'

'Yes. A woman. She sounded young. She said I was in danger and should go immediately to a neighbour and stay there until you arrived, and to leave the door unlocked to prevent damage if they forced their way in.'

Harry stared at her. What the hell was going on? Was this Ballatyne working behind the scenes, putting someone on to Jean as a precaution? He remembered the young woman who'd been watching them in Victoria Embankment Gardens. Maybe that was who the caller had been. If so, why hadn't he said anything just now?

'She said we were colleagues?'

'Well, not exactly.' Jean looked confused. 'But she said it was for my sake and yours, and you were on your way.' She looked at him, eyes wide. 'What's going on? You don't know who she is, do you?'

'I can guess.'

'Never mind. Did you see the other men?'

'What others?'

'Two older men. They're in a grey car down by the shops. They arrived just after the woman called, and I was looking through the window for you. They crossed the road towards the building, so I slipped out the back and left the door open as she'd said.'

Harry let out a long breath. This was all moving too fast. Behind him, Rik was standing by the corner of the building, studying the street. 'Harry.'

Harry moved alongside him. The FedEx truck was gone. It had been concealing a grey Renault parked further along the street. Two men were sitting inside. Both looked big, one with short hair, the other bald.

Zubac and Ganic. It had to be.

Instinct made Harry glance up the street behind him. A police car was approaching. He recognized one of the Armed Response Unit Volvo V70 vehicles. Remembering the Bosnians' disregard for the police, and their likely response when they saw the car, he stepped out from behind the building and started walking along the street, his semi-automatic cradled inside his jacket. Rik followed and crossed the street to the far side.

They were thirty yards along, walking in parallel, when the men in the Renault sat up and the engine burst into life. It was unclear whether they were reacting to Harry and Rik or the police car. Seconds later, the Renault was reversing at speed, side-swiping a scooter parked at the kerb, then it performed a handbrake turn and raced away after the red Kombi.

The police car, caught by a line of school children on a

pedestrian crossing, sat helplessly, then roared off in pursuit. But they were already too late.

FORTY-FIVE

'The two in the red van were low-level messengers,' said Ballatyne. He called later that day as Harry was heading home. Rik had made his own way earlier, to continue the hunt for Tan. Jean had agreed reluctantly to stay with friends for a couple of days, and Harry had seen her safely delivered to make sure she wasn't being followed.

'Who for?'

'Not sure. But they led the undercover unit to a C'emal Soran, a shopkeeper in Hackney. He's clean here, barring missed opportunities by the Serious Organized Crimes Agency or Five. But they've got quite a file on him in Sarajevo. He was suspected for years of being a freelance quartermaster for a number of gangs, supplying weapons and cars. Unfortunately, with all the fighting, they didn't have the resources to get hard evidence. He got out ahead of an investigation and so far, nobody's been able to come up with reasons enough to bring him up on charges. Call me prejudiced, but I doubt he's changed his spots. We're doing a thorough check on him right now.'

'Who were the two in the van?'

'Family members, that's all we've got. No papers on file, though. They claimed they knew nothing about nothing, jobbing decorators waiting for a pick-up until you arrived and started waving guns in their faces. They looked terrified, according to the officer who interviewed them, but he thinks that was down to Soran hovering in the background like the angel of death.'

'Soran? Or Zubac and Ganic?'

'Good point. All three, probably. The cops didn't have reason to search so they had to pull back after talking to the two young ones. In the end, they had nothing to hold them on. My guess is they'll be out of the country by morning.'

'And no signs of Zubac and Ganic?'

'No. Nothing obvious at the ports, anyway. They've probably gone to ground until the fuss dies down.' He paused. 'Any idea what their plan was?'

'With Jean? No.' Harry didn't like to think what would have happened if the two men had taken her. The message would have been simple: back off and stay that way. Whether that would have resulted in getting Jean back in one piece was a moot point. He doubted it somehow; the Protectory seemed to be playing for keeps, and getting him off their tail would have been a high priority.

Ballatyne continued, 'We're going to spring a surprise on Soran this evening, just for the hell of it. SO19 are going to raid the shop. If you want in on it, be my guest. You might find something. I'll let you know where and when.'

'Thanks. I'll be there.' The answer was automatic. This had gone too far already, and Harry wanted to get the men responsible.

'You didn't get far with Fort Knox, I hear.'

'Not yet. Why?'

'I had a call from the State Department. Seems Major Dundas carries some weight in the corridors of power, courtesy of a brother-in-law who's a state senator. He complained about interference from the British, namely you, and they're currently assessing how much to share with us.'

'Dundas is an idiot. I asked for a check on a name, that's all.'

'Right. I think rubbing Bradley Manning in his face was a bit harsh. They're all a bit sensitive about that young man. Still, I'll leave it with you to sort out.'

Harry rang off wondering if the real purpose of that exchange had been to get him involved in the police raid on Soran. As for the message from the US State Department, he didn't hold out much hope of getting any further cooperation from Garcia. The lines would have been instantly shut down. But why the reluctance to help? All he was looking for was a name.

He was surprised, therefore, to find an email waiting for him at home. It was from someone calling himself candlepoint81 at a Gmail account, and the message read:

Master Sgt Gregory C. Turpowicz ('Turp') – b. 1968, Ft Worth, Texas – served 101st Airborne Div (Air Assault) Ft

Campbell Kentucky – served Kosovo 2000 – Iraq and Afghanistan – wounded 2003 (Iraq) and 2008 (Afghanistan) – listed as deserter January 2010. Believed to be Canada or Europe.

It had to be Garcia, Major Dundas's assistant at Fort Knox. Harry was wondering why she should have contacted him via an anonymous email account, when he scrolled down and saw another line of text.

This soldier has been de-classified as NFA (No Further Action).

There was no signature. Harry was convinced the message came from Garcia. He debated dialling Fort Knox again, but decided against it. If Garcia was operating as some kind of whistleblower, he didn't see that compromising her would help. But it still didn't explain why Dundas and the State Department were being so coy. And what did an NFA classification mean? Had Turpowicz come back in? Or was he dead?

His phone rang. The number was withheld.

'Mr Tate?' A woman's voice, cool and efficient, Home Counties smooth. Faintly familiar.

'Yes.'

'I'm calling on behalf of Richard Ballatyne. He wonders if you could meet him in Victoria Embankment Gardens, same as last time. Thirty minutes from now. Can you confirm?'

'Make it forty,' Harry said automatically. He cut the connection and rang Ballatyne's number. A man's voice picked up.

'He's not here. Can I help?'

'No, thanks.' Harry couldn't think why a personal meeting was necessary simply to exchange information about a police raid, but Ballatyne was clearly comfortable at keeping up their contact. If that led through the Bosnians eventually to Paulton, he'd be stupid to throw his dummy from the pram just because he didn't like being tugged around. Even so, he felt uneasy and rang Rik and told him where he was going.

As he stepped outside the building, he met one of his neighbours. Mrs Fletcher lived on the ground floor and saw herself as the local neighbourhood watch. She was fencepost slim and seemed permanently dressed in an elegant long coat and scarf.

'Mr Tate,' she greeted him. 'Did your visitor get hold of you?'

Harry was forced to stop. The manner in which she blocked his way indicated that it was more than just a passing question, and he wondered if she had ever worked for the Security Service. 'What visitor was that, Mrs Fletcher?'

'The young woman I saw coming down the stairs earlier today. I didn't recognize her, and when I asked if I could help, she more or less brushed me off. I must say, you try to help people and they respond with rudeness.' Her expression was accusatory, as if Harry was in the habit of consorting with riff-raff.

'Can you describe her?'

'Just a young woman. Reasonably well dressed, early thirties, I'd say. A business person, perhaps, maybe an estate agent?' She fixed him with a stare. 'You're not thinking of moving, are you?' She made it sound like jumping a sinking ship.

'No, I'm not.' It must have been one of Ballatyne's people, he decided, and made a mental note to check. He went to move past Mrs Fletcher, but she touched his arm, a tentative smile hovering around her eyes.

'A few of us in the block are having a coffee morning later this week. We were wondering if you would like to come. Maybe we could get to know a little more about you. Say Thursday?'

Harry wondered how to refuse without upsetting her. She was only being neighbourly, and telling her to mind her own business was a bit strong. She and her coffee table irregulars had undoubtedly discussed him at length already. Instead he said, 'Sounds very nice. But Thursday is my day for gun practice.'

FORTY-SIX

Victoria Embankment Gardens held its customary gathering of desperate smokers, leisurely tourists and a growing flow of early homeward-bound commuters. Harry was early, having hit the underground on the run just as a train was arriving.

He did a tour of the area, checking the access paths before entering the garden. There was no sign of Ballatyne or his posse of outriders, but that didn't mean he wasn't waiting nearby. Georgio's restaurant apart, he wondered if the rumours surrounding the Vauxhall Cross collective weren't true; that like some rare breeds of wild cat, they rarely revisited the same place twice.

He approached the bench where he and Ballatyne had sat last time. It was vacant and he took a seat at one end and stretched his legs. Maybe a few minutes alone would be good for his thought processes. If he could just get rid of the minor prickling feeling on the back of his neck, he might almost manage to relax.

'Hello, Harry.'

The prickling feeling intensified. He recognized the voice. It was the young woman who had called to set up the meeting. But that wasn't why his internal alarm bells were ringing. The recognition came from further back, when it had been face to face and unencumbered by the distortion of a phone line.

As she sat down beside him, he turned and looked her in the eye.

It was Clare Jardine.

FORTY-SEVEN

Harry stared at her, wondering what had brought this cold, calculating killer back into his world at this particular moment in time. Whatever, he doubted it would be good news.

'Got a moment?' she said chattily. 'We need to talk.'

He wanted to refuse, to walk away and not look back. But he couldn't. He had to know what she was doing here. The last time he'd seen her, she had been sitting on the Embankment alongside her former boss, Sir Anthony Bellingham, Deputy Director (Operations) of MI6, moments before she killed him by slicing into his femoral artery.

'Why not?' There would be no Ballatyne, then. No wonder her voice had sounded vaguely familiar; he'd heard it often

enough in the flesh. It must have been Clare who had warned
Jean about the Bosnians, too. The realization that she knew that
much about his private life was deeply unsettling.

'Sorry, Harry. Secret squirrel habits never die, do they?' She
patted his knee. 'Still, this is nice.' She was dressed in a smart
leather jacket and slacks, and looked fit and capable . . . and to
Harry, quite lethal. Her hair was cropped short and her face had
lost the drawn look he remembered from his last sighting of her
on the way back from Red Station. But then, he reminded himself,
she had still been getting over being shot at. That kind of experience has an effect on people.

'What do you want?'

'You're going after Paulton.' It wasn't a question.

'Where did you hear that?' There was no point denying it; she
probably had an inside track on security matters and knew roughly
what was going on, even if not the fine details. Professional links
made in the service were not always easily broken, no matter
what the circumstances. And Clare's circumstances were that if
she were spotted by the security establishment, she would go
away for a long time. They didn't like their senior people being
murdered within sight of the building, no matter how badly they
might have deserved it.

'I've got friends. They don't condone what I did, but they
understand.'

She hadn't taken her hand from his knee, he noticed, and it
was now covered by a folded newspaper. He got a memory flash
of her sitting alongside Bellingham not very far from this spot,
and felt a sudden tightness in his belly.

'You slotted a senior figure in SIS,' he reminded her. 'That
kind of thing catches up with you sooner or later.'

'Maybe. Maybe not. Be honest, Harry, didn't you want to do
the same? He tried to have you topped, for God's sake.' Her
voice was low but there was a sharp brittleness he didn't recall
from their last meeting, and a faint tic beneath one eye.

She was right, though. He'd thought about it many times since,
and wondered what he'd have done if Clare hadn't got there first.
Paulton had already disappeared by the time they returned from
Red Station in Georgia, getting out just ahead of the invading
Russians. Turning in Bellingham to the authorities and relying

on them to take appropriate action wouldn't have been enough; the man had the connections if not to evade punishment altogether, certainly to avoid its more damaging extremes. In the end, he would have disappeared into a quiet retirement, countering the token establishment slap on the wrist by claiming that he had done it all for Queen and country.

'How do you know about Jean? And my address?' he added. The mystery caller Mrs Fletcher had seen. It had to have been her.

'Same friends, how else? The intel community is the biggest gossip mill in the world, you know that. Bunch of floppy lips, most of them.' She shrugged. 'There are no secrets in our profession, Harry. I even know what you're up to. The Protectory is for real, isn't it? Who'd have thought . . . a branch of the Samaritans for deserters and conchies.'

'How did you know to warn Jean?'

'I'd tried making contact at your place, but the resident dragon down the hall put me off, so I decided to think laterally and asked around.'

'It's hardly public knowledge.'

'Oh, come on . . . you know what I mean. Like I said, nothing's totally secret, is it?'

'You trawled Six's files.' It was the only way she could have known . . . unless she had friends in Five, too.

She gave him a teasing smile but didn't deny it. 'It's what they trained us to do, isn't it – use whatever assets we have? She looks nice; just your type. Bit too elegant for my tastes, though.'

'I'll be sure to tell her.' She was trying to annoy him. 'How did you spot the two watchers?'

'The two wannabes in the red van?' She rolled her eyes. 'God, they were too obvious. So obvious, in fact, that I scouted around and saw the others. They looked the real deal. Tough job you've got on, Harry. Is it your way of laying ghosts?' Suddenly the humour was gone and she was searching his face for something, trying to read his expression. 'Is that it?'

'I'm doing what I can, Clare. It doesn't explain why you're here, though.'

'Simple. I've got ghosts, too. And Paulton was part of setting up Red Station. Maybe I don't forgive as easily as you, or maybe

I'm just a bad-tempered, hormonal bitch. Call it what you like. I'm hoping you won't get in my way, that's all.' She shuffled a little closer to him on the bench seat and smiled, a hint of perfume overlaying the metallic smell from the river. She tightened her hand on his thigh. It was a strange gesture of intimacy given their last meeting, which hadn't been particularly warm, and the fact that she had no interest in men. Indeed, her reason for being banished from MI6 in the first place had been due to falling victim in a honey trap, where the intended target – a woman – had reversed the roles with career-damaging consequences for Clare.

Then she moved the newspaper to one side and looked down. Harry couldn't help it; he did the same.

She was holding a powder compact, silvered and elegant and entirely ordinary. In fact it was very ordinary, an accessory nobody would look at twice, wouldn't even give a passing thought to. Except that this one had an extra, sinister facility beyond the cosmetic: it housed a three-inch razor-sharp curved blade now protruding from the edge, retractable at the push of a button. And the blade was resting against Harry's inner thigh.

FORTY-EIGHT

'You haven't lost your taste for cold steel, I see.' Harry tried to remain calm. He'd seen what Clare could do with this thing. If he tried anything she'd cut him before he could move an inch and be gone before he could raise the alarm.

'Sorry, Harry. Try to call out or pull away and you know what I'll do. You'll bleed out before they can get you to hospital . . . and I won't hang around to help.' She continued smiling but it stretched only as far as her mouth. 'I really don't want to do that, though.'

'What do you want, then? I'm sure it's not to go over old times.'

She licked her top lip. On any other woman at such close

quarters, the gesture might have been almost erotic, a promise of things to come. On Clare it gave him the shivers because there was nothing in her eyes. Where there should have been shades of colour and sparkles of light, there were bottomless pools.

'I want Paulton. Simple as that.'

Harry shook his head. 'Paulton's mine. You got your revenge with Bellingham.'

She lifted both eyebrows. 'I see. Somebody handed out reserved tickets, did they? I don't recall agreeing to that.' The pressure on his leg increased steadily, and he braced himself. 'I don't think you understand, Harry. This isn't open to negotiation. I just want to tell you that.'

'Hey, look who it isn't!'

A figure sat down alongside Clare, less than a foot away. She had been so intent on Harry, she hadn't noticed his approach until it was too late.

It was Rik Ferris, wearing his sling and carrying a mug of coffee.

Clare turned and looked at him. But the pressure of the knife stayed on Harry's leg, a measure of her self-control. She looked to her front again, momentarily surprised, then said calmly, 'Fuck off, Ferris. This is a private chat between grown-ups.'

'Yeah, I know. But it's a bit difficult, see.' Rik placed his mug on the bench alongside him and scratched his chest. He was wearing a leather jacket over one of his more colourful T-shirts. He slid his good hand inside the sling over his other arm, then smiled. Their shoulders were almost touching, and Clare must have sensed something, some unseen movement undetectable by anyone else. Or maybe it was expression in Rik's eyes. She dropped her gaze and fastened on the inside of the sling itself.

'Heckler and Koch nine millimetre,' he told in a mock whisper. 'Eighteen-round magazine; if I miss you with the first one – which I think is hugely fucking unlikely, to be perfectly honest, even for me – I'll get you with the rest.'

'My,' she said in mock admiration, 'you have grown up into a big, bad boy. I heard about what you did to that girl in St James's Park.' Her face hardened, taunting him. 'Get off on shooting women, do you?'

'Only the ones who piss me off.'

'Then you should study your ballistics; you pull that trigger and a nine mil will go right through me and into Harry . . . probably through him and the next person, too. So screw you, baby face.'

'Fair point.' Rik nodded without turning a hair. 'Very fair. Only I did study ballistics and these rounds carry a reduced charge. They're also loaded with soft noses, so you'll cop the lot.' His expression this time was every bit as cold as hers. He leaned closer, nudging her shoulder, and whispered, 'Take the blade off Harry's leg or I'll fucking shoot you in the ribs, you stroppy cow. You know what that'll do to your insides, don't you? Then where's your revenge got you?'

An age seemed to pass. Clare didn't move, evaluating the likelihood that he might be bluffing. Her eyes were fixed on Rik's face, seeking a hint of hesitation, of weakness. For Harry, waiting for the blade to turn and open his leg to the bone, it was too long. He batted her hand away and shifted sideways before she could move, leaving her marooned, with Rik too close for her to retaliate.

Along the path, a man in a smart suit was watching them, a mobile phone in one hand. He'd probably picked up on their body language, seeing a woman bracketed by two men and misinterpreting the situation. Harry almost wanted to explain who, if anyone, was in real danger here, but he doubted the man would believe him. If this carried on any longer, it was in danger of going public.

'It's over,' he said quietly. 'Leave it.'

Clare closed her hand with a faint click and the compact disappeared. 'OK, boys. I get the message. You can't blame a girl for trying, though, can you?' She stood up and looked at Rik with a tiger's smile. 'You'd better watch it, Ferris. You've been mixing with him too long.' She glanced at Harry. 'And you, big feller; call me, won't you?' She turned and walked away, back straight and heels clicking on the pathway.

'Reduced charge?' Harry muttered, watching her until she disappeared out of the gardens. He didn't entirely trust her not to suddenly turn and start blazing away. 'Where did that bullshit come from?'

Rik looked pale. He picked up his coffee and took a sip. His hand was shaking slightly. 'I was kidding, wasn't I? Christ, I wasn't about to start blasting away out here – and she knew it.'

Harry's mobile buzzed. 'That's the thing: I don't think she did.' He checked the screen. Ballatyne. 'What's worse, neither did I.'

FORTY-NINE

'Y ou trying to be coy by any chance?' Ballatyne sounded tired. 'You call and don't leave a message, my boys see that as a bad sign. Says an asset's feeling nervy and leaving a trail for others to follow.'

It was the second reference to an asset in quick succession; the first had been by Clare Jardine. 'Nervy's right; I got a message to meet you on the Embankment.'

'Couldn't have. I was busy.'

'I know that now.' Harry told him about the phone call and finding Clare Jardine waiting for him with her trusty little knife.

'That could have been nasty. She did Bellingham like that, didn't she?'

'Thanks for reminding me.' She had also cut the man's throat, Harry remembered. Artistry with a blade in the blink of an eye. He felt an echo of a twitch in his leg at the lack of expression on Clare's face and the thought of what she might have done had Rik not been there. He had no compunction about confirming her part in her former boss's death because she had been caught on CCTV in the act. It had earned her a place on MI6's Most Wanted list.

'What did she want?'

'Paulton's head on a plate and me to step aside. But not in that order.'

'She'll have to join the queue, won't she? How did she seem?'

'Tense. Angry. I'd say she's got issues – and an accurate inside track on what you and I are working on. She found Jean, she got my home address and phone, and she knows pretty much up to the minute what I'm doing. She even knew you were out of the office.'

'Christ, what a bloody nerve. We've got a chatterbox in the woodpile. I'll put out an alert and set off a security trawl through her old section.'

'Good idea. But it was Clare who spotted the Bosnians and warned Jean to get out. I've moved her to a safe place just in case.'

Ballatyne grunted. 'Next thing you'll be telling me is Jardine's not all bad.'

Harry wasn't that naïve. 'She helped Jean because she wanted to get to me. That doesn't mean she wouldn't roast me if the situation came up.' He realized he was still holding the newspaper which Clare had left behind. She must have thrust it at him as she stood up. Or maybe he'd grasped it subconsciously – he couldn't remember.

Ballatyne had switched topics. He gave Harry the address of a shop in Dalston Lane, and the name and contact number of an officer in SO19, the Metropolitan Police firearms unit. Harry dug out a pen and wrote it down in the margin of the newspaper. It was that day's copy of *The Times*. 'Be there at eleven thirty tonight. They're going to turn Soran's place upside down. They'll probably find nothing but it might be a good idea if you were in attendance.'

'What do you expect to find?' He flipped the newspaper round. Something had been written across the lower half of the page, just above the political and military engagements for the week. It was a mobile phone number.

'Anything or nothing. Soran's clever enough to stay below the radar, but even clever people get careless. If he thinks nobody's going to touch him, it's time to show him otherwise. Keep Ferris out of it, though. SO19 don't need any walking wounded as bystanders.'

Harry switched off and found Rik watching him over the rim of his coffee mug. He handed him the newspaper and tapped the number written down. 'Any chance you could find a subscriber name for that? It's probably a disposable but try anyway.'

'Sure. You off somewhere?'

'I've been invited to a party.' Before Rik could ask, he stood up. 'Sorry – grown-ups only. And you've still got Tan to hunt for.'

'Spoilsport.' Rik didn't look too upset at being left out, though. 'I've got a couple of ideas about her . . . something a mate suggested. I'll shout if anything comes up.'

Other than a few early drunks and late workers, none of whom were paying any attention, Dalston Lane was reasonably quiet when Harry walked along the pavement and tapped on the passenger window of a transit van with a cleaner's logo on the side. A scattering of other unmarked vehicles indicated that SO19 were here in numbers, with a perimeter tight enough to stop anyone from leaving the area if they needed to. As the window went down, he caught the mixed aromas of coffee and body odour and heard the clink of metal from inside the van.

'Harry Tate,' he said softly.

'Good to have you along.' The man in the passenger seat was heavily built and wearing a helmet and dark boiler suit. He was holding a large metal battering ram, known as a 'universal key' between his knees. He nodded towards the front. 'The boss is along the street in the control car. He asked if you could stay back until we go in and the way's clear. A unit will block the front of the shop and we'll hit the rear. Less likely to get cut by flying glass that way when I use this.' He jiggled the ram up and down and gave Harry a brief once-over. 'You ever done this before?'

Harry thought back to the last time he'd kicked a door in. He'd been holding a weapon then, and ready to shoot anything that moved. Although he was armed now, this wasn't quite the same. 'A few times. But I'll stay out of your way until you're in.'

'Fair enough.' The man half turned his head. 'Col? Refreshments for our guest, if you please.'

A hand came out from the back of the van clutching a small plastic cup. It was steaming and smelled of coffee.

'We've got ten minutes, Harry,' said the voice behind the cup. The side door slid back. 'Climb in and get that down you.'

Harry thanked him and climbed aboard, nodding to half a dozen helmeted and suited men sitting patiently in the dark. The tension in the air was palpable and someone was humming quietly. He sat and drank his coffee in silence; they didn't need conversation, and probably had him tagged as a Whitehall watcher sent to monitor proceedings.

His phone buzzed. It was Rik. 'No joy on the mobile number. You want me to try it to see who answers?'

'Don't worry, I'll try it later.' He switched off at a burst of static on the vehicle's radio, followed by the order to approach the premises and for cars on the outer perimeter to close in. Harry was surprised by the numbers involved. Ballatyne must have called in some big favours to get this level of help, and was taking no chances. Even if it came up empty, it would send a powerful message to Soran and his associates that they were under the spotlight.

He let the men out and climbed in alongside the driver, who sensed his impatience and glanced at his watch. 'Give it a minute or so and they'll be in.'

Harry lowered the side window. From eighty yards away, the coordinated shouting of the teams at the front and rear of the shop, followed by the ram hitting the back door, sounded very loud. It immediately set dogs barking in adjacent premises, and caused one or two lights to go on along the street. Most, however, stayed off; not everyone was keen to be seen joining in the public spectacle, preferring to watch under cover of darkness.

Harry stepped out of the van and walked along the street to the front door, where an officer was standing guard. Two of his colleagues were kneeling on a struggling figure in the middle of the shop, while a third was checking behind the counter and racks with a large flashlight. Harry stepped past them and walked through to the back room, his nose twitching at the spicy atmosphere, where he found a senior officer standing alongside a large man with a bald head. Two armed officers stood in the background. From overhead came the sounds of a search in progress.

'You break my property, you pay,' said the balding man, as something tinkled and a man swore. The man's voice was dull with sleep, enhancing his heavy accent, and Harry thought he recognized the familiar tones of the Sarajevo district of Bosnia and Herzegovina. He'd heard them too many times before, ranging from friendly to downright hostile, ever to forget them. Mostly the latter.

The officer sniffed and looked at Harry. 'You want a word with him?'

Harry shook his head. Questioning the man wouldn't help; Soran would undoubtedly use every lever he could to plead a case of unlawful entry and an invasion of his privacy. 'I'll take a look around, though,' he said, and walked up the stairs. He found several officers conducting a room-by-room search, piling anything of interest at the top of the stairs for removal in evidence bags. Most of it looked like junk, although there was a replica automatic pistol which looked real enough to fool anyone.

The living quarters were cramped and dark, the air heavy with cigarette smoke and the smell of cooking. It was a man's space, with no signs of a woman's touch. Harry knew instinctively that their chances of coming up with anything concrete leading to the two Bosnians who had killed Pike and Barrow and tried to get McCreath were slim. Whatever secrets Soran had were probably well concealed.

He returned downstairs and found the officer and Soran sitting at the room's central table. Soran was spinning a mobile phone with his forefinger, while the officer was asking about the two young men questioned earlier.

'They have gone home,' Soran muttered disinterestedly. 'They do not live here.'

'Home? Where's that?'

Soran shrugged. 'I don't know. Young men, they move all the time . . . change place like I change shirts.' He scowled and waved a hand, the matter of no importance. 'Why should they tell me? I am not their keeper.'

'They work for you?'

'No. They are painting, decorating . . . many jobs like that.'

'What about phone numbers?' said Harry, after a nod from the officer.

'I do not know.' Soran looked up at him. 'Who are you?' He jerked his head at the officer. 'His name I know. Yours I don't.'

It was a delaying tactic, a distraction. Harry ignored it. Instead he picked up the mobile phone from the table and pressed the call button. It showed the last few numbers dialled. He read them aloud and the officer jotted down each one in a notebook.

'Hey!' Soran rounded on Harry, stabbing the air with a stubby finger. 'You cannot do that! Is private property. I complain through my solicitor.'

Harry gave him a cold look. This man had helped the two who had been watching Jean, had probably provided material assistance to Zubac and Ganic. 'You go for it.' He read out the last of the numbers listed, then tossed the phone back on to the table and walked through to the back door, which was sagging off its hinges, courtesy of the metal ram.

Outside, a collection of eager young faces had gathered at the rear gate. From the comments made, he got the impression that they were not unduly upset at seeing C'emal Soran being turned over. He ignored them and made for a small outhouse to one side. It had a substantial door which was out of keeping with the ancient, porous brick walls. It was locked. He went back inside and asked Soran for the key.

'Is lost,' the Bosnian replied without even looking at him. 'Is nothing much in there – storeroom only. I never use.'

Harry nodded, wondering if Soran was being obstructive for the hell of it, or playing a delaying game. 'In that case, you won't mind if we open it for you, will you?' He looked at the officer, who called out for the man with the battering ram and told him to break down the door.

Three heavy blows and the door caved in. It revealed a storeroom with white walls fitted with metal racking piled with cardboard boxes. A camp bed and an armchair were the main anomalies, along with a kettle, milk and two mugs with traces of cold liquid in the bottom. Packets of sugar and tea and an open packet of biscuits lay nearby. Harry touched the kettle with the back of his hand. Difficult to be certain, but he thought it held traces of warmth. Someone had been in here recently. Maybe this was where they had planned on holding Jean, to use her as a bargaining chip.

The man with the battering ram was watching him, and caught on quick. 'I'll get one of the guys to take the temperature,' he said, and spoke into his radio.

Harry nodded. If nothing else, it would prove Soran was lying about the key. He flicked up the thin mattress on the camp bed. Nothing but canvas and the stale tang of unwashed bodies. The armchair was stuffed with foam, lumpy, misshapen and stained, but that was all. He nudged it to one side, then bent and picked up something lying on the floor.

A triangular metal ring.

There was nothing else to see, so he asked the officer to bag up the mugs, biscuit packet and kettle for prints and DNA testing, and left him to it.

He walked back into the building and dropped the ring on the table in front of Soran. It was clear by the man's expression that he recognized it for what it was. So did the police officer, whose jaw dropped.

'This is a pull ring from an M84 stun grenade,' Harry announced. 'It was found in your locked storeroom along with traces of recent occupation. Hours recent, in fact. This, along with chemical and DNA analysis, is going to put you right at the centre of an attack on a south London police station by Zlatco Ganic and Milan Zubac, where at least two officers were shot dead.' He turned to leave, while the officer took out a plastic evidence bag and placed the ring inside, his face grim at what Harry had revealed.

Soran was looking sick and licking his lips. He said nothing.

'You should have got your people to clean up properly,' said Harry. 'Big mistake.'

FIFTY

'Employ undisciplined thugs and that's what you get, in my experience.' Paulton was uneasy at the news of the abortive attempt at lifting Jean Fleming. They should have had her by now. And Tate, too, as he would have galloped to her rescue like an eager bloodhound, no doubt about it. Instead it had fallen apart, following on from the widely circulated news of a terrorist attack on London's Brixton police station, resulting in the deaths of two officers and the serious wounding of several others. No group had claimed outright responsibility for the raid, but two or three were hinting at it in an attempt to gain credibility. As a separate issue, news of a late night police raid on a house belonging to the Bosnian community in the east of the city was just filtering out, although Paulton had already heard the latest details from a contact in London with connections to the Metropolitan Police.

He, Deakin and Turpowicz had relocated once more while awaiting developments in London and the search for Lieutenant Tan. This time they had moved from Nürnberg to a conference centre hotel near Ghent, in Belgium. Groups of businessmen were the norm here, and the three of them would pass unnoticed amid the comings and goings of corporate parties and trade delegations. The grounds were extensive, encompassing a large lake surrounded by woods, and guaranteed privacy. But it was also close enough to major roads should they need a rapid evacuation, something Paulton had insisted on.

Colin Nicholls had not joined them. He had retreated further into the background, claiming to be busy scouting for Tan and checking on other deserters. It left the other three to look after the current business, a move openly welcomed by Deakin. His irritation with his colleague had been growing more evident, and he had begun to voice his impatience with Nicholls' lack of energy and his reluctance to trade on the skills of the people passing through their hands. It had been slowing down his own plans to take the Protectory up a level and place it on a more commercial footing, something which had attracted Paulton to join him in the first place.

'They've never missed before,' Deakin muttered. He was staring into space, unsettled by the repeat failure of his two Bosnian guns.

'Perhaps because they've never previously delegated the work you pay them for to people with no experience. Did they even get inside her flat?'

'Yes, but something had alerted her. She'd disappeared and left the door open.'

Paulton lifted an eyebrow. 'Really? It allows them in but they don't break anything in the process. Clever move.'

Deakin looked sour. 'Isn't it just? Are you sure this Fleming woman doesn't have training? Only it was odd she should bug out just before they arrived.'

'She most likely saw 'em coming, that's why,' growled

Turpowicz. He had said little after hearing of the latest setback. 'Those guys blend into the background like a pair of silverbacks in a toy store.'

'Cut the sniping, will you?' Deakin snapped. 'I hear you – you don't like Zubac and Ganic. I get that. But they have their uses.' He slumped back in his chair, chewing his lip in frustration.

'If you recall,' Paulton put in smoothly, before Turpowicz could argue back and escalate matters, 'the whole idea was to draw Tate out by threatening his girlfriend. Then they could have dealt with him. We've now lost that advantage. Tate will have moved her to a safe house and he'll be on his guard against further attacks.'

'So what do we do?' asked Deakin.

Paulton hesitated before replying. He'd been disappointed at Deakin's reliance on the Bosnians and their decision to involve others without consultation first. That was where Deakin lacked management experience, in his opinion. Maybe he'd been out of the army command structure too long. He should have insisted on the two Bosnians being the only ones in play. That way any exposure through mistakes, such as using amateurs, was minimal, as was the trail back to Deakin and himself. 'We try again, only sooner rather than later. Perhaps the last method was too sophisticated for your pet thugs. I suggest we use them to make a more direct assault and get Tate out of the picture for good so we can get on with business.'

'Direct?' Deakin looked uncertain. 'How direct?'

'The surest way to defeat an enemy is to hit them when they least expect it.'

'Which is?'

'Tate's a soldier, with a soldier's mind-set. After a win, the victors invariably let their defences down. It's human nature. With a man like Harry Tate, it's ingrained. He won't expect us to try again so soon.'

Turpowicz sat up, his face showing understanding. 'Harry? *Harry?* Christ, I *knew* it. You've had this guy Tate tagged from the moment you saw his face. You *do* know him!'

Paulton wanted to bite his tongue. He'd said too much, allowed his need to exert some control over the situation to take over. However, he had survived worse verbal calamities in tougher

company than these two men. He recovered and spread his arms
with barely a break in his stride. 'Mea culpa, gentlemen, mea
culpa. I admit it, I fibbed a little, if only because it didn't seem
relevant at the time.' He held up both hands to ward off their
protests. 'Let me explain. Please. Tate used to work for me. He's
no more a warrant officer than I am – he's a former MI5 officer
who was discharged in disgrace.' He sniffed. 'A little shooting
incident which killed two civilians and a police officer.'

'So why's he still working for the government?' Turpowicz
demanded.

'Because he's deniable, Mr Turpowicz. If anything goes wrong
. . . well, he's not on the books and nobody knows he exists.'
He stared hard at the American who was looking ready to argue.
'Isn't that what Blackwater was all about with their security
contractors? Sorry – Xe, I believe they now like to be called.
Strange name, but that's PR for you.'

'Tate was one of yours?' Deakin was staring at him. 'Christ,
George, you promised me you were clean . . . that they'd forget
all about you. That's why I agreed to let you on board. There's
no risk, you said. Now you've got an intelligence operative on
your tail! Where the hell does that put us?'

'Actually, that's not what Tate's doing.' Paulton's voice dropped
a level, pitched deliberately low so that the two men were forced
to listen. He was surprised they could be manipulated so easily
in this way. Even so, he was on a knife's edge and knew it. If
he didn't convince them very quickly that he had some control
of the situation, they might easily decide to cut their losses and
turn against him. 'I'm reliably informed,' he continued firmly,
'that he was taken on by the MOD for one job and one job only
– and that was to look for Lieutenant Tan. Tate's strictly freelance;
a contractor. They do it all the time when they're short of
manpower.'

'That's supposed to make us feel better?' Deakin didn't sound
mollified. His body language was tight, his movements betraying
his impatience and a need to take action.

Paulton continued quickly, 'Tate's a plodder and always was.
He follows orders but he's no great strategic thinker. Tan was
clearly judged to be too high a value asset to leave out there, so
they called in Tate to go after her and bring her in . . . something

he has been singularly unsuccessful in doing, let me remind you.'

'You'd better be right about that. We've managed to stay below the radar for a long time now; I'd hate to find I was suddenly exposed because you were top of the Security Service's wanted list.'

'I wouldn't be too happy, either,' Turpowicz added darkly. 'Which makes me wonder why you're talking about taking him out. Surely that'll make them mad enough to come after us?'

Paulton smiled. They were coming round, albeit slowly. 'Precisely the opposite. Too much trouble at a time when the MOD is already under scrutiny over lavish spending, equipment shortfalls and desertion rates, and they'll shut down the operation and focus their efforts elsewhere. Believe me, I know the way the drones in Whitehall and the Security Services think. Jumped-up bean counters, most of them; they don't have the stomach for trouble unless it's publicly or politically popular – and hunting down deserters has never been either of those. Half the population doesn't care about soldiers on the run and the other half doesn't want to know. Not the right form, y'know.'

'All right.' Deakin stood up, shrugging off his earlier mood. 'So how do we get this bugger off our backs once and for all?'

Paulton looked satisfied at having got them both onside. 'Simple. I'll give you the home address of Tate's protégé, a man named Ferris. All you have to do is get your men ready. Only this time, no subcontracting the job out to kids or hoping to catch Tate in a drive-by shooting. This is warfare, not a gang-bangers' spray-fest. Lift Ferris – he's an IT button pusher, so he'll be no problem – and Tate will follow. He's too much of a white knight to leave Ferris out there. When he moves in, your thugs kill them both and we've got a clear field to carry on our work.'

Deakin looked unconvinced. 'But that will expose Zubac and Ganic. Tate will be looking for them.'

Paulton's response was cool. 'Sadly, yes. But that's what they're for, isn't it – to take the risks? After all, better they go down than we do.'

FIFTY-ONE

'I need to speak to General Foster.'

Ballatyne didn't express any surprise at Harry's early call the following morning. Maybe, Harry thought, he'd been expecting this all along. Especially as Foster was reported to be in London to talk to an important parliamentary select committee about the progress of supplies and equipment for troops on the ground.

For Harry, talking to Tan's former boss was the next logical step in the search for the missing lieutenant. She would have been the general's shadow every pace he took, in Kabul and elsewhere, closer than most and always there whenever she was needed. It was what good aides did: anticipating the unexpected, operating at elbow's length yet mostly unseen, advising, noting, observing – another set of eyes and ears for their superior. In such circumstances, General Foster would have got to know the young officer better than most, would have acquired even subliminally some information about her that might help them find her. Would have gained, perhaps, an insight into what made her tick.

'What's wrong, having trouble sleeping?' the MI6 man muttered tartly.

'No. But I am having trouble tracing Vanessa Tan. I might get a lead from talking to Foster.'

'You can't,' Ballatyne said finally.

'Why not?' Harry mentally dusted himself off for a fight. This official habit of creating firewalls around figures of power and influence was not going to help, not in this situation. He needed to talk to anyone who had known Tan recently. Her school and university days were gone, her family was non-existent and it was likely that anyone who had known her before her army days would not recognize the person who had gone to war. Without talking to the one person who had been closest to her, he was no further forward in even guessing where she might have gone since jumping the fence.

'Because he won't talk. Sorry, Harry, it's not on the agenda.'

'He won't or he won't be allowed to?'

'You'll have to find another way.' The tone was adamant, final. End of discussion.

Harry cut the connection. He thought he knew what was going on: Foster was being protected from any potential fallout associated with having a key member of his staff deserting. When in doubt, close ranks.

Time to bluff his way forward.

Stepping into the Ministry of Defence Main Building felt like deliberately walking out into rush-hour traffic in Trafalgar Square. In spite of the impressive amount of light coming through the glass acreage of the new development, Harry felt a darkness about the place, although he knew it was his imagination. He headed for the enquiry desk under the watchful eye of the security guards and flipped his Security Services card at the bristle-haired man on duty. It was just nine fifteen and there were a lot of people about, something he was hoping to turn to his advantage.

'I'm here to catch General Patrick Foster's press briefing,' he said. 'Last minute assignment.' He'd been surprised to find how easy it had been for Rik to access the General's timetable.

The receptionist nodded and ran Harry's card under a scanner. It would probably light up all manner of screens in the MOD and Security Services, but Harry was past caring. What could they do to him other than chuck him out? 'Room 16A on the ground floor.' The receptionist nodded towards the security screens and returned his card. 'Through there and turn right, sixth door along. He's been talking about fifteen minutes already.'

Harry nodded and passed through the body scanner, then submitted to a security wand check before getting the OK to proceed. So far so good.

He arrived at 16A and stepped inside. The room was light and airy, concealed lighting giving the feel of a conservatory. General Foster was standing behind a lectern facing the door, gesturing towards a screen to one side showing a schematic of force distribution numbers against a background map of Afghanistan. The figures looked impressive, a multiple array of ground capabilities in various colours, an image of the country flooded with personnel. But Harry knew they were less than full; putting up detailed figures of how many men, women and machines were in theatre was as far beyond the instincts of the MOD as asking them to pull their own teeth with pliers. Whatever this press talk was meant to achieve, it was unlikely to be giving anyone – least of all the press – an accurate breakdown of UK and Coalition commitments in the fight against insurgents, but rather a political feel-good image for public consumption.

Foster was droning, his voice dry and automatic, and Harry guessed he was here under orders, to put a man-on-the-ground gloss on the situation for the media. While he would be accustomed to talking, the press was unlikely to be his favoured audience. Like most military men, he would be happier talking to fellow professionals, using a direct language far removed from the discreet, carefully micro-managed words he would be using here and being watched by MOD suits to ensure he didn't depart from the agreed script. Generals before him had done so, and the control now was far tighter than it had ever been.

Harry checked the room. There were fewer than twenty in the audience, most of them photographers. It must have been disappointing for the MOD press office. Flying in a general all the way from Afghanistan should have generated a lot more interest, but maybe it was an indication of just how much information the press now had on a daily basis; they didn't need to queue up to see the main man himself to know what was truly going on.

Harry couldn't see the faces of those sitting in front of him, but he felt sure there was nobody he'd recognize. He slid into a chair and waited.

The talk ended a few minutes later with a few desultory and pre-prepared questions from the media pack. Then a woman from the press office stepped forward and said, 'That's it, ladies and gentlemen, I'm afraid we have to wrap it up there. General Foster has a very busy schedule. There are briefing notes by the door for you to pick up on the way out. If you would like to take photos now?'

Harry waited while the snappers did their job, before they headed for the door in a flying wedge, eager to send in their photos and copy and get to the nearest pub. As the numbers diminished, General Foster collected his papers together and walked down the aisle between the rows of chairs, head bent listening to an aide feeding him his next agenda item. As the officer neared him, Harry stood up and showed his Security Services card.

'General Foster, if you have a moment?' He was relying on a tone of authority to cut through the inevitable smokescreen around the general and confuse the suits and aides into letting him speak long enough to gain the officer's attention.

Foster slowed, eyeing the card and then Harry, his concentration broken. He stopped.

'What is it?' Up close, he was tanned and lean, exuding confidence and gravitas. He would have to, given his job, Harry thought, and realized he was only going to get one punt at this.

As he opened his mouth to reply, a minder in a suit tried to intervene, placing a hand on Harry's chest and pushing without even bothering to look at his card. 'That's not possible. Step back. Apply through the press office in the approved manner.'

Harry looked down at the hand, then eased it away, applying just enough pressure on the tendons with his thumb to draw a gasp from the man. He dropped the hand and looked straight at General Foster, estimating that he had about five seconds before the minder got over his surprise and wounded pride and yelled for back-up. Another three and security guards would be jumping all over him. 'General, I need to ask you about Lieutenant Tan. Have you any idea where she might have gone?'

Foster's eyes were a dark shade of green, Harry noted, full of intelligence and, no doubt, the weightiness of his position in the war against the Taliban, coupled with his role as a military diplomat. But there was a disturbing blankness in there, too, echoed by the frown edging his brow, and Harry experienced a moment of startling revelation.

The general said, 'Sorry – I think you need to speak to personnel on any issue like that.' Then he was gone, surrounded by his acolytes, and Harry was left with two large security guards hustling him towards the exit.

As he stepped out into the sunlight over Whitehall, Harry realized he'd been wrong. His assumption about the senior officer being protected from any fallout and therefore off-limits to Harry was way off-target. The simple fact was, General Patrick Foster, Deputy Commander Afghanistan and Lieutenant Vanessa Tan's immediate boss, hadn't got the faintest idea of who Harry had been talking about.

FIFTY-TWO

'Cutting it fine, Harry. I was beginning to have my doubts about you.' Clare Jardine answered Harry's call on the fifth ring. She sounded amused and even faintly smug, as if she'd been expecting his call all along. 'I'm glad I was wrong.'

'What do you want?' He was only fifty yards from the MOD building, and curiosity had got the better of him.

'Come on, don't be like that.' Her voice took on a more businesslike tone. 'Look, sorry about the teasing. If we work together, Harry, we can both get what we want. I help you, you help me, friends forever.'

'I'm listening.'

'Not over the phone. There are too many ears in this city for my liking. Choose somewhere public if it makes you feel safer.' The amused tone was back, giving Harry cause to wonder at Clare's mental state, her mood veering from one extreme to another in the blink of an eye.

'All right,' he said. 'Horse Guards Parade opposite the lake. Fifteen minutes.' Horse Guards, where armed police were stationed in cubicles, watching the government's back and the passing public. If Clare was thinking of trying any of her knife work there, she'd have to be suicidal.

Her laugh echoed down the line. 'Horse Guards is good. But fifteen? From where you're standing right now, Harry, it should take about four minutes, tops, a fit man like you. Don't be late . . . and don't bring the Milky Bar Kid or I might have to give him a slap.' Then she was gone, leaving him with a prickly feeling on the back of his neck.

He refused to turn round and look; he didn't want to give her the satisfaction.

Five minutes later, Clare joined him on the edge of the parade square, within sight of an armed police guard. She was dressed this time in pressed trousers and a smart jacket, every inch the office worker on a break, fitting easily into the background the way she would have been trained. She carried no bag, he noticed, but that didn't mean she was harmless; he'd seen how quickly she could move and how she could produce her little compact knife faster than many sleight-of-hand artistes.

'Mmm . . . clever,' she congratulated him, eyeing the guard. 'You really don't trust me, do you? And after everything we've been through. I'm almost hurt.'

'No, you're not. Tell me why I should trust you.'

'OK. Fair point. Straight down to business, then.' She set off at a dawdle along the pavement, keeping a body's width apart from him, hands clasped in front of her. Amazingly, she looked almost demure, as if butter wouldn't melt. 'I know Paulton is working with the Protectory,' she announced. 'Don't bother asking how, I just do. He's a wheeler-dealer and he must have seen them as a prime source of money. Only he doesn't have any secrets of his own to sell, does he? Who the hell cares about MI5 stuff that's over a year out of date? And officers or agents he was running have long been pulled out. But he has contacts in all sorts of unlikely places. He must have been storing away names for years, hoping that one day he'd have a use for them. He might not have planned on this kind of use, but he's resourceful; he knows how the Protectory works: they get their hands on a few prime military personnel who are desperate for a new life and safety away from guns and bullets and IEDs and whatever crap they call their home life, and sell whatever they've got in their heads.' She paused for breath; she'd been talking fast, a professional pitch to sell the idea of chasing Paulton and not letting Harry go. And was that a hint of desperation in her voice?

'That's the Protectory. Where does Paulton fit in?'

'Simple: he's got something to bring to the table. He knows people who know people and he can get buyers for the kind of stuff on offer. The Protectory's problem is they don't have the reach or the contacts and never have. They're strictly small-time; soldiers cut adrift, looking to flog off a few details here and there. Negotiating without a gun is not their strong point, and they've probably been ripped off plenty of times. Paulton's argument is that he can get them in front of some real buyers . . . and in the process take a nice cut for himself. It's a neat fit.'

She was right. Paulton had been in the security and intelligence game a long time. It was a world away from the kind of spheres Deakin and his friends inhabited. The kind of information that had passed across Paulton's desk over the years would have included names, positions and locations of people looking to get hold of whatever Britain and her allies were developing in tactical equipment. Names men like Deakin and Nicholls would never even have heard of.

But he still wasn't sure how knowing this would get him to Paulton. Clare answered that in a way he hadn't been expecting.

'I don't want to tell stories out of school, Harry, but you know Ballatyne's playing you, don't you?'

He stopped, forcing her to do the same. He knew this might be a ploy, Clare playing SIS-type mind games to drive a wedge between him and Ballatyne. Divide and rule, as old as the hills. Yet a part of him found it difficult to contradict her outright. 'Go on.'

'They're only using you for one thing: to track these guys down so they can take them out. They don't have the manpower to do it themselves, and don't want to get their hands dirty if it all goes public and shit-shaped. So they've dressed it up, with Paulton now in the frame in the hope that you can kill two birds with one stone. They knock the Protectory out of the game, you get Paulton . . . everyone's happy.'

'How do you know this?'

'I told you: I've got friends. They have connections. Word is that a dribble of information has been coming out of the Protectory for about three months now. Bits here, snippets there; nothing huge, but it's enough to tell them what the group is doing. At first the government didn't want to know; they looked on the Protectory as no more than rumour, a small group of ex-army misfits not worth bothering with. Then about a month ago the decision was taken to shut them down.'

'Why?'

'They were becoming the stuff of legend; celebrity renegades, would you believe? Robin Hood and his merry men in desert camos. You know what squaddies are like; coop them up in forward operating bases for weeks on end and they'll talk up Jack the Ripper as a hero. Make it a group helping out deserters and they're like the X-Men and the Magnificent Seven all rolled into one. It gives those with even a vague notion of jumping ship the idea that it might just work if they had somewhere safe to run. That's not good for morale.'

'Neither is killing deserters who refuse their help.'

'It might have pushed the MOD's thinking along a bit, but I don't think that was the catalyst. Why would the MOD care about the odd dead deserter? As far as they're concerned, it's a problem solved. Close the files, delete and move on.'

The MOD's decision had nothing to do with Tan's disappearance, either, Harry realized. If what Clare was saying was true, Tan had kicked off at least three weeks ago now, some time *after* the decision had been made to go after the Protectory. But why? Coincidence, or simply a realistic anticipation that the longer the conflict in Afghanistan went on, the situation could only get worse and more high-value targets would leave and be chased down for what they could sell?

'These friends,' he said, turning to continue walking. Too long in one position here and the police would begin to take an interest. And he hadn't finished with Clare yet. 'Are they in Six or the MOD?'

She shook her head with an enigmatic smile.

'OK. The information coming out of the Protectory . . . do they know who's leaking it?'

'The main money seems to be on a guy called Colin Nicholls, formerly a major in the Intelligence Corps. He went missing about eight years ago while on leave from Iraq. He found his way into the original Protectory, which was just a bunch of guys helping each other stay below the radar. But they weren't selling anything, not like now.'

So far, so correct. 'Why Nicholls? There are others in the group.' He told her about the American, Turpowicz, as an example.

'There are thought to be half a dozen regular members, spread all over, but I don't know any names. Nicholls probably has the best background for feeding information through the system to the authorities without being traced. Maybe after all these years, he's developed a conscience – I don't know. What they have picked up is that he's become disenchanted with the way the others in the group are taking it and wants out. His messages have been sounding increasingly despondent.' She paused. 'Hasn't Ballatyne been telling you all this stuff?'

'No. You know they'll go after your friends, don't you?' He wasn't giving away any secrets; Clare and her contacts might be a little naïve to think they could pass her information for ever without being caught, but they weren't completely stupid. In the end, something always gave whistleblowers away, if only the whistleblowers themselves, victims of over-confidence or inflated egos. 'They'll go on a rat hunt and clear them out.'

'I know that. So do they.' She sounded subdued. She must have been harbouring the knowledge for some time. 'They've been thinking of leaving, anyway. Time to move on.'

They had come as far as Birdcage Walk. Harry turned about, then stopped.

'Thanks for helping Jean, by the way.' It was something he'd been meaning to say. It would never be enough to make them friends, but it warranted something of a truce between them, if not quite full trust.

'No problem. You helped me in Georgia, got me out of there when you could have left me behind. Consider us quits.' She looked and sounded sincere. Another mood swing or a glimpse of the real Clare? He still wasn't sure.

'Quits.'

'So what now?'

'I thought you were going to tell me. You seem to have a lot of facts.'

'Basics, that's all. What I do know is, after what happened at Jean's place, you must be top dog on the Bosnians' hit list. They're probably feeling bruised by that failure. We neither of us know where Paulton or the Protectory are hiding out, but from the Bosnians to them is a fairly straight jump, wouldn't you say?'

'Find the Bosnians, find Deakin and Paulton?' It was a

tantalizing thought, but offhand he couldn't think of another. He'd already staked himself out as a goat once, so he might as well try it again. 'Where can I find you?'

'You have my number. Just call and I'll come running.' She smiled archly and walked away, her heels going click-clack on the hard ground.

His phone buzzed. It was Rik.

'Harry, I've got something on Vanessa Tan. But you're really not going to like it. She's dead.'

FIFTY-THREE

arry sank into a chair in Rik's flat, and felt a wave of tiredness wash over him. They were too late. The Protectory had got to her after all. But why kill her? 'How did it happen?'

'She died in a house fire.'

'When?'

Rik paused for dramatic effect, then said, 'Six years ago.'

'*What?*' Harry was stunned. If Tan was recorded as dead, then how—?

'It was in Huntingdon, in a squat used by animal rights activists. The others knew her only as Vanessa, a supporter. The police never managed to match it to the address in north Wales, so she was named as Vanessa X by a local newshound. I only spotted the name by chance in a local newspaper archive. There's no photo but the activists gave a good description. One of them said she had a faint Welsh accent.'

Harry sighed. At least it explained what had happened to her after university. 'That must be when they made the switch.'

'Well, maybe not. That's the weird thing.' Rik sounded excited. 'When I was still searching for anything related to Lieutenant Tan, I went through every record I could find on the command structure for ISAF in Kabul. There were pictures of all the officers, from every national force represented – puff pieces, mainly, with links to their careers, training and so on, who they knew, what sports they played, everything but who they were sleeping with. There were even shots of the support staff, right down to security guards, drivers, admin workers, chefs and valets. The only person consistently missing was Tan.'

'Nothing?' It wasn't impossible but it seemed highly unlikely that one person – even an impostor working by design – could have missed a military photo session every time.

'There were a couple of entries listing Lieutenant V. Tan as an aide to the Deputy Commander, but no pictures. She doesn't appear in any of the group shots, background photos or staff registers. There's no sign of her in shots of the command staff with local tribal leaders or ministers, which there would have been if she had the local languages. Can you imagine what the more politically correct wonks in the MOD would have made of that one? Here's a young woman in a key position in a war zone . . . blah, blah, blah.'

He was right. It would have made political capital good money couldn't buy.

'Even the gallery of leaving parties at the time has nobody who remotely resembles her,' Rik continued. 'Blondes, brunettes – even a redhead or two – but not a single Anglo-Chinese. I checked the rosters for rotations in and out; nothing there, either.'

'Regimental records and officer training?' Harry asked, although he could guess the result there, too.

'She's on the strength, but listed as on temporary secondment to ISAF – but no photo. There's a V. Tan on the officer training rolls, but no further details. It's like she was a cipher; there but not there.' He took a deep breath and added, 'I, uh . . . I also took a peek at the MOD flight manifests for trips out to Afghanistan and back.'

Harry looked at him. 'You did what?' That was dangerously close to restricted territory. Troop movements were jealously guarded for basic security reasons: find a particular member of the military on the move, and you were within an ace of knowing which regiment was going where. Find a specialist and you knew what the concentration and focus was going to be. Allowing access to that sort of information also exposed individual personnel to danger and security leaks.

'It's OK,' said Rik quickly. 'I didn't leave a footprint. I used a relay through the regimental records office. It'll stop dead at a terminal with open access. She wasn't on any of the manifests. No outs, no returns.' He sat back, pleased with himself.

'Good work. So what's your conclusion?'

'This Vanessa Tan was just a name on a list. A real looker, but not a real person.'

Harry stood up and did a turn around the room. Was that the real answer to this? That Vanessa Tan had been impossible to find because her entire existence had been a hoax? A fabrication? It hardly seemed credible, but stranger things had happened. If it were true, it explained why Ballatyne hadn't wanted him talking to General Foster, and why Foster himself had looked totally blank on hearing her name. He hadn't been included in the plan.

Then he had an idea and cursed himself for being slow off the mark. He'd missed an opportunity to get here much faster than this. What was it Mrs Crane had said about her?

'. . . as if she might make up for being a bit plain by having a string of letters after her name.'

If there was one thing he wouldn't have called Vanessa Tan, it was plain. He found Mrs Crane's telephone number and rang her.

'Mr Tate?' She sounded surprised to hear from him. 'What can I do for you?'

'Mrs Crane, do you have a PC?'

'Well, of course. We're not in the Stone Age up here, you know. I was just using it, as a matter of fact. Why do you ask?'

'I want you to look at a picture and tell me what you think.' When she agreed and gave him her email address, he got Rik to send her the jpeg of Vanessa Tan from the memory stick.

Moments later, she said, 'Right. Got it. Just let me open the attachment. I don't suppose you've found her, have you? Oh . . . goodness.'

'What's wrong?'

Mrs Crane sounded puzzled. 'Who is this?'

It was all Harry needed. But he had to have confirmation without feeding her any hints.

'Do you recognize her?'

'No, I don't . . .' She hesitated, then said, 'You think it's Vanessa, don't you?'

'You tell me.'

'Sorry, Mr Tate, but I think you've been given the wrong information. Whoever this woman is, it's definitely not Vanessa Tan. Not in a million years.'

After thanking Mrs Crane and hanging up, Harry sat down to consider the possibilities of what they had stumbled over. Suddenly several bits of the puzzle were falling into place. The unexplained disappearance of a very bright and promising young female army officer; the absence of any solid background details, friends or family; the lack of any clues to her whereabouts.

'How the hell did they do this?'

Rik shrugged. 'Easy enough, given time and access.'

'Could you do it?'

'Sure. Whoever set this up would've been on the inside, with a lot more facilities, but I could manage, given time and some privacy.' He smiled knowingly. 'I could get your name in there if I had to. Put you on the general staff, all braid and creased trousers.'

'How?' Harry felt sure he was going to regret asking, but he had to know. And Rik was the only one who would tell him.

'I'd have to access certain servers and files which I won't frighten you with by naming, then I'd go in and enter your name as having served, say, on the HQ staff in Desert Storm. I'd throw in a few photos of you sitting on a gun turret and smiling, or enjoying a brew-up with the lads in the desert, then link it all in with your regimental records. And if I was really clever, which I am, I'd make sure your name was included in movement records from the UK to Iraq and back; maybe even add a bit of gloss by showing you'd been evac'd out and treated in hospital for shrapnel wounds.' He sat back and grinned. 'Everyone loves a hero with some metal ballast. It's not really that hard – just a matter of filling in blanks.'

'But the photo.'

'That's where they fell short: they wouldn't have had a recent shot of Tan, so they just took the first one they could get of an Anglo-Chinese woman of roughly the same age. Maybe they managed to get hold of any existing shots of her as a girl and wiped them. What they didn't reckon on was that you'd show the file photo to someone who'd known her, or that that anyone would bother looking beyond the basic facts they'd put on the records.'

Harry swore. He'd been on one long wild goose chase. There never had been a Lieutenant Tan. The original had died in a fire after leaving Cambridge. And now he knew why: her place in the big wide world had been taken by a fiction – an invention – used to lay an elaborate bait for the Protectory. It wouldn't have taken much; false entries in the army records, a glowing CV that painted a picture of a high-flyer with an elephantine memory, and the closest possible connections to the high command in Afghanistan. And just enough detail to make her seem real if anyone should run a cursory check.

'There's a clincher,' added Rik. 'I checked Tan's original application to university – her real one. She never studied languages, and even if she'd been to Kabul, there's a reason she wouldn't have been pictured with locals: in contrast to the old cobblers you were fed, she couldn't speak Pashto or Dari. She had some Cantonese from her father, and a bit of French, but that was it. And there was no record of a special memory to help her graduate, either. Whatever qualifications she got, she'd had to work hard for.'

They'd done it in a rush and got careless. Pasted together a past which didn't exist for a woman who was dead, snatching bits of reality and painting on a fabricated history. A giant Photoshop representation of a make-believe life. It wasn't going to stand up long to close scrutiny, but that would never have been the intention. It was all smoke and mirrors. Once they'd identified the dead woman in the house fire – which only MI6 would have had the time, clout and purpose to do – the house and phone must have been kept active to show anyone who cared to look that she still existed. Clever.

He stood up. Ballatyne; before this went any further, he had a lot of talking to do. Before leaving, however, he told Rik about his meeting with Clare off Whitehall.

Rik was sceptical. 'She's poison, you know that. Anyone could cut a man like she did Bellingham isn't right in the head.'

'I know. But she's told me more than Ballatyne has, and right now I need all the help I can get. If her friends in Six come up with anything substantial, it could save a lot of time.'

'He's another one, Ballatyne. He's strung us along – and for what?' Rik scrubbed at his hair, making it even wilder than it looked normally. 'Great game we're in, isn't it? Our friends turn out to be our enemies.'

Harry couldn't argue with that. It was in the nature of the people who worked in the intelligence business: only tell people as much as they need to know, and even then, make sure very little is the full unvarnished truth.

'I'm going to see him. Find out what's going on.'

'You want me there?' Rik looked hopeful. 'I could hold your jacket.'

'No. I'd like to keep it civilized – but don't go anywhere.'

Rik spread his arms, forgetting to wince at his wound. 'Where will I go? This is my existence. I'm beginning to feel like a laboratory rat. Nothing ever happens.'

Harry grinned at him. 'Be careful what you wish for,' he said, and left.

FIFTY-FOUR

'There are reasons we did it this way, Harry. I'm sorry I couldn't bring you in on the fine detail, but my hands were tied.'

It was an hour later and Ballatyne had agreed with surprising ease to a meeting. They were back in the Italian restaurant off Wigmore Street, the minder on the door and a car outside. 'It was decided to have the tightest possible list of people in the know, restricted to me and a maximum of four others, including the IT specialists who fed the Tan background data into the official records. Any wider than that and we would have been no closer to knowing who was leaking the names of deserters out to the Protectory. I don't include you in that, of course.'

'Big of you. So what's the story?'

'The government and MOD have been concerned for some time about the desertion figures. They're rising all the time, especially with the casualty rates in Afghanistan. That by itself

is containable, given some attention. But what nobody had reckoned on was deserters turning round and selling what they knew.
It's happened occasionally before, but strictly small-time stuff.
Trouble is, we've now got a situation where ordinary soldiers
are in possession of some amazing technology and equipment,
from weapons through to IT and tactical data; stuff that other
countries would love to get their hands on. Not just countries,
either. Terrorist organizations like al-Qaeda trade on equipment
and information, too, selling to the highest bidder. It's the new
form of spying, with a touch of spin.'

'I get the picture.'

'Some months ago, we heard the Protectory had got hold of
some information from a naval weapons specialist who'd jumped
ship. A young bloke who'd got an attack of conscience and didn't
like what buttons he was expected to push in the event of a
serious conflict. He told his mates how he wanted a new life and
new ID, and had heard how to get them, through this group called
the Protectory. They thought he was fantasizing, and so did we;
campfire stuff as you called it, a load of romantic tosh. By the
time anyone realized it, and before he could be hauled ashore
for questioning, he'd disappeared while in dock in Gibraltar.'

Harry said nothing. It was already sounding familiar.

'Fortunately for us, he turned up two months later in Morocco,
stoned out of his brain and homesick. But he was telling an
interesting story. The Protectory had sat him down in a room
with an expert in weapons technology and drained him of everything he knew. It took ten days, by which time he realized what
they were doing, and took off when they relaxed their watch on
him. As we now know, he was a lucky bunny; he'd have probably ended up dead under a culvert somewhere once his useful-
ness was over. As it was, he gave us the first leads into what
Deakin and his pals are doing, and from what he told us, it was
clear they knew a lot more about him than he'd have ever put
on Facebook. The kind of detail that could have only come from
his naval records.'

'They had someone on the inside.'

'In the MOD. It was a clever move: they'd get instant news
of a deserter, along with a summary of their job, background and
rank, and be able to make a decision about whether the runner

might be useful to them. After that, they'd make an approach, offer salvation and suggest a trade. Some worked, some didn't. It was decided at that point to get serious about the Protectory and shut them down. Our problem was finding them; as you know, they're very good at hiding themselves.'

'So you decided to draw them out using a dead woman as bait.'

Ballatyne didn't look ashamed at what they had done. 'Get a grip, Harry; you know how it goes. Tan had no family, no real friends. Nobody got hurt.'

'That doesn't excuse it.'

'Maybe not. But we needed something to draw the Protectory out of their hole. A heavily embellished half-truth was the best means of doing that. Tan's name came up by chance during a police investigation into animal rights groups. She'd died in a fire but her full name was unknown. Given her facial characteristics, it was thought she might have been part of a Chinese work gang who'd got split off from her friends and merged with the animal rights mob as camouflage. We dug around and found out stuff the local police hadn't, and it led us to a full name and address. By then her mother had died leaving her the house and a small pot to keep it going. We took over the management of the house and phone for background, gave her a glowing legend into the army, then let loose the AWOL story to see if it would draw the Protectory – and the person doing the leaking – out of the woodwork.' He smiled thinly. 'You can now see why I didn't want you speaking to General Foster. He wasn't in on it.'

'So I gathered.'

Ballatyne looked annoyed. 'You spoke to him?'

'I tried. He didn't have a clue what I was talking about.'

'I'm not surprised. It was for the same reasons that I didn't want you chasing after "Tan" as a possible sleeper for the *Guoanbu*. It was a natural conclusion to come to, given her apparent ancestry, but it would have blown up in our faces if you'd started digging around in that nasty little Chinese puddle. It was all part of the overall picture.'

'And did the Tan story work?'

'Yes. We wanted to see how quickly the Protectory would latch on to it. We started out by feeding the false story through a limited circulation inside the MOD to see who would take the bait. As I said, sorry that had to include you, Harry, but I had no choice.'

Harry bit down hard on his instinct to tell Ballatyne what he thought of him. It would serve no purpose. They'd played him, but they had played the MOD insider and the Protectory even more. He also understood why; they'd needed to put a stop to the Protectory's trade in sensitive military data and personnel. To do that effectively, they had to plug the leak of information on deserters at source – inside the MOD. A small skirmish in the fight to protect the nation's secrets.

'Who took the bait?'

'Gordon Cullum. He was well placed, as it happened; he had access, opportunity and motive. He'd got disenchanted over the years and accumulated a mess of property debts, and was facing retirement on a pension that wasn't going to take him anywhere. It turns out he was a buddy of Major Colin Nicholls. They'd worked together in Northern Ireland years ago, running an undercover bargain-basement car-hire business renting out disposable vehicles to bad boys from the Real IRA. All part of the army's plan to keep tags on what cars were going where. Worked brilliantly for a time, too, but they got blown and had to duck out fast. Cullum says Nicholls first contacted him two years ago. Just a call for old time's sake at first. Then he started leaning on him, citing their service together in the back streets of Ulster and how he needed a favour. That didn't work, according to Cullum. So Nicholls got him to go to a meeting in Amsterdam, and who should show up but Thomas Deakin. He got all hard-nosed and presented Cullum with a list of his debts and proof that some of the money from the undercover car-rental business had stuck to his hands, and how it would look if a copy landed in the corridors of Five, Six and the MOD. Cullum saw the writing on the prison wall and folded. The rest we know about. He systematically plundered the MOD files for every deserter and disaffected squaddie, trooper or officer he could find. They were all targets for Nicholls and Deakin, but the more specialized they were, the better their chances of making a trade.'

'If the target played along with them.'

'True. Not all of them did. Pike and Barrow were certainly two recent unlucky ones.'

'What did Cullum get out of it?'

'So far? About thirty thousand quid, give or take. Hardly worth losing his job and pension over, but he must have thought he'd be in it for the long haul. Fortunately for us, he was no better at hiding his illicit money than he was at managing his debts. Our internal bloodhounds put two and two together and suddenly he was centre stage.'

'How did they do that?'

'He got careless and left an audit trail. They latched on to it.'

'Cullum knew what I was working on.' He wondered whether – or when – the information had filtered out to the Protectory.

'Yes. But he didn't connect the dots. He'd have known Six wouldn't have been involved in this unless it was something too sensitive for Five to be running. And bringing in an outsider like you only strengthened that possibility. What he didn't know about was Paulton's connection with the group. Nicholls must have deliberately kept him out of the loop on that one. All he had was a changeable phone number and various Hotmail addresses for making contact with Nicholls or Deakin.'

Harry wondered if Cullum had really been that naïve. Given his knowledge of Harry's history with Paulton and Red Station, an episode that would have been office gossip among long-time Fivers, and the fact that Harry had been brought in to look into some military absconders, it would not have taken long for a man of Cullum's experience to deduce what was going on. Or maybe his financial straits had blinded him to making those kind of connections.

'So what happens now?'

'We're playing Cullum. He stays in touch with the Protectory or he goes to jail for a long time. The longer we can keep them unaware of what we know, the better our chances of reeling them in. But we don't have long; this has got to end sooner or later, but we don't want any more information finding its way into the hands of the Chinese, Russians or anyone else with an axe to grind. And we still want Paulton.'

'And in the meantime they think Tan is still out there?'

'Yes. The big prize.'

'And your own insider?'

Ballatyne looked momentarily blank. 'Sorry?'

'There's been a trickle of information coming the other way
– from inside the Protectory. You said so yourself. Was that a
bluff as well?'

'Not entirely.'

'What does that mean?'

'There've been bits of information, but never enough to help
us pin anyone down. The language used sounds like it could be
Nicholls, but it's been coming in through an unusual medium.'

'Unusual?' Harry prompted him. It was an MI6 trait, he knew,
to keep everyone, even their friends and assets, in the dark wherever possible. It was standard tradecraft, the need-to-know principle. The downside was that it kept people isolated who very
often should have known what was going on further down the
line.

'The United Nations Internal Oversight Services office. We
have no idea why; it could be that the source once had a contact
there or feels it's the safest way of passing information out. The
IOS investigates breaches of conduct and security. Although this
business doesn't involve UN personnel, they've been taking this
information seriously and passing it on as a matter of concern.'
He pulled a face. 'Sadly, it didn't stop with us; the Americans
have the information, too, although they've shown no great
interest so far in doing anything with it. Probably because it
involves British forces.'

'And he's still feeding information out?'

'He's been a bit quiet of late. We're wondering how long he's
got.' If Ballatyne was concerned about the fate of the inside man,
he was hiding it remarkably well.

He stood up and took a slip of paper out of his pocket, then
placed it on the table in front of Harry. It held an address in West
Sussex. 'We've had one bit of luck: Soran's got several lock-ups
for keeping stock, most of it genuine. He acts as a wholesaler
for household goods in and around London. But there's one place
he was rather coy about. In fact, he denied having anything to
do with it until we showed him a rental agreement. Then he
caved. It's one of several units on an abandoned World War Two
airfield; Nissen huts the old War Office forgot about.'

'What does he use it for?'

'Nothing he was ready to admit to. He said it was just another storage facility for supplies in the southern counties, to save trucking stuff all the way to and from London. I don't buy it. If the buildings are that old, they'd be no good for storing anything valuable, and too out of the way for regular deliveries. The site is by a section of disused railway line in West Sussex. Remote enough to be ignored, close enough not to disturb the neighbours.' He gave Harry the directions. 'I haven't told the local cops because they'd take several hours to make their risk assessments, then stamp all over the scene. If you're still on board, you might want to take a quiet look instead.'

Harry picked up the paper. He was still on board and Ballatyne knew it. He hadn't come all this way simply to give up out of an attack of the snits for not being consulted fully. But after this, that was it. No more.

'Watch your back, Harry,' Ballatyne added. 'Even if Deakin and his friends have forgotten you, the Bosnians won't have. They've got memories like elephants and they hold a grudge like nobody else on the planet.'

Back outside, Harry called Rik. He still wasn't fit enough yet, but they were a team. He had every right to be in on this next phase. There was no answer. Must have gone stir crazy and slipped out for some air. He rang Clare. She picked up immediately.

'You ready for some action?'

'Ooh, Mr Tate,' she trilled in a tarty voice. 'You say the sweetest things. Where are we going, then?'

'West Sussex.'

'Nice. Are you bringing your big gun?'

Harry ignored her. She was trying to wind him up. 'Where do I pick you up?'

'I'll be at your place,' her voice returned to normal, 'when you get back.'

Get back? He glanced around, an uneasy feeling crawling up his neck. It would never have surprised him if she was watching him from across the street. He hung up.

His phone rang immediately. Number withheld.

'Yes?'

'. . . *Tate? Got* . . .' The signal dropped out. The voice had been male, gruff, and too brief to recognize. It rang again before he could move. '*Tate . . . again . . . your . . . friend.*' A jumble of half words, then a burst of static and it was gone again.

He rang Rik. Landline and mobile. No reply.

Something was wrong.

He grabbed a cab and was halfway to Paddington when a text message came through. This time there was no mistake, no garbled words. He told the cab driver to head for his place. He had something to pick up. He looked at the screen again and felt his stomach clench tight.

'*We have your friend. You help us or he dies.*' An address followed.

It was Soran's storage facility in West Sussex.

FIFTY-FIVE

A narrow farm track led off a secondary road below the A264 in West Sussex towards a cluster of fields dotted with small clumps of woodland. Harry drove down the track, suddenly reminded by the swish of grass on either side of the track near Schwedt, where Sgt Barrow had died. The atmosphere here was very different, though; green and scenic, a pleasant rural setting with none of the history of the former Iron Curtain, a British haven where nothing bad could happen. Or maybe that was wishful thinking.

He stopped along the track and got out, studying the fields on either side. All he could hear were a few birds and the subtle swish of wind through the trees and hedges.

Clare joined him and surveyed the surrounding fields. 'Good location. It's miles from anywhere.'

'Precisely. Soran's probably used this place before for bringing in his people. His place in Hackney was clean; he had to have somewhere else he could use for storage on the way back from the coast.' He nodded towards a dark shape just visible between two oak trees at the end of the track. 'Looks like a building.' He walked to the rear of the car and took out his gun, checking the load. He handed Clare a second semi-automatic and a magazine.

She gave him a quizzical look. 'Aren't you worried I might shoot you?' She inserted the magazine with practised precision. It set off a glint in her eye which he recalled from their time in Georgia. Some people were just turned on by guns, he decided. Or knives.

'What would be the point?'

'Fair question.' She waved the gun, head cocked to one side. 'A little bird told me you're carded. Is that true?'

'Yes.'

She looked scornful. 'So you've taken the Queen's five-penny piece. And after all they did to you.'

'It doesn't mean anything.' Less than he'd thought, in fact, other than being dragged into fights he'd rather not have.

She rolled her eyes. 'Tosh, Harry Tate. This is meat and drink to you and you know it.' She shook her head. 'You're more complex than you pretend.'

He took out his mobile and brought up the text message from Zubac or Ganic. He held it up so she could read it. She looked at him wide-eyed, and for the first time, he thought he detected a sense of seriousness in her eyes.

'Christ, why didn't you tell me?'

'Would you have still come?'

'Yes, actually.'

'Why?'

'Because all roads lead to Paulton. Isn't that why you're doing this?'

He set off without answering her question. If she was going to shoot him, now would be the time. But he was counting on her wanting Paulton too much to do it just yet. 'Keep a lookout,' he murmured, 'and try not to shoot any members of the Ramblers Association.'

They left the car and moved down the track, arriving at an open gateway and a cluster of small outbuildings on a level patch of ground. Harry stopped in the shade of an oak tree and studied the layout. He counted five buildings in all, darkened by age and neglect, some sprouting grass from the roof. They

still looked usable, and seemed too structured to be farm buildings. He soon realized why; the ground they stood on was at
the head of a north–south stretch of land which must once have
been a runway. Any brick or concrete buildings had long since
been demolished, but someone had obviously forgotten about
the Nissen huts used as sleeping quarters or storerooms. Whoever
now owned the land had profited by renting them out for temporary
storage or as workshops.

He glanced at Clare and nodded towards the left-hand buildings. She slipped away without a word, the gun held two-handed
in front of her. He didn't wait to hear if there were any shouts
of alarm, but started walking around the other side, eyes on the
window panel in the door of the nearest hut.

Empty. The missing pane showed an oil-stained floor and
an old workbench, the interior walls festooned with cobwebs.
It hadn't been used in years. He skirted the building and
approached the next one, feeling the hard standing underfoot,
with cracks and crevices in the concrete caused by the passage
of time.

Also empty and with a hole in the roof. He glanced across
and saw Clare moving away from a hut on her side. She shook
her head to indicate nothing found, then stepped up to the next
one. She peered through the window and shook her head again.

One more left.

Harry stopped.

The last hut was a dozen paces away, set slightly apart from
the other four. Something about it looked different. He gave Clare
a warning signal, and she hunkered down by the wall of the hut
she had just checked while he gave this last one the once-over.
Unlike the previous huts, this last one had a newer door and no
window. The roof also looked solid and the grass around the
doorway had been flattened by regular use.

He waited, listening for any alien sound above the breeze. A
couple of skylarks were kicking up a song high above, and an
unseen tractor was clattering away in the distance. Disturbingly
ordinary. If the Bosnians were in there, they would catch him
flat-footed before he got halfway across the open space towards
the door.

To hell with it. He stepped out and moved at an angle towards the hut, which would make it hard for anyone inside to draw a bead on him. Then he cut back in and fetched up against the door. No shots and he was still upright.

He tried the handle. Locked. He walked around the back, checking for a second door, and found a grey Renault tucked in against the rear wall. The bonnet was up and a pool of oil had spread out on the ground underneath.

Clare joined him. 'Looks like they ran out of luck.' The keys were still in the ignition. She leaned in and gave them a twist. The engine made an unpleasant noise but refused to catch. 'Seized up.'

Harry walked back to the door. 'Sorry, Mr Soran,' he muttered, 'but needs must.' He kicked hard at the panel alongside the lock. The door gave slightly and he kicked again, driving it back until it smacked against an obstruction on the inside.

A wave of musty air came out to greet them, overlaid with body odour and cigarette smoke. Harry stepped inside. Anyone here would not have locked themselves in, waiting to be caught.

The interior was dark. A large battery-powered camping lantern stood on a workbench just inside the door. He switched it on. A pile of wooden crates stood at the far end, with cardboard boxes standing on pallets to keep them off the floor. The floor itself was bare concrete. Against the walls halfway down the hut lay four camp beds, two on each side. A nylon sleeping bag lay on each one with a bare pillow at the head. Two mugs stood on the floor, and an ashtray was perched on an up-ended rubber bucket.

On one of the other beds lay a crumpled T-shirt with a vivid orange starburst pattern on the front. Harry walked across and picked it up. He had only ever seen one like this; Rik had been wearing it. He'd left a clue.

He checked the cardboard boxes, which looked new. Video game consoles with a brand name he'd never heard of. Probably cheap rip-offs if Soran was risking leaving them here. The wooden crates were just small enough to have come through the door, but were heavy, and nailed down tight. He left them. Whatever was in them could wait. He went back out to where Clare was waiting.

'Anything?'

'No. Rik was here, though.' He walked around the outside of the hut, scanning the ground. The grass was shorter here, and clumped haphazardly where it had pushed through the concrete. Further out, though, on the edge of the old runway, it was longer, untouched by vehicles or humans, shimmering in the breeze like waves in the sea.

'There.' He pointed to where twin lines ran through the grass towards the far end of the runway, the passage of whoever had walked down there showing darker than the rest. One line was broader than the other, with occasional kinks, as if someone had stepped off the line they were following.

Or he was being dragged.

'Come on.' Harry set off, leaving Clare to decide whether she wanted to come or not. He wasn't sure why the Bosnians had taken Rik with them, but it could only have been as a bargaining tool if they ran into trouble, or to use him as a last throw of the dice before they bugged out. Whatever their reasoning, it was a short-term thing; this could only go on so long before they wouldn't need him any longer.

'This isn't a random route. They've come this way for a reason.' Clare spoke just behind him.

She was right. It was too direct, too purposeful. Nobody in their position would head out into the fields like this on a whim. They'd be drawing him out and making for a back-up vehicle, somewhere not too far away. Deakin and Soran would have provided for that. They would want both men out of the country so they couldn't talk.

'We'd better hurry.' Clare sounded calm and controlled, her breathing steady. Harry reminded himself that she would have been through a tough training course with MI6, including close quarter combat exercises and live firing. Scenarios such as this would have been part of the curriculum, played out with as much reality as they could muster.

But that was training. It was nothing like the real thing.

FIFTY-SIX

They reached a wire fence, sagging in places, the posts canted at odd angles. On the other side was a railway cutting. The disused line Ballatyne had mentioned. The banks were carpeted with wild flowers, overgrown with bushes and brambles, spilling over in a frenzy of free growth all the way to the bottom.

Harry studied the area, noting where someone had slid down through the grass at one point, bending and crushing the stems, the way a man might if his hands were tied and he was unable to keep his balance.

He stepped over the fence and stood for a moment before venturing down the slope. If the Bosnians suspected someone was after them, they would be waiting at the bottom. Although on higher ground, the pursuer would be vulnerable, committed to the long slope with nowhere to hide but soft bushes and nowhere to go but down.

It would be like a turkey shoot.

'I'll go first,' said Clare. She joined him and then stood by his side, staring at the ground below and no doubt thinking the same thing.

It was a trap waiting to be sprung.

'No,' he said. 'We do it together.' He pointed to where a path had already been flattened, where Rik had lost his balance. 'I'll take this, you take a spot further along.' He set off without waiting, knowing that to argue was to waste time. Rik couldn't have long left.

He slid down the slope by degrees, waiting for the slightest movement, the merest hint of sound. It might be all they would get. Zubac and Ganic were skilled on terrain like this, and would have trained and fought in open country as well as woodland. They had the skills and the motivation, and too much to lose to play safe. They would kill at first sight.

Harry reached the bottom and studied the terrain. The metal

rails and sleepers were long gone, the ground now flatter, but scattered still with stone ballast which made walking uneven. There were signs of regular use, however, and he guessed this was probably part of a hiking route. He fervently hoped nobody was going to come this way today.

He waited for Clare to join him, then turned east. 'Grinstead is this way. If we follow the line, we'll find them.'

He led the way, with Clare following a few paces behind. They stopped every now and then, listening, checking the bushes ahead for signs of disturbance, for anything that shouldn't be there. Overhead, the skylarks were becoming a distraction, and Harry wondered what the penalties were for shooting them.

They came to a bridge. Brick built and sturdy, with metal parapets and ornamental panels, it rose up above the track, throwing a shadow and dwarfing the surrounding bushes and trees with its sheer bulk. There was no sound of traffic passing over its length, only the birdsong, now distant and faint.

'Unused,' Clare murmured.

Harry said nothing. If there was anywhere to spring a trap, it was right here. Plenty of hard cover, lots of shadow, good vantage points from on high, tailor made for killing.

He heard a creak of wood.

They had passed an ancient grit bin a few yards back. Made of metal, with two wooden batwing-style doors set at an angle, it was a piece of railway detritus, abandoned and forgotten. Warped now and long since peeled of any paint, the doors were shut.

Except now they were moving.

'*Down!*' Harry turned, bringing up his weapon, instincts and training kicking in. He found Clare standing in his way, and stepped sideways to get a better line of fire. She moved back, trying to drag her gun round to bear on the target, but stumbled on a piece of ballast and lost her balance.

The batwing doors flew open, and the tall figure of Ganic uncurled from inside, grinning triumphantly. He had waited for them to pass before making his move, and now he had them cold. He was aiming at Harry, whom he clearly thought was the bigger danger. But as he squeezed the trigger, one of the doors fell back against his leg.

It was enough to distract him. The gunshot was loud in the

cutting, the bullet so close to Harry's head he swore he felt the wind of its passing.

He stood his ground and returned fire. Two shots, an echo of a third, and Ganic was flung backwards, trying to stay upright, a shocked look on his face as twin red spots showed on his shirt front. He dropped his gun and fell back into the bin, the doors disintegrating as his heavy body crushed them flat.

Clare had cried out. It took Harry a moment to realize that he had only fired twice. Clare had not fired at all.

But there had been a third shot.

He turned. Clare was lying across the track, a bright splash of red on her stomach. She had dropped her gun and was scrabbling in pain at the ground, trying to get up, and staring at Harry, eyes wide in desperation and shock.

'Don't move!'

Harry froze. Slowly turned his head. It was Zubac, standing just clear of the bridge and holding a semi-automatic. It had been a classic ambush. Zubac must have been waiting in the safety recess under the bridge, with Ganic taking the rear.

Zubac stepped out from the bridge, feet crunching on the scattered ballast, motioning with his free hand for Harry to drop his gun.

'Drop the gun, Englishman, or I'll finish off your bitch right now.'

Harry did so reluctantly, bending slightly to allow the gun to drop carefully. Misfires could also kill. It would be too humiliating to be gut-shot by his own weapon.

'What do you want?' He had to keep Zubac talking. Talking was good. Talking allowed for distractions and negotiations. Talking meant life.

'Want?' Zubac was looking at Ganic's body, slumped inelegantly across the grit bin that had been his hiding place. If he was upset by the death of his friend, he showed no emotion.

'Yes. You didn't lead us down here for nothing. You could have been away and gone by now.'

'True.' Zubac shrugged and looked up at the sky. The skylarks had gone silent. Only the tractor droned on, ragged and distant. 'It is pleasant here. Tranquil. Is that the word – tranquil?' He dropped his gaze to Clare. 'Help me and I won't let her suffer.'

Harry glanced at Clare, who was groaning softly. Fresh blood glistened wetly on her blouse, with a trail running down her side. If he didn't get help soon, she would die.

'Help you how?'

'Out of the country. With you I can get across the water.'

'Why me? Hasn't Soran got you a way out? Deakin? Nicholls?'

Zubac stared at him, a flicker of surprise crossing his face. 'You know a lot, Englishman. Maybe too much. Maybe I should kill you right now.' He lifted the gun and took the first pressure on the trigger.

FIFTY-SEVEN

'So far so good, then.' Paulton nodded. Deakin had just relayed the news that Ferris was in the bag and a message had gone to Tate letting him know. He and the others were walking around the lake at the conference centre, avoiding the other groups taking a break from their meetings. Chatting with corporate windbags was the last thing any of them wanted to do right now.

'As long as Tate does what you said he will.' Deakin picked up a stone and flicked it into the water. 'You've got a lot more faith in him than I have. What's to stop him screaming for the cops?'

'Because it's not in his nature. I know the way he thinks, believe me.' Paulton was now relishing the fact that they were depending on his knowledge of Harry Tate to do the right thing. It meant the balance of influence had shifted, allowing him to play a more guiding role in what would follow. 'He'll trot after Ferris alone because he's been conditioned to do so. It's all he knows.'

'But if he doesn't?' Turpowicz insisted.

'In that case, there will be a messy confrontation with the police or Special Forces and I fear your two thugs will not return to their homeland. And Ferris will be another casualty of police action.' He eyed Turpowicz keenly. 'In which event, Mr Turp, I think we might have need of your specialized military skills.'

'Me?' Turpowicz stopped walking.

'Yes.' Paulton turned and glanced at Deakin for support. 'Of the three of us, you alone have the freedom to travel to the UK without lighting up half the security or military networks in the country. You're what some of my more hip, cool and trendy former colleagues call a "clean skin" – unknown to anyone and able to move freely without arousing interest.'

'Why the hell would he need to do that?' Deakin asked. He sounded torn between the desire to remain in control and fascination at what Paulton was saying.

'Damn right,' Turpowicz echoed. 'I like it just fine on this side of the Channel, thanks.'

Paulton kept his eyes on the American's face. It was a trick he'd learned when about to propose a dangerous course of action to a subordinate. It lent gravity and confidence to the implied request that was about to follow. 'If the Bosnians fail to stop Tate, then you will have to step in and take over. Unless, of course, you've been out of practice too long?'

It was a risky way of provoking a positive response, not least because Paulton wasn't sure what Deakin's reaction would be at having matters taken out of his hands like this. Except that it made absolute sense – and he was certain that the former US airborne sergeant's pride would not let him back down.

'He's right.' Deakin nodded after a few moments. 'We have to get this turkey off our tail. We've already used up three of our five days, and we don't need Tate on our case along with the Chinese. How about it, Turp?' He waited for his colleague to agree.

Turpowicz stared at them in turn, then tilted his head. 'Sure. Why not?'

Paulton smiled broadly. 'Good man. Shall we go and celebrate, or do you need to go off into the woods and practise those silent kill techniques which I know they teach at Fort Campbell?'

Turpowicz didn't return the smile. 'No need. Once taught, never forgotten.'

FIFTY-EIGHT

'It's not just me any more,' said Harry, thinking fast, eyes fastening on Zubac's and trying to drill into his brain. 'The word is out; the Protectory is going to be ripped apart anytime soon. Their time is up along with anyone associated with them: Deakin, Turpowicz, Nicholls, the lot. For you, using any of the conventional ports is out of the question. They'll be watching every exit from here to Inverness.'

Zubac slowly relaxed his grip on the gun, flexing his fingers around the butt as a frown knotted his brow. The barrel dipped as he absorbed what Harry was saying. Then, 'You better hope not.' He shifted the gun and angled it down at Clare's head. 'Or I shoot her right now. You think I care about shooting a woman? She is nothing to me. We did it all the time where I come from. It was sport.'

'OK. OK.' Harry wanted to call his bluff, but he couldn't take the chance. He'd seen what Zubac was capable of. He lifted a hand to placate him, anything to stop him pulling the trigger. 'Let me think how. First, though, where's the man you took?'

Zubac blinked. 'Ah, you mean your colleague, the boy?' He tilted his head back towards the bridge. 'Him I nearly forgot. He's fine. He's my other insurance, in case this one dies too quick . . . or you refuse to help.'

To emphasize his point, Zubac reached down and placed the gun barrel against Clare's forehead. He took the first pressure on the trigger as Clare stared up at him, looking helplessly past the gun. 'You like this woman, Englishman? Huh? She's not pretty already; this will make her even less so, I promise you. Difficult to like her much then.' He grinned, showing yellow teeth. 'But at least she won't fight back, yes?'

Harry didn't say anything. He was too busy trying not to look at Clare. Her right hand was moving. He told himself that it was probably a subconscious motor motion, a reaction to shock and pain drawing in the muscles. God knows what she must be feeling.

'There's no need for that,' he said. 'I'll help.' It was bullshit, of course, as they all knew. Zubac would no more allow them to go free than he would give himself in to the police. First Clare, then Rik, then Harry; all expendable in exchange for his freedom. And with Harry, Zubac had a score to settle. 'So what was the plan, then, before this? If you've got a vehicle, it would help.' Keep him talking, opening the idea that he could get away even now.

'There is another car with fresh plates. In the town called Grinstead.' Zubac had trouble with the 'Gr'. 'One kilometre east from here, by crossing . . . but not used any more. You understand, crossing?'

'I understand. All you have to do is walk along the track until you reach it.'

Clare had brought her hand down to her hip, moving with excruciating slowness. It must have been agony. Harry kept his eyes on Zubac's face, demanding his full attention. He had no idea what Clare was up to, but if she could distract him long enough . . .

'That's easy enough. You get the car and then what? What did Soran say to do next? What was the plan?'

Zubac spat to one side. 'Soran is going to be dead man,' he muttered. 'The Renault he gave us was supposed to be good. It was shit machinery with shit engine, fit for scrapyard. So maybe there is no car in Grinstead and he cheat us. That is why you will help.'

Christ on a bike, Harry thought. What a time to lose confidence in your supply line.

'There will be other cars, no problem. I can get one.'

Clare's hand had disappeared. She was now trying to move her body, to roll slightly. Was she going for a back-up weapon . . . or was the pain so acute that she was trying to ease it? Whatever, the final movement was sufficient to catch Zubac's attention.

He glanced down with a muttered query.

Harry began to move, his gut lurching. It was no good; he would be too late. All it would take was the pressure of Zubac's finger—

Fortunately, Zubac was even slower to react. Clare gave a

grunt and her hand came out from under her body trailing a glint of silver. She brushed the back of Zubac's hand, leaving behind a heavy veil of blood as the blade of her compact knife sliced deeply through the skin and extensor tendons. The Bosnian cried out in pain and tried to pull the trigger, but his fingers were useless and the gun fell on to Clare's face. As it slid to her side, she scooped it up in a flash and thrust it into his chest, screamed furiously, and pulled the trigger twice in quick succession.

Zubac was thrown backwards by the force of the shots.

By the time Harry got to her side, Clare had dropped the gun and was nearly unconscious. He made her comfortable and checked her airways were clear, then tore off his shirt and used his belt to hold a wad of the cloth against the wound.

As he worked on trying to save her, she watched him, her eyes unnaturally bright. If there was a message in there, he failed to see it. But then she whispered something and it was simple, desperate.

'Help me . . .' Then she passed out.

Harry took out his phone and rang Ballatyne's office.

'One woman with a gunshot wound,' he told the man who answered, and gave him his location. 'She needs urgent medical attention. Ground access is rubbish – a chopper would be quicker. Tell them to look for a railway cutting near a bridge. Landing area is good.'

'Understood, sir. Air ambulance on the way. I'll tell Mr Ballatyne. Any opposition likely?'

'There was – they're both dead.'

'Very good, sir.' The man cut the connection and Harry switched off his phone, not sure if his final words had been an acknowledgement or a congratulation.

Rik. He had to find Rik. Must be under the bridge if Zubac had been telling the truth. As he scooped up his gun and stood up, Harry glanced back along the track, eyes drifting towards the grit bin where he had shot Ganic.

But Ganic was no longer there.

FIFTY-NINE

Harry jogged across to the bin, staying low. The skin on his neck was prickling with anticipation, expecting the slam of a gunshot. But nothing came. He scanned the area, hoping for some signs showing where the Bosnian had gone. How the hell had the man survived the two shots? He must have the constitution of an elephant.

But he wasn't bulletproof. There were blood spots on the ground. More on the remains of the bin's wooden doors and the grass leading towards the slope. It didn't look as if he was bleeding profusely, but still more than enough to have slowed down or stopped most men in their tracks.

And no sign of his gun.

A tangle of bushes littered the slope, some at head height and covered with greenery. Too dense to see anything clearly until you were right on it, by which time it was too late. If Ganic was up there waiting, it would be suicidal going up after him. He'd have done this kind of fighting before. All the Bosnian had to do was wait and Harry would walk right on to his gun.

He turned towards the bridge. He had to find Rik, or Ganic would have a bargaining tool and they'd be back to square one. And somehow he doubted Ganic would be as patient or as talkative as Zubac.

He stopped before going in, trying to see inside the shadowed structure. It was probably forty feet wide, the ground clear as far as he could see. But there were bushes and weeds growing along the base of the walls, ideal cover for a man to lie in wait. If Ganic had worked his way round and was already in there . . . Harry shook his head. Pointless worrying. After all, what else was he going to do – turn round and walk away? This had to bloody end some time.

He stepped forward, braced for a movement, a sound. According to the close quarter combat instructors many years ago, it was more a feeling you had to look for, a shift in the atmosphere that gave a hint of the threat to come. If the opposition was good enough, they'd make no sound, have no need to move until they were ready. But the air around them would shift, and that was what they had to look out for. The good students used their instincts and tuned in immediately, picking up the signals. The bad ones ended up dead. At the time, Harry had thought it was instructor mumbo-jumbo, thrown in to make them try harder. But he'd soon learned different.

He heard a groan, then a scrape of sound, like fabric rubbing on something. It was coming from the far side of the bridge, behind the wall.

Was it Ganic, wounded and desperate, but willing Harry on so he could kill him?

It was Rik, arms tied behind his back and ankles held by a wrap-around of rope. Just enough to hold a man still. He looked groggy, his body limp, but he jumped when Harry bent over him. Then recognition flooded his face and he relaxed.

'Took your bloody time, didn't you?' he moaned, shaking off the ropes when Harry loosened the knots. 'I thought I was going to have to fight them off all by myself. Jesus, I've got a headache. That bastard Zubac . . .' He rubbed his eyes. 'Sorry. They came knocking not long after you left. I thought it was you and opened the door. Next thing I knew I was having the shit kicked out of me. I don't remember much after that.' He looked up with a start. 'Where are they? I heard shots.'

'Zubac's dead. Ganic's free and roaming but wounded. Lie still – you might have concussion. There's a chopper on the way. We need to get back to Clare.' He put a hand under Rik's arm and helped him up.

'Clare? You mean slice-and-dice Clare, the MI6 sushi chef? What's that crazy bitch doing here?'

'Saving our bacon, mostly, so stop moaning, you little tick – you owe her. She took a bullet.'

Rik made a sound, stumbling on shaky legs. 'Long as I don't have to be bessy mates with her. She gives me the creeps.'

They emerged from the bridge and crossed to where Clare was lying. Her breathing was uneven, but she was hanging on.

'Christ, that looks bad,' said Rik. He looked shocked, dropping the antagonism in an instant. 'Is she going to make it?'

'Only if they're quick.' Harry stood and listened, wondering where the chopper would come from. For Clare the seconds were ticking away.

Rik found Zubac's gun. He checked the load, cleaned off some dirt, then sat down on the ground and looked up at Harry.

'This was a fuck-up, wasn't it? All of it. Was it necessary?'

Harry shrugged. He didn't know any more. They hadn't found the Protectory or Paulton, and one of their tame orcs was out there somewhere with a gun. He took out his mobile and called Ballatyne. This time the man himself answered.

'You on another killing spree, Harry?' he said drily. 'I'm not going to have to send you back overseas, am I? The ambulance should be there any minute, by the way. What's the damage?'

'Clare Jardine's badly wounded, Rik's bashed up but moaning and one of the Bosnians was playing possum. He's out there somewhere, bleeding, but armed and mobile.'

'Don't worry, there's a police chopper somewhere above you now. Got a camera on board so good he can spot the freckles on a rabbit's arse. Moment they see Ganic they'll have him picked up by a Special Forces team.'

'No,' said Harry quickly. That was the worst thing they could do. 'Let Ganic run.'

'Say again?'

'They have a car waiting ready to go. They were trying to get back across the Channel. Ganic wasn't the brains of the outfit; that was Zubac's role. Ganic's a soldier. All he knows is they had to get out of the country – he won't be thinking about why. With Zubac dead he'll concentrate on getting back to Deakin . . . and Paulton.'

'Can't do that, Harry. The man's a cop killer.' Ballatyne sounded adamant. 'We let him get among the public with a gun and we'll all end up in Parkhurst. There could be a bloodbath.'

'Then get me to him before he can go anywhere.'

'To do what? You're not the executioner here, Harry.'

'He'll tell me where Deakin is hiding. Pinpoint his location and get me close behind, and I'll follow him in before he gets anywhere public – but you have to be quick.'

'Then what?'

'Then it's over.'

*   *   *

Ten minutes later, Harry was seated in the body of a British Chinook fitted out with medical equipment. He could do nothing but watch while the crew of army medics got on with their job, evaluating the extent of Clare's injury and keeping her alive before they took to the air. She was still losing blood from the bullet wound in her side, and her skin was a frightening shade of grey. The chief medic was on the radio feeding through the details of her wound and current state ready for their arrival and Clare's transfer to an emergency unit, while his colleagues busied themselves monitoring her condition and keeping her as still as possible against the build-up of vibration as the aircraft got ready to lift off.

Across from Harry, Rik was staring at her, his face a vivid array of colours from where Zubac and Ganic had subdued him for transport to the abandoned airfield. He had a patch of blood on his chest, but a medic had pronounced it a minor leakage from his shoulder wound which, Rik had explained, was caused by a carefully placed kick from Ganic on the way down.

One of the helicopter crew members waved at Harry and signalled for him to get out. Harry unclipped his belt and jumped down, and the crew member hurried him away from the noise and dust of the down-draught.

'You're to wait here,' he shouted. 'They've spotted your man less than half a mile away. He's down and not moving. Another helicopter will pick you up in three minutes. Stand well back and keep your head down.' He clapped Harry on the shoulder and jumped back into the fuselage, then the Chinook wound up and lifted off, enveloping Harry and everything around him in a stinging spray of soil, dust and tiny bits of gravel.

SIXTY

Ganic was lying to one side of the trail, face up, arms flung out to his sides.

As the police helicopter assigned to pick Harry up slid alongside the old railway cutting, Harry could see that the

Bosnian's hands were empty. He checked the cutting in each direction. Nobody about. But just beyond where he was lying, the remains of an old vehicle crossing were just visible where a track met the railway at right-angles.

There was no sign of a getaway car. Zubac's suspicions had been correct: Soran had failed to keep to this part of the plan.

'Drop me here,' he said, pointing to the top of the slope leading to the track, where long grass would make a soft landing and give him some cover if Ganic was still a danger.

The pilot nodded and lost height, and Harry dropped from the doorway and rolled, feeling the impact through his legs. He stood up and took out his gun, then stepped over the wooden fence rail and crouched at the top of the slope just above where Ganic was lying. He hadn't moved.

The helicopter pulled away, the down-draught fanning the surrounding vegetation and lifting Ganic's jacket.

Harry mentally crossed his fingers, then slid down the slope. Holding his gun two-handed, he fixed the sights on the man below. Any movement and he was going to start shooting, and to hell with Ballatyne's reaction.

He breathed a sigh of relief when he saw Ganic's gun lying nearby. Too far for the Bosnian to reach out for it, even if he'd wanted to. It was covered in blood, with a trail of bright red splashes leading back in the direction of the bridge. Ganic's shirt front was awash with red, too.

His eyes were open, watching as Harry approached. He showed no expression. But a blink showed he was still conscious.

'You're a tough man to stop,' said Harry.

'Fuck you, Englishman.' Ganic's whisper was faint, his Adam's apple bobbing up and down. 'You lucky.'

Harry squatted down alongside him, showed him the gun. He felt no emotion at seeing this man down; Ganic had planned on taking Jean and killing Rik, and had a long list of bodies to his name, including the officers in Brixton. In the grand scheme of things, his time was long overdue.

'Where's Deakin?'

A red bubble formed at the corner of Ganic's mouth. He shook his head and coughed, his face twisting with pain. The bubble popped and a string of reddened saliva slid down the side of his chin.

'Come on, what's the point of defending him? Deakin stiffed you; he left you here with no car and no way out.' He nodded in the direction of the crossing, which he could just see from here. Ganic must have seen it, too, before he fell. An empty track with no car in sight. It had probably been the last straw for a dying man. 'What do you owe him?'

Ganic swallowed, but said nothing. The helicopter had gone, and Harry guessed it had landed to conserve fuel. Overhead the skylarks had started up again, and a pigeon added its melancholy tune to the landscape.

'Milan?' The man's voice was fainter, his breathing faster. 'Where's Mil . . . Milan?'

'He's dead.'

Ganic's eyes swivelled. 'You?'

'No. Not me.'

'Then . . . the *woman*?' He tried to laugh, but choked noisily instead.

Harry waited for him to recover, and his breathing to settle. 'He took his eyes off her.'

Ganic coughed, liquid burbling in his throat. 'Bloody fool,' he murmured. 'He always talked too much.'

'Deakin,' said Harry, sensing Ganic's clock was fast running down. 'Where do I find him? And Paulton.'

'Do not . . . know . . . Pault . . .' Ganic swallowed. 'Turpowicz. American airborne . . . Nich . . .' He seemed to run out of names, as if it had all been too tiring.

'But Deakin. Where does he hide out?'

Ganic's head flopped sideways. For a moment, Harry thought he'd gone. But when he bent closer he was surprised to pick up a flutter of breathing. 'Deakin . . . is English . . . asshole,' Ganic whispered.

Then he died.

SIXTY-ONE

Two days passed during which Clare Jardine hovered between life and death, her every heartbeat monitored in an intensive care centre. The bullet from Zubac's gun had done a lot of damage, causing serious blood loss. But she was tough in body and spirit, and the consultants finally emerged to pronounce her past the worst. It was expected that she would survive as long as no infections set in.

There was also the revelation that Osama bin Laden had finally been run to ground in Pakistan and killed by US Special Forces. There had been no let up ever since the news broke, and every broadcast brought fresh details about the capture and the ramifications for the West.

Harry wasn't sure whether to be relieved or satisfied about either event. Bin Laden himself was a distant figure, more newsfeed image than a real person. The danger facing the West came from radicalized followers who were unknown and therefore highly dangerous, and likely to want to make a statement of support.

As for Clare, he still wouldn't trust her as far as he could jump, but she had saved Jean and himself when she didn't need to, and he was grateful for that. She had also unwittingly saved Rik Ferris, who had grudgingly given her a thank you in acknowledgement by sending her a new powder compact made of bright-pink, girly plastic. No blade attached.

'She can recover in a prison ward,' Ballatyne announced tersely. He had called a meeting at Georgio's. Ballatyne's male minder was in tow as usual, and gave Harry a familiar nod.

Harry was dismayed by the comment. 'Isn't it a little late in the day for that?'

'Jesus, hardly. She killed her boss, a serving MI6 officer, remember? That's a long prison term right there.'

'Oh, you mean her boss the corrupt, murdering MI6 officer who wanted us both dead,' Harry pointed out evenly. 'She did us a favour and you know it. Bellingham would have walked, otherwise.'

Ballatyne looked mildly shocked. 'Surely you're not defending her, Harry. Did she get under your skin that much?'

'No. She saved my life and she saved Jean. Call me old-fashioned like that, but I can't help it. You'd do the same.'

'Maybe so. But the law's the law.'

'Bollocks.' Harry leaned threateningly towards him. Ballatyne's minder got to his feet, although it was to pour himself a glass of water. He raised the glass in the background in a mock salute and grinned, then turned away. 'What's the point of locking her up? It won't accomplish anything.'

Ballatyne shrugged. He appeared to have no ready argument, which made Harry question how serious he had been in the first place. 'Maybe not. I'll see. No promises, though.'

Harry sat back. It was something at least.

'Nicholls has come in, by the way,' Ballatyne told him. 'Bumped into a group of Intelligence Corps officers at Frankfurt airport and suffered some kind of a mental trauma. Luckily one of them took it seriously and they hustled him away to a medical unit where he was treated and shipped back here. No idea when he'll be able to talk coherently, if ever, but at least it's another one down.' He chewed his lip. 'No sign of Deakin or Paulton, though. And if Nicholls knows, he isn't saying.'

'And the American?' There had been no mention of Turpowicz.

'Ah, well there we have some news. He's been taken off the American AWOL list. He walked into Grosvenor Square the day before yesterday and asked to speak to the US Embassy's Army Intelligence liaison. He's probably out of the country by now and on his way to the brig . . . or whatever they call it over there. Good riddance.'

'Do we know why he came in?'

'No, and right now they're not telling. He'll go through a period of questioning, so we might find out later. But I'm not holding my breath.'

'No problem. We'll keep looking.'

Ballatyne shook his head and looked suddenly uncomfortable. 'Actually, that's why I called you here.'

Harry waited. He sensed something wrong in the atmosphere.

'There's no point continuing, I'm afraid. You're being stood down. This operation is now terminated. We've been given other priorities.'

'Like what?' Harry didn't bother hiding his annoyance. He could guess what it was, in which case he didn't expect Ballatyne to answer. But he was surprised when he did.

'Blame Osama. Ever since he got himself caught and killed, all agencies have been ordered to focus on watching for a back-lash from his supporters. Sorry, but it can't be helped. Our remit just got broader and our budgets still got slashed. We'll have to leave Paulton and Deakin for another time.'

'Why can't we do both? They're out there preying on deserters and selling secrets, and we have to stand back and let them do it? It doesn't make sense.'

Ballatyne shrugged, his face hardening. 'It rarely does, Harry, you know that. There's nothing else I can say.'

'But they'll be vulnerable now. With Nicholls gone and Turpowicz off the board, they'll have to reorganize. And Turpowicz must have jumped for a reason. He was either disillusioned or felt threatened by something – maybe the direction Deakin was taking them in. If we can put the squeeze on him, we stand a good chance of finding out where they are.'

It was like fighting smoke. Ballatyne merely shook his head and repeated what he had said.

'Fine,' Harry said at last. 'I'll look for them myself.'

Ballatyne shrugged. 'I can't stop you doing that, of course. But you'll have to do it without my help. Sorry. Orders.'

'What about Cullum?'

'He was threatened with being dropped from a very great height, but he doesn't know anything. They made sure of that.'

Harry gave up. It wasn't Ballatyne's fault. He decided to walk home, hoping to shed his anger by pounding the pavements. It wouldn't do his shoe leather much good, but the exercise might make him feel a little less like wrecking something.

As he rounded a corner on to Euston Road, his phone rang.

'Harry Tate?' The voice was American. 'My name's Greg Turpowicz. Is there any chance we could meet? I'd like to talk.'

SIXTY-TWO

'Have you heard from the Screaming Eagle yet?' Paulton walked into Deakin's room without ceremony, sniffing the air like a bloodhound. He was referring to Turpowicz, using the 101st Airborne's nickname. Dressed in a neat suit and tie, the executive abroad, he strode across to the window overlooking a large expanse of lake and studied the landscape. It looked fresh and clean under the early morning sunlight, inviting a brisk walk. 'He was supposed to keep in touch, wasn't he?'

Deakin shrugged. 'He's not a rookie; I don't need to hear from him every couple of hours. What's the problem?'

It had been two days since Ganic had failed to respond; two days since they had received confirmation that both the Bosnians had gone down, apparently without revealing any information. Dead before they hit the ground, according to Paulton's contact in the Met Police.

'The lack of reassuring information is the problem,' Paulton murmured. 'He was supposed to get close to Tate and deal with him for good. He has all the information he needs. I'd just relish hearing that he has done that.'

Deakin lifted an eyebrow. For once, he seemed quite calm, while Paulton was the edgy one. They had remained in position, safe in the knowledge that nothing would go wrong, and neither of the Bosnians knew where they were, so could not reveal their location, even if they survived. Turpowicz, on the other hand, did know, although Deakin had professed continued faith in the former American soldier's ability to stay out of trouble and keep his mouth shut even if he was questioned.

'You need to chill, George,' he said. 'Turp will do the business.' He grinned malevolently. 'He has a vested interest in doing things right, anyway. The Yanks are a lot less forgiving of their deserters than the Brits; if they should happen to find out where he is . . . well, he'll spend a lot of time banged up.'

Paulton looked at him. 'Tom, if I didn't know you better, I'd

say that sounds as if you've applied a little undue pressure on
our American friend. That's a bit risky with a man of his background, isn't it?'

'Not really. Turp knows which side his bread is buttered.'

'I'll take your word for that. Only I would like to hear that
he's still in the game . . . merely for my own peace of mind, you
understand?' He waited, eyebrows lifted, until the other man
nodded with a sigh.

'OK. I'll call him.' Deakin took out his mobile and touched
speed dial. It rang several times before being picked up. 'Turp?
How's it going? Have you completed the transaction yet?' He
listened, eyes on Paulton, then said, 'Sounds good to me. You
know where to meet up once you're done? Good.' He switched
off the phone and smiled. 'He knows where Tate is going to be
tomorrow morning. He'll do it then. Believe me, I've seen his
work before. Tate's dead meat. Satisfied?'

SIXTY-THREE

'One of these days I'll have a proper meeting in an office
with an appointment and everything,' Harry said, as
a tall, thin man sat down beside him. 'Who are the
flat tops?' He was referring to the men he'd spotted trying to
blend in with the tourist crowd in Kensington Gardens. They
were not doing too well, and were too fit and smart, in an overtly
military kind of way.

'They work for US Army Intelligence. Don't worry about
them, Mr Tate – they're pretty harmless.' The man smiled. 'As
a matter of interest, how many can you see?'

Harry didn't need to look. One was stationed under the trees
against the backdrop of moving traffic along the Bayswater
Road; a second was standing by the Round Pond watching two
swans; and two more were on the move along the Broad Walk
in front of Kensington Palace, but never straying too far and
trying not to look directly at Harry and his new companion.
'Four.'

The smile dropped. 'Four it is.' The man held out a hand. 'Greg Turpowicz. It's good of you to meet with me.' He sounded relaxed and genial, a man with time on his side. His hand was dry, the grip firm but with the underlying power of a man who kept himself in good physical shape.

'Good's got nothing to do with it, Master Sergeant. I need information.'

The American looked stunned. 'You know my background?'

'It wasn't difficult. The accent couldn't have been Deakin, Nicholls has had a brainstorm and turned himself in, and I'd know Paulton's voice anywhere. You were the only one left. And,' he continued, waving a finger in a circular motion, 'there are a few of our own flat top equivalents in the neighbourhood, too. Just to see that you play nice.'

Turpowicz couldn't help it; he glanced around the park. 'I don't see 'em.' One of the watchers picked up on the look and started to move, but the American shook his head to warn him off.

'They're here, take my word for it. If this was a film, you'd be able to see at least three red dots dancing on the front of your shirt.'

Turpowicz struggled not to glance down, and gave a nervous laugh. 'I'm impressed. You must have connections.' He watched two heavily built men in tracksuits walking a string of large dogs, and a small Asian woman almost being pulled off her feet by another pack. 'Is it true that this place is crowded with Russian agents? I hear this is where they come to do their drops and stuff.'

'Only in books. What do you want?' Harry didn't want to exchange small talk about this place; he'd been forced to shoot dead the last person he'd been here with. Joanne Archer, a rogue Special Forces soldier, had shot Rik Ferris and turned her gun on Harry while attempting to kill a former Iraqi cleric in St James's Park. He'd been left with no choice.

'You off my back would be good, although,' Turpowicz waggled a hand, 'it's kind of academic, now I'm back inside, so to speak.' He added quickly, 'Uh . . . what'll happen if I reach into my pocket?'

'Do you need to?'

'Just asking.'

'Well, then, nothing . . . as long as you do it slowly.' He waited but Turpowicz had changed his mind. 'You did a deal with the military, didn't you?'

'Yeah, sort of. How'd you know?'

'I checked with Fort Knox and got blanked. And the US military wouldn't assign a four-man protection team if you were still out there and running.'

'Blanked?' He frowned at the word. 'Oh, you mean the runaround.' He smiled. 'All this time with Deakin and I still don't get British slang. But "blanked" I like. Says what it means.' He crossed his legs. 'Yeah, it's true, I did a deal. I also heard you'd been checking up on me. How did you pick up my name?'

'McCreath heard the abbreviation. When Fort Knox got tricky about telling us who it might refer to, I knew there had to be something to it.'

'But they didn't give you my full details, right?'

'Not directly.' Harry wasn't about to dump Garcia in the pan. She had done what she thought was right, for her own reasons. 'We bugged Major Dundas's desk. He talks as he types. Very sloppy security.'

Turpowicz made a noise with his mouth. 'Seriously?'

'What do you want? You want to trade with us, too?'

'Not exactly. I want to give you Deakin. Interested?'

'Why? His activities are nothing to do with the US military. The nearest he came to US army personnel was you.'

'That's correct. Let's just say that I have my orders.'

'Go on . . .'

Turpowicz shifted in his seat. 'You're right, I made a deal with the military. Full disclosure for a light sentence. I tell them – and you – what you want to know, and I get my life back in maybe ten months' time.' His voice was flat, matter-of-fact, a recital. He might seem relaxed, but there was a tension about him like a ripple in the air.

'How did they make contact?'

'I got careless one night in Germany several moons back and ran into a couple of undercover military cops. I was already having doubts about Deakin, so I told them I was in contact with the Protectory and suggested I could be of use. They made some calls. The answer came back to let me run as long as I stayed in touch. I had no choice – I said yes.'

'Interesting,' said Harry. 'So to get this straight, even though you stood by while Deakin and his two bulldogs murdered at least two British army personnel, made an armed raid on a British police station and killed three police officers, tried to kidnap a close friend of mine, actually abducted and beat a colleague of mine and shot a woman, you get to walk away for being a good boy?'

'Hey – that wasn't any of my doing,' Turpowicz protested heatedly. Then he dropped his voice. 'I had no control over what Deakin was using those two psychos for. Most of the time he never said what they were doing until it was done.' He pounded his knee angrily. 'I reported what I knew as soon as I could, every time.'

'What was the response?'

Turpowicz said nothing, so Harry said, 'They told you to play along, didn't they?'

'I couldn't help it, man!' For the first time, the American sounded passionate, his voice low. 'I didn't trust Deakin not to get suspicious and set Zubac and Ganic on me. And I wasn't exactly in the clear with the military, either. The message was simple: I either stuck with it or they picked me up and I'd be doing serious time in the military stockade at Leavenworth. So I agreed to go along with it.'

'Nice people you work for.' It was easy to condemn the man, although Harry could see his dilemma. A rock and a hard place. 'Was that the deal – a lighter sentence?'

'Pretty much. It was all I had worth asking for. I figured they were worried about US military personnel being sucked in and used to trade military secrets. I had to look out to make sure it didn't happen.'

'How?'

'Easy. The moment anyone showed up, I had to report it in. They'd have been lifted immediately. Fact is, no one did. Our runners all bug out for different places and keep their heads down. Deakin and Nicholls were strictly after their own, although I reckon Deakin would've got round to trading US personnel some day. He doesn't like to let the grass grow – and he's impatient to make a big score.'

'Who were his clients?'

'I only ever met one. The rest he kept close to his chest, did all his own trading. When I first met up with them, Nicholls was the one who found the people and Deakin did the selling. Then gradually it changed, and Nicholls became less involved, especially after Paulton showed up. I liked Nicholls but he was a sick man. I wasn't surprised when he cut and run.'

'What was Paulton's position in the Protectory?'

'A partner, I guess. He showed up one day, and he was in. Deakin claimed he had the inside track on contacts of foreign governments where they could sell stuff, and that made him the golden boy. Personally, I reckon he was aiming to stage a take-over.' He shook his head. 'He was a manipulative son of a bitch, I know that. Subtle, though, so you didn't notice. He never came at anything head on, know what I mean?'

Harry knew all right. 'How did you pick up on it?'

Turpowicz grunted. 'Because I'm a simple guy from a farming background. I don't deal in subtleties and I take people as I find them. Paulton was too smooth. I just know a mover and shaker when I see one. I didn't like him from the moment I met him.'

'Good. We have something in common. It didn't seem to bother him, trading secrets and personnel for money?'

'No. I think he got a real kick out of the whole idea, like it was getting one over on teacher, you know?'

'You said you met one client. Who was that?'

'Wien Lu Chi. Chinese, Deakin said, one of their middlemen. Smooth as a snake and probably as dangerous. That was a few days ago.'

'In Bremen.'

Turpowicz looked shocked. 'You knew?'

'Yes. And they're right – television puts pounds on a face. What was the trade?'

'We deliver a Lieutenant Tan – some highly placed aide to the Deputy Commander of your forces in Kabul – in return for a lot of money.'

'How much?'

'A million bucks. Deakin was doing a hard sell, saying he had access to this woman, and the guy lapped it up.'

'Was Paulton there, too?'

'No. He was meant to be, but he cried off at the last minute; said he was tied up.' He sighed. 'I was against the whole deal, but when Wien handed Deakin a case full of money as a down-payment, there was no going back. He gave us five days to come up with the goods.' He shook his head. 'It was insane; no way were we going to find her that quick. We didn't even know where to begin – there was no sign of her anywhere.'

'I'm not surprised,' said Harry. 'She never existed.'

A brief, frozen silence during which Turpowicz looked stunned. 'You're kidding!'

'She was a ghost, laid to draw in the Protectory. You shouldn't feel too bad – even Deakin's man in London fell for it.' So, he almost said, did I. But he decided that would be too much information.

Turpowicz shook his head. 'Christ, were we ever suckered. In that case, you'd better move fast if you want Deakin and Paulton. If they're still out there, anyway. I wouldn't lay much on their chances when the Chinese get to hear about Tan. They've probably gotten them in their sights already.'

'How did you manage to get away without them being suspicious?'

'It was their idea . . . well, Paulton's, actually.' Turpowicz looked a little sheepish. 'He wanted a fall-back plan in case Zubac and Ganic failed to stop you. I was nominated to step in and do it instead.'

Harry nodded. 'And you agreed with that?'

'Sure. I'd already had contact with Army Intelligence, using a link with the UN. Soon as I could, I told them I was coming in.' He rubbed his hands together. 'They agreed, but said I had to come in to London, brief your people on everything I knew about Deakin and his crew, then return to the States. But I wanted to meet you, too. I may be a failed soldier, Mr Tate, but I'm no assassin.'

Harry didn't believe him, but there was little he could do about it. There had been other deaths attributed to the Protectory, and Turpowicz must have been around at the time. Maybe he just had a well-developed instinct for survival. If the Chinese really wanted to get antsy with Deakin over the money they had paid, it was unlikely they would bother coming after Turpowicz once he was in the States.

He wondered how long Deakin had got left.

'Where are Deakin and Paulton?'

Turpowicz gave him the name of a conference centre near Ghent, in Belgium. 'It's a hideaway place he's used before. Lots of privacy. They'll be there two more days, then they're gone. Deakin's using the name Phillips, Paulton is Goddard.' He blinked. 'Is that us done?'

Harry reached into his top pocket and took out a small black box. He'd got as much as he needed from this man. How Ballatyne used it was up to him. 'Pretty much. This has been transmitting ever since you sat down.'

Turpowicz looked stricken, and glanced down to his side involuntarily, his mouth working. 'Jesus . . . they'll kill me for this.' He swallowed and reached into his side pocket and produced a similar sized box to the one Harry was holding. 'They told me I had to use this to block any signal . . . I forgot.'

'Technology,' said Harry. 'It's a bitch, isn't it?'

SIXTY-FOUR

The Auberge Grand Lac was a glorious misnomer. More chateau than inn, it had clearly been added to in a variety of ways over the years resulting in a mishmash of conflicting styles, and it now resembled something with a touch of Hollywood. Shrouded by several acres of woodland around a large lake, it was billed as a conference centre with leisure facilities, seclusion guaranteed, with one road in and out along a looping stretch of narrow pink tarmac. The road in ended at a large open gravelled space out front with discreetly marked strips for guest parking. Several outbuildings linked by covered walkways were described on their website as a gym, guest rooms and a swimming pool with, further over, a group of tennis courts and a golf course.

Harry stopped the hire car just inside the gate, where he could get a clear panoramic view of the grounds and buildings. The place was impressive. It spoke of ample funds and devotion to a cause, which was the provision of facilities for those with means and the need for secluded discussions in surroundings untroubled by everyday life.

'Nice place,' said Rik Ferris. He had discarded his sling and was dressed in conservative slacks and a plain shirt and jacket. 'Selling state secrets must pay well if Deakin's lot can afford to stay here.'

Harry used a small pair of binoculars to check the area around the main building. A few business types were wandering around, probably on a break from their meetings. A patio on one side of the building held a scattering of chairs and tables, with more people gathered around a trestle table serving coffee and biscuits. Cameras were located on the roof at various points, and flood-lights, too, at ground level.

But no security guards, he noted. At least, not obvious ones.

He checked the tree line, which stood at least two hundred yards from the nearest building. A narrow track ran between the two, cutting across part of the golf course. Probably an access road for maintenance or deliveries. A few players were abusing balls out on the greens, but in a refined, easygoing way; no doubt the top dogs of the corporate world, enjoying a round or two while the juniors did the talking and meeting inside.

'Come on,' he said, and got back in the car.

They drove to the front entrance and parked out front. A shuttle emblazoned with the centre's name was loading cases and passengers, and Harry scanned the faces out of habit. Tired-looking, but smiling, checking out and heading for home after a gruelling few days. A grey Mercedes was ticking over near the road, the Asian driver standing by the door. He looked alert and fit, too watchful to be an ordinary chauffeur or taxi driver. Harry was reminded of Ballatyne's words when the MI6 officer found out where he was going.

'The place is used by foreign diplomats, so don't go shooting anyone we like.'

It had taken a lot of persuasion for Ballatyne to allow Harry to proceed, but he had thrown in the right amount of help where it was needed, on the grounds that it wouldn't cost anything.

Harry left Rik outside and walked past the shuttle bus and through the front entrance. Inside was all marble and glass, soulless as a hospital foyer, only quieter. He approached the desk and asked to speak to the manager. The receptionist nodded and hustled away into a rear office, returning with a bristle-topped man with sad eyes and the look of a professional problem solver.

'Yes, sir? May I help?'

Harry showed him a card with a name on it. It held a telephone number which was a direct line to a senior member of the Belgian Interior Ministry. Ballatyne had assured him that it would clear the way should he need it, and that the Belgians had been advised of his visit but would keep only a watching brief.

He could tell by the manager's reaction that the name was familiar.

'If you ring that number,' Harry said quietly, 'you will have confirmation of our credentials. In the meantime, could you tell me if two guests by the name of Phillips and Goddard are still here?'

The manager nodded eagerly. 'Of course, sir. As a matter of fact, I have already had a call from the ministry, advising me of your . . . visit.' He glanced sideways but there was nobody close by. 'I would merely ask that you be discreet, please. We have trade delegations here from Hong Kong and Singapore and I would not wish to upset the atmosphere.' He simpered. 'They are like wild birds: once frightened, they rarely come back.'

Harry nodded. That would explain the driver out front. 'Don't worry – I'm totally house-trained. Are the men still here?'

The manager turned and caught the receptionist's attention, and they went into a brief huddle. When he came back, he said, 'Indeed they are, sir. Mr Phillips is in L24, overlooking the lake, and Mr Goddard is in G18, overlooking the golf course. I am advised by Leon, our customer reception captain, that Mr Phillips is down by the lake. He saw him walking in that direction earlier, accompanied by another visitor.'

'Thank you.' Both together. It would be easier than hunting them separately. Harry began to turn away, then stopped. 'Another visitor, you say. Not Mr Goddard?'

'No, sir. The gentleman called just as you are now, and asked to speak to him.' He gestured towards the reception desk. 'The customer reception captain checked with the room service chief for you just now. Mr Goddard is still in his room. He was heard talking on the phone just a few minutes ago.'

Harry thanked him for his help and walked back outside to join Rik. Which one first – Deakin or Paulton? His instincts were pulling him towards his former boss, but getting Paulton wouldn't close down the Protectory.

The shuttle bus had gone and the Mercedes was pulling away along the exit road, elegantly powerful. There was one passenger in the back, in shadow. As the car passed by, the driver glanced across, and Harry felt a mild frisson of something pass between them. It was like a small current of electricity, and he knew he'd experienced it before. But where?

Then it came to him: Ballatyne's minder in Georgio's restaurant, the first time they'd met. It had been the unspoken recognition between fellow professionals.

'Christ, surely not.'

'What?' Rik looked at him.

'The lake. Deakin's down by the lake.'

They ran across the forecourt and over a belt of immaculate lawn past the corner of the building. The lake was spread out before them, the sunlight glinting off the surface, a scattering of water birds throwing small shadows as they floated on the mildest of ripples. A jetty jutted from the bank, with a handful of small boats tied up alongside. Benches were spread out at intervals around the perimeter of the lake, each one sheltered by small open-box surrounds of privet hedge. Only one bench was in use, and that was away from the approach road, with its back to the woods.

Harry led the way across the open ground, eyes fixed on the person sitting on the bench. It was a man in casual dress of shirt and pants. He looked relaxed, slim, one arm along the back of the bench, the other hand in his jacket pocket. He looked as if he might be dozing, no doubt lulled by the warmth of the sun's rays and the reflection off the water.

Thomas Deakin.

Harry wasn't taking any chances. He reached for the gun in

his pocket, conscious that Rik would be moving away to one side to cover him. Ballatyne had moved mountains and called in debts to ease the way for them both to be armed. But he'd added strict instructions that the weapons must be used only in extreme circumstances.

Harry moved closer and said, 'Deakin. Show me your hands.'

There was no response.

'Deakin, show me you've heard and understood.'

Then he realized that they were already too late.

Deakin's eyes were closed, but not in sleep. A trickle of blood had run down the side of his face and stained his shirt collar, and was already attracting a small buzz of flies. The blood was coming from a dark hole just above one ear.

SIXTY-FIVE

Harry felt the hairs move on the back of his neck. He forced himself not to look round; it wouldn't have done any good, anyway. If the man who had shot Deakin was watching from the tree line and had Harry in his sights, there was precious little he could do about it now. Instead, he checked the other side of Deakin's head. No exit wound. He inspected the wound again. Powder burns were visible around the entry point. Not a rifle from the woods, then.

This had been an execution, up close and personal. Pointed. He remembered what Turpowicz had said about the Chinese middleman, Wien Lu Chi. '*Smooth as a snake and probably as dangerous.*' This was Deakin's payback for not coming up with the goods in time. Or maybe they'd realized they'd been sold a pup. The Chinese wouldn't have got their down-payment back, but that would be of less immediate interest than saving face – and sending out a warning to others. Nobody messed with them without paying in full.

Rik joined him and stared at Deakin's body. 'You reckon Paulton did this?'

'No.' he said. 'It's not his style.'

Harry was looking towards the access road, where a flash of movement had caught his eye. The grey Mercedes was approaching the gate, unhurried and sleek. It slowed almost to a stop, and Harry saw the oval of a face turned towards them in the rear window. He'd only caught a brief glimpse as the car had passed by, but he'd got an impression of a slim figure, neat and of middle years, dressed in a suit. He'd have blended in perfectly with the trade delegation the manager had mentioned.

He toyed with calling the authorities, but decided against it. From here to a motorway intersection wouldn't take long in the Merc, and by the time a helicopter got overhead, they'd be in among thick traffic or have switched cars. Operations like this weren't carried out on a wing and a prayer; they had too much to lose if they fouled up. Maybe the centre's security camera would pick up the number plate and show the faces of the driver and passenger. Or maybe not.

'Come on. There's nothing we can do for him.' He turned and walked back towards the hotel. He'd call it in from reception. It would take the gloss off the manager's day, but there was no hiding a murder.

First, though, there was something else he had to do.

George Paulton had an instinct for danger, honed over many years operating undercover in extreme conditions. It was usually signalled by a prickling of his palms, and the last time he'd experienced it, the feeling had saved his life. He had learned never to dismiss it.

That prickling was with him again and he knew he had to leave. Right now.

He was accustomed to living out of a small bag, ready to move at a moment's notice, and there was no sign of panic as he toured the room, checking that he'd left nothing behind. He used a damp cloth to wipe down everything that he'd touched since the night before, when he'd done another such check, as much a way of easing his impatience than adhering to a self-imposed security routine.

He'd spent the last hour or so trying to get hold of his contact in the Met, and another in MI6, to find out what was happening about the hunt for the Protectory. But neither of them was answering. This lack of knowledge meant he was operating blind, unable to see even part of the picture, let alone all of it. Now it didn't really matter; it was time to go.

When he was ready, he stood for a moment, settling his nerves. Then he scooped up his bag and headed for the fire escape at the rear of the building. Deakin would be taking care of the bill, so he had no reason to go near the front desk. It would be unwise, anyway, to appear in the front foyer, since the danger, if his instincts were correct, would be centred right there.

He considered Deakin for a brief moment. The former soldier was out walking somewhere, but intuition told him that going in search of him was not an option. Deakin would have to look after himself.

He hurried down the rear stairs, a rush of excitement building in his ears. He didn't know the source of the danger, but whatever it was, whether the Chinese Deakin had dealt with or Harry Tate, every instinct told him it was very close.

In the ground floor stairwell he passed between pallets of provisions, stacks of conference chairs and folded tables, all waiting to be moved. The atmosphere and décor here was strictly utilitarian, sombre and cool. Figures in white jackets scurried about, not even bothering to look at him. They were back-of-house workers and he was plainly a guest in their view, so they would have no reason to interact.

He stepped outside. Saw a scattering of staff cars and two trucks making deliveries, tail lifts down and boxes stacked. Drivers and kitchen staff intent on their work and someone shouting in Flemish. Otherwise, nobody paid him any attention. He walked across to the edge of the building and looked round the side, where golf course was spread out before him. He could just see one end of the car park and a portion of the access road at the front. And parked on the edge of the line of cars was the hire car he and Deakin had used to get here. He studied it for a few moments, hearing a vague, internal alarm. And wondering.

He walked along the side of the building, stopping as a young man in a porter's jacket stepped out from a recess in the wall, puffing out a final lungful of smoke and flicking away the stub of a cigarette.

Paulton smiled and the man coughed, face erupting in a flush as he was caught out in his vice. Impulsively, Paulton stopped and said, 'I wonder if you can help me?' He needed a distraction at the front of the building, and what better one could there be than a porter on an errand?

'Yes, sir?' The man smoothed his waistcoat, no doubt relieved that he wasn't in trouble and might even earn himself a tip.

Paulton took his keys out of his pocket and a couple of crisp notes from his wallet and gave the porter some instructions. Then he handed him his bag. The youth nodded, although he clearly didn't fully understand, but his expression also said that the amount of money he was being offered was enough to do away with any doubts he might have had.

He hurried away to do the guest's bidding, leaving Paulton waiting, his nerves jangling.

Just then, his phone rang, startling him. He answered it and listened, then said, 'I know that. I think he's already here. For the future, I'll call you when I need to. This number's out of action as of right now.' He cut the call, then stripped the back off the phone and took out the SIM card. He bent and pushed the square of plastic into the ground, then tossed the two halves of the phone into some bushes and walked away.

SIXTY-SIX

Harry used the room service chief's pass-key to open Paulton's room. There had been no response to knocking, so he had asked the manager to give authorization to enter. He stepped through the door, his gun drawn, and walked around the room, checking the bathroom and a walk-in wardrobe. The décor was plush, restful and very expensive. His feet sank into the thick carpet, reducing his footsteps to a whisper. The place was clean; even the wastebaskets were empty. Only the rumpled bedclothes and some water pooled in the shower-tray betrayed the fact that anyone had stayed here last night.

They had missed him by a whisker. Paulton had been here,

according to the manager, making phone calls. Something must have spooked him. He looked out of the window on to the golf course. He couldn't possibly have seen Deakin being shot, not from here. So what, then?

He checked the drawers and wardrobe, anyway, a brief exercise which, as he expected, told him nothing. The room had been sanitized, the work of a true professional. There was nothing left to indicate who had actually stayed here.

He went back out into the corridor and followed the international signs for the fire escape. They led to the rear stairway and he hurried down, his feet echoing in the stairwell. On the way, he called Rik who was waiting out front.

'He's gone. He must still be around the place somewhere. Look for anyone leaving – and watch your back.'

'Got it.' Rik kept the connection open and Harry could hear his progress as he passed groups of people talking and a door slamming close by. Harry came out of the stairwell and passed through a fire exit door to the outside. The staff car park. A few cars, a couple of trucks and their drivers, a young man in overalls and carrying a toolbox, a porter throwing a bag into a small red Fiat and climbing behind the wheel, two kitchen workers wearing aprons, lighting up cigarettes.

He walked towards the corner of the building, which would take him to the front car park. Paulton must be here somewhere, he told himself. He couldn't have vanished into thin air—

The explosion when it came was loud and flat, shockingly out of place in these surroundings. It echoed around the building, sending a brief tremor through the structure and a rush of birds scattering off the roof. Others lifted in panic from the trees beyond, bursting away in all directions. Someone shouted and a brief scream was shrill, but with shock and fear rather than pain.

Harry ran out into the open, searching for the source of the noise. At first he could see nothing. The acoustics here weren't helping, with the main building, the outbuildings, the lake and the trees all combining to disperse the sound and confuse the senses.

Then he saw a spiral of smoke lifting into the sky towards the front of the conference centre and heard a babble of excited voices. Staff and guests came piling out of the rear of the building, some still holding kitchen implements, others clutching coats and bags, no doubt fearful of a terrorist attack. Amid the clutter of people, a car started up and drove away. The porter who'd been getting in moments earlier.

He walked out on to the golf course, from where he could see the road leading away from the front car park towards the main gate. He stopped in amazement.

The remains of a vehicle was sitting across the road like a gutted animal. The wheels were intact, but the bodywork was in flames, part of the roof gone, black smoke boiling from the inferno and trailing into the sky like a long, dark flag. It was – had been – a saloon car, dark in colour. That was all Harry could tell. Now it was a ball of fire, the flames already eating hungrily at the car tyres and adding to the black smoke billowing out and drifting in angry clouds across the surface of the lake.

Rik joined him, shaking his head.

'What happened?' Harry asked.

'No idea. I saw it leave the car park, then *bang* – it got a hundred yards away and went up.' He glanced at Harry. 'That wasn't an accident.'

'I know.' Harry turned and watched as an authority figure in a suit began to restore order at the rear of the building and hustled the staff back indoors. Beyond the building, a couple of golfers had been frozen in their game, and were standing awestruck, eyes on the flaming car.

The only movement was a small red Fiat on the narrow track, just disappearing into the trees.

Harry grabbed a young man in a porter's waistcoat coming from the front of the building. 'This road,' he said. 'Where does it go?'

The man shrugged. 'Is for staff, sir. And deliveries. It goes to the outside – to the road.' He pulled away apologetically. 'I am sorry, but I have to look for Mattheus, my colleague. He was here but is missing.' He turned to continue towards the kitchens.

The porter, getting into the car.

'Wait.' Harry stopped him. 'What did your colleague look like?'

The man stopped. 'Young . . . blond, with glasses. And wearing one like this.' He pointed at his own waistcoat. 'Why?'

Harry shook his head. 'Sorry, nothing. I thought I might have seen him.'

He turned and looked at the trees where the Fiat had now disappeared. The porter he'd seen at the Fiat had been older and heavier. He hadn't seen his face because his back was turned. But his waistcoat had been stretched across his back. Too tight for a presentable fit in a place like this.

'What was all that about?' said Rik.

'Paulton,' Harry replied, and nodded towards the trees. 'He traded cars with a young porter named Mattheus. He went that way.' Then he turned and looked toward the smoking debris of the car along the exit road. 'And Mattheus got the wrong end of the deal.'

He felt a sense of defeat. Paulton had slipped away with moments to spare. It left him wondering how the former MI5 man had known they were here; how, right now, he'd suddenly judged it was time to go. Instinct born of experience, and maybe a sixth sense about what had happened to Deakin, had been enough to warn him away from his car, too. He would have known the Chinese weren't likely to forgive being misled by the Protectory.

'Why the bullet for Deakin,' said Rik, 'but a car bomb for Paulton?'

'It just worked out that way,' Harry guessed. 'They were playing the odds. They'd have got them both in the hire car, anyway, but they wanted to make a specific point with Deakin.'

Rik shook his head. 'They did that all right. But how did Paulton know?'

'He's smart and experienced; he's been around the block. He'd have known playing with the Chinese was risky, and if they showed up here, they'd know who was with Deakin and they'd come prepared.'

'That's cold, though, using the porter like that.'

'Yeah, well, it's what he does.' Harry felt tired. He couldn't quite believe that it had merely been fear of the Chinese that had made Paulton run. If he'd known they were so close, he would have alerted Deakin, too. But he clearly hadn't done that. Something else must have added to the urgency to leave right away.

Then he recalled what the manager had said, about the man he knew as Goddard being in his room. *'He was heard talking on the phone just a few minutes ago.'*

If he was on the phone, was he making a call . . . or receiving one? A call telling him to get out if he valued his freedom.

'He was warned off,' said Harry with absolute certainty, and walked back towards their car. He could already hear the wail of sirens in the distance. Their presence here had been noted, and even with the benefit of the phone link to the Interior Ministry, it would be preferable not to be here when the police arrived. He started the car and turned towards the back road, away from the burning wreck out front.

'Are we going after him?' said Rik. He took out his gun and checked the magazine. 'First thing we should ask him is who he's getting his information from.'

'I'd like to know that, too.' Harry slowed to allow two golfers to cross the road, hurrying to see what the explosion had been about. Paulton, like Clare Jardine, clearly still had friends. Friends who were prepared to go out on a limb for him.

'But we are going after him.' Rik slapped the magazine back in place and applied the safety.

They reached the main road. Two hundred yards to their right, three police cars with lights blazing were making fast turns into the gate to the conference centre. A fire truck was hard on their heels. The smoke from the burning car was beginning to drift across the carriageway. Harry wondered if the cops had passed a small red Fiat going the other way. He debated going after it, but decided not to; Paulton had a head start and would already be losing himself in the suburbs, most likely on foot by now and blending in with the populace the way he would have been taught. The odds of finding him were far too slim.

Ballatyne's words came back to him from the briefing in Georgio's. *'We rarely get the resolution we crave.'*

He shook his head. He wasn't prepared to believe that, not yet. He and Paulton had some unfinished business. But there were times when you had to pick your battles.

'No, we're not going after him. Not this time, anyway.' He turned on the radio and tuned in to a music channel. 'But we will.'

'So what do we do?'

Harry considered it. He could see a bar-café sign along the road. A bit too close for comfort, but there were plenty more within a few minutes' drive.

'Have you ever tried Trappist ale?'

Rik shook his head, puzzled. 'No. Why?'

'You should. It'll blow your socks off. Straighten your hair out. Curl your teeth. Put lead in your pencil.'

'This is not some kind of date, is it?'

'No. Call it an end-of-assignment party.'

Rik put the gun away and nodded. 'In that case, it's your shout.'

Harry nodded in agreement, then turned left and drove away.